THE GOODBYE LIE

Volume One in
The Goodbye Lie Series

Jane Marie

greenlightWRITE
Oklahoma City
United States of America

The Goodbye Lie is Copyright© 2000, 2004 by Jane Marie Harkins Malcolm, dba Jane Marie.
ISBN 0-9749182-2-9 (pbk)
ISBN 0-9749182-3-7 (ebook)

Library of Congress Control Number: 2004104182

First Edition
2004

greenlightWRITE - http://www.greenlightWRITE.com
Oklahoma City, Oklahoma
United States of America

Printed and distributed in the United States by Lightning Source, Inc.
1246 Heil Quaker Blvd., LaVergne, TN, USA 37086
http://www.lightningsource.com

Printed and distributed in the United Kingdom by Lightning Source UK Ltd.
6 Precedent Drive, Rooksley, Milton Keynes, MK13 8PR, UK
http://www.lightningsource.co.uk

Amelia Island, Florida is last in the chain of Atlantic coast barrier islands that stretch from North Carolina to Florida. Just south of the Georgia border, it is named for Princess Amelia, daughter of George II of England. The island is 32 miles northeast of Jacksonville and is naturally protected from hurricanes (most of the time). It is just 13 x 2.5 miles in size with an average temperature of about 70° F.

Birthplace of the modern shrimping industry, the Victorian seaside City of Fernandina Beach has a population of some 10,700 and is the only city on Amelia Island. Fort Clinch State Park, a pre-Civil War fort, sits on the northern tip of the island overlooking Cumberland Sound.

TO MY FATHER, LEO MICHAEL HARKINS,
AND ALL WHO ENCOURAGE

"We lie loudest when we lie to ourselves." Eric Hoffer

"Fiction is the truth inside the lie." Stephen King

Sultry Summer 1882

Chapter 1 – *The Goodbye Lie* by Jane Marie

The girl's body flew through the air.

Moments earlier, she'd been riding her black stallion down the beach. Conscious only of thoughts of her job at the local newspaper, the girl languishing on her horse's back gave no response to the urgent cry, "This way! Ride this way!" Nor did she hear the distant shouts, sharp whistle or even the pop of gunfire that followed - though her animal perked his ears at the faint warning.

When the growl of her own hunger invaded her contemplation, the girl realized the hour had grown late. More importantly, the wind was beginning to swirl. She was alert now to her surroundings and noticed the sea birds struggling against invisible air currents. She listened hard for the usual humming of native insects as strands of her hair tangled in the blustery breeze, but all she heard was the ever increasing whine of wind and pounding surf. Overhead, low-running clouds in a queer yellow domed sky shrouded a heavy sun dropping in the west.

Noir's unexpected whinny stunned her, and she nearly toppled from the saddle. He reared up, forelegs scraping the air as he sought imaginary rescue. His sleek black hide glistened and the ebony animal bolted forward, taking his mistress with him. The horse was uncontrollable with fear and the girl could smell his terror despite the churn of the atmosphere. As his eyes ballooned with dread and frothy panic dripped from his mouth, his rider called to him, "What's the matter, boy? You should be used to a little wind and rain. It's Florida, after all." She patted his powerful neck in useless reassurance only to be interrupted by a thunderous roar of nature's authority.

Then the girl's head snapped to the right as her eyes took in the ghastly sight of three white waterspouts sprinting just above the ocean's boiling surface. Lightning charged the sky as pricking needles of rain began drilling the rough sea. The girl rallied all her strength. Winding the reins around her gloved hands, she held tight, flattening herself along Noir's length as he galloped full-fury, trying to out distance death. She refused to look again at the monstrous funnels gaining on them. She knew their purpose - to take them as partners in a heinous pirouette of extinction.

The girl gamely chose to spend her last breath in prayer, "Dear Lord, please ..."

Then everything stilled as she was struck from behind and cast to the ground.

In the tiny Southern town of Fernandina, Florida on Amelia Island, little Marie pleaded, "I want my tiptoes to touch the roof, Daddy. Please push me a little harder." Pale pigtails flew back from the three-year-old's sweet face. While the ropes of the swing creaked, she strained to reach the ceiling to add her personal scuffmarks to the scarred planks, the same as her older brother and sisters had done over the years.

Her father, Carroll Michael Dunnigan, had built a chair swing in the barn for his youngsters so they could actively play, even when it rained. He rarely refused his children anything if he felt it would not harm them and if it was within his power to give. "To my mind," he told his wife, Ella, "There's no such thing as spoiling a child. That's why they're put on this earth."

Miss Ella found she was married to the most intractable husband created when it came to his four offspring. She'd discovered why Michael was so indulgent by listening to infrequent stories of his childhood. Over the years, he'd revealed pieces of himself in dribs and drabs. His parents, she'd learned, had said, "No," more often than not to nearly all his wants, big or small. Their reasons were most probably economic, considering the times and the size of their family, but those denials had permanently marked Michael. His reaction was irrational generosity. Whatever the reason, it was difficult to fault a man for such a characteristic. Unless, that is, you were the mother of his children.

"Now, Michael," always Miss Ella's reply, "If the children receive all they ask for, how will they contend with life when things don't run their way? They've never known real hardship or consequence."

"Nonsense! Would you wish on them what we've been through? With the war behind us, we're finally all living in hog heaven. Now stop your frettin'. They'll cope. Dunnigans always do."

Miss Ella hoped she had instilled a sense of the practical in each child despite the fairytale life provided by their adoring father.

Turning to leave the barn she asked, "How did you happen to come home so early today? It's just now five o'clock. Are things going well in the world of architecture?"

He knows supper our evening meal is always served at six, she thought, unless there's a potluck supper at church or some other social event. Then again, it could be that his already bulging belly demands an earlier feeding.

"What's the use of being the boss, Miss Ella, if I can't play a little hooky with my baby here?" His tone was short. This was certainly one of his hungry moods coming on.

"I'll see if I can't hurry up your dinner, Michael."

"What? You mean it'll be a while?"

"Yes, darling," she responded in as sarcastic a voice as his question deserved. "If you'd listen to your wife occasionally, you'd hear her say she has a few things to do besides following the timetable of her husband's stomach."

He reacted with a snort.

"Today, as substitute choir mistress, I was called upon to make last minute changes in this Sunday's schedule of hymns because Miss Bayer is out of town visiting her grandfather and Mrs. Lingenfelter is having her baby."

Her husband grumbled in disgust. Unable to stay cross with him for long, she offered, "If you'll give me ten minutes, I'll pull some cornbread from the oven and slather it with apple butter for you to nibble on. That should tide you over for a bit until I'm sure the soup is done."

"You know how I hate it if the beans are the least bit hard," he cautioned.

"We only hate the devil," Marie announced.

"Yes, baby girl. That's right. See there, Michael. It's true what they say about little pitchers having big ears and our little pitcher hears everything. Don't think she doesn't."

Michael replaced his grimace with a smile and kissed his youngest child on the cheek.

Miss Ella shook her head at her sometimes moody, but very wonderful husband, thinking how lucky she was to have him. Back inside the aromatic kitchen, she checked the steeping jelly kettle of peaches, stirred the pot of salt pork and bean soup, and cleared a spot for the hot cornbread among the fresh radishes and onions. It had been such a peaceful afternoon. Too peaceful, she realized.

Where was Jack Patrick? Her only son, age eight, was usually so noisy she knew his whereabouts every minute. She left the kitchen, went down the long hall past the stairs, and entered the front parlor to find her mother, Hettie Eckert, known to all as Grammy. Grammy was swaying in her rocker, intently working on a braided rag rug, and there was Jack

Patrick, sneaking up from behind, scissors in hand, about to cut the soft wild-hair wispies from his sainted grandmother's head!

"Jack Patrick!" yelped his mother.

Calmly placing the shears back in the sewing basket, he stated, "Mama, I hope lightning flies through the window and kills the cat. I'm innocent!"

She knew exactly how innocent he was. She allowed the boy to dash out the front door before he caught her laughing.

Fortunately, since Grammy's hearing was not quite as keen as it once was, she was oblivious to her grandson's near attack, figuring only that his mother was yet again reprimanding the boy for his usual mischief.

Leaning against the wall, Miss Ella thought back to yesterday, remembering her middle daughter, eighteen-year-old Breelan, as she'd mimicked Grammy in the construction of her own rug. Over the last few weeks, Breelan had torn three-inch strips of cloth, folded their frayed edges inward and sewn the long thin tails, one to another. She had arrived at the final step of braiding and stitching the tails into a flat oval rug, when her mother had overheard her say, "This will be my scrap mine of colorful memories. I've made it from the worn dresses and torn trousers we've saved, Gram, just like you taught me. When I have my little girl, I want you to show her how to make your rugs, same as you've shown me."

Miss Ella hoped her mother would still be around in the time it took Breelan to have a child old enough to learn the art of rug making. And interestingly enough, Breelan seemed certain her child would be a girl.

"Whenever I look at my rug, I'll think of this pretty dress." Breelan pointed to the tail made from green plaid taffeta. "I couldn't wait for Carolena to outgrow it so it would be mine. Its lace petticoat was edged in red satin ribbon. I'll tell you a secret, if you promise not to tell Mama."

"I promise, honey," Grammy had conspired.

Miss Ella knew she should have left the parlor, but so loved to witness the closeness of the two that her heart had frozen her feet in place.

"When I was twelve, I had a teacher named Mr. Gregor. Until him, all my instructors had been old. He seemed much too young and handsome to hold such a post. Hoping he'd fall in love with me, I strategically sat at my desk, adjusting my skirt just a tish, so the edge of my beautiful petticoat peaked out. If he noticed, he never said a thing. But I think now that was my first real attempt at flirtation. I was thrilled by the possibilities that might develop, even at such a young age as that. Pretty shameful, huh?"

The sound of Marie's chattering had interrupted Miss Ella's eavesdropping and she never did hear Grammy's answer. Whatever the response had been, Miss Ella was certain it was given with wisdom.

Her thoughts back in the present, Miss Ella frowned at the idea of her children growing up. Once Carolena, the oldest, was born, she and Michael waited to have more babies until after the terrible fighting of the War Between the States was over. They were successful due to Michael's absence during the conflict and a bit of his Irish luck, to be sure. Today, she had two lovely young ladies all grown. She didn't want to lose her daughters, have men take them away, yet that was what had happened to her when she left Pennsylvania to live with Michael in Fernandina. And she was glad of it. When you had love, no matter if that love was peaceful or chaotic, you had the world.

Lighting the lamp hanging above the large enamel sink, she moved quickly to light another over the eight-foot pine worktable, trying to fire them both with the same match. Miss Ella was a creature of habit so she filled the crystal pitcher with cold well water from the red hand pump on the drain board, despite the recently installed indoor water faucet. As she rinsed the radishes, she decided it was time to have the children wash up for supper.

Carolena, twenty-one, was upstairs reading a book she'd borrowed from the lending library. Her mother had watched her maneuver up the steps to her bedroom, arms loaded with books. Miss Ella sometimes questioned whether a professor could read all that literature - let alone a young woman - in the two-week period allotted. Her daughter had never failed to complete the challenge.

As she checked the simmering soup, Miss Ella felt a burst of pride as she recalled how Carolena had recently graduated from Florida Women's College in Tallahassee. Living back at home and wondering what to do with her life, this daughter had considered the usual teaching positions available, but hadn't the patience. She'd thought of nursing, but hadn't the stomach. Currently, to the delight of her father, she was fascinated with architecture and design. Between the public library and the Dunnigan private library, there certainly were enough books on those subjects to keep her interest fueled.

What opposites Carolena and Breelan are, their mother mused. Carolena Michele. I'm glad we named our first-born after her father since she has his golden coloring. Her honeyed hair and moss green eyes fit with her delicate emotions and serious, studious ways, but we don't see her straight, white smile often enough to suit me. Breelan Jane's ivory skin and dark brown hair are more like mine, and she's so easy going, she never gives us a bit of worry. If only she cared more for her studies, but it's writing stories that appeals to her.

Picking up a water glass and polishing off the fingerprints, Miss Ella was reminded of how many times her girls had fought over whose turn it was to set the table. Too often their frequent bickering turned nasty. They went from jamming freshly ironed clothes beneath one another's blankets to putting old horse teeth in mashed potatoes. Miss Ella hoped they'd soon outgrow all of the perceived infractions of sibling statutes and childish laws before they wore their parents plum out.

Miss Ella caught sight of Jack Patrick and Marie in the back yard intently observing their mongrel dog, Blackie-White-Spots. Leaning over the sink, she looked out the window, likewise fascinated by the animal stalking his own shadow in a slow motion kind of movement.

The calm was short-lived. "Mama! Mama!" hollered Marie running into the kitchen to hide in her mother's skirts. "Jack Patrick's gonna make me eat cheese!"

"What's wrong with that, child?" her mother puzzled. "You love cheese."

"No ma'am, I don't. Not no more. It's made from buffalo tongues! Jack Patrick told me so!" she whined, wrinkling her nose and sticking out her tongue.

Miss Ella peered through the screen door to see her son retrieve a cube of cheese from his pocket. Picking off dirt or lint or both before inserting it into his mouth, he puffed his cheeks and grinned widely to proclaimed his triumph at having snagged the last piece of cheddar by telling tales to his little sister. But this was nothing new.

After her mother explained the origin of cheese to her, Marie was clearly relieved. She crawled into the cupboard under the sink, much involved in a mysterious conversation of baby talk and gibberish.

"All my children have loved that hidey-hole of yours, Marie."

"Wanna play, Mama?"

"I'd love to, dear, but I have to finish supper."

Miss Ella washed the last of the mixing bowls and watched her husband loosen his tie. Michael got down to talk to his son, now playing in the sand. She dried her brow with the corner of her apron, thinking how oppressively still the outside air seemed and how muggy it felt.

"Now where has Breelan gone off to, Marie? She knows it's her turn to finish setting the table. At least I think it is."

Abruptly, the rustle of the wind picked up. "Stay in your special spot for Mama, baby girl. I'll be right back." Miss Ella dashed to the front welcome hall and threw open the screen door. Standing on the eastern side of the wraparound veranda, she wanted to deny what she saw and feared most. The leaves on the trees were turned upside down and the daylight was sheathed in an unnatural saffron color. "Sweet Jesus! Where's my Breelan?"

Chapter 2 – *The Goodbye Lie* by Jane Marie

Water splattered Breelan Dunnigan's face. She gasped for air, but was unable to fill her lungs. Was she drowning? She tried to paddle her way to the surface, when she realized she couldn't move her arms. Was she pinned beneath some massive tree? Fluttering leaves were teasing her lips unmercifully. But there were no trees on Amelia Beach. Completely confused, she panted for breath.

Slowly raising the lashes of her sapphire eyes, she tried to blink away the rain that continued to pelt her skin. The broad shoulders of a man lying on top of her were blocking her line of sight. "What are you doing? Get off me! Get off!" she sputtered, insulted and frightened, all the while trying to flail any part of her that was free. "Oh! When I tell my people ..."

Her words were choked off as a huge hand came down across her mouth. The palm was callused and smelled masculine. The hand was powerful and could easily hurt her if that were the intent of this stranger. Alarm spun harrowing possibilities of her fate. After being nearly flattened, was she to be robbed and murdered? What had she done in her short life to justify such a finish?

"Madame," shouted the shadowed voice over the rush of the rain and the pound of the breakers. "By the saints, though it is a lovely mouth, I am hard pressed to free what I expect is a malicious tongue. My patience is gone, and I will not be called down by you or anyone." He paused. "I shall remove my hand if you will simply thank me."

She nodded willingly. Upon removal of his hand, she spat forth, "Thank you? Thank you for groping and smothering me?"

"To my disappointment, you're an ingrate as well as a shrew," he said more sedately than he felt as he watched droplets of rain drip into her eyes from the tips of his dark hair.

Starved for oxygen, Breelan desperately pushed against the strong chest. To her surprise, the man rose to stand over her. She momentarily forgot the weather and her fear of him, to think how graceful his movement for a man of his size. But her involuntary reflexes wouldn't wait, and she dragged the cool, wet air deep into her chest, again and again, instantly beginning to feel alive and instantly, too, discovering how bruised she felt. Springing to a sitting position, she tried to preserve her dignity since she figured she had precious little of that left.

"Ingrate? Shrew? No one has ever called me such dreadful names," she ridiculously argued at him into the storm. Breelan was about to continue her tirade when she remembered why she sat wet and rumpled on the beach. She wasn't sure just how much time had passed, but she recalled the advancing waterspouts and grabbing for Noir's mane. "Noir! Where's Noir?"

Dread struck the man as he frantically looked about for another, trying to wipe the rainwater from his eyes to see more clearly. With such a fanciful name, he automatically assumed he was looking for a girl named Noire. "How old is she?" he asked, his eyes scraping every surface visible to the horizon until he'd completed a full circle.

"Who?"

"Noire!" Impatience sounded in his voice.

"Noir is a he and what difference could it make how old he is? He's mine, and I'll die without him." The girl's wet face paled as her chin quivered with worry.

Unreasonably, yet immediately, the man's heart dragged a few beats at her dramatic words of passion.

"I'm sorry," he hollered over the weather. "All I see is your horse standing up there on the dunes."

"Where?" She saw as she spoke. "Oh, Noir! Darling Noir!"

Relief flooded the man as it did her, but for very different reasons.

Breelan scrambled to her feet and began a dash in Noir's direction only to be stopped by the man's hand on her wrist.

"Turn loose of me! Can't you see he needs me?" she cried, her saturated gown defining her slight shape for him.

"Yes," he said. "Go to him, but go gently. He's been through a lot himself. You may frighten him more."

"Me? Never!" Still, she reduced her approach to a slow walk. Nearing the rigid animal, trying to speak as softly as she could yet loud enough for him to hear in all the wind and rain, she said, "Noir, my brave boy. You'll be fine now. Breelan is here with you."

The man heard her words in the air current blowing his way and whispered her name. "Breelan." Despite the assault of the slapping gale still upon them, he watched this girl, this woman, fascinated. Her dark matted hair had long ago won total freedom from any combs she may have been wearing. When dry and struck by sunlight, he guessed it show a sparkle of copper.

As Breelan reached for the reins, the horse reared back. The man tensed. The girl stood her ground, pacifying the animal with endearments. When recognition of his mistress finally cracked the barrier of disorientation, Noir visibly relaxed.

"That's my boy. I'll take care of you now. Come, darling. Come on."

The man listened hard to hear her words, wishing they were addressed to him. How would she speak to a lover if she could so cherish this creature? "I must be crazy. I've been without a female far too long," he told himself softly. It wasn't only that he found her physically captivating. Something about her agitated and irritated him at the same time. The sensation was unfamiliar yet almost pleasurable, and he swore he'd discover why.

This was his second trip to the usually beautiful little community of Fernandina, a thriving island city in the Deep South. The first town in Florida across the Georgia line, it lay naturally protected on Amelia Island at the mouth of the St. Mary's and Amelia Rivers. Naturally protected, that is, from most hurricanes, he mused, but not waterspouts and tornadoes. He'd marched through here on his way to battle the Federals during the war. Now he'd discovered a better reason than the lovely seascape around him to frequent the place. This girl.

He hoped she was unmarried. While examining her for injuries a few moments earlier, he'd purposely felt for a ring through her black riding glove and found none.

Breelan ran, leading Noir back to where the big man was holding the reins of his own dark mount. She placed one foot in her stirrup. Looking over her shoulder, she said quickly, "I've no time, let alone desire, to catch my death in this rain in order to visit with strange men."

"Are you sure lack of time and the weather are why you're in such a bloody hurry to leave me?" Although equally drenched, the same as she, he teased her, not wanting to see her go.

Breelan began to mount Noir when her leg buckled. A strong arm caught her round her waist. Surprised yet relieved she hadn't hit the ground, she tried to turn and face him. He held the shapely miss fast against him, enjoying the feel of her softness.

"Must I again tell you to let me be?" Breelan quizzed, infuriated. "I've got to get home to see about the others!"

Hearing this, he released her at once. "What others? Your family?" His concern was apparent.

"Yes. They may be in trouble."

"You are obviously in little condition to help anyone. Let me take you where you can rest, and I'll be glad to check on them for you." He feared what they might find and wanted to spare her any heartbreak.

Breelan knew what he was trying to do for her but said, "No. There's no time for debate. I'm fine."

Doubting, he reluctantly nodded, realizing another unpleasant exchange would follow if he pursued his point. "Very well. But I'm going with you," in case you need me again, he thought.

"All right. All right!" Breelan yelped. She recognized her rudeness and chose to ignore it. She couldn't be bothered with any more apologies. Too many minutes had already been wasted bickering. "Please help me onto my horse."

He did as asked, handling her booted foot. She swung her right leg over the saddle and he caught a glimpse of her petticoats. A shiver reverberated inside him.

In a moment, Breelan was hurtling north with the Atlantic Ocean on her right. She ignored the still lashing rain and snarling thunder. The heavy drops left indentations in the soft, almost saturated sand. Before her lay a four-foot wide, eight-foot deep furrow chewed perpendicular to the ocean by the might of a swirling funnel, she guessed. The relentless waves were filling its depth. It was her turn to give a shudder at how closely the danger had struck. With no hesitation and with the grace of Pegasus, Noir jumped the trench, landing smoothly on the other side.

Following, the man watched them fly, girl and animal as one. He admired her fearlessness, her determination, and her skill on horseback. In particular, he admired her loveliness. Bedraggled, she would probably call herself at this moment, but he could see beyond that to her beauty.

Faint laughter and music were coming from the new Strathmore Hotel with its ocean front rooms. The guests had obviously chosen merriment and wine over bothersome tornadoes. Breelan ignored them. She jerked Noir's reins to the west to cross the sand dunes, driving through thick sea oats to find the main road into town.

An unmistakable howl sounded. Breelan spied another funnel cloud about a mile away, this time skimming the treetops and heading in the direction of her house! God Almighty! It never took so long to get home, she thought. It feels like the earth is spinning backward beneath us and we're getting nowhere. Keeping to the road that ran through the marsh grasses, she careened left onto a side street marked Dunn Road. She led the man three quarters of a mile until he saw two grand houses all alone on the right. They were differently shaped, but somehow a pair, as if they had been designed by the same architect.

Breelan passed the first with slight concern. Her attention seemed to be focused on the second. She entered the crushed oyster shell drive, taking no notice of the sharp sound of Noir's hooves digging into the rough texture. Sharply pulling at her horse's bit, Breelan bounded from his back to tie his reins to the still standing hitching post.

She paused briefly to take in the destruction from the tornado. With a soft moan, she saw where the live oak tree was split in thirds. It was lying passively as if too old and tired to stand upright any longer. The Charleston-green shutters from the house lay splintered on the shimmering glass-strewn lawn. Only one set of her mother's old rose-colored draperies was left hanging. Twisted, they blew out the empty twelve-foot window frame at the southeastern end of the house. The wooden sign reading Dunnigan Manor was jammed crossways near the top of the evergreen that was surrounded by undisturbed marigolds and periwinkles.

Breelan's trembling was intense as she envisioned what was inside the walls of her home. Her thighs felt weighted by her fatigue and drenched garments and also from the sucking mud and sand underfoot. Mama will surely scold me if I track any of this wet mess inside, came her ridiculous thought.

With one hand on the latch, she breathed deeply, steeling herself to meet the inevitable.

Chapter 3 – *The Goodbye Lie* by Jane Marie

The squeak of the front door was the only accompaniment to Breelan's pounding heart. She couldn't stand the quiet and spoke. "We're all supposed to go to the center of the house if we ever hear a twister coming." She thought of the thick-legged mahogany dining table the adults used as shelter and the matching buffet cabinet for the children.

Engrossed in her worries, Breelan started at the sound of the man's voice, "Were this any place but Florida," he reflected, "they'd all be hunkered down in the root cellar."

She scoffed at his comment because they were in no other place but Florida and realized that the near dark of evening was descending upon the house. "I need a candle," Breelan said. Wary, she crept her way along the wet entrance hall to the parlor. The man, hearing nothing, feared the same as she.

"Daddy? Mama? Please answer. Tell me where you are. Carolena? Marie? Jack Patrick?"

Then, a sound. A raspy sound. A moan. Then another.

"Daddy!" Breelan recognized his customary muttering. Hope flooded her heart. "I'm here! I'm here!" she cried. "Quick, find me a match," she ordered as her hand automatically landed upon a cool, slender candle in the box hidden behind the music stand above the pump organ's keyboard.

With two fingers, the man pulled a match from his waistcoat pocket. Hoping it was dry enough to fire, he flicked his thumbnail and there was light.

Breelan blinked quickly at the sudden brilliance, impatient for her eyes to adjust. She ran from the front parlor and into the dining room, her hand shielding the precious flame. Her mother's black patterned carpet undulated with woven bouquets of yellow and pink roses tied with powder blue bows. It danced, alive with broken pieces of shattered windowpane, on the wooden floor beneath the massive dining table. Breelan dropped to her knees to see her father wag his shaggy gray head out from under the rug, as if trying to regain reason. The man's arm reached around Breelan, throwing back the heavy textile to reveal three adults. Her daddy was covering her mother and older sister with his own large frame.

Breelan brought the candle closer, setting it down on the polished floor. She saw the gash on her father's left temple along with the bloody freckles.

Miss Ella cried, "Breelan, are you hurt?"

"No. Oh no, Mama."

Carolena's voice quivered the same as her body. "Mama, is it over? What about the babies?"

It was then the pounding of tiny fists on the inner door of the buffet sounded reveille. Everyone scrambled, ignoring the glass chips slicing skirts and britches. Breelan was the first to reach for the polished brass knob and fling open the cupboard door. There, perched atop the family's best Irish linen was Jack Patrick, one hand in the process of hammering for response, the other around his little sister, Marie. They were frightened, but each masked their fear with a relieved smile. Breelan scooped them out, pressing their heads to her breast. With tears streaming down faces, the family laughed and cried, as murmurs of gratitude were sent heavenward.

"Bree, let me go. You're soakin' wet and squishin' me! I'm all right," hollered Jack Patrick, indignant at being cradled by his big sister.

"Like brother, like sister," said the man, smiling.

"Who's that, Bree?" asked Marie, her tiny finger pointing at the large, soggy stranger standing in the dining room.

Looking over at him, Breelan answered, "Well, I don't really know."

Her father and mother eyed one another then looked from Breelan to the man.

"We passed on the beach, and he was insistent upon following me here to make sure everyone was safe."

"Don't you think we should crawl from beneath this table and take stock?" asked Michael.

"Yes, but before anything else, we need hugs," pronounced his wife.

Miss Ella stood as erect as a five-foot-tall woman could, her face cloaked in thanksgiving, loving each child in turn until Breelan was in her arms. "Oh, sweetsie. We were so worried with you out there in the storm."

"There was a baby waterspout clear out on the horizon, but it wasn't even close to me. I was lucky."

The man raised one eyebrow, but understood her reason for the understatement.

"What about the others, Mama?" Breelan asked, anxious with concern.

"We just heard them shout they were fine. As soon as we tend your Daddy, we'll check on them." Of course Miss Ella was anxious to make sure her people out back were indeed safe, but now, because of the flow of blood from his wound, she worried her husband's head injury might be more serious than it first appeared.

Michael was leaning against the table, steadying himself. Miss Ella took his arm, preparing to guide him to the nearby chair.

Sensing an immediate need, the stranger lurched forward and rescued Mr. Dunnigan from a fall to the floor as the older man's knees collapsed. "Here, sir, may I lend a hand? You've taken a mighty blow to the head," said the man tactfully.

"I'm fine. No need, no need," Michael offered, convincing no one.

"Now Daddy," Breelan spoke, "let him help. He's here and may as well be of some use."

Michael thought to reprimand his daughter for her discourteous remark, yet felt too weak to bother.

Sitting beside him, Miss Ella brought the candle close, examining the wound, all the while shouting orders. "Jack Patrick, find more candles and a candelabra. Marie, bring Mama two clean towels and be careful not to trip on them. Carolena, heat some water and bring soap and the medicine chest. Breelan, my sewing basket."

When all had scurried away as directed, the man produced a silver flask from his inside coat pocket. "Excuse me, ma'am, but may I donate a bit of brandy to ease the pain?"

Miss Ella was hesitant. She looked hard into the eyes of this man she'd never before seen. With her husband indisposed, a stranger in her home should conjure up concern. Inexplicably, she felt she could trust the fellow. "Yes. Thank you, sir. I'm sure Mr. Dunnigan will be quite agreeable to your offer." Lifting her husband's chin she said, "Sip this brandy, my love." With no aversion, Michael gladly drank the liquor, raising his own hand to the flask.

All supplies requested were delivered to the freshly cleaned table. Having the situation under control, Miss Ella said, "Thank you, all. Now, leave your father in peace while I tend to him, and be careful of the glass. Carolena, watch over the children, please."

"But Mama, may I go round and see what damage has been done? Breelan can look after Jack Patrick and Marie."

"No, dear. You take the little ones out into the kitchen and feed them. I want Breelan and her gentleman friend to check on the others."

"Mama!" a shocked Breelan protested. "My gentleman friend? I don't even know him."

Strange. Miss Ella would even trust this man alone with her daughter. She was certain he would never physically harm her. Anyway, Breelan would be within screaming distance of the house if the need arose. But it wouldn't. The mother quickly spoke, "We will make proper introductions as soon as I've cared for your daddy, and we know for certain everyone is safe. Go along. Hurry now!"

"Yes, ma'am." Throwing a sidelong glare at the man, Breelan challenged him to follow as she carried out her mother's charge.

"What others are we looking for, Miss Breelan. How many more are there?"

Breelan gave no response. She heard her name on the man's lips and the sound of it stirred her senses. Concentrating to recover her composure, she sprinted down the hall, through the kitchen, out the door, and across the back porch. Her strength renewed upon knowledge of everyone's safety, she ignored the three steps and jumped straight to the ground to follow the wide stone path past a rose garden hardly touched by the wind and a sturdy cabin, barn and laundry house. "Hey Clove. You okay?"

"I am, Miss Bree," answered a middle-aged black man coming out of the cabin. "You'd best be checking on Gram and Peep before they kill each other. I can hear 'um squabblin' again already."

The man gave a wave to Clover who returned the gesture and disappeared into the barn. In the twilight, the dwelling Breelan headed toward appeared to be a miniature version of the big house. They heard someone crying and through the window could see a lamp burning. Little damage seemed to have occurred compared to Breelan's residence.

"Grammy? Peeper? It's me. You both all right?" Breelan called out as she pulled open the screen door that formerly possessed wooden scrollwork in diagonal corners. Now, it sagged on its hinges, plain and broken.

Grammy was hastily drying the tears on her cheeks, and Peeper was sprinkling wood ash on the bristles of her toothbrush.

"How often do I have to tell you, Peeper," scolded Grammy, "if you don't stop brushing your teeth every time you get nervous, you'll polish the enamel clear off of them."

"Quit pesterin' me. I don't get nervous and a girl's teeth can never be too white," the old woman responded, unconsciously forgetting she was up in years. Turning to Breelan, Peeper answered, "Yes, child. We're fine. We're just a little tuckered is all, except for this big toe a mine. It's all swole-up like a poison pup." Setting aside the dentifrice she said, "Think I'll be a needin' one a my elixir-fixers afore long. Gram, I know we got plenty a borax and bran for a foot soak, but did I see ya use up the last of the iodine?"

"You know well and good I did. I poured it across that scratch you got from the chicken wire. Although it wasn't much of a scratch," Grammy explained to Breelan, "Peeper insisted I use all that was left in the bottle. If she'd have let Clover mend the cage when he wanted to, she wouldn't have gotten hurt in the first place." Turning back to Peeper, "And you can't remember anything from one minute to the next. You'll be asking me what your name is any second."

Breelan watched Peeper reach for her clay pipe as she pulled one knee toward her ample chest to caress her aching appendage. It amazed the girl that a person of seventy-two years was capable of such physical agility. Peeper was the family's resident character, a true hypochondriac enjoying some fifty years of bad health.

"I forgit sometimes and so do you," Peep defended. "Just the little things. I remember what's important. Don't be telling me I don't."

Breelan ran to Peeper, encircling as much of the dear woman's large girth as she could reach in a hearty hug.

Breaking away, she crossed the small kitchen to embrace her grandmother. "You okay, too, Grammy?"

"Yes, dear. I'm too tough to let a little old twister get me down."

Breelan knew her grandmother well though, and realized this last episode had scared the pea waddin' out of her. "Everyone's fine up at the big house."

"Praise the Lord and amen," prayed Peeper.

"Daddy has a cut to his forehead," continued Breelan. Alarm tensed the elderly faces and she wished she'd said nothing about it. "But Mama's tending him and he'll be fine."

"All the same, I best be for goin' up and aiding your ma," insisted Peeper. "My treatments is knowed for miles, ain't they, Bree?"

"Yes'm."

Peeper unfolded herself and waddled over to the animal regally perched on the second shelf beside the store of canned tomatoes. Monstrose, the playfully malevolent, no-tailed marmalade cat was grooming himself in a most undignified position. Teetering on her good foot, Peep picked him up cautiously, since it was not his idea, and carried him to Grammy for petting.

"It's nigh onto dark now, Bree, so wait 'till tomorra ta run over to your cousin's," Peeper told her. "If'n their place is a shambles, won't do no good ya seeing it tonight. All I can say is that it's a good thing your Aunt Noreen and the family is out of town in Savannah or else we'd be alistenin' to her wailin' all night long. I could turn a deaf ear ta her silly sufferin', but I don't like it none when somethin' worries your Uncle Clabe and the children. He's a good man. Smart, too. I even like that handyman, Joey, he hired last winter. Joey don't take no guff off'n your aunt. Heck, he'll have their place back in shape afore ya know it. Anyhow, go check on our animals and help Clover if'n he needs it."

"And invite that sod-soaked fellow waiting outside to supper," Grammy suggested. "He looks as if he could do with some of your mother's cooking."

At Breelan's hesitation, Peeper urged, "Go on. Do as we're atellin' ya. I'll look after Grammy. We'll be up ta the big house shortly."

"The devil you say!" Grammy fired back. "No one need watch over me. Why, the way you two hover, you'd think I was some wild phlox and you were a couple of humming birds. Now git, Bree! And get out of those wet clothes quick as you can or Peeper'll be spreading one of her fiery mustard plasters on you, and then you'll know it!" counseled Grammy.

Monstrose let lose a soft suffer-sound, not appreciating a second disturbance when Grammy stood up and he landed on the floor. Grammy went to the unbroken front window, lifting it for air. When the sash slammed down, she fetched a wooden spoon to prop it up.

"Make room for me, too, old lady," whined Peeper as she elbowed her way beside Grammy. Then two curious faces peered out of the opening after Breelan and Breelan's companion.

Chapter 4 – *The Goodbye Lie* by Jane Marie

Ever fascinated by Peeper and Grammy, Breelan had temporarily forgotten about the man walking beside her until Peep mentioned him. He'd waited outside, looking in through the doorway. "Why didn't you come in?" she asked.

"I thought better of it. Your Grammy and, uh, Peeper, is it? They probably weren't in the mood for entertaining anyone."

"I'm sure they would've been glad to meet you. That was considerate, all the same."

"They seem like nice ladies. Are they both your grandmothers?"

"We think of them like that. Actually, only Grammy is my real grandmother. She's my mother's mother. The two of them have become fussing friends the last nine years since Pap, my grandfather, passed away. Grammy left Pennsylvania and came to live with us then, insisting on staying out of the way. That's why she lives in the little house.

"Then there's Peeper. I'm told that before I was born, Peep heard my daddy, a young and upcoming architect, had taken a wife and wanted a lady's helper for his bride. Peeper's daughter had died in some awful railroad accident, so she was alone. That little lady back there, as big around as she was tall, marched right up to Daddy's door and applied for the job. Peeper adopted my parents on sight, caring for Mama and my sister, Carolena, while Daddy was away to battle."

"Is that right?" he asked, taking in as much information as she wanted to give him.

"It was Carolena who gave her the name Peeper. Daddy could never convince Peeper that times would get better once the war ended, that she wouldn't have to watch her pennies so closely. He used to tease her, saying, 'Is that a little bird I hear? Cheap, cheap, cheap.' Carolena gave her own baby talk translation, 'Peep, peep, peep.' Hence, the nickname. Peeper never complained about it because she hated her real name anyway - Gaylee Maud Clegg."

Breelan knew she was chattering. It must be nerves, she concluded. Then again, she'd never had a case of nerves before in her life.

"Did I see you waving to Clover?" she asked.

"The man coming out of the cabin? Yes."

"Clover Williams is our hired hand. More of a wonderful friend, really. With Daddy at his office downtown so much of the time, we needed someone to lend a hand with the heavy chores. Clover's been with us since just before I was born," Breelan replied, suddenly realizing she'd been giving out her family history to a stranger.

"Now that's a particularly fine looking rooster," the man noticed as they surveyed the barnyard.

"Oh, that's Sir Chick-N-Scratch. I'm the only one he allows to hand feed him sunflower seeds. I predict it'll be a while before he lets me to do it again, though. He'll chase the other chickens, peck at the dog and cats, trying to get even with everyone and everything for any imagined weather damage to his beautiful feathers tonight."

The man laughed easily in the twilight and Breelan could see tiny lines running from the corners of his haunting eyes. She tried to mentally reconstruct the earlier incident on the stormy beach. He must have seen Noir bolt and raced upon us unheard, she thought. I know Noir would never throw me, no matter how frightened he was, so he had to have pulled me down to the ground, willing to take the blows from the tail of the devil himself. I owe him my life.

The moon escaped from its cloud captors to better light his face. It was a smooth face, no beard, no moustache. The skin looked dark, like that of someone who loved the out of doors, not like those draftsmen at her father's office who worked inside all day. His deep-set eyes could be nothing but the richest cocoa. His jaw was so square, Breelan almost reached up to touch its angle, the line of it broken only by the cleft in his chin. His nose was surprisingly straight, considering the small uneven scars he wore at his hairline, across his right cheek and on his neck, just below his right ear. That face had seen many a scrap in its thirty-odd years, she guessed. The dark hair was full, damp, and wickedly wild from the weather, yet it suited him. His mouth was drawn tight again, but might be most inviting, should the right moment occur. In all, a more handsome rescuer, she couldn't envision. Standing in front of him, she had to look up to see into his eyes. He was easily a head taller than she. She liked that. Why did it matter? She shrugged to herself.

Nearing the barn, he spoke. "You were right."

"Concerning?"

"Your horse. Once he laid eyes on you, he calmed down. It's a fine thing to be trusted."

"Sir," she paused. Silence lay on the still, clammy air. She took a huge swallow of her pride to say, "I'm deeply ashamed."

Wondering, he remained quiet.

Lowering her chin, eyeing the sandy dirt, she went on. "I didn't understand at first awakening that you'd protected me. I assumed you were a robber or murderer - or worse."

As soon as those last words escaped her lips, her head snapped up to catch a coarse sparkle in his dark eyes. She saw the corner of his mouth lift slightly and felt her face flush. Before she lost her nerve, she fired off what needed to be said. "Therefore, I apologize for my behavior. And thank you."

Not verbally responding to her contrition, he nonetheless appreciated it, gladly reversing his earlier judgment of ingrate and shrew. He could see how uncomfortable groveling left her, so he continued his observation of damages. "The barn seems intact," he pronounced. "It does look like the horses nearly kicked out the stalls though."

"How terrifying it must have been for these poor innocents." Giving an ardent caress to the velvet nose of the first horse, she cooed, "There, doesn't that feel better, Clip? And here's a scritchy-scratch for you, Clop. I can't ever forget my Clopper, can I?" As Breelan patted the withers of the two gray mares that pulled the family buggy, she explained, "Daddy is forever letting the little ones name the animals, sometimes to our embarrassment. We were stuck with a yellow canary named Crinkle whose feathers twinkled in the sunshine and a clumsy collie named Dog Flop who was always tripping, or flopping, as Marie called it."

"That's pretty cute."

"Maybe. It's just kind of embarrassing to say, 'Here Dog Flop,' to get your animal to obey." She realized how silly she sounded and laughed.

"Do you still have Crinkle and Dog Flop?" he inquired, finding the names amusing as well.

"No. I wish we did. A cat got Crinkle when Marie let her out of the cage, and a buggy ran over poor Flop when he was lying in the driveway after dark."

"That's too bad."

"Noir! I forgot all about him! He's been tied out front since we got here."

The man followed her, helping tend her horse when she'd let him and grateful all the while she couldn't read his mind, at least not yet. What kind of spectacle would the world behold if she knew his plans for her future? He'd seen her pinned down and come back spitting fire. She wasn't a shrew. She'd been confused about the circumstances. She thought she was fighting for her honor. He'd seen her dread at the possibility of injury to her family and her relieved tears at their safety. And far too briefly, he'd

27

felt her heat when he'd held her on the beach. He guessed this woman was capable of deep passion, passion on a par with his own. With an indefinable certainty, he decided she would be his one day. But not yet. She would first have to realize they were meant to be together.

After conferring with Clover, Breelan was finally assured that except for scattered branches, shingles, buckets and washtubs, the grounds were secure. She pronounced the outdoor chores completed for the night, but there was still the rest of the house to investigate. Breelan took a candle from the stock in the vestibule and the couple entered Michael's study. An ancient tree limb lay across the desk. Paper was blown everywhere. Books lay tossed about, open and torn.

"It'll take patient straightening," assessed Breelan as she noticed the last drops of kerosene dripping slowly from the saturated wick of an overturned lamp onto Miss Ella's oriental rug. "We'll never get the smell out of here," she worried, as the man righted the lamp. "Let's go upstairs. How much worse can it be?"

What was this stranger doing in her family's house? Admittedly, he didn't seem as out of place as she felt he should. Breelan sighed.

"You said something?" he asked.

"No. Just thinking to myself is all."

He leaned in and whispered, "Never let it be said I interfered with your personal thoughts about anything or in any way."

Had he emphasized the word personal? "Are you assuming I was thinking of you in some intimate fashion? Why would I? Don't be insulting!"

He laughed then.

Spinning on her boot, she hiked her muddy skirts and ascended the staircase. Her wet under things were ice cold on her skin by this time, and she felt a chill.

The man saw her shiver and wanted to warm her. Of course and unfortunately, it was out of the question.

Hearing a crunch underfoot, Breelan glanced over her shoulder to note the large oval of glass was gone from the front door. Its remains lay in shards on the carpeted stairs and carved banister. Breelan dared not touch the rail. "Be careful of your hands on the balustrade."

"Yes, thank you," he replied, having already seen the glint of the glass.

Breelan headed straight for her parent's bedroom, the first room on the left at the head of the stairs. Raising her candle, she let out a squeal of relief. There was the bed with its eight-foot headboard of polished cherry wood. It was embellished with two burled-walnut hearts angled outward.

The peak formed a broken pediment enhanced by carved oak leaves. She ran her hand along the low footboard, outlining the raised medallion in its center with her finger. "This bed belonged to my great grandmother. She gave it to Grammy, and Grammy shipped it down from Pennsylvania for my mother and father. Many children have been born here. By rights, it should go to Carolena because she's the oldest, but she doesn't care a fig about such things. She's an intellectual."

"And you're not smart?" he questioned.

"Oh, I get by. When it comes to book smarts, though, I can't compete with my sister. Textbooks have never held a fascination for me. I gave up competing to get Carolena's perfect marks in school. I did only what was necessary."

"Sounds like one of two things to me," he figured aloud.

"What would they be?" she asked, masking her beauty with a sarcastic expression.

"Well, either you're lazy ..." She stiffened at the insult and he motioned for her to remain silent. "Or you've other things you deem more interesting and important on your mind. I'd be willing to bet a great deal it's the latter, because you're certainly not stupid."

That was a compliment! Or she hoped it was. Why did it matter? "I do enjoy writing stories. Since that comes easily to me, I've never considered it to be a particular measure of aptitude."

"Stories? What kind of things do you write about?" Without waiting for an answer, he added, "Someday, I'd like to have a look at one or two, if you'd let me."

She was flattered anyone other than her immediate family would be interested in her scribblings. Flattered, yes, but also apprehensive for her written words were no detailed insight into man's behavior, nothing so serious as that. They were simple stories. "I don't know why I even mentioned them. Besides, they wouldn't hold your interest. I like best to write about feminine fancies."

"Do you mean love stories?" When she looked away, embarrassed at the sheer frivolousness of her subject, he told her, "Not all men are solely involved with guns and fighting or gambling and drink, you know. Although I do admit to dabbling in those vices a time or two in my life."

Deciding to denigrate his character as her defense against his surprising appeal, she commented, "That admission doesn't come as any surprise to me. I don't know if you're a gambler or a drinker, but it's clear you tote a gun, and those scars on your face indicate you've participated a time or two in fisticuffs."

He smiled at her choice of words. "Is that bad?"

Why did I ever bring up the subject of my idiotic writing, Breelan asked herself? It makes me uncomfortable enough just being around him. Lord Almighty! Look where I am! I'm alone in a bedroom with a man I know absolutely nothing about! With that realization, Breelan's degree of discomfort increased a thousand-fold.

"I ask again. Is it bad I've been out in the world a few years longer than you?"

He wasn't close to her, but his gaze pinned her stationary, as if her ankles were encircled with unyielding leg irons. Breelan's lips thinned as she forced herself to refrain from speaking. She wanted to say, "No. In your case, I don't imagine it is. I would say you were a man who'd experienced much in life and one who is probably capable of handling most any situation." But she didn't.

He could see some sort of internal struggle going on within her, so didn't force her to answer his last question. Dismissing her pensive look, he said, "Tell me. What does your sister being intelligent have to do with her not wanting this bed?" He was glad himself to have changed the subject back to her family.

After a relieved breath, she explained, "Carolena is always reading, so much so I told her someday it would fry her brain. She's curious about everything new. She refers to family heirlooms as clutter and fuss. She isn't particularly sentimental."

"And you are?"

"Yes, I am. The older I get, the more I love my relatives and their history. Maybe it's because of the things I've learned about war. Daddy doesn't like us to hear him talking about it, but we eavesdrop anyway. No matter how secure you may feel one minute, no one knows the future. Anything can happen. Look at the sudden storm today. I guess that's what makes life interesting. Still, who or what can you really count on?"

Breelan expected a cynical and snide remark in return and was pleasantly surprised when he responded, "You can count on the ones who love you."

"If you mean my family, I know they'll always be there for me. I'm very lucky that way. It's the people who aren't your blood kin you have to trust out of necessity, like a husband or wife. How does anyone ever decide whom to marry and feel sure about it? Right now, the idea frightens me out of my skin."

"When the time is right, you'll know without a doubt that you've chosen the right man for the rest of your life. You'll do it out of instinct."

30

"Instinct? That doesn't sound very romantic. It almost sounds more animalistic than human." She was becoming uneasy again.

"Maybe, but so natural."

"Well, anyway," Breelan shrugged him off, "the bed may be mine someday. I remember coming up here years ago and telling Mama this bed was too sacred to sleep in."

The man studied the bed and smiled as his imagination reeled.

Breelan remembered her mother smiling at her comment back then, too.

Inhaling deeply, he stood tall, clearing his head of ideas he couldn't yet allow himself to dwell upon. This was not the time. One day. "I hope you inherit it. I believe it suits you."

"Do you really think so?" she happily replied in her innocence.

"Yes. The carved hearts say much. Only those who love and are loved are meant to lie here."

"That's just how I feel!"

"It's something on which we shall always agree, Breelan," he said, casting her a powerful look.

What was so different about this man that made her feel strange? The way he phrased his words? The way she caught him watching her?

"We should check on the other rooms up here."

"After you."

This time she thought he almost seemed glad she moved away from him. Men, she thought, are certainly peculiar.

Except for broken windows, they found the second floor nearly free of damage. Descending the stairs, they were once again in the welcome hall. They passed through the double pocket doors and entered the parlor. Breelan and the man could hear the family in the kitchen. Grammy and Peeper had joined them.

Breelan had forgotten there was no glass left in the windows. She dropped the hand shielding the flame of her candle and a puff of wind blew out her light.

"Oh, dear," she said in frustration. "I need to find an oil lamp so this won't happen."

She quickly turned seeking another match, and the man stepped into her. She was knocked off balance, but he caught her arm and steadied her. Holding her close, "I don't mind if the flame goes out. I like you in complete darkness. Of course, I can't see your pleasured expression when it's dark."

Twisting in his arms, she said in disgust, "You're always needlessly touching me."

"Most women don't seem to mind."

"Most women?" She'd heard of men who spent time with many women, but that was when they were young. This man was certainly old enough to be married. His days of running after different girls should be over unless he was a widower or a philanderer. Yes, she'd known him long enough to classify him as a philanderer, snagging every fast trick his barbaric bulk craved. Without thinking, she clicked her tongue in his direction.

"What is that intriguing little sound you make? I'd be happy to investigate its source."

Her teeth clamped. "You're maddening! All I require from you is another match."

"Certainly, my beauty."

"I'm no beauty and, if I were, I surely wouldn't be yours."

"But you could be." Holding her to his chest, his fingers spread across her slender back.

She felt her breasts compress against him. His palms were hot as they heated her skin clear through the damp fabric of her dress. Being this close, she either had to rest her head on his chest or raise her face to his. She chose to look him in the eye, preparing to bestow a scathing attack upon his character.

His lips hovered over hers. She remembered that same fluttering sensation on the beach earlier. Had the cause been the warmth of his breath against her mouth? Now, it seared that mouth, in short rapid bursts. Her breathing paced even with his. He smelled of leather and bay rum cologne. He smelled good.

They froze in that posture, each silently stamping the feel, shape, and scope of the other on their memories. They were startled apart by the loud cursing of her father.

"I'm sorry, darling," consoled Miss Ella. "We really must close this wound. Only one last stitch. Only one more." Her tone changed. "If we take any longer, your head will heal of its own accord, and we wouldn't want our daddy to have a nasty scar. Isn't that right, children? Have another sip of brandy, dear." Her agitation was plain. Miss Ella disliked any encouragement of intoxication, particularly in front of the little ones. In this case, she deemed her husband's cursing and ill temper were worse. Anything to get beyond tonight.

"Grammy, would you please help Carolena put the babies down now they've seen just how brave their father is?" asked a weary Miss Ella. "I know we spoil them, but Michael insisted they watch if they wanted and, naturally, they did."

"Give me Michael's shirt, Miss Ella," said Peeper. "A little paste of starch and water on that there blood stain and tomorrow it'll just brush away, good as new."

The conversation continued from the kitchen, but the man and the woman in the parlor heard nothing more. He reluctantly widened the distance from his mouth to her lips. Still holding her, he quizzed, "You realize, don't you, a moment more and I would have had my kiss?"

"Your kiss? To my understanding, a kiss belongs to neither one nor the other. A real kiss is to be shared."

"Is that the opinion of an experienced lover?" he mocked, his voice husky. "I think not."

She was livid! Was she so unappealing he thought she'd never even been kissed?

He continued before she could speak. "But you are right. When we kiss, it will be shared. I promise."

So, he did find her attractive. That was better. Still, she could not allow such intimate comments from a stranger. "We will never know because you will never again get the chance. Guaranteed."

"And I will see you wrong. My opportunity will come. And when it does, you won't fight me."

"What conceit!"

"Conceit hasn't a thing to do with it. Only simple mutual desire," he replied. "Then again, there's nothing simple about desire. You'll learn."

"Ugh! Just light this candle and let me go!"

"As you wish."

Breelan had been clinging to the man without realizing it. When he stepped back from her, she lost her balance.

Observing only, he offered no assistance as she righted herself. He walked by her, placing the match in her hand as he passed.

She slowly turned to discover he was outside on his horse and quickly gone from her sight. The light wind landed his dust upon her through the gaping window. She opened the buttons at her throat, frantic for a deep breath.

She heard her mother's voice calling from far, far away. "Breelan, would you light a fire for us, please? The storm certainly cooled things off. You aren't still in those wet clothes, are you?"

She began to set the kindling, but there was no need for more heat in the house. To Breelan, the air was stifling.

Chapter 5 – *The Goodbye Lie* by Jane Marie

Seashells held the floral table spread in place, victorious in their defeat of the early evening's breeze that persistently tried to lift it from the picnic table. Grammy passed out Peeper's brown sugar pralines as Miss Ella poured more iced tea for any takers. Everyone was sunburned from the previous day's activities, but that couldn't stop a Dunnigan family get-together.

While the children played in the near distance, the last of the supper conversation returned to yesterday's Fourth of July festivities. "I ran into old friends in town who I hardly ever see," Michael was saying. "Guess they heard it was to be one grand celebration. I don't think they returned home disappointed."

"Probably not, but it was so hot," Aunt Noreen Duffy whined. "Just like today." She dipped her cotton napkin in what was formerly iced water and dragged it across her cheeks, forehead and around the back of her neck.

"Thank goodness for the sea air blowing so much of the time. It makes things more bearable," soothed Miss Ella.

Her sister-in-law responded with an, "Oh, Ella, you always find the silver lining. Sometimes it's almost irritating."

"Don't ya be talking bad about Miss Ella, Noreena," snapped Peeper in defense.

Clabe Duffy jumped in to try and salvage the situation before his wife got too nasty. "From my office at the bank, I watched shopkeepers decorate the downtown for days. I can only guess how relieved they were that last week's tornado stayed east of town near us and didn't touch them."

"Too bad it tore your place up so badly and spared our home," Aunt Noreen preened, as if her family had been passed over because they were divinely ordained. "It's a mystery of faith. One just never knows where God's hand will strike next."

Peeper's lips disappeared into her mouth in an immense effort not to say she knew where her hand would like to strike - and it was across the face of the fat lady at the end of the table.

Clabe was determined to prevent a battle. In an attempt to distract the combatants, on he went. "Did you see where they even had the ships' masts in the harbor gussied-up with red, white and blue?"

"Oh, thank you again, Michael, for my patriotic umbrella," Grammy chimed in.

"Mine, too," Peeper added. "It was sure in keepin' with the occasion."

"Frankly, I must say they were poorly made. I'll bet if we open and close them more than a dozen times, they'll come all apart."

"They were meant for temporary usage, Noreen." Clabe was becoming annoyed and quite weary of her complaints.

"Did you see the man dressed like George Washington standing in that tiny row boat?" asked Carolena, sitting with the grownups where she felt she rightly belonged and not off with Breelan and their cousin, Nora. "He was there when we arrived and still there when we left!"

Clover was usually a listener. Not today. "My favorite was the tightrope walking pig. I thought I'd never stop laughin'."

"I want the pig. I want the pig!" demanded Marie.

"The pig has gone off to entertain other people, honey," her mother explained.

"I want the pig! I want the pig!"

Clover picked up the little girl. "Hey now, Marie. Let's go see if we can find your brother and Warren Lowell. Your Aunt Noreen would most likely want to know where her son is, I'm thinkin'."

Noreen leaned close to Clabe and whispered, "Does the hired man mean I don't keep track of my children?"

Her husband's response was a brusque shake of his head indicating the negative.

Appeased as usual when she was in Clover's arms, Marie hugged his neck. She forgot the pig and asked, "Horsie?"

With no effort, he swung her around to sit on his shoulders and away they went, both bouncing and giggling.

"I think it's about time that little girl realized she can't always get her way."

"Mind you own business, Noreena. Don't you be a tellin' the Dunnigans how to raise their youngin's."

"Peeper, would you and Grammy get the children washed up for bed while Carolena helps me finish taking the dishes and food back inside? Frankly, I'm still worn out from last night. What with us waiting until the very last fireworks were shot off, then having to fight the crowds to get back home, I didn't get to sleep much before midnight."

"It's Breelan's turn tonight, Mama. She's always making excuses why she can't do her everyday jobs."

"I know for a fact, Cary, that she did your part of the ironing on Monday."

"Well, okay." As Carolena stacked the dirty china, she forgot her crabbing and let her mind fill with better things. "I can't get over how

36

beautiful the fireworks were. It seemed as if the angels had hung a huge mirror in the night sky when St. Mary's held their pyrotechnic display the same time as we did ours. The river between the two towns reflected everything."

"How lovely, Cary," Grammy concurred. "Breelan's handbell choir was a wonderful touch, too. Maybe next year, though, they should play before the fireworks begin instead of trying to accompany them. Half the time they were drowned out by the loud explosions."

Michael, needing to walk off his supper of fried catfish double dipped in cornmeal and garlic, excused himself from the table as his interest in the conversation dwindled. "Care to join me, Clabe?"

Quite relieved to have an excuse to remove himself from his wife, Clabe was beside his brother-in-law in an instant. After a few steps, Michael spotted a stinging nettle. Concerned that his children might be deceived by the pretty white flower and pick it, he used the toe of his shoe to push it over, then tugged on the stem, pulling it up by the root. A short toss landed the weed beneath a low-growing evergreen where his babies couldn't prick themselves.

Straightening his back, Michael surveyed the grounds. "I was just thinking of my oldest brother, Fitz. I thought I'd never recover when he and my Ma and Pa died from that goddamned yellow fever five years ago, but you do. You have to."

"Rose and John were fine people. And Fitz was so generous. Reminded me a lot of you, Michael."

"Kinds word, Clabe. I don't think I'm anywhere near my brother's equal, but I'm working on it. Anyway, a lot of Fitz's generosity had to do with him never marrying. He focused all his energies on his carpentry business. Any profits he made went to the family."

"To give this very land we're walking on to his brothers and sisters when each of you reached eighteen, and then to keep paying on it until it was paid off, well that was nothing short of magnanimous. I don't know how many times I tried to get him to let me take over payments. He wouldn't hear of it."

"Hell, I tried just as often as you did," Michael said. "He refused me, too."

"It used to embarrass me that he was buying the land I lived on. It took me years to understand that giving Noreen a section of his property was his way of trying to keep his family together."

"I wonder if our baby sister, Kathleen, and her family will come back from Washington someday and build. Her section is waiting."

"You've always said that's her plan. What about your brother John?" Clabe asked. "Do you think he might return to Fernandina someday even though he's sold his acreage?"

"Probably not. I believe he's content in Pennsylvania teaching school. I only hope the man who purchased that land doesn't ever build a house. I like my wide open spaces."

They walked to the fence and Knocker, the goat, one of two of Clover's crew who helped keep the grass a respectable length, came over to greet them. "I would have liked to buy his section if I'd had the money at the time," Clabe told Michael.

"I wanted to as well. Let's face it. We were flat busted back then." They both laughed, remembering their days of scrimping and sacrifices. Michael stopped to rotate his gaze around Fitz's original parcel of land. "Has it really been twenty-three years since I graduated from the University of Georgia? You know, had I not gone to Philadelphia on that architectural foray, I would never have met and married Ella Eckert, the pretty little freulein from Pennsylvania. A chance meeting became a certain union."

"It was six months later that your baby sister, Noreen, married me."

Michael finished the sentence, "A prominent banker from Jacksonville."

"I not sure about the prominent part," Clabe said with sincere modesty. Looking up, "I've often marveled how distinctly different our houses are, and yet you designed them both. Duffy Place is basically a brick cube, but with that bay window running its height, the square cupola sitting in the middle of the crossed hip roof, and all those asymmetrical features you added, it looks European. You called it Italianate, didn't you?"

"Italianate it is. You're a good student."

"You're a good teacher. To me the place has a visual strength as well as actually being sound. Had the tornado hit my home directly, I know the windows would have blown out, but I'd bet that would have been about all."

Michael turned to his own sturdy home as he had a hundred times over the years. "Most of the repairs on the manor are complete. I'm glad it's back to the way it was. Do you recall how Miss Ella originally fought adding all the fretwork, thinking it would look too busy? In passing, I mentioned that it reminded me of her fancywork. After that, she liked it."

"Women are hard to figure."

"You got that right."

"I wonder if Miss Ella will ever want to change the house color from yellow?"

"She isn't too fond of change, so probably not. The fact that she had Clover paint the front door Charleston green surprised me. When she gave me the claddagh doorknocker for Christmas last year, she said its brass would look best against a darker color instead of the white. Said it would better show off its meaning of friendship, loyalty, and love."

"She was right. It stands out. Pretty much makes an overall statement that all those things abide within."

"We hope so. Hey, did I tell you I was afraid it would take forever to match the decorative verge board that twister took off if the lumberyard had to cut it? Then one of the men from my office said he thought he knew someone who might have some of the same pattern stored out in their barn. And he was right. I couldn't believe my luck."

"I guess that means you're not the only guy in town who likes the Gothic Revival style."

"Clabe Duffy, honest to God, I'm impressed. If you ever get tired of counting money at the bank, you've got a job working for my architectural firm."

Happy in his occupation, Clabe said, "Thanks, pal, but I think I like being your friend. If we worked together, who knows what might happen?"

"I agree. It'd be a mistake. We're both too independent."

"And too damn old to change our ways."

Or change much of anything else, Clabe thought, trying to count his blessings. Life would be perfect if his wife were more like Miss Ella. He'd resigned himself to the fact she never would be, and that was that. "We're pretty lucky, you and I, Michael. Thank goodness for our children. My Nora might be a little scatterbrained, but she's so very loveable. And Warren Lowell, child from the Land of Awful ..." Michael eyed Clabe, surprised he would admit such a thing. "Hey, I can say it because he's my son. That boy could use a daily body beatin'. Once in a while just isn't enough. So long as his lenient mother has her way, that's how it will remain. Our only hope is someday he'll grow up to be an honorable man."

Michael understood the shortcomings of his sister and although he heartily agreed, he refrained from saying so. He did enough bad-mouthing of Noreen on his own. He didn't need encouragement. "I've got a monster boy of my own. You don't think we were that bad when we where kids, do you?"

Clabe looked over. "Of course not."

Each was sure he was worse than his son and silently pitied his parents for having had to endure his antics.

Together, they walked over to Jack Patrick's dog. "Hey there, Blackie-boy." Michael removed his waistcoat to fling it over his shoulder on one finger. The dog, tail wagging, jumped at his leg in happy answer. "Get down. Get down! I guess you'll never learn any manners," Michael stated as fact. "Heck, we love ya any how. Come on." He patted Blackie on his well-padded ribs a few times, and the dog followed the men back to where the last of the family remained.

Putting his arm around his still beautiful bride, he said, "I've been thinking on how blessed we all are, Miss Ella. The look on your face tells me it's happiness you've been thinkin' of, too." He kissed the tip of her slender nose.

"You're right, Michael. Surely you know after all these years you're the cornerstone of that happiness."

"Twenty three years is but a light kiss on the cheek of time, my darling." His wife looked away so he wouldn't see the mist of tears forming in her eyes.

Michael and Clabe moved on toward Ella's zinnia bed. Aunt Noreen had gone home, the mosquitoes having chased her away, and Miss Ella took a moment to herself to rest quietly. Breelan, the blue-eyed brunette and Nora, her green-eyed, redheaded cousin were sitting in the crook of the huge magnolia, their "talkin' tree," as Peeper named it, conspiring. The two were more than close, forget they were kin. They'd grown up living next door to one another, gone to the same school, and done most everything together. They made few decisions without each other's counsel.

While the girls chatted, Miss Ella remembered their charmed childhood, how they played hour upon hour with dolls or Chinese checkers, cat's cradle or double-Dutch jump rope, and croquet. They'd even had a secret club.

"They're doin' it, again!" Jack Patrick pointed to his sister and cousin. "The Squint Sisters are doin' it again."

"Jack Patrick, leave the girls alone. Aren't you supposed to be getting ready for bed?"

"Ah, Ma. I'm not tired. Heck, it's not anywhere near dark yet."

"Alright. Then go and tell Clover to put you to work finishing the chores," Miss Ella ordered. "Now."

"Yes, ma'am." He dashed off, still calling Breelan and Nora names. "Bye, Slice Eye. Bye, Sliver Lid."

Miss Ella crossed the yard to talk to the embarrassed parties. "What can I say? Your brother can be a dickens, Bree. Sorry, Nora."

40

"Oh, we're used to it. The worst part is we've been working so hard not to squint and he knows it. Why is it we're the only two in the family who have this affliction?"

"Affliction? I would hardly call closing one eye slightly in defense of the sun an affliction. And you're not the only people who do it. We all do sometimes. It's a natural reflex, but I understand that right now this is of great concern to you both. You won't believe me, but in a year's time your worrying will be forgotten. Still, it's just one of many things you two share. It's part of what strengthens your bond to each other. To tell the truth, I think it's kind of charming. Really, I do." Miss Ella could plainly see the girls wanted to believe her yet were having difficulty. "Just continue to wear your bonnets to shade your eyes."

"Blackie-White-Spots, get away from them leftovers. They's for tomorrah's supper!"

At the sound of Peeper warning the dog away, Miss Ella said, "Got to get inside and put Marie to bed." She turned to see Clabe and Michael sitting on the brick wall corralling her flowers. "Michael," she called out. "I'll be in the house."

He waved her way and continued his talk with Clabe as they sampled Michael's latest batch of blackberry cordial. "Since I've been adding sweet milk to the brew, then letting it sit for twenty-four hours, the end product is beautifully clear. I just have to be careful pouring it off into another decanter. None of the milk and sediment can get into the fresh bottle. What's your verdict on the wine?"

"I'd have to say it's guilty of smoothness and sparkle. An excellent effort, Michael," Clabe answered. He presented his glass for a refill while he swished the libation around his mouth, trying to reach every taste bud with its sweetness.

The men were interrupted as Jack Patrick held up a cloth sack. "I brought you a present, Daddy. It's a bag of gold that Warren Lowell and I mined from the sandbox. We've never seen any gold before this. We just heard you and the other men talking about it. It smells pretty bad, but it's the right color so that means we're rich! And now that we're rich, can I have a BB gun?" He turned to his uncle. "Warren Lowell wants one, too."

"Jack Patrick!" Grammy was hollering out the window.

"I gotta go. Bye."

Still holding the sack in stunned silence, Michael offered a weak, "Thank you." Jumping down from the wall, "I'd best be burying this gold, Clabe," he chuckled. "I'll do it behind the barn. Don't want to hurt the boy's feelings. I'd bet you'll have the same thing waiting at home for you. I do believe the next time the children go to play in the sandbox, they'll find a tarp covering it to prevent any further feline deposits, if you get my meaning." With that image in mind, they went their separate ways for the evening.

If the older adults were watching the near-adults, the near-adults returned the glances with much less curiosity. "Your mother is so grand, Bree," Nora told her sincerely. "I hope you realize how lucky you are."

Feeling bad for Nora because Aunt Noreen could often be difficult, Breelan tilted her head and smiled at her cousin. "I am lucky. Remember, my mother is always available for you, should you ever need her."

"I'm glad," was all Nora could get out. She didn't want to think ill of her own mother so she said the first thing that popped into her mind. "Older adults often discuss such intolerably boring subjects."

Squirming to make herself more comfortable on the tree trunk, Breelan agreed as she mindlessly bit off the edge of one of Peeper's sugary deserts. Hearing a sudden scream, they turned to see a limping Marie, struggling toward Peeper for sanctuary. Her cousin, Warren Lowell, was gaining on the tot.

"He kicked me again," groaned Marie, showing Peeper the dark bruise already discoloring her tiny leg. Warren wore special corrective shoes with steel braces in the toes. It gave him delight to brandish his weapon at girls, big or small.

"Warren Lowell!" shouted the old woman. "The devil's makin' his book and you're in it!"

"Clabe," called Noreen, who had reappeared at the Dunnigan home in time to join the hubbub, "Clabe, remember he's just a little boy. Offer it up."

"I'll offer him up!" snapped her husband, happy he was able to witness the crime and dole out the proper punishment for once.

Breelan and Nora laughed behind their hands as they watched Warren Lowell's over-sized father laboriously chase him round the pink climbing rose trellis, over the azalea bushes, between two light blue flowering plumbago plants, and eventually into the Duffy barn where the razor strap hung.

"Now that we're grown," said Nora, suddenly serious, "It's time we travel. Just the two of us."

"There's plenty to do right here in Fernandina. Since I work part time for Major Fairbanks at *The Mirror*, I get all the latest news down at the paper, even if it only has a weekly circulation. It's very exciting for me to see my articles in print. Maybe they're not the most important ..."

"I, for one, think it's very interesting to hear whose crab won the race at the beach."

"You're sweet for saying that," Breelan said sincerely. "But you know I work at the paper mostly to hone my writing skills. It's hardly a career in journalism since the small amount they pay me might as well be sand. Maybe someday it might develop into something, though. Besides, I'm in no particular hurry to leave our hometown. Sure there're great places and people to see and meet out there, but I adore Fernandina. I plan to settle down here. Daddy has already told us children we can build a house on his property if we choose to. And I do."

Nora continued when Breelan didn't say anything more. "Before we turn around, we'll be married and won't have any freedom to go places. We'll be busy taking care of our own families. Now is our chance."

"Mmm," commented Breelan.

"I was thinking about going to New York City to visit your Aunt Coe. It's been years since we've seen her. It would only take a week by steamship."

Breelan thought a moment about what Nora was saying. "You might be right. Our time to marry gets closer every day. And if we want to tour and have any adventures as unattached ladies, this would be a sensible way. Oh, let's be honest. We're talking about affairs of the heart, aren't we?"

"Yes. What else is there of any consequence?" Nora shrugged. "Men. That's where my interest lies. If I have to leave town to find the fellow for me, then so be it. Heaven knows, there isn't anyone here that makes me pot-gugged and saucy."

"Shh. Do you want your mother to hear you? She'll never let you go then."

"You're right. You're right. We must remember deportment at all times. At least until our parents give us permission to go."

"Nora, dear cousin, you are a pistol."

As the sun slid down behind the trees, the girls revised and refined their plan of attack, and their ever-attentive families wondered if and when the reason for this particular parley would be revealed.

Chapter 6 – *The Goodbye Lie* by Jane Marie

The week passed. Again the Dunnigans and the Duffys were outdoors, sitting about, digesting. This time the occasion was the completion of two blue-painted picnic tables that Michael had just built. With the release of a latch and support on either side, each tabletop tilted and became the back of a bench.

A hearty beef roast, poked with garlic chips and stewed in coffee, had been prepared by Grammy with assistance from Miss Ella. Near to bursting, they all enjoyed the peach cobbler Uncle Clabe had suggested Aunt Noreen bring as her contribution. The steaming peaches melted the vanilla ice cream that ran in rivulets over the slightly soggy golden crust.

"I have to say," continued Uncle Clabe, "I've run against a stump when it comes to you girls going off to New York City unchaperoned, with only one another to rely upon. Who knows what manner of skunks will be on the ship or board it when it docks in Charleston and Baltimore and Philadelphia? Or even worse, who knows how many Billy Yanks you'll run into or how they'll try and rook innocent young ladies like yourselves? Oh, excuse me, Miss Ella. I meant no disrespect."

"I know you didn't, Clabe," replied Miss Ella graciously.

"Good gravy!" an exasperated Nora sputtered.

"Nora Ruth Duffy, you'd best be polite," insisted her mother, lifting one brow and lowering the other in a disciplinary attempt at body language that only made her face appear lopsided.

"Yes, ma'am, but ..."

"Let's all calm down," Miss Ella said.

Aunt Noreen's gaze focused on her sister-in-law. Unnecessarily pointing out Clabe's shortcomings, yet again, his wife noted, "We must not comment negatively upon the Yankees. How many more years will it take before we can put that War of Northern Aggression behind us? We've all learned to love Miss Ella and her people, even if they are Yankees and not good Catholics to boot."

Michael was on his feet and ready to order his sister off his property. His wife took hold of his sleeve and tugged at him. Struggling to give Noreen the benefit of the doubt, she whispered, "It's alright. Really it is. She doesn't realize she's being unkind."

"It's about damn time I let her know then. The reason people are rude is because other people let them get away with it!"

Clabe and Nora stayed stoic. They had no words of excuse to offer Miss Ella and Grammy. Peeper was delighted Michael was going to give that grump Noreen her comeuppance and in front of everyone, too.

Grammy was plain mad. "And they say it's Yankees who are rude," she muttered.

Aunt Noreen's attention was captured. She sat with her fingers laced in front of her as she tried to conceal her excitement. "Tell, tell, Michael. Who was rude?"

"It's hopeless, Michael," Grammy flat out admitted.

Throwing up his hands, he sat back down with a thud.

Aunt Noreen realized her brother was not going to reveal the perpetrator, so made what she considered to be a noble statement. "It's good of you not to speak ill of anyone, Michael. Our mother would be proud."

"Lord, God Almighty!" Peeper said. "I ain't feelin' so good. I might lose that slimy peach cobbler of your'n, Noreena. It weren't no good anyhow. Ya don't cook it long enough. Ya never do. The syrup is runny."

"Why, Peeper Clegg! Who gave you the right to criticize my cooking? How many times have I had to endure those nasty crab cakes you make with stale oil? And how many times are they served burnt black because you're too cheap to throw them out?"

"I'd rather be tight-fisted with my money than spend so much of it my poor husband has ta stay away from home ta earn enough ta pay my bills. Or is it 'cause he just don't want ta be around ya?"

Breelan's thoughts drifted away from the squabbling and centered on her mother. Breelan understood her mother was uncomfortable when conversations like these arose. She remembered way back when she was little, when they didn't visit with her cousins as readily as they did now. Because Miss Ella was a Lutheran, her people from Germany, and not an Irish Catholic like the Dunnigans, tension abounded. Breelan understood Miss Ella had taken instruction in the Catholic faith in an attempt to resolve the problem, but she had chosen not to convert. The priest had called her a heathen, nearly causing Michael to leave his own church. His wife urged him to adhere to the faith of his fathers by explaining that this particular priest was only a man, and a foolish man at that. They both knew she was no heathen. Since she agreed to raise her children as Catholics, and they all attended mass together - partly because there were few Lutherans in town - the family prejudice had diminished. But clearly, to one in particular, it was not gone completely.

Breelan always figured her father was straight-laced and conservative, yet as she grew older, she realized what a break with tradition it had been for him to marry outside his religion. To ignore his family's objections was something to be admired, she decided, a true act of courage. She was awakened from her reverie by Nora's elbow to her ribs.

"Ladies, please," Miss Ella scolded the women like bad children. "I wasn't raised around such unpleasant exchanges, and I don't think we need expose our daughters or ourselves to any more. Let's get back to the subject at hand. Our girls plan to go to New York City."

It was Breelan's turn to persuade. "You allowed Carolena to visit Auntie alone."

"That was different, out of necessity, and you know it," answered her mother. "Your Aunt Coe was ill and needed someone. I was unable to travel in my condition with Marie on the way. And too, Carolena was mature and going there on an errand of mercy, not a frivolous romp. You'll have to do better than that, Bree."

Carolena sat smiling, not saying a word, just watching her sister and cousin squirm. It took all Breelan's willpower not to snarl at her big sister.

Breelan thought fast. "Daddy, you can put us on the ship yourself and talk to the captain! You know, have him keep an eye out for us. Surely we'll be safe, don't you think?"

Nora couldn't endure her own silence any longer. "Mother, Daddy," she smiled sweetly toward her folks. "Breelan's Aunt Coe and Uncle Fries can meet us at the pier in New York City. And we'll wire you as soon as we dock. After all, I'm nineteen now and will use the same excellent judgment I exhibit in all things."

Her parents eyed one another. Miss Ella bit her lip. Michael quickly took out his handkerchief and masked his laughter with a few spurious sneezes.

"Bless you," bestowed Grammy with a straight face.

"Ah, thank you," choked Michael.

Clearing his throat, Clabe spoke, "All right girls, leave us in peace. We'll discuss the matter and give you our decision shortly."

"Does Carolena get to stay?" Breelan wanted to know.

"Yes. Your sister has been there and can advise us about any concerns she may have. Now go on so we can settle this thing, dear."

"Yes, Uncle," Breelan obeyed.

Nora closed her case with, "I love you, Father," and the two walked off to await their fate.

"We were in for sure until they let Carolena stay," Breelan sighed. "She'll discredit everything we've said. I don't think we have much of a chance. And by the way, that last 'I love you' was a bit obvious, don't you think?"

"Nah, parents gobble that sort of thing up. They can't help themselves. Have a little faith," comforted Nora.

"I'll try." But Breelan was ready for disappointment.

"Well, I've done it," Clabe told Michael as they sat on Clabe's front porch.

"What's that?" Michael asked as he kept his eye on Warren Lowell, most particularly on Warren Lowell's deadly feet, since he and Jack Patrick were playing pickle in the middle and Marie had been given the role of the pickle.

"I sent the letter off to Waite Taylor, captain of that passenger liner, like we talked about. I mailed it to Charleston. According to the harbormaster, it's the next scheduled stop on his run. I asked him if he would be personally responsible for our daughters on their first trip to New York and back. For a fee, of course."

"Of course. I guessed you'd get around to writing it eventually, once you let the facts of my investigation sink in. He's been in and out of here for sometime, according to *The Mirror*, since Fernandina is a regular stop for the *Gentle Comfort*."

Peeper was delivering a plate of her lemon pecan muffins to the Duffys, taking pity on poor Clabe since Noreen's reputation as a notoriously poor cook was alive and well. It was a mystery where the man was getting food good enough to keep his middle as round as it was. She decided to save that question for a time when Noreen really made her mad. She giggled to herself, knowing how the insult would jab her archenemy a good one. Overhearing, she felt inclined to ask questions. "What investigation would that be, Michael? That captain man? Wha'd ya find out?"

Michael refrained from rolling his eyes. He would never tell Peeper that some things should be left to the men of the family. It would have been a waste of time anyway. Peep would hound him until he told her what she wanted to know, so over the years he'd learned to just give in. "Only good things. Waite Montoya Taylor is the sole child of a Venezuelan heiress, Carla Montoya, and an English seaman, Kenneth Waite Taylor. He was raised in the Florida Keys and sailed the Caribbean with his father until his mother's passing when he was fourteen. He continued his education and then joined the Confederate Army at sixteen. I understand his father wanted him by his side to fight the Yankees at sea, but Taylor chose to stand with the lads from his class on land. He served with the Third Florida in the Battle of Olustee. It's west of here."

"I know where Olustee is. I ain't never been there, but I read the paper, ya know. What other good stuff do ya got about him?"

Impatient and persistent, that was Peeper. Michael went on. "Just that he received a battlefield commission raising his rank to lieutenant. His father, however, didn't fare so well. He was killed when his vessel was rammed broadside by a sinking Federal supply ship. They say that since that time, his son vowed to have a career at sea, no matter what manner of ship he served on, in honor of the man who'd shown him the wonder of the waters. After the war, he earned his shipmaster's license and eventually became the youngest captain in the history of the transatlantic shipping company, Atlantic Eagle Cargo Lines. For a dozen years he commanded a regular run between Baltimore and South Hampton, England, delivering lumber, turpentine, cotton and phosphate. I understand he wanted a change, so built his passenger ship, *Gentle Comfort,* named in memory of his beloved mother, and he's been running the *Comfort* along the eastern shore of the United States ever since. That brings us to the present."

"He's got my stamp of approval, boys. Now, quit all this jawing and have yourselves some muffies while they's still hot."

"Yes, ma'am," the boys answered in unison.

Breelan and Nora desperately awaited the captain's answer to Clabe's letter. A dozen days later, Nora heard the tin whistle of the postman announcing his delivery. "Howdie, little miss. I think I've got that special letter you've been wanting."

Forgetting herself, she grabbed the mail from him, let out a, "Thanks, Mr. Stanley," and ran into the house. Throwing open the library doors, she cried, "Daddy, it's here! It's here!"

Clabe carefully sliced the edge of the envelope with his letter opener, withdrew the note and read aloud.

26 July 1882

  Dear Mr. Duffy,

I regret the delay in answering your request to oversee your young ladies. My mail always has a time catching me. I would be honored to be responsible for their safety. Please contact me when they are ready for travel. I will meet you all at the dock in Fernandina and escort them aboard personally.

Your servant,
Captain Waite M. Taylor

P.S. This will be my privilege. No fee is required.

Clabe smiled, determining the captain was a man of character. Then he nodded and returned the letter to his eager daughter.

Without even reading it, Nora was out the back door, down the steps and flying across the yard to Breelan's house. Forgetting to knock, she burst through the Dunnigans' kitchen door.

"Land sakes, child!" squawked a startled Grammy. "Haven't you got a 'good morning' for me?"

"Sorry to be rude, Gram, but the reply to my father's letter just arrived!" she breathlessly responded and bounded up the stairs. "We're going to New York City!"

Nora found Breelan in her bedroom with Carolena who was rummaging through a glass compote dish, which held a mix of ribbons, combs and other hair toys. Carolena was asking, "Why is it you always end up with all the hairpins in your room? If it's hot like today, you are well aware I put my hair up to get it off my neck. When I go to get my pins and don't have enough to finish the job, I know just where to find more. Are you some kind of compulsive hairpin hoarder?" the big sister interrogated.

Not wanting to defend herself, yet not willing to let this last comment pass uncontested, Breelan told her, "My hair is thicker than yours and it takes more pins to keep it up. Can I help it if Peeper puts the extras she finds around the house in here? If you have a problem with that, take it up with her and don't bother me about it. And I'd appreciate it if you'd stay out of my room."

A spontaneous reply left Carolena's lips. "Believe me when I say I'd never step foot in your sanctuary if you'd ..."

Used to the sisters' bickering, Nora interrupted their silliness. "We're going, Bree! We're going!" Nora blurted out, tossing the note at her cousin and flopping down on the double bed.

"So you wangled yourselves a trip to New York," Carolena said, hinting they'd done something underhanded. "Just be sure and mind the captain, children. I wish I were going along, but only to see him pull you over his knee and give you a whipping when you don't obey."

"Oh, dry up, you big pile of dung!"

Carolena laughed at the silly insult. "With that sort of mature retort, Breelan, you're sure to stay out of trouble," and she left the room wearing a cherubic expression.

"Just ignore her, Bree. Her mission is to get your goat and we won't let her, no matter how much she teases."

"You're right. Back to business. How many trunks should we each take?"

"That's the way! My insides are all fluttery. I've already packed two in hopes we'd go!"

Chapter 7 – *The Goodbye Lie* by Jane Marie

Centre Street traffic was at a standstill. From the vantage point of separate carriages, it looked to the Dunnigans and the Duffys like an overloaded log wagon had split an axle in the middle of the street. Uncle Clabe pulled his rig beside Michael's, knowing the women would want to talk to pass the time.

"The port is so alive with activity this morning," observed Breelan, her excitement motivating her eyes to wander.

Nora frowned. "It's too crowded. I hope we won't miss the boat."

"We're plenty early enough, darlin'," her father comforted. "Schooners are pulling out a little late this morning because of last night's heavy rains, but the sun's shining and the river's plenty enough flat. Even if we have to walk you a few blocks to bypass the mess ahead, you'll make it."

"I hope this good weather holds for their trip, Miss Ella," called Aunt Noreen from beside Clabe. "I worry. You know how I worry."

"Yes. I know. It was good of Grammy and Peeper to stay behind with the little ones," Miss Ella mentioned, trying to take Noreen's mind away from herself. "They wanted to see the girls off until I explained it would take three buggies to accommodate everyone. Then they understood."

"Mama, it's not like Bree and Nora are going abroad," remarked an exasperated Carolena, quite tired of all the fuss. "It's just to New York City."

"Well I, for one, am concerned that the captain referred to us as young ladies in his note," stated Nora. "I think he figures we're children. If he tries to treat us like babies, it will spoil everything."

"I'm sure when he sees how grown up you are, he'll be your protector and not a nursemaid," consoled her father.

"I hope you're right," agreed Breelan.

"To my way of thinking, Miss Ella," Michael whispered, "no amount of supervision would be too much."

Breelan turned back to the east to check for herself that the sun was still shining and that no clouds were threatening a storm. Her right eye squinted, as was its natural propensity, because the brim of her bonnet was not deep enough to sufficiently shade her eyes. She scolded herself and pulling her hat forward, forcing both eyes fully open. Since it was eighty-some degrees already this morning, her choice of a cotton walking gown of tiny forget-me-not flowers was a wise one, she decided. "Mama, thank you for sewing the new blue braid at my hem."

"It's an old trick Grammy taught me, honey. Your skirts will last twice as long that way. I wasn't sure if you'd finish crocheting your gloves in time, but you did. And your reticule is just wonderful, Bree. I love the brooch you've pinned on it. It's always so nice when your handbag matches your gloves. It's the little extras that count. Noreen, did you see where Breelan has gone to the trouble of lining her bag?"

Reluctant to ever offer too much tribute, Noreen loudly whispered, "You must be careful with praise, Ella. You'll make her nervous."

"Nervous!" Michael heard his sister's incomprehensible instruction to his wife, which caused his head to snap angrily in her direction. "Noreen, what in your misguided mind ever told you to say such a thing? Praise makes children proud and confident, not ..."

Miss Ella was patting his arm. He took her meaning to not waste his breath as he had so many hundreds of times over the years. Would he ever in this lifetime get used to Noreen's inane advice? He seriously doubted it.

Nora fidgeted in her gown of pale yellow voile. Peeking from her marigold colored sash was a small bouquet of velvet violets accenting her nearly slender waist. "I can't get comfortable in this bonnet. First the ribbon chokes me. I retie it, and then it's too loose. Oh bother! I'll just hold the stupid thing in my lap."

"What about the sun and your eye?" her mother warned.

"The devil can have the sun and my eye as well!" Having misspoken, Nora rapidly apologized for her comment before one of her mother's inevitable lectures was launched. "Sorry, Mama. We'll be on the ship in a few minutes anyway."

Taking hold of his wife's hand and squeezing it tighter than was comfortable, Clabe looked down to wordlessly instruct Noreen to hush.

Getting his message, but not liking it, Noreen snatched back her gloved fingers and crossed her arms around her ample bosom to sulk.

By this time, enough logs had been cleared to allow traffic to proceed.

Spotting the *Gentle Comfort* was not a difficult task, seeing as how it was longer than a three-masted schooner, half-again as tall, and its name was spelled out in black letters two feet high. "What a lovely steamship!" Breelan proclaimed. Admittedly, her knowledge of such vessels was limited to Sunday sailboat rides around the marina "to blow the stink off," as her father always called it. She looked forward to going on board and actually seeing the inside of it - or her. Yes, she remembered she'd heard that ships were referred to as females. No matter. Her attention was diverted as Michael pulled as close to the gangplank as he dared without running over the rushing passengers. He halted the two grays, Clip and

Clop, glad he'd had Clover put blinders on them to insure they would remain calm and not jostle the ladies. Clabe pulled his buggy up behind.

A boy of nine or so hurried over to Michael. "Hey mister, can I take your trunks on board for ya? If you please." He had clearly added the last in hopes of a fair-sized tip.

"Yes, son. We've got several. Mind, they're heavy."

"Nah," the youngster responded as Michael watched him maneuver them onto a dolly with wheels and then push all the baggage up the incline.

"I'll wait here," said Carolena, opening her parasol. "The dock is too crowded. Now be sure and write, girls. Keep us posted on your antics, hear?"

"We will," answered Breelan. "Bye, sis."

With Breelan and Nora each centered between their parents, the pair of threesomes walked toward the gangplank like soldiers drilling.

Breelan could see the back of a tall gentleman at the base of the boat ramp where it met the dock. Men and boys all jumped at the mere gesture of his hand. She assumed he must be Captain Taylor, her keeper.

I'll be pleasant enough in front of Daddy, she decided, but once Nora and I are on board, well, I see no reason to be overly solicitous just because he's doing a favor for my father. After all, we're not paying him a cent, so I'm sure he won't care one way or the other. She pushed to the back of her mind the fact the captain's favor had granted her the liberty of traveling to New York City and that it had been her own suggestion as well.

The sound of tearing fabric caught her ear. The braid on her hem had hooked on a rough plank. Daughter, then mother, then father halted to inspect the severity of the tear.

"Captain Taylor?" Clabe called out, pulling his wife and girl around the paused Dunnigans.

The big man turned, the obligatory smile of a captain greeting his passengers on his lips. His gaze saw first the trio of Nora and her parents. He tipped his hat and offered his hand to Clabe. Then glancing beyond them, he spied Michael, Miss Ella and Breelan. Surprise and delight lit the sparkling dark eyes that belonged to the man who had delivered Breelan from the deadly tornado!

Upset that her trim had pulled loose nearly the entire width of the back of her skirt, Breelan fussed under her breath, "Oh, rats! Just what I want to do, repair a hem on my holiday."

"Why, my dears, I can scarcely believe our luck!" beamed Michael.

"Sir," the officer acknowledged fondly. Removing his hat, he bowed low from the waist, confirming his identity. "Captain Waite Taylor."

"Captain, you may remember my family. Mrs. Dunnigan and Breelan and that's my other daughter, Carolena, over there in the buggy."

Carolena smiled brilliantly, returning his wave once she recognized the captain.

"Certainly. It's grand to see you all again," he replied, his stare quickly returning to the young lady in the floral gown who appeared to be somewhat flustered.

Upon spying the captain, Breelan forget her irritation at the ruined hem. She realized she was blushing as she recalled the feel of his embrace in the front parlor, an embrace that had excited and puzzled her. How might he act toward her aboard ship? And all the way to New York City, too? She'd put him in his place when last they'd met. It wouldn't be difficult to straighten the man out a second time if he forgot himself.

Captain Taylor saw Breelan's expression change from confusion to what he suspected was determination. Or was it obstinacy?

Her conviction faltering, Breelan dropped her gaze to her fumbling fingers intertwined with the chain-stitched strings of her purse.

"You were off and gone so quickly, we were unable to thank you properly," Miss Ella said, much relieved this was the man who would watch over her daughter and niece.

"The hour was late, and I knew everyone needed rest after their ordeal."

"Sissy," Michael said to Noreen. "This is the man who helped us after the tornado last month. He saw to it that our Breelan arrived safely home and then proceeded to check on our property, helping to calm everyone. I was indisposed and the captain gallantly offered aid." Touching the fading scar on his forehead, Michael remembered the swallows of brandy warmly, his throat becoming suddenly dry.

Disregarding the current subject, Aunt Noreen spoke. "This is your first passenger ship command, I'm told, sir. I pictured a much older man in the critical position of captain." Her face reddened slightly at such a personal remark regarding his age. However, she figured using the word "critical" offset it. In any case, it had to be commented upon.

Shocked at his wife's obvious distrust, Clabe glared at her. "Miss Noreen, really! The single fact that for years this man commanded cargo ships that crossed the deadly Atlantic is recommendation enough for us to trust his skill at maneuvering a passenger vessel up and down the coast."

Still worrying that this fellow was a little too attractive to be chaperoning impressionable girls, Aunt Noreen looked at her daughter and immediately recognized a case of fascination in Nora's eyes. Clabe, like most men, never did catch onto such matters until it was far too late. But what was there to do now? The die was cast. Unless, of course, she made a commotion and forbade Nora to travel. How could she keep her child here without giving some sort of explanation? They would all demand one. She could suddenly take ill, and Nora would get a case of the guilts and stay by her mother's side. No, that wouldn't work, Noreen thought. Just two days ago Doctor Tackett had pronounced her fit at her annual physical exam and, foolishly, she'd told everyone.

Aunt Noreen crossed herself, promising to attend morning mass daily until the girls arrived home. Speaking softly, yet intending that her words be plenty loud enough for the captain to hear, "There is a great deal of difference between inanimate cargo and the emotional intricacies of living passengers. I will have to put all my trust in the Almighty to get the children safely to New York City."

"Trusting in the Lord is always the best way, Mrs. Duffy," concurred Captain Taylor who showed no signs of offense.

Miss Ella placed a reassuring arm around her sister-in-law's thick back. "Really, Noreen, it will be just fine. Do you think we'd let the children go if we didn't trust the captain completely? You know us better than that."

Checking a nearby line, a young crewman interjected innocently, "Ah, go on, Cap'n. Tell the good folks how they give ya a medal for valor on the battlefield so's they can rest easy."

Casting a searing look toward the sailor, notice was sent and received to get to work but, more importantly, never to interfere again unless asked. The face of the crewman dropped at the harsh lesson. Realizing the lad had merely meant him a compliment, Captain Taylor eased his stern expression. "Go along, Billy-Boy. We'll soon be shovin' off and there's plenty still to do."

The anguish on the boy's face disappeared at hearing his given name spoken by his commander. "Yes, sir! Aye, sir." The incident was forgotten as quickly as it had occurred, and the crewman dashed out of sight, whistling.

Turning again to the captain, "Yes, yes. We would love to hear of your citations in battle, sir," Aunt Noreen pressed.

Waite Taylor spoke, but only to resolve the debate. "Ma'am, I was just one of many stalwart fellows who received commendations. I discovered fear makes a boy into a man overnight, and a man will often surprise himself when forced to the wall, doing what must be done."

"Well said," lauded Clabe.

55

Directing interest from himself and glancing at his pocket watch, the captain stated firmly, "We must get the young ladies on board and be underway shortly if we're to ride the high tide and depart on time."

There it was again. Young ladies. Breelan could have spit. Nora looked unaware of much of anything except that she was in love and ready to follow her captain anywhere. She'll snap out of it the farther from home and the closer to New York City we get, Breelan reassured herself. She'll find something and someone else to attract her there.

"Nora, did you remember to pack your turpentine and apple vinegar liniment?" Aunt Noreen pestered.

"Yes, Mother."

"Good. And what about the lime water? You haven't forgotten what the lime water is for, have you?"

"No, Mother. The limewater is an all-purpose antidote," Nora recited from rote. "And yes, before you ask, I even have the green tea." How very anxious she was to escape this foolishness.

"That's my girl," Aunt Noreen replied proudly explaining to everyone, "The green tea is for dysentery. One needs to be prepared."

"Mother, please," begged her daughter, embarrassed to the bone.

The two families hugged and kissed while Waite Taylor watched and listened, enjoying the scene. He particularly watched the girl with the rich dark hair peeking from beneath her bonnet and envied Miss Ella for her daughter's arms about her neck.

Counsel came from all quarters.

"Do whatever the captain recommends."

"Eat slowly so you won't get seasick."

"Contain your laughter."

"You must not appear ignorant of good manners."

"Retire at a decent hour."

"Be gracious when the steward offers his comforts to you."

"Stay together."

"Be particular in making the acquaintance of strangers, and let no one thrust his favors upon you."

"Sit on deck only when the sun is behind the clouds and for heavens sake, don't fall asleep reading or you'll dry up like old prunes."

"Yes. Yes, of course. We promise. We will," the girls replied, lifting their skirts with one hand as was proper. They walked up the incline, waving and throwing kisses to their parents just as the ship's whistle sounded.

Before taking his place at the helm, the captain reassured the anxious parents one last time, "On my honor, I'll return them to you."

"Thank you," said Clabe.

His two hands encasing one of Captain Taylor's, Michael declared, "We're trusting in you. God go with you all."

Chapter 8 – *The Goodbye Lie* by Jane Marie

Once the captain made sure the ladies were settled in their stateroom, he left them. He had never looked directly at Breelan. He'd been attentive to Nora's chatter and most cordial, wearing that unnatural smile on his lips that Breelan had seen at the waterfront. Since they'd come aboard, she was surprised he'd made no comment concerning their previous encounter. It must have been my imagination on the beach and at the house, she decided. There was really nothing seriously intimate between us. Just a trifling is all. That, combined with anxiety from the storm, got me needlessly fired up over the whole thing.

As Amelia Island became a thin line on the horizon, the girls stood at their porthole, each thinking private thoughts of the same man. "Breelan," Nora piped up. "You've not made a sound since we entered this beautiful room. Just look around you." She indicated the well-appointed surroundings as she leapt onto the lower of the two single berths to test the mattress. "No offense meant, but how I'd like to be sharing this room with the good captain, instead of you."

A pall spread over Breelan's complexion.

"Really, if we're to become women of the world, we must start thinking like them. Don't be so shocked, Bree. I meant share it with him once we're married."

Nora had it all wrong. Breelan wasn't shocked by her reference to the sleeping arrangements. She was astounded because moments before in the passageway, looking into the cabin with Waite standing beside her, she'd had that very same notion. However, in her fantasy, his wife was not Nora. Breelan swallowed. "I really don't think Waite Taylor would make a suitable husband for any nice girl."

"Why on earth not? After all, he's a war hero. He saved your family from the tornado. And my father kept going on about how honorable he was to have refused any payment when it was offered for watching out for —"

Breelan cut her off in the middle of her summation. "You needn't plead his case before me, Nora."

"Well, my woman's intuition is running overtime, and I know he'll be fantastic as a husband, father," Nora, speaking more softly, added, "and lover."

Breelan shook her head. "I'm just saying we'd better be careful. Hell's bells, we've only been on board a few minutes and you've got yourself married and settled down. What happened to the adventures we were going to have?"

Nora conceded, "You're right about that. I must keep myself available for opportunities. All the same, I'm going to leave one eye on him just so I'm ready when he makes his move."

"You're a wonder." Breelan added with an imitation Irish brogue, "And where would ya be keeping your four leaf clover that will be bringin' ya the luck of love?"

In the spirit of the moment, Nora replied, "Don't ya be teasing your own kind, dearie. I'm feeling good things from that god of a man, and it's for sure he'll be wild and warmin' the bed of one fortunate colleen. The only questions bein' is who and how soon?"

Breelan hoped her laughter would hide her similar thoughts.

Once their valises were emptied, gowns hung in the wardrobe and toiletries assembled neatly on their dressers, the girls decided to stroll the promenade deck. Each one carried a book to appear casual, not wanting anyone to suspect this was her first time away from home. And though they had eaten only a light breakfast of toast and tea, their stomachs were unaccustomed to the gentle rise and fall of the ocean. Being outside seemed like a good idea.

Sipping the cool water urged on her by the attentive steward, Nora spoke between deep gulps of sea air. "If I don't soon feel better, I'm afraid I'll fire and fall back right here over the rail. What a humiliation that would be." Her hand was pressed to her chest, trying to stem the sour taste in her throat.

Breelan smiled at the picture she envisioned of Nora until her own stomach began a serious churning. Breelan's distress grew as the captain passed their way, this time looking directly into her face, recognizing at once the reason for her pasty pallor.

"I'm sorry if you're having trouble adapting to the sea," he tried to reassure. "Give it a spell and before you realize it, you'll both think you're already in New York, strolling the fair city. The planking of the *Comfort* will feel that firm."

"Thank you for your interest, but we're quite fine," Breelan responded curtly.

"Maybe you are, Bree. I'm sure not. I'm feeling rotten. Does this ever happen to you, Captain?"

"Not too much anymore. When you've been sailing as much as I have, your body acclimates itself."

59

"May I show you to the chairs over there under cover of the deck above? You'll be out of the glare of the sun, although its effect is charming on each of you." While he indicated a line of a dozen wooden chaise lounges with yellow and white-stripped cushions, the girls didn't know whether he was teasing them or sincere. Nora chose to believe him. "Do you really mean it? We always thought our habit of squinting made us look odd."

"No, anything but."

You flatterer. You phony flatterer, Breelan judged.

"Thank you, Captain." He offered his arm and Nora eagerly accepted, casting a smug smile over her shoulder in Breelan's direction.

"These seats will give you the best view, I think. May I suggest you don't read, at least, until you're feeling better? There's something about the eyes moving back and forth and the stomach moving up and down that isn't too compatible."

"Shows how much you know," Breelan sassed. "These aren't books for reading. They're for autographs!" Immediately, she chewed her lip for admitting they were looking for famous people. She might as well have announced aloud that she was the most unsophisticated and unseasoned person aboard! In her haste to ridicule the captain, she'd embarrassed herself.

He masked his smile as Nora tried to cover her idiot cousin's remark by simply ignoring it. "We'll certainly follow your experienced advice," she said.

"Good morning, ladies."

"Good morning, and thank you, again," was Nora's response.

Breelan rose above her folly and found her manners. "Yes, thank you."

Waite nodded slightly.

Waite? How long have I been thinking of him as Waite, Breelan quizzed herself? Well, Waite is easier to say to myself than is Captain Taylor.

Then she asked, "Nora, if he was a lieutenant during the war, why is he called captain now?"

"Because he's the captain of the ship. Naturally." This was a guess on Nora's part, but seemed logical enough. "Let's just lie back, close our eyes and drift off. I know whose face will be in my dreams. How about yours?"

"Here we go again."

And they giggled despite their queasiness.

Captain Taylor stood at the helm of the *Gentle Comfort* after having safely piloted her from the low-lying coastal savannah. Concentrating on the history of the local lighthouse in the distance to clear his head of thoughts of the girl, he struck up a conversation with Catfish, his first mate. Catfish O'Halleran, former skipper of the Green Water Gertie, was a craggy old sailor, with a deep whiskey voice and eyes the powder blue of a husky dog. His russet curls were often the envy of women who, to a person, immediately decided their beauty was wasted on such a scrounge. Catfish always stood close and looked hard at people. Strangers declared him dimwitted. Acquaintances knew better.

"Hey Fish, do you know much about that lighthouse back there?"

Catfish was always interested in whatever young Waite had to say. He'd sailed with Kenneth Taylor and had known the boy since his father was lost at sea. He and Waite were steadfast friends. The old salt probably had more knowledge than anyone around when it came to the ports on the Atlantic coast, but he sensed the captain needed to talk so he patiently indulged him. Catfish cocked his leathery face to the right to catch a better earful.

Moving to the chart room behind the bridge, Waite double-checked his vessel's course while he spoke. "The other evening in the ship's library, I pulled out a ragged old volume about this area. It talked about 'the Amelia Light,' as the Fernandinians call it, and how it's been here on the north end of the island at the Amelia and St. Mary's Rivers entrance since 1838. Even though the brick tower is only 60 feet tall, it sits on the second highest elevation of the entire east coast. That puts the lighthouse 107 feet above sea level. You can see her glow 19 miles out."

"Is that so?" Catfish said, interested. He knew sea lore and geography, but didn't know exact figures. He always felt Waite to be a smart man, smarter than himself. "Go on. This is real educational."

"Let's see. I think it said there're 58 hand-hewn New England granite steps to the prism room and, originally, there were 14 whale oil lamps that were replaced with a third order Fresnel lens. A cable and weight system is wound by the keeper and that rotates the lens."

The workings of a lighthouse were common knowledge to sailors, but Catfish let Waite continue the lesson.

"The thing has two walls. There's an exterior wall that's 22 feet across at the bottom and 10 1/2 feet at the top. The interior wall is a straight nine foot cylinder all the way up." Looking over at the old man, Waite realized Catfish was being overly attentive to his ramblings. "Anyway, I found it fascinating."

"Yup, prit-near the most fascinatinest thing I ever heard meself."

Waite burst out laughing.

"At least, it's good to see you smilin' for a change. Dad blasted, if you ain't been a mean cuss since that tornado they had here a month ago. I've been scrapin' together my courage and fixin' to talk to ya about it. What's grievin' ya, Waite?"

"Have I been all that bad? So bad that even you have to worry about what you say to me? You can talk to me about anything, Fish. Anytime."

"Then don't take exception to what I'm about to say, but is it that little gal that just come on board, the one with all that mess of pretty brown hair? I seen the way you looked at her. Are you girl-sick, son?"

Waite tensed, ready to tell Fish he was wrong and to mind his own goddamn matters. He caught himself before he'd uttered a curt word. He'd never been disrespectful to his friend. No woman was going to make him behave so now. Because of their past bond, Catfish had every right to offer his opinion and Waite was obliged to listen. He walked over and closed the door, not wanting any others to hear his personal business. "Ever since that night on the beach, the night of the storm, I haven't been able to rid my thoughts of her."

Fish hadn't heard Waite speak so of any female before this.

"Her features are before me no matter where I look." Waite needed to tell someone and his soul emptied itself. "When I found her on the shore, I was dumbstruck by her beauty. At first, it was all physical, or so I figured. As soon as I rode away from her, I knew better. I felt possessed by something more than want of sex. I've a feeling inside that tortures me because it craves a like response from her. Something isn't complete without her.

"But hell, she's too young for me. I've tried hard, real hard, to convince myself she was too inexperienced for a reckless sea dog. Too innocent. That I'd hurt her, be too rough with her body and her mind. Didn't you find it strange that I had business in Savannah every trip south these last weeks? That I asked you to take command of the *Gentle Comfort* on her runs to and from Fernandina? You picked me up on the return north and never said a word. You must've suspected something, Fish."

"I guessed you'd tell me when you was good and ready. I didn't want to push none."

Waite kept on. "Just to be in her town was an ordeal, but I had to take control. I had to face things. When we arrived yesterday in Fernandina, all my resolve left me. That's why I stayed aboard. I wasn't just reading. The truth is I was studying, investigating where she comes from, trying to get closer to her somehow. The more knowledge I acquired about her background, the worse I wanted her. So I purposely started drinking last night until I passed out. With enough liquor in me, I knew she'd be safe from the wild man who wanted to pound on her door in the middle of the night and take her away for himself.

"This morning, with damn near the worst hangover I've ever had as a reminder of my determination, I was prepared to be strong and leave town without ever attempting to see her. I was counting the minutes until we pulled out, until I escaped Amelia Island. You can't know how shocked I was when she arrived at the foot of the dock, her father handing her over to me! It was her uncle, Clabe Duffy, who corresponded with me. I didn't know the name. I swear to God, I had no earthly idea she was one of the girls I was to watch over. Now she's here, aboard my ship, and so is temptation. I don't know what to do."

Waite turned his back and peered out at the water. Catfish could plainly see his captain was drained. "What I have to say might not be too comfortin' at first, but hear me out, would ya? Yes, this gal is young. Yes, she's probably inexperienced. Fact is, you'd best face it. One day, someone will come along and change all that."

The thought of another man touching Breelan made the muscles cramp in his forearms as Waite clenched his fists to stone.

"Then why in God's good name shouldn't it be you? Don't knock yourself, boy. When the time is right, you'll know how to handle this girl, how to treat her with respect and ..." Catfish turned the color of blood from embarrassment, the only time in his long life, "And bring her to maturity. You're the best and most honorable man I know."

When the time is right - Waite had said that very thing to Breelan the first night they'd met. "Thank you for the kind words, old friend. But suppose she wants no part of me. So far she hasn't been what you'd call receptive, let alone interested in me."

"The only way you'll find out is to test the waters." He chuckled at his seaman's pun. "I have a feelin' those hateful looks she was throwin' at ya could be turned to sugar if ya just give it a chance. I say talk to her soon. I don't know if the crew is up to much more of your moonin' around. You're mean with longin' for her, Waite. 'Sides, we all have eyes, and she's might near the fairest lookin' maiden I've seen round here in a long while. There's bound to be a pack of beaus houndin' her at every turn. Remember, he who hesitates, gets run over."

Waite weighed the older man's comments carefully. Those comments were welcome because it was exactly what Waite wanted to hear. He'd

63

needed permission somehow. Or was it assurance that he was doing no wrong? Whatever in hell it was, he'd soon find the right time to tell Miss Breelan Dunnigan of his serious attraction - before he was aced out by some other lucky bastard.

Chapter 9 – *The Goodbye Lie* by Jane Marie

After a spell, Breelan slowly awakened and as promised, felt much relieved of her ailment. However, her eyes didn't want to open to let in the brilliant reflection of the sun on the water, so she languished happily, listening to the sounds of the ocean around her. Interrupted by the low tone of a man's voice, she heard him speaking to another.

"A pair of lovelies."

"Especially the one in the flowerdee dress there. Look at that shimmering mass of hair."

Lids lifting, Breelan peeked into the bright light of day. Shading the glare away with her hand at her brow, she saw two whispering men looking straight at her! They were casually leaning against the rail of the ship, taking her in. Nora, too. And all while they'd slept! What gall!

She reached over and shook Nora.

"What? Go away," Nora fussed, enjoying her snooze.

"Nora, wake up. Now," Breelan muttered, not removing her gaze from the men smiling at her.

Shaking Breelan off her arm, her eyes only half-open and puffy from sleep, Nora grouched, "I'm awake. Believe me, I'm awake."

"We're being stared at. Look over there." That was all it took. Fully alert and straightening herself in the chair, Nora returned a grin.

Annoyed, Breelan ordered softly, "Don't acknowledge them."

"Why on earth not?" Nora asked, wiggling only the corner of her mouth. "We're here for experience and these men appear to be quite capable."

"What happened to your undying love for Captain Taylor?"

"Well, if he misses his chance with me, then it's his misfortune. I can't wait my whole life."

Breelan guessed about two hours had lapsed by the lower angle of the sun since Nora had told of her great affection for the captain. She shook her head and smiled.

That smile was a beacon to the onlookers who advanced on the girls at its unintended invitation. "Ladies," the males said in near unison from the foot of the lounges.

The taller, blonde man spoke, "We couldn't help noticing how peaceful you two looked."

"And enchanting," added his darker, slightly shorter friend.

"The rolling sea must have lulled us to sleep," commented Nora. "May we introduce ourselves?"

On her guard, Breelan nodded.

"This is Will Akins and I'm Trip Clelland. We're on our way home to Connecticut."

"Connecticut? Then that makes you Blue Bellies!" screeched Nora, but mostly for show because, if she were honest, the war was history and these fellows were exceptionally attractive. Besides, she and Breelan were, this very moment, en route to Yankee country to visit Breelan's family there. So she figured, after a fashion that made Breelan's relatives her relatives, since the two were first cousins. And it simply wouldn't be proper to be rude to your own kin. Yes, Nora was certainly glad that darn fool war was over.

"I'm sorry, Miss, that you're disturbed by the fact we're from the north," said Will. "May I point out that it's been some years, I believe, since peace was declared? And, too, that no one has control over his or her birthplace, now do they?"

"I suppose a person can't help where their people are from," Nora submitted magnanimously and hurtled forward with introductions. "My name is Nora Duffy and this is my cousin, Breelan Dunnigan. We're from Fernandina, Florida."

"How do you do?"

"Glad to make your acquaintance," the darker man replied properly. "We're with the military."

"You're soldiers?" asked Breelan. "What are you doing on this ship?"

Recognizing her suspicion, Trip replied sharply, "If we were deserters, would we tell you we were with the military?"

Feeling the tension, Nora jumped in, "Of course you're not. We're just curious because you aren't wearing uniforms."

"We're on leave to visit my folks. We decided to go civilian and in style aboard the *Gentle Comfort*," said Trip.

"Breelan has family in New York City. We're going to stay with her aunt and uncle for a month." Nora was much too forthcoming with information to suit her cousin.

"Should we happen to be in New York City, for whatever reason, might we perhaps call upon you there? We are introduced."

"We don't even know you," Breelan stated matter-of-factly.

"Well, we have a week on board ship to remedy that," parried Will.

"We'll see," said Nora batting her lashes.

"May we sit down?"

"You've paid for the privilege, same as we have," Breelan snapped.

Before a shoving match could start between the two men, Trip quickly captured the lounge chair next to Breelan's, leaving Will no choice except to take the seat beside Nora. He accepted genially, but Trip, knowing his friend well, could see the envy in his eyes.

Isn't this lovely? Here we are, thought Breelan, sandwiched between two dandies. What would Daddy think were he here to witness this display? After a reasonable period of small talk had passed, she urged Nora to the cabin, explaining their need to change for dinner.

"Perhaps we'll see one another there," said Trip.

"Perhaps. Good day."

Trip took Breelan's hand in his, "Good day to you, miss."

Nora smiled at Will. Returning the same, he bowed before her as Breelan latched onto her elbow, propelling her cousin in the direction of their stateroom.

After the girls departed, Will told Trip, "You know, had I been quicker and grabbed the other chair, I'd be the one wooing sweet Breelan, instead of you."

"Maybe," Trip replied politely, sure the beautiful brunette would have chosen him in any case.

Once in their cabin, "Breelan, I'm surprised at how unsociable you're being, dragging us away just when we were getting to know those boys," Nora complained.

"I'm not unsociable. They were moving a bit too fast for me. I simply wasn't comfortable."

"Ha, not me. I'm certainly looking forward to dinner."

It was then Breelan saw the square white envelope that had been slipped under their door. "Look," she said pointing, and Nora rushed over to pick it up. Tearing into it, she read aloud:

The honor would be mine if you would dine at my table this evening. Seating takes place at 8 p.m. RSVP by way of the steward.

Sincerely,
Captain Waite M. Taylor

Nora glanced at the envelope for the first time. Carefully piecing it back together, she was gratefully able to see it addressed to "Misses Duffy and Dunnigan."

"Let me have a look, please," Breelan gently demanded. She was strangely pleased at having been invited. Still again, she found herself doubting the captain's sincerity. Examining the note, she touched the embossed insignia of the *Gentle Comfort* at the top of the heavy bond stationary. "As I suspected, it's in pre-set type. It's a form letter. Obviously, the captain is merely being polite. He undoubtedly has stacks of these. All he does is sign them. His table is bound to be huge, seating twenty-five or more people, so everyone will eventually have a chance to dine with him sometime during their travels. Then they can all brag to their friends and high roll their enemies about having supped with his highness, our glorious skipper."

"Mercy Maud! I've never known you to be so distrusting and sarcastic. It may well be a form letter. Still, it's a privilege to be asked the first night out. This invitation will make a wonderful addition to my scrapbook. Whatever is the matter with you, Bree? Why are you acting this way?" Before Breelan could respond, Nora went on. "I'll write a short letter of acceptance right now. I want you to check the spelling before I give it to the steward, just in case. I'm excited, Breelan. You be, too."

"Oh, I am really. I guess anticipation and planning for this trip tired me more than I realized. I'm sorry I've been such a grump about things. Come on. You write the letter. Then we'll help each other decide what to wear." As Breelan moved to hug her cousin, she saw the sparkle in Nora's eyes and was glad she'd overridden her reservations about this evening, if only to make her roommate happy.

As Nora wrote, Breelan began work on her hair. While she labored, her worries returned. She hadn't overridden any uncertainties. She'd simply put on her best face. Sitting at the vanity, she peered at her image. Her expression detailed her feelings and she hoped no one would guess the specifics. She was anxious about dinner with the captain. Maybe he'll ignore me like he did when he escorted us to this room. Whatever happens, I've got to keep my composure. I've got to.

At three minutes of eight, with Nora heralding the time every quarter hour, they declared it appropriate and proper to depart their stateroom. Both girls looked in the mirror one last time for reassurance. Nora was pleased with herself. Her auburn hair was swirled at the nape of her neck, covered by an appealing salmon-colored snood speckled with green leaves. Her dress, too, was salmon, setting off the natural roses in her cheeks that were reflected in the gleam of the pale peach potato-shaped pearls around her neck. Her parents had given her the jewelry to distract her when she'd fallen from a horse and broken her wrist last year. Nora didn't enjoy the occasional resulting stiffness where the bones had mended, but she took pleasure in her lovely necklace.

"I look pretty."

"Yes, you especially do," agreed Breelan.

Tying her hair in rags was rarely necessary for Breelan since she had a naturally soft wave. Tonight she'd simply pulled her hair back from her temples, securing it in place with the tortoise shell combs presented to her by her father when she'd turned fifteen. Her glorious locks hung in long loose curves.

Breelan's gown of green watered silk was trimmed with a three inch wide embroidered yellow lapel that bordered the neckline, forming an X across the low bodice and hanging to the floor. Her only jewelry was an elegantly simple necklace of sparkling green peridot stones. She felt stylish and sophisticated. After all, she was a woman of eighteen.

Chapter 10 — *The Goodbye Lie* by Jane Marie

The evening air was still sticky, although somewhat cooler as, arm-in-arm, Nora and Breelan walked the deck to the dining salon. Sounds of violins playing The Last Rose of Summer drifted toward them, as savory smells of temptation beckoned. Two seriously professional young men in white uniforms attended double glass doors etched with a frosted menagerie of romping sea creatures. Behind those doors, glistening oil-painted murals portraying marine life floated on a background of soft blue-green flocked wallpaper. Lazy sea cows, bounding dolphins, a massive sperm whale, teasing sea lions, and schools of colorful fish darting among coral, all appearing to be alive. The gentle creatures seemed to summon the passengers to join in their fun. Candle-filled crystal chandeliers hung overhead, their swing barely detectable. The room shimmered in the scattered mirrored panels to leave Breelan beguiled.

Then she spotted Waite and the magic disappeared. It hadn't been difficult to find him. A particular presence surrounded him, a presence that immediately indicated he was in charge. She'd felt unsettled the moment she realized he'd been watching the door.

"There's the captain, Bree, at the head of the table," said Nora. "And see, his table isn't anywhere as big as you thought. Only one, two, three - twelve seats, though still too many for my taste. Doesn't he look grand in his uniform?"

"Uh-huh." Hearing but not listening, Breelan followed her cousin as they wound their way through the maze of tables that wore covers of sea-mist hued linen. The china was pure white like the chop of a foaming ocean. The silver service and crystal stemware contributed to the sparkle of the hall as if it were a giant jewel box belonging to King Neptune.

Candlelight twinkled in the depths of the captain's eyes when he greeted Breelan and Nora. "I'm so pleased you accepted my invitation, ladies."

"You are most gracious to invite us, Captain," said a mesmerized Nora.

Breelan's lips curved tentatively. This was the way she remembered him, attentive and handsome.

"How are you, Miss Breelan?" he asked.

"Just right," she replied smartly.

"I'd have to confirm that assessment."

Why did he have to agree with her? On the other hand, had he disagreed, she probably would have started blubbering on the spot. She was a crazy woman. That was the only explanation possible.

"Please, may I introduce you to my other guests?" He began with the gentleman on his right. "You may already know Major George Fairbanks, editor of your own *Florida Mirror* newspaper."

Amazed and gladdened, Breelan offered her hand. "Major Fairbanks! I'm astounded we're on the same ship!"

"Good to see you, Breelan."

"My father and the major have worked together promoting the new buildings going up back home," she explained.

"How lovely to see one of our own," Nora nodded.

"Thank you, dear," he replied. Turning back to Breelan, "You've neglected to mention you've done a little work with me yourself."

"Oh?" Captain Taylor was curious.

"Yes. Only a few articles." She was embarrassed at the fuss over her silly stories. And she hoped their particular subject matter, like the return of Kylie Kildare's stolen wagon or the prize winning eleven-inch tomato grown by Francis Bushy, wouldn't be mentioned.

"I'm impressed. I would think that quite an opportunity for someone your age. Particularly, since you're a girl."

"Whatever do you mean by that?" Her back was up.

"Breelan." Major Fairbanks felt the need to interject. "The captain is right."

Her eyes flared fire at her boss as well as the captain.

"I don't take just anyone on my staff, especially if their father is a friend. Nepotism is a dangerous thing. It can only cause trouble in the long run. No ma'am, I hired you because you're a damned good - oh, excuse me, a darned good writer. You only need experience. And, of course, that will come with time and practice."

Addressing everyone at the table, "Since we're a weekly, we need to be sure all our articles count. With the events of seven days from which to choose, we certainly need no filler. We use strong stories from strong reporters."

Looking directly at Breelan, "And I consider human interest stories as strong and necessary. They're the heart, the humanity of a paper. Let me say that Miss Dunnigan is only one of two women working for me. I aim to remedy that when I find more of her kind. I'm sure she'll develop quite a following before long."

Breelan dropped her gaze to the floor from all the praise.

"I'd bet she has quite a following already, George," Waite said devilishly.

The editor tried not to smile as a look of anger from deduced disrespect darkened Breelan's face.

"May we meet your other guests, Captain?" said Nora, much aware of her cousin's ire.

"Certainly." Waite proceeded to introduce those around the rectangular table. "Mr. and Mrs. Charles Ralston. They've been spending time with their daughter in St. Augustine, Florida. She's just had her first child, I believe." The new grandfolks nodded, their faces radiating pure joy. "There at the end of the table is Judge Prindeville. He's on his way back to Buffalo. He's been down here meeting with potential political backers. They're trying to persuade him to run for the Senate from New York."

All within earshot applauded him, Nora among them, although few knew his political stance. "Do you all realize," she asked everyone, impressed by the stature of the man, "that we've just been introduced to someone who might know someone who might know the President of the United States?"

"Are you convinced yet, Judge?" asked Breelan, her mood lifted as she sensed the stirrings of a story.

"You may be seeing an announcement in the major's paper any day. You never know in the intriguing world of politics." As he answered his brows raised and out fell his monocle. It bounced off his protruding belly to land with a clink on his empty dinner plate.

"My goodness, Judge," Nora addressed him. "You're very lucky your monocle didn't break. Must be because it's so thick."

Exasperated at her uncomplimentary comment, he huffed once and opened his mouth to berate Nora, Breelan was sure. "I realize I'm a newcomer, Judge, but I would certainly enjoy the opportunity to draft an article about your campaign." That is if Major Fairbanks will permit it, she thought to herself. She'd have to ask her employer after they'd dined.

"Find me later, dear, and we'll talk about it."

His lascivious examination of Breelan was apparent to everyone except his innocent victim. Waite wanted to throw the disgusting idiot over the side. He'd have to keep an eye on the old coot.

On up the left side of the table, the captain continued. "May I present the recently-married, Mr. and Mrs. Miles Kirkland. They're returning from their honeymoon in Daytona Beach."

"We've been married six weeks today," announced young Kirkland, brightly. His bride blushed attractively, fiddling with the fringe on her lightweight summer shawl.

The pink color of the couple's complexions from the Florida sunshine left a body, to Breelan's mind, looking healthy, even if it wasn't the fashion.

Or was their hale and hearty coloring from lovemaking? Glory be! Now, I'm thinking like Nora! She focused on what Waite was saying.

"We're awaiting the arrival of three more guests as you no doubt deduced from the empty chairs. Being a cub reporter, Miss Breelan, I'm sure you're always on the lookout for clues, are you not?" came his mocking question.

Why was he deliberately trying to humiliate her? Breelan ignored him, rising above his taunting. She was certain it was what her mother would have done.

"Ah, here is one of those guests now." He offered his hand to a beautiful woman who seemed to glide into the room in a clinging gown. "This is Miss Leona Visper, world-renowned singer and actress. I'm sure you've caught her photograph in magazines if you haven't been fortunate enough to see her perform on stage. We're honored she's chosen to travel to New York on our ship."

Nora and Breelan were somewhat in awe of the blonde with the stunning assets. They'd heard of her. Who hadn't? She was very attractive, but very obvious, too. The revealing bodice of her coal black evening dress was blatantly meant to encourage gazes from the men. All, that is, except Mr. Kirkland who was much too absorbed with his new bride. And that's exactly as it should be, Breelan noted.

The beauty spoke, "Enchantée, everyone." Singling out Breelan and Nora, she added, "You too, girls." Her salutation carried a superior tone to it. She recognized Breelan's splendor and didn't enjoy any rivalry. "This is your first trip at sea, I assume?"

"How did you know?" asked Nora.

"By the stars in your eyes, my dears. You look like children in a toy store, birthday money in hand, all aglow with anticipation and unable to decide which plaything to try next."

"I may be young, Miss Visper is it?" Breelan pretended ignorance of the woman's fame and defended herself against this unprovoked attack on her worldliness. "I can only say I sincerely hope by the time I reach your age, I'm not as haughty as you appear to be by that condescending statement. Oh, and speaking of playthings, once a toy belongs to me, I have it forever. I always take excellent care of what is mine." Even Breelan wasn't quite sure what she'd meant by her last remark. All the same, she was glad to have said it.

"My, my. You're a bold one. Now see here, child, no need for a fit."

Softening her voice and smiling brilliantly, Breelan replied, "I merely endeavor to correct your misconception of my life's experience.

Admittedly shorter than your own, that experience has taught me to correctly assess people," firing a sharp glance at her prey, "particularly when someone is clearly desperate from fear of female competition."

Competition. It seemed a natural assumption on Breelan's part. Looking at Miss Visper in her showy attire, only one conclusion could be drawn. The actress possessed a vain and most probably vulgar attitude. Breelan grudgingly admitted the woman was quite ravishing. Yet the more she studied her, the more the entertainer's eyes and mouth seemed too small for her large head. Covering her smile with her glove, Breelan desperately wanted to tell Nora of her appraisal. Unhappily, this wasn't the time. Perhaps men did find this female attractive because they were swayed by the superficial. It was her pretentious manner that left Breelan cold. She deemed it her self-imposed duty to her fellow women to bring the hussy down a rung or two, should the chance arise.

"This is nothing," voiced the captain. "You should see Miss Dunnigan when she's really furious. Take my word for it. I've been personally roasted by her." In truth, he was most pleased by Breelan's powerful defense. He wasn't sure what the underlying cause was for this catfight, since, to the best of his knowledge, these two had only just met. He sensed it might be over a man. Could that mean Breelan was thinking about him? Unquestionably, that would make for an interesting voyage.

Breelan pressed her lips into a hard line. She dare not speak more angry words lest she prove Waite's point that she was some sort of hothead. Her control over her fluctuating emotions was minimal. She was feeling like a small rubber ball shot from a cannon, ricocheting from floor to ceiling to walls with no prospect of slowing its irregular course.

Waite endeavored to calm the ruffled coats of the two lovely felines by moving on with the evening. "Shall we all be seated?" He held the chair for Miss Visper. The entire table was aware that the verbal skirmish was over, at least for now.

The girls noticed fresh gardenias on their dinner plates. Charmed, each pinned the flowers to the bodice of the other as Waite said, "Apparently, the remainder of our party has been detained." He glanced at his gold pocket watch with the ivory carving of a sailing ship on its case.

"Beautiful watch," pronounced Major Fairbanks.

"Yes, isn't it? It was my father's," Waite explained simply, becoming lost in fond memories for several silent seconds. He recalled the softening of the strong face of the man who reared him as he offered his only son his watch on the occasion of Waite's sixteen birthday, just days before the boy left to fight for the Southern cause. With a snap, Waite closed the watch, then ordered champagne. As he stood to toast the voyage, he was interrupted by the arrival of his last two dinner guests.

"Captain, please pardon our tardiness. We were attending to business and time got away."

Waite offered his hand to Lieutenants Trip Clelland and Will Akins. The soldiers looked dashing in their Federal blue uniforms.

"I understand how things can easily turn all consuming and take over one's life," Waite mumbled, looking at Breelan.

The captain then made quick introductions. When he got to Nora and Breelan, Will interrupted, "Fortunately, we've already met," he said directly to the young girl in green with as much charm as he could marshal.

"We plan on becoming well acquainted with these ladies by the time this ship arrives in New York," Trip divulged, his gaze, too, on the beautiful brunette.

Breelan didn't particularly enjoy the way Trip tried to insinuate himself into her life so rapidly, but she smiled sweetly at him. She couldn't have Miss Visper thinking she was incapable of flirting with the best of them.

The actress resented the handsome soldier's attention toward the girl. She herself should be the star in every production, professional and personal.

Waite, witnessing the exchange between Breelan and Lieutenant Clelland, was unreasonably displeased with his steward for having chosen this peculiar combination of dinner companions the first night of the voyage. Offering no visible reaction, he tapped a knife on his crystal goblet. The room halted its banter and people turned in their chairs to see who was calling for their attention. The captain raised his glass, saying, "To the journey ahead," and the other passengers returned the toast. Taking his seat, "The chef tells me my men caught some excellent thirty pound silver kingfish today as we pulled into the main channel leaving Amelia Island."

"What baits are the boys using, Captain?" asked Mr. Ralston.

"Live pin fish and fresh cigar minnows."

"Ah, well …"

Miss Visper surmised Mr. Ralston was about to reminisce over his own fishing triumphs. "Waite, let's do order now. I'm ravenous. If we fiddle much longer, I may just charge the kitchen and save myself." She chuckled at the picture she'd presented. What would her fans think of her waiting on herself? How outraged they'd be. Why, she hadn't been without servants since she'd grown into a young woman and men showered her with whatever she demanded.

"We couldn't have that." The captain looked up and immediately an attentive waiter advanced.

As dinner progressed, Breelan found it necessary to continuously excuse herself to Mr. Ralston as her left elbow brushed his right one. "It's awful how bothersome being opposite from everyone else is," she explained. "Mother tried to change everything to my right hand as a child, but I'd just put it down and pick it back up with my left."

"Don't worry, my dear. We'll manage fine," said the understanding gentleman.

"May I make a suggestion?" The captain had overheard Breelan's predicament. "Major Fairbanks, I'm sure, would be agreeable to changing seats with you, Miss Breelan. That way you won't have to annoy Mr. Ralston, and you won't find it necessary to continue apologizing."

"Oh, no need. No need at all," began Mr. Ralston.

"Please, Breelan, come along and take my chair, won't you?" asked the major.

Before she had time to respond, Waite instructed the staff to exchange place settings and Breelan was seated on his right. This humiliating commotion caused the other guests in the room to turn and stare once again.

She doubted things could get much worse until her good and faithful cousin, draining her second glass of champagne, made known, "They seat her at the end of the table at home to solve this problem." Nora giggled. "Her father is always telling her to 'pull in her wings' whenever she elbows someone." Miss Visper let out a huge and unladylike guffaw.

Completely mortified, Breelan despised the world. Her eyes on her plate, she dared her tears to overflow. People would think her a child after this infantile to-do. She was angry with Nora for such a remark, angry with Miss Visper for howling at her expense and angry with Waite for causing an uproar.

"There. Everybody will be more comfortable," he concluded.

"Everybody but me," she whispered through clenched teeth.

"You said something?" he asked her.

"I said nothing to you," she replied a little more loudly than she'd intended. Though the food was probably delectable, Breelan's appetite had vanished as she tried to analyze why Waite was being so dreadful. By the time the marbled pureed fruit and whipped cream fool dessert arrived, her composure had returned, thanks to the persistent and surprising charm of Trip Clelland. Breelan found herself smiling at his small talk, which he'd directed at her. By asking about her family, he'd brought her out of her misery without her realizing it. When Waite questioned her, attempting cordial conversation, her answers were abrupt as she tried not to even look at him.

Waite understood he deserved her coldness. He'd set out to purposely disconcert her, testing and proving her vulnerability. She was fragile in so many ways and despite the advice of Catfish, he was still concerned he would be too intense for her. But oh, how he regretted the pain he'd caught in her eyes the only moment she'd glanced his way. He hated hurting her, truly hated it.

"The melodies are marvelous, Waite." Showing off her musical acumen, Miss Visper announced, "First a grand march, then *Home Circle*, a schottische, and *Song of the Mermaid*, a voluntarie, and now *Mosquito Waltz*." How appropriate a serenade with which to be leaving hot and buggy Florida, she wanted to scream out. Oozing confection with each word, Miss Visper leaned forward, displaying her physical wares to the captain and any other takers.

She's inviting Waite to dance, for heaven's sake, discovered a startled Breelan. A lady would never ask a man to dance. Of course, Miss Visper need never fear being labeled a lady.

Breelan watched Waite falling for and slipping in all that invisible syrup. Offering his hand, captain and actress regally walked to the parquet dance floor. The only couple there, they began to swirl in great sweeping circles, waltzing one, two, three, one, two, three. How graceful, thought Breelan. I must give him his due. Waite is so erect in his posture, shoulders broad, arms strong. Miss Visper's feet need never touch the ground. The couple swayed together in perfect symmetry. I envy her. Lord Almighty! I envy her? Oh, I do. To be able to dance with such a partner. He'd make any girl look like a prima ballerina.

Now that the dancing had commenced, others filled the floor. "Miss Duffy?" Will offered his hand across the table, and Nora smiled in acceptance. Mr. and Mrs. Ralston's dancing was almost motionless as they remained in the center of the dancers, allowing the more agile couples access to the outer circle of dancers. Among them were Mr. and Mrs. Kirkland, laughing and thoroughly enjoying themselves and the discovery of one another.

Trip asked, "If you don't mind being seen in the arms of a Yankee soldier, Miss Dunnigan, may I have the next dance? From the program, it's to be the *Linden Quickstep*. Are you up for it? You certainly look as if you are."

"Yes, Lieutenant." Nora's right. I won't be left out of this night, Breelan decided. I'm ready now, now that I understand the game. We'll see who wins what. Her confidence was back.

Trip had come around to her side of the table and was pulling out her chair. His smile was bright, his blue eyes friendly. He was a very appealing man.

Breelan was finally having a glorious time. She loved to dance. Her father had taught his older daughters to waltz while Miss Ella played her pump organ. Breelan pictured the plaque on the pedals that read "mouse-proof" and chuckled.

"I'm so glad you're enjoying yourself, Miss Dunnigan."

"I am. I am. I was thinking of my family."

"I'd hoped you were fancying my company and thinking only of me."

"I am enjoying your company, Lieutenant Clelland." She deliberately neglected adding she was thinking what a fine dancer he was, judging she should withhold further compliments. Breelan had been somewhat concerned when they'd walked to the dance floor. Had she noticed him favoring his right leg a bit? It certainly didn't show in his dancing. She realized she liked toying with this man in blue.

"Please call me Trip. Titles are too cumbersome."

In most instances she'd agree with him. In most instances. It was not the case with Waite. She would always call him Captain Taylor to his face. She welcomed the safe feeling of detachment it left in her.

"Trip it shall be. Please, call me Breelan." And he held her secure, leading her in wild spins around and around. She threw her head back as she laughed softly, her hair covering his uniformed forearm.

Waite was completely aware of Breelan's movements. He wanted to kiss the ivory of her flawless bare shoulders. But when he saw the lieutenant's arm tighten around Breelan's waist, Waite's desire turned violent as he imagined ripping the soldier's arm off at the elbow. He resented the man, any man, holding her, let alone holding her as close as this gent was. Trip's body pressed intimately against Breelan's green dress, separating her skin from his by only a few thin layers of silk and cotton. His officer's white-gloved fingers entwined themselves in the ends of her satiny brown hair. At least, his actual flesh wasn't in contact with hers, Waite consoled himself. He was glad a gentleman always wore gloves when dancing so as not to soil a woman's gown with perspiration. He'd considered many customs foolish and a waste of time. Not this one. For this social edict, he thanked the stars.

"Waite, darling," Miss Visper spoke a second time. "You're not listening to me, are you?"

Caught. He was having difficulty tearing his eyes from Breelan. He asked, his tone mocking, "Leona, do you think I'd dance with a woman and she not be the center of all my attention?"

"I think one thing. You're most engaging and you know it. Any woman who allows herself to love you is demented. You'll only break her heart."

"You flatter me. But I think the excursion to that point would be an escapade not to be missed," he suggested, stroking her mind, using her. He excused his selfishness because he knew she wanted him. He needed a woman tonight and she was an alluring, if somewhat obvious creature.

"I could do with a little excitement," she said suggestively. "I've been working much too hard. I'm not speaking of my acting. That I revel in. It's all the pesky fans. It wears a girl out, I tell you. They're everywhere. That's why I so look forward to the privacy of my cabin. No polite pretense." Then whispering close, "There, I can be what and who I want," she added, "for whichever man I choose."

Waite endured her babble. She would give him relief later.

It was Breelan's turn to notice the *Comfort's* captain with his partner. I read somewhere that flirting is a gentle art, Breelan remembered. The way she rubs herself against him may be attractive to some people, but we should scrub her face with soap and a rough cloth. I'd guess we'd see then just how dark her lashes and how red her lips really are.

Looking into Breelan's face, a concerned Trip asked, "Miss Breelan, what happened to that smile? Have I stepped on your toes?"

"Oh, no. The music is nearly ended. Let's sit down and sip more champagne, shall we?" Nora and Will were still dancing, as were Mr. and Mrs. Ralston. Breelan peeked at Waite and Miss Visper over the rim of her champagne glass. She remembered wanting to talk to Major Fairbanks. Turning, she called to him down the table. "Major, do you have a minute for business?" He nodded and came to sit by her. "Trip, excuse me a moment, will you?"

"Certainly," he said graciously, "but only a moment. The music tonight is meant for you, the most beautiful creature in the room." He left them to talk in peace.

"I see you're quite popular on this ship," remarked her editor.

"It's all very innocent."

"I wouldn't be so sure, Breelan. Take it from a man who thinks of you like a daughter. There are several hungry males on board, so please, please use good sense. For me?"

"You're making much too much out of casual conversation." His expression appeared very serious, so she said, "I promise to be careful."

"Fine. Now, what business was it that you wanted to speak of with me?"

"It's about Judge Prindeville announcing his candidacy for the Senate. I was hoping you might let me write an article for the paper," she confessed.

"Truthfully, I would be glad to have you submit your notes to me, but between the two of us, I think the judge is all show and no go."

She was puzzled.

He went on, "For years, every time there's an election he spouts how his party wants to draft him as their candidate. I believe it's mostly wishful thinking on his part. I'll let you know if there's a real chance for a campaign." Looking as disappointed as she felt, he said, "Don't you dare let that blowhard spoil your voyage. There will be many opportunities for you to write. Trust me."

"You're right, I guess."

"Now go have some fun, but not too much fun, ya hear?"

Breelan brightened at his tease.

"If you'll pardon me," her mentor told her as he kissed her cheek fondly, "I believe I'll try a few hands of poker at the gaming tables." Shrugging at his lack of choice, he asked the judge, the only other unoccupied male at the table, to join him. They were off to enjoy the balance of the evening with the queen of spades, potent whiskey and dizzying cigars, which, as Breelan had often overheard her father say, had surely been rolled on the tender thighs of Cuban maidens.

Trip slid into the seat beside her. With his gloves hanging neatly from his belt, his bare hands were concealed beneath the table skirt. "May I call on you tomorrow?"

She felt his hand covering hers and it was warm. On her third glass of champagne, she replied, "Lieutenant, if I'm seen only with you, every one will think we're a couple."

"I'd like us to be."

"Then no other men will approach me," she said with wide-eyed sincerity.

This becoming miss was more fascinating than any of the girls Trip had had of late. She was special, her beauty, her pride, her naïveté. He found himself unable to leave her alone. "Just promise me dinner tomorrow night, and we'll let all else take care of itself."

"Well, I will have the entire rest of the week free so, oh, I guess I can say yes. But only for tomorrow. Remember now, only tomorrow," she warned him, recklessly ignoring her tipsy faculties and enjoying these new sensations caused by the grape. So this is why people drink. It's fun. I feel happy and silly, like I'm on a slow spinning merry-go-round. One could readily become accustomed to this, I imagine.

Waite observed that both Breelan's and Trip's hands were out of sight. "Leona, let's sit awhile and let the others show off a bit."

"I suppose it would be kind of me to let them try and shine," she bragged, knowing full well, it was the gods' own truth. Waite and Miss Visper joined the attractive couple at the table, Trip in his blue uniform, Breelan in her beguiling gown.

"Tired, are you?" asked a hostile Breelan of Miss Visper. "Trip and I were enjoying ourselves. Alone. Weren't we, Trip?" She didn't care that she was being hateful. She determined she had the upper hand over the singer. Waite can see I'm no one to take on from the way I handle someone as famous as she is.

Delighted at how closely Breelan was following his scheme for her, Trip cheerfully responded, "Why yes. We definitely were."

His wide smile goaded Waite, forcing him to restrain his temper. This is ridiculous. Get your mind off her, he lectured himself. For a man in charge of a ship, command of your own feelings is sorely lacking. Waite turned his body and fully faced Leona. She talked unceasingly and loudly of her upcoming engagement at the Golden Tower Theatre in New York. Her costumes, her song and dance numbers were detailed in such depth, anyone caring to listen would be able to play understudy.

"I'll be happy to sing for everyone, Waite, after I rest my voice one more day. I've been taking this new remedy recommended by a fellow actor. It's a mixture of cut-up Indian turnip and whiskey, three or four doses a day. Makes my throat feel like silk."

Little wonder, he thought, and your mind like mush, as well.

Breelan needed a diversion. Watching Mr. and Mrs. Ralston still on the dance floor, she said dreamily, "I hope when I'm their age, my husband will be as devoted to me as he is to her."

Waite had an ear out for Breelan's voice and gratefully interrupted his conversation with Leona. As if awaiting her statement, he responded immediately, "If the love is true, he will be."

Breelan looked into his deep black eyes. She had to speak for fear she'd tumble into their depths in the silent moment that followed. "You talk as if you know of such things, Captain Taylor. Have you ever been in love like that?" she asked boldly.

"Bree!" an astounded Nora piped, returning to the table in time to catch her cousin's personal query, asked in public no less. Right or wrong, all were awaiting the captain's answer.

He welcomed the challenge in the question and was about to respond when the orchestra struck up the chorus of Good Night Sweetheart. Everyone began to murmur the same "I hate for the evening to end" sort of phrase, some sincerely spoken, some not so. Veiled whispers of later assignations were audible if one took the time and had the curiosity to notice. Normally, Nora and Breelan would have been interested in all the intrigue of the night. Now, they had intrigue of their own and it was glorious seasoning for them.

Breelan stood a bit unsteadily on her feet. With concerted effort, she straightened herself. "Thank you, Captain. The dinner was delightful."

"I'm glad you enjoyed it, Miss Dunnigan. May I then assume I'll see you at my table again tomorrow night? And you too, of course, Miss Duffy. I did promise your fathers I'd keep an eye on you."

"What? Her father hired you, Waite? How very sweet!" Leona was rubbing in Breelan's youth for all it was worth, intuitively aware of Waite's attraction to the pretty little package of a girl and equally aware of his attempts to resist her. The actress would do her part to discourage any interaction between the two. She wanted all of him in her cabin tonight, including his thoughts.

Ignoring the gloating performer, Breelan stated matter-of-factly, "I'm afraid I will be unable to dine with you tomorrow, Captain Taylor. You see, Lieutenant Clelland, Trip, and I have already made arrangements." She left her last word hanging in the air for anyone wishing to pluck from it whatever meaning they chose.

Waite's jaw tightened. "No offence intended, Lieutenant, but do you think that wise? After all, this is Miss Dunnigan's first time." His words, too, hung there with hers in bold invisible letters, their essence clear on so many levels.

"Let me assure you, Captain, I will protect her with my life."

"I'd rather be the one to kill my own snakes, thank you very much." Swaying, Breelan turned abruptly. "Lordy, this is plain silly. Evening everyone. Nora, are you coming?"

"Yes, Bree," and she exited the dining room on Will's arm, following the moderately weaving path of her cousin and Trip.

Waite barely controlled his anger, "Look at her. She's sure-enough drunk. And worse yet, she's with that lousy Billy Yank."

"Simmer down there, boy. You're jealousy is blazing," the blonde beauty pointed out, jealous, too, for her own reasons.

"You're crazy. She's my responsibility and that's all. Come on." Waite grabbed Leona's hand, none too gently, and pulled her along behind him out into the dark sea air.

She followed eagerly because right now she didn't care about what or whom he thought. Leona wanted him in her bed tonight with all the magnificent power and fury he possessed.

Chapter 11 – *The Goodbye Lie* by Jane Marie

The following days aboard ship were full of activity. There were picnics on deck, shuffleboard, fishing tournaments, bingo, bunco, board games and card games from euchre to old sledge to poker. Amusement, proper and improper, was available, with one's degree of pleasure regulated only by one's conscience.

Everything was accompanied by music. Piano recitals, string quartets, full concerts. Miss Visper gladly gave her rendition of requested ballads and operatic airs, leaving most with a tear in the eye. Her believable sincerity as well as her ability to provoke raucous laughter proved the woman was indeed a talent.

The *Gentle Comfort* worked her way north, pulling into Savannah, Charleston, Wilmington, Baltimore and Philadelphia. There were brief shopping and sightseeing trips while new passengers boarded and old passengers disembarked. As the ship neared New York City, Waite was half crazed from envy of Lieutenant Clelland. It seemed Breelan had wasted all her waking hours with the young officer while avoiding the ship's captain. Waite found little solace in the company of Leona Visper. Despite the physical relief she provided, she did nothing to ease his mind. Waking and sleeping, Waite was plagued by stark portraits of Breelan wrapped in another man's arms.

Waite realized he had set Breelan apart from other women for more than her beauty. Simply, he felt she was fated to be his. Not his property, Breelan would not allow it and he wouldn't want it. To rein her in, to stifle her, would be unnatural. He only wanted to enjoy her. He'd searched for her without knowing it for so long. Her soul was conceived to complement his. He was certain of it.

Hell, maybe I'm a fool, he counseled himself. Maybe she'll laugh in my face at the thought of us together. But surely she can feel the air thicken when we near one another. Before she leaves this ship, I have to find out where I stand with her. And as if responding to his private hopes, Breelan was suddenly in front of him in the narrow passageway leading to the *Gentle Comfort's* chain locker.

"Oh, good day, Captain," she spoke politely, masking any signs of the headache she carried with her from the previous night's imbibing of too much drink. "I'm probably not supposed to be in this part of your ship. Apparently I've taken a wrong turn somewhere and can't find my way out. Could you please point me in the right direction?"

Waite desperately wanted to tell her of the irony in her question. He could point her in the right direction if she'd let him. His direction. She projected a cold, stiff manner and he didn't like it. Any of it. But what could he say?

"My cousin and I will soon be disposed of and will no longer be your worry. I'll report your attentive service to my father and uncle. A job well done."

"I've only ever thought of your well being. I'm not sure the lieutenant is as trustworthy as you seem to think he is."

"Must I repeat," she raised her voice in frustration, "I don't need a keeper!"

"Maybe not." His answer was sharp. "However, I'm just that so long as you're on my ship."

"Mercifully, that's about to come to an end - at least for a month. And I thank the good Lord for it, too," she said, raising her gaze heavenward.

His shadowed eyes were angry as he pulled her roughly into him. He held her close for a long slow time, feeling her heat, searching her face, inhaling her soft perfume.

She stood there apprehensive and anxious, confronting his intense scrutiny. The fight in her was gone.

"Why do you hate me, Bree?"

His words assaulted her to stunned silence.

"Damn it all! Answer me," he commanded.

"All right, then. I don't hate you."

Relief invaded him.

"I'm frightened."

"Frightened of what?" He couldn't guess who or what was threatening her and alarm pricked his nerves.

"Of you." She looked down at his arms wound so tightly about her she could only breathe in shallow gasps.

Taken aback by her response, he loosened his hold on her somewhat. "You hardly know me, but I swear you need never be afraid of me. I will only ever care for you." As he continued to breathe her in, he mindlessly commented, "You should not smell so sweet."

Breelan responded with a proud smile. Was her perfume alone enough to drive him mad? What power woman had over man and what a thrill this power gave her. Her fear of Waite was forgotten, as she understood she had the upper hand.

"You were never meant to wear such a light scent." His warm breath carried his words to her ear. "That fragrance is for old women and little girls. I have in mind something heavier for you, richer. It will better match the complicated woman you are."

"What?"

He seemed not to notice she'd spoken and went on. "There are two very diverse personalities beneath that satin skin of yours. The public you is ever the definitive lady." He amended his description, thinking of her verbal attack on Leona. "Most times, that is." Ignoring her wriggling, he elaborated on his observations. "But there's a wild vein that tangles and turns throughout the private you. I predict that it's demanding, and from the reckless look I've seen in the depths of your eyes, it craves to be loosed. And soon. I only hope I'm the one and only man you reveal your hidden self to. You won't regret it. Not for a moment."

Breelan was outraged! "I'm a lady through and through, the way my mother is and Grammy, and Peeper, too! You're right about that. But some wild streak? I'm not wild. You don't know what you're talking about. You can't be wild and still be considered a lady. All the best books say so!" How very wrong she'd been. She hadn't any power over Waite Taylor. Perhaps other men. Certainly not him. He mustn't know she'd been so foolish and conceited. She came back at him the only way she knew how. "Your impudence is unpardonable! To speak of such an intimate subject as my perfume, let alone some concealed inner madness I supposedly possess. You only wish I were like that Visper woman, easy and cheap, so you can be low and disgusting with me, the same as you are with her."

He wanted desperately to shake her, to make her shut her mouth and listen to reason, his kind of reason. He wanted to explain, to clarify. "That's where you're wrong. It's cold and common with someone you have no feeling for. When there's mutual ..." Exasperation squelched his good sense. "If you're so sure you don't have a wild streak, that you're a full time, stiff necked female who wouldn't lift her skirt higher than her shoelace for fear a man might think indelicate thoughts about her foot, then prove it to me. I just don't buy it!"

"Gladly. Shall we begin with this?" She drew back her hand to strike him, to hurt and embarrass him as he had her.

He was alert, too quick to be taken by surprise with her weak and completely predictable gesture. He laughed at the sheer femininity of it all, loving every second.

Then, his face darkened. "Has he kissed you yet?" Waite demanded, straining, checking his desire to do the very thing his question asked.

Breelan didn't need to inquire to whom he was referring. "For God's sake, that's my business."

86

"For God's sake, it's my business, too."

"Why?" she whispered so quietly he couldn't hear, but read the word as it formed on her lips. Neither would get their answer this night as voices approached, accompanied by reality.

Waite swiftly released her. His manner was once again formal. "Forgive me, Miss Dunnigan. I've forgotten myself. Take a right at that corner. Go straight until you find the stairs. Go up three flights and ask a steward where your cabin is. You do remember the number, don't you?"

Her eyes narrowed.

"Good. I'll take that as a yes. When we dock, I'll wire your father you've arrived safely in New York City. Try to stay out of mischief on your holiday, won't you? We'll meet again on your return trip to Fernandina."

"What a horrid way to end a vacation, another excursion with you!" She wrinkled her nose and curled her lip at him. She heard his laughter as she walked away. Her brain told her how glad she was to be leaving him, yet her lips whispered, "Goodbye, Waite."

Waite remembered Breelan's voice in the passageway. It sounded so cold and distant. As he'd held her close, had her eyes said, "Goodbye?" No. Not to him. Or was his wanting so strong he imagined she'd return his feelings with the same intensity?

He looked down from the top deck upon the scene below, the way he would have watched a production on stage from the highest balcony. He had transferred his two feminine charges to Breelan's Aunt Coe and Uncle Fries Dresher, who happily accepted them.

Breelan had looked back once, too far away for the ship's captain to read her face. She was gone now. Out of his sight, out of his care, out of his hands. And she wanted it that way. Whether it was Clelland or another man, Waite's confidence was wavering. He cursed himself for not telling her of his deepest feelings. So much could happen in the month's time she would be in New York.

Chapter 12 – *The Goodbye Lie* by Jane Marie

With all the receptions, teas, shopping, sightseeing, theater and visiting that Aunt Coe arranged for her guests, Breelan and Nora didn't spend one bored moment in the massive city called New York. They couldn't get enough excitement. Two girls from the South needed plenty of mighty tales to tell when they returned home. Breelan didn't cotton to fabrication of any kind except in her writings of fiction. Any stories she told would be the bare truth with no invented frills. That is, unless there was a most compelling reason, one that absolutely necessitated a falsehood for a good end.

"I can't sleep another wink," said Nora. "I felt sure I'd hear, pardon me, we'd hear from Will and Trip. I'm truly surprised their interest was so superficial. If that's how they want it, then it's their loss, not ours. I won't give them any more worry." She was holding back tears and bravely continued. "There's so much left to see and do, and we have only two weeks more to do it all in. Up and at 'em. It's about time we were well and creakin'."

"You're absolutely right," agreed Breelan, leaping from her bed with a lively spring.

They dressed and hurried downstairs to the hearty breakfast simmering in Aunt Coe's cheery kitchen, papered in yellow and white stripes. There was no skimpy fare here.

"Good morning, girls," greeted Aunt Coe. "Come, set un eat yourself full. At our table, you're welcome."

"Is that the kind of talk Aunt Ella calls 'Pennsylvania Dutch,' Auntie Coe?" Nora asked.

Answering for her mother's sister, Breelan said, "It sure is. Mama and Grammy sound like that once in a great while. It's delightful to hear."

"Good morning, my lovelies," said Uncle Fries, feeling left out. "I must admit a man would live longer were he to see visions like yourselves every morning of his life. Gets the old heart started." Before either girl could return the gracious reception, he went on hospitably. "Your aunt is a cruel good cook, and I've just the belly to prove it. How's about some flap-jacks and sow bosom hot off the fire, ladies?"

"Mr. Dresher!" his wife wailed in embarrassment. "If the girls should repeat that kind of vulgar language when they're home, why, their mothers would forbid their visiting us ever again!"

"You've got your way of speaking and I've got mine, Coe darling."

The misses giggled over his feeble attempt at disarmament. "Don't fret, Aunt Coe. We realize Uncle is just being a wag. Daddy does the same thing to Mama to get a rise out of her." And Breelan exchanged an understanding wink with her uncle.

"All I can say is he had better stop his devilment if he wants any conversation or company with his wife in the near future."

"Yes, dear. I surely would miss your musical timbre, were it deprived me," Fries answered, his response absent of any contrition.

Fries and Coe Dresher wrangled like this on a regular basis. He teased. She scolded. It was the pattern of their long marriage. Breelan imagined it might be their secret to keeping their union alive and lively.

"Pour some of your aunt's singular maple syrup over your cakes, girls. She orders a gallon every year and then rations it out only to special folks."

"With all these fine victuals you're serving us, Auntie, I shan't fit into my frocks by week's end," Nora worried as she poured on the rich, sweet liquid.

"I can guarantee you two will walk, ride, and play off any weight you might gain at my table. We have so much more planned for you."

The twist of the front doorbell interrupted the morning's discourse with an insistent ring. Uncle Fries rose to answer the call and returned to the kitchen carrying a small white envelope with the words Miss Breelan Dunnigan, written in a sweeping style.

"A small boy delivered this note for Bree," announced her uncle.

A tiny thrill assaulted her as she was handed the paper rectangle. The embossed return address read The Langford Hotel, New York City. She opened it carefully, all eyes upon her.

"I can't stand it. What does it say?" demanded Nora.

The recipient looked up at the anxious faces then read:

Dear Miss Dunnigan and Miss Duffy,

We apologize for the short notice of this invitation. However, family appointments have kept us quite busy since our arrival in Connecticut. We have just now come to New York City this very morn. If you could see clear to honor us with your presence tonight, Lt. Akins and I would sincerely enjoy your company for dinner at The Gallery 708 Restaurant. We've been told it is the newest and most popular establishment in town. If we hear no word of regret, we will call for you at 8 p.m.

Ever hopeful,
Lt. Trip Clelland
Lt. Will Akins

Exposing only a calm exterior, Breelan was inexplicably disappointed and excited all at once. Nora on the other hand never could hide her feelings and let loose a long and loud sigh of relief, fearing she had not been included since the envelope was addressed only to Breelan.

"Really," blustered Aunt Coe, "You both realize it isn't proper to ask a lady out unless sufficient time is allowed for her to check her social calendar. Manners are minor morals, you know."

"Yes. You're right, ma'am. They have explained their difficulty in getting away any sooner, though," said Breelan, afraid her aunt would refuse permission to go. "They've been delayed because of family obligations. And we always say any man who reveres family, well, odds are, he's a fine man." Breelan recalled how her own mother had sold the idea of the good Captain Taylor to Aunt Noreen using a similar tactic, his aiding the family during the tornado.

"I don't know. These men hadn't ought to be so presumptuous," judged her uncle.

"They're not at all. It's only that they realize we won't be here for much longer and they don't want any more time to slip by, I'm sure. They've traveled clear from Connecticut to visit us. Surely, it would be next to rude to refuse to see them. And remember, they weren't insistent, only optimistic that we would join them. Shall I read that part again?"

"No, Breelan. I heard it the first time, thank you very much," said the older gentleman.

"Please. Oh, please," she pleaded.

"Yes, please." Nora felt her assistance was essential.

"Very well. I find it difficult to say no to my girls."

His wife, looking concerned, crossed her arms and tapped her foot, fretting.

Breelan beamed at Nora, although she did have a slight case of the guilts, whining as she had to her aunt and uncle like that. Knowing they had no children of their own, she found it easy to get what she wanted from them. Still, tonight would be the highlight of her trip. Enthralled, she failed to see the heavy suspicion in her uncle's eyes.

"What to wear? What to wear?" happily yammered Nora as she picked through the armoire in the pink painted guestroom. "How about this soft cherry tulle? No, too much frou-frou. It looks like the party dress of a six-year-old. Besides, I'll blend into the wall and you'll never find me." Still investigating the possibilities, "There is this lavender with the orchids embroidered across the skirt. No, too matronly. Ah, this is the ticket. The midnight blue. Dark enough for mystery and sophistication, and low enough to tantalize."

Breelan sat quietly on the bed watching with unseeing eyes. Tonight would be special and not just because of the fancy dinner. She would be with a man who had been places, who was a professional military man with countless adventures behind him. This officer was charming and very nice-looking to be sure. The whole idea of him pleased her.

"The blue for you, did you say?"

Nora nodded. "The blue it is."

"Then I'll wear my burgundy brocade," Breelan decided.

"Let's remember every detail about tonight, Bree, so we can share the experience with all the girls back home. I usually can't remember exactly. I remember around. But this night feels different. Even I don't think I'll forget anything."

With Aunt Coe's advice and assistance, the girls were regal and ready to depart at five minutes to eight. "Now, dears, you wait here in the bedroom until I call you to come down. Your uncle and I promise to collect you as soon as your young misters arrive. Then we can all have a little chat to get to know them better."

"Thank you, Auntie," they said together.

Nora continued to primp and Breelan did likewise, inspecting herself in the oval cheval glass. She tilted the full-length mirror just enough to see the gathers of her gown hide the black slippers that emphasized her small feet. Her filmy stockings, secured with eyelet lace garters accented with light blue ribbons, felt like gossamer clouds against her skin. In the gaslight, the rich claret of her dress radiated iridescent shades of the rainbow. Long white gloves accentuated her wrists and the forearms that led to her powdered shoulders. While her throat sparkled with her own delicate garnet necklace, she also wore the antique garnet earbobs unearthed in Aunt Coe's jewel casket. Those now dangled delicately from Breelan's lobes as her mahogany brown hair sat intricately coiled atop her head. Purposely permitted strands of loose hair hung teasingly at the nape of her neck. As she twisted one, then the other around her index finger, it came to her how often she'd complained of the weight of her thick hair. So many times she'd whined about wanting to cut it a more manageable length until a stranger in Dotterer's Grocery in Fernandina had told her, "Anyone can grow hair, but not everyone can grow beautiful hair like yours." It took this compliment from an outsider before she appreciated one of her father's favorite fractured Shakespearean quotations. "When a woman combs her hair, she imitates the motion of the stars." She was glad now she had left it as long as it was.

Breelan's mildly arched brows, like her mother's, defined blue eyes that tipped up slightly at the corners on her oval face. And those hateful freckles across the bridge of her nose didn't appear quite so hateful to her anymore. In this light and on this night, they were almost alluring. The short scar her own baby fingernail had inflicted on her cheek was well hidden in the crease of her smile. Her mouth was small. "Bird lips" had been a childhood taunt. Now, leaning in for a better view, she might be considered downright kissable. Despite her present appeal, the awful boy who had mocked her at fourteen for being flat-chested came to mind. She hadn't realized any inadequacies before he'd enlightened her. She'd been a late bloomer and anguished over it because of him. No more. Fully grown, she felt almost beautiful.

One extra spritz of the flowery toilet water Waite hated and she was ready. "There. And I don't give a fig whether you like it or not," she said in a defiant tone to the man in her mind. Glancing at the square-faced clock on the nightstand, she cried, "That clock must be fast. It can't be 8:20 already!"

"What?" Surprised, too, Nora had been lost in her own imaginings.

"How dare he be late on our first outing!" Breelan was piqued. Then, "That sounds so self-centered. Trip obviously has been detained. I only hope it's nothing serious."

"Me, too," agreed Nora, her brows drawn.

Idling the time away while they waited, the girls went into Aunt Coe's room to examine their skirts another time in the petticoat mirror fastened across the bottom of her bureau. "Remind me when we get home," Nora stated, "to investigate the circumference of our ankles. I read somewhere that a man is put off by thick ankles. If we determine that one or the other of us has that acute condition, we must pledge to walk the beach more frequently to tone and thin our legs. Do you agree?"

This struck Breelan as ridiculous, but offering no dissension she said, "Yes, whatever you think best."

At half-past eight, they descended the stairs. There sat Uncles Fries, looking none too thrilled, as the old grandfather clock struck, marking the time.

"Uncle," said Nora, nervously sitting beside Aunt Coe on the crushed velvet settee. "You're a man. You know how occasions arise over which one has no control when you're a slave to something or someone else's schedule." Nora jabbered, succeeding only in creating more concern. "Why, I'd bet when you were courting Aunt Coe, you were late a time or two."

Uncle Fries cut her off. "Breelan and Nora. While you are under my roof, I am charged to treat you as my daughters. You have the obligation to respect my wishes as you would those of your own fathers. When these Trip and Will characters come to the door, if they ever do come, I will send them packing. Can I make it any plainer?" Looking at two quivering chins, he stood resolute.

Chapter 13 – *The Goodbye Lie* by Jane Marie

With tears and fierce pleading from the girls, and apologies and excuses from the men, Uncle Fries was too inexperienced a foster father to have the strength to say no. As he stood on his front porch in the drizzling mist to watch the covered carriage with its exterior driver pull away, he realized this particular mode of transport allowed the soldiers privacy to use worldly wiles on their unsophisticated companions. He guessed that at this very moment, the carriage walls were reverberating with flattery, laughter and implied sincerity.

After two hours and forty-five minutes of worry by a pacing uncle and a fidgety aunt, the foursome arrived home, pointedly one half-hour earlier than the expected midnight. It was clear to Fries and Coe that the sole purpose of this more than prompt arrival was meant purely to pacify the elders. And it worked. They were surprised and moved by the obvious attempt to amend their earlier opinion of the soldiers. The next morning when flowers were delivered to Aunt Coe along with an invitation for luncheon for the entire family, hearts and minds were mended. The days and nights which followed were full with fun. Couples fun.

The two couples experienced a world of excitement. They visited Coney Island Amusement Park and sipped cream sodas between whirling rides and games of skill and chance with a chicken managing to beat Breelan at tic-tack-toe. They attended a magic sideshow where a young boy billing himself as Harry Houdini, The King of Cards, amazed all eyes.

They dined at Delmonico's famous steakhouse and went to the horse races. They relished the rollicking musical, H. M. S. Pinafore, by the famous team of Gilbert and Sullivan, which was enjoying a three-year run in New York City.

Breelan and Nora even managed a day trip to Connecticut to meet Trip's family. Breelan found Hannah and Roy Clelland to be lovely gentlefolk. Over dinner, they'd explained the origin of their son's given name. His mother wanted him to be named for his father, but his father didn't want the confusion of two men with the same name in the same house, since he'd experienced that problem growing up. So Trip was short for triple, the third. And the girls learned Will's history, as well. Orphaned at six, Will had been taken in by the Clellands to be raised as their own. Since Trip was an only child, Will was a welcome addition to the family.

With every meeting, Breelan discovered Trip to be more attractive. When they weren't together, he sent a daily messenger with suitable gifts, all of which were to be carried, eaten or looked upon. Aware of the proprieties, Trip understood that a gift to be worn was too personal and certainly too improper to accept. One day the present was butterscotch candy. On another, an envelope of lily-of-the-valley seeds was accompanied by a note saying he didn't know if the warmer weather in Fernandina was conducive for this particular specie's growth, but it might be fun to give the seeds a try. Then, it was the sheet music to *Vanishing Moments*. He'd penned along the margin:

> *We danced to this song the night we met.*
> *A time remembered, I shan't ere forget.*

Later, a scented lavender stick tied with pastel ribbons was discovered on the porch. Finally, Trip surprised Breelan with a charcoal drawing of them both, side-by-side on a swing. He wrote how he'd described her beauty to the artist. The resulting resemblance was remarkable!

The most exhilarating event of all was the ride in a hot air balloon. Two days before they were to set sail for Fernandina, Trip turned his back to Nora and Will and the man in charge of controlling the basket in which they all flew, and took Breelan's hand. Up there in the blue of a cloudless New York City sky, he said, "What I'm about to disclose may shock you."

"At this point, Trip, nothing you can say or do will surprise me. I've had such grand times and seen so many new and marvelous things, I don't know how I'll ever be able to thank you."

"Thank me? You make this easy for me. The only way you can thank me is to marry me."

Had she not been holding onto one of the ropes of the basket in which they floated, Breelan might have toppled over the side.

"You'll be leaving soon, and I need to have your decision, Bree. Yes, this is unexpected. That just makes it all the more wonderful and exciting. What do you say?"

When Trip had kissed Breelan for the first time in a rowboat in Central Park, she felt shy and unsure, yet she liked the way he made her feel. The new sensations weren't wild and uncontrollable inside her the way Waite had said they'd be, and she dismissed the captain as an insulting and crude lifelong bachelor.

Now, her head was reeling. Whether it was lack of oxygen from being up so high or pure adrenalin from dropping to the ground so quickly, Breelan needed a cooler head than her own.

As soon as they were alone, she talked things over with Nora. Vicariously thrilled by her cousin's temptation, Nora could think of nothing to dissuade her. She encouraged the marriage wholeheartedly. In the space of several hours, Breelan wired her father, saying she wanted to marry a man from the *Gentle Comfort*.

Michael Dunnigan's answer was absolute. He was appalled, and told his daughter to wait until the family got to know her fiancé better. They needed a proper courtship and betrothal while the wedding banns were posted. After sufficient time, they could be married and blessed by Father O'Boyle at home in St. Michael's amid relations and friends as was appropriate.

But Breelan Jane Dunnigan was a stubborn American girl. She disobeyed her father and disappointed her mother for the first time in her life. She eloped with Trip.

Breelan insisted on a church wedding, however. The two couples rode horseback to the tiny town of Sayville, New York. There they found Father Conroy, pastor of Saint Agatha's, a small, impoverished Catholic parish. He willingly performed the ceremony for a much-needed fee of two dollars. With Nora and Will as maid of honor and best man respectively, Breelan and Trip were married at 4 p.m. on a cloudy and sticky Tuesday afternoon. Hardly had the vows been spoken when a cleaning woman removed the drooping bouquet of wildflowers from the rough hewn wooden altar, declaring, "Old man Marron died and the pastor and flowers are needed to preside over the burial before the remains get ta stinkin' in this Indian Summer heat."

It hadn't been the wedding Breelan had seen in her daydreams, but it was done now. She was Mrs. Trip Clelland. She kissed Nora and hugged Will, telling them to wire her family with her good news when those two returned to New York City that evening. Breelan had been grateful she wouldn't be present when her father read the telegram announcing his daughter was married. She prayed and kept on praying he wouldn't disown her for her deed.

"It's a short ride to the Birch Bark Inn, Bree," Trip announced. "It's nearby, so we can get up early tomorrow, ride hard, and catch the *Gentle Comfort* just before she sails."

"That sounds fine." How unfortunate Daddy booked round trip passage on the *Comfort*, Breelan thought. Any ship but that one. Well, she'd have her mind on things other than Captain Taylor, now that she was a married woman.

To her disappointment, the Birch Bark Inn was coarse and unwelcoming. Breelan saw a rowdy array of men in various degrees of inebriation when she entered the barroom. She guessed there were probably nasty smelling rooms upstairs where drunken men could sleep off their liquor or take a fast trick. She'd learned of prostitutes and such from a yellow-cover, one of the forbidden books the girls had passed around at school. Until now, she'd never personally seen anything as base as this place in her life. Once she was alone with Trip though, Breelan was sure he would make things all right.

Trip stopped at the counter and ordered a bottle of red wine from a bartender secured behind iron bars with his precious stock of alcohol. "Since champagne is unavailable, this will just have to do," Trip explained. Bottle in one hand, her overnight satchel in the other, he proceeded her up some squeaking, concave-worn steps.

"What about the rest of my luggage, Trip? In my haste, I forgot all about it!"

"That's what I'm here for, Bree, to take care of you. I talked with Will, and he'll make sure your luggage gets aboard the *Comfort* and is waiting for us."

The late afternoon light showed dust hanging golden in the dead air of the dismal square room. The small double bed, her marriage bed, was shrouded with a worn coverlet. Upon closer inspection, "Look at the once beautiful quilt, Trip. I think the faded pattern is Duck's-Foot-Stuck-in-the-Mud. It's sad to think it's found its end here. How many wasted hours were spent making it?"

He offered no response, and she hadn't really expected one. She was nervous and trying to keep some conversation alive. Near the window, a crudely printed sign with an arrow pointing down read Fire Escape. In a knotted pile lay an old frayed rope, one end tied to the spindly leg of the single dresser. Breelan laughed. "What little weight that rope would hold and what little use it would be to any poor soul who might need to exit this room quickly. Their chances of jumping and breaking a leg would be equal to this rig." She loosened the top button at her throat. "Trip, could you open a window? We need some fresh air."

His efforts failed. "It's no use. It looks like the sashes were painted shut a hundred years ago. Listen, it isn't a palace, Bree. Don't think I don't know that, but we'll make the best of it." A minor argument of some kind could be heard coming from downstairs, but Trip ignored it, unconsciously raising his voice to make sure she didn't miss a word he was saying. "We'll look back on this and tell our children how their parents were so in love, they ran off and married. Come on. Let's have some wine in celebration." He found two glasses on the bedside stand. Holding them to the fading light, he wiped the insides clean with his neckerchief, and handed a half-filled glass to his bride. "To our life together. May it be long, with many babies to carry on for me."

She had never before spoken of children to a man. But this was no ordinary man, she reminded herself. This was her husband. She would have to get used to such discussions. She sipped her wine and watched as Trip drained and refilled his glass several more times. Breelan lit the candle on the dresser as night entered the room.

Trip stood and reached for her, and she went willingly. He fumbled with the rest of the pearl buttons on the front of the bodice of her pale blue dress, her wedding dress. The alcohol had made his fingers clumsy. There was no turning back at this point. While Breelan removed her dress, Trip poured the last of the wine into his glass, then into himself.

He looked up from the empty tumbler and said, "Before we start things we won't want to interrupt, we need another bottle."

"Do you think that's necessary?" asked Breelan sweetly, standing in her camisole and petticoats.

Trip seemed unaware and uncaring of her state of undress. "Of course, it's necessary. This is a special occasion! I'll be right back," and he exited, leaving her alone and uncertain. She heard him holler from the top of the stair to the barkeep, this time asking for whiskey. He returned triumphant, holding high his purchase as if he had been chosen to receive the last available bottle. Ignoring his bride and grabbing a glass, Trip poured and then downed the strong-smelling liquid. He sat back on the sagging bed, propping himself up with both pillows. His words slurred, he said, "Let me see you, Bree. All of you."

She hesitated. "Not like this. Please."

"What do you mean not like this? I'm your husband. This is my right. Do as I say."

Trembling, Breelan closed her eyes and tears trickled from beneath her lashes. A chill ran through her as she removed the last of her clothing. Although it was still suffocating in the room, she felt as if she would never again be warm inside. She fully understood the definition of humiliation, wanting to die from disgrace. Trip was silent, staring at her nakedness. She loathed him and herself for letting this happen to her. With courage drawn from where she didn't know, Breelan breathed deeply, ignoring the stench of the place and opened her eyes, ready to face her husband's hungry examination.

Trip was passed out across the bed, empty glass still in his grip! To Breelan's amazement, her greatest emotion was relief. Shouldn't I be disappointed? Aren't honeymoons supposed to be glorious? Banishing all thought but escape, she threw on her clothes and as gently as she could, collected a few coins from the pocket of Trip's trousers. He didn't move a muscle, and she was more than pleased. She'd pay him back by letter once she got home and out of this nightmare. Closing the door softly behind her, Breelan fled, only to stop mid-stair as a silence fell over the barroom. All eyes took in the unexpected comeliness descending into their depths. Breelan soon realized that in her haste, her hair had almost completely fallen free of its pins and her dress was left open, gaping at the neck. She covered her shoulders with her cape and pulled it tight under her chin.

"Hey girlie. What's the matter? The gent can't keep up with ya?" asked a man with no teeth in his head. Between belches, he sucked and chewed the corner of his unshorn moustache making sickening smacking sounds.

Another voice from somewhere in the dim room bellowed toward her, "How's about a try with somebody else, missy? I ain't never had no complaints yet!"

"Ah, you're crazier than a shit-house mouse, fester-head, if you think that beauty would look your way twice!"

Vile laughter and boorish remarks scorched Breelan's ears. She tried to run from the tavern to her horse outside. Men grabbed and pinched at her as she attempted to pass. She felt a hand on her breast, stopped, and slapped a mean, hairy face as hard as she could. Her wrist was seized and curled behind her back as a monster breathed down on her, his breath so sour, she wretched from the odor. When he squeezed her jaw with his grimy fingers, she turned her head, opened her mouth, and bit out a chunk of his right arm. He wailed in agony as she spit out the bloody flesh and muscle, stone cold to his suffering.

"Mercy! If that don't take the socks off all!"

"The bitch has left her brand on you for life, Pearly!"

"That woman needs some learnin'!" Vulgar comments were hurled around the pub, accompanied by hoots and applause.

"Yeah, Pearly. You teach her good. This place could stand with a little entertainment."

"Hell, Pearly Nast ain't nobody to be givin' lessons, but I'm willin' ta watch if I have ta."

"Then, it'll be my turn."

"No. I seen her come down them stairs first. That makes her mine! No cabbaging allowed."

"I say I get first dibs, or I'll twist off your skull and piss down your neck!"

"You all had best back away 'cause I'm fixin' ta knock the crust clean off your bony asses!"

A vicious fracas broke out, turning the entire place lethal as fists, chairs, and glass all flew. Though Breelan was no longer the main attraction, the monster of a man still had her upper body trapped against him. She reached wildly for any weapon she could find and felt a cold steel hairpin, the last, holding her tangled tresses. With strength fueled by fear, her free hand hit dead center on its target between the man's legs. He expelled all the foul air from his lungs onto her face. The revulsion she experienced was worth the look of pure pain on his hideous features as the hog bristles on his ears stood straight out. He fell to the floor and she bolted for the door, jumping clear of the bodies and debris accumulating from the fray.

"Pull it out! Pull it out!" shrieked her victim.

"You pull it out yourself, Pearly. I wouldn't touch that thing with your brother's hand, let alone mine," some non-sympathizing soul shouted across the bar.

"Like to see what she'd do if something really got her mad as a blind bull!" The drunken creatures bayed with hysterics.

"Pass me more of that there bug juice, man!"

"Sing us another chorus of Hand Organ Gallop, Pearly. It'll be the only enjoyment you'll be havin' in that department for a mighty long time!"

Revolting laughter poured out the door after Breelan. She ran to the stable, threw a saddle over the horse she'd ridden to the inn, and galloped away, trying to out-distance the evil images and ghastly echoes she feared she'd forever recall.

Chapter 14 – *The Goodbye Lie* by Jane Marie

Alone in the darkness, Breelan saw the Big Dipper overhead and thanked God it was a clear night. She found the North Star, then headed due east toward the ocean. At least, she hoped she was headed east.

An unexpected memory appeared inside her mind. While she and Nora readied themselves for their first dinner engagement with Trip and Will only two weeks earlier, Aunt Coe had read aloud from Martine's Hand-Book of Etiquette and Guide to True Politeness. It was her aunt's second bible, a miscellany of decorum. Whenever she questioned the suitable response to any social circumstance, out it came.

> *Be careful to reach home in good time. Let nothing induce you to be out after dusk or when the lamps are lighted. Nothing but unavoidable necessity can sanction such acts of impropriety.*

This had to be classified as exactly that, an unavoidable necessity.

As Breelan rode, the wind of flight slapped at her body, awakening her to the consequences she'd deliberately ignored. She'd wrapped herself in Trip's devotion and relied upon it, the way her mother relied upon her father. Do I love Trip? Really love him? Can he possibly love me and be so selfish? Am I just angry and ashamed that he didn't have enough concern or respect for me to stay awake on our wedding night? That he'd rather drink liquor than make love to me? And I had the conceit to think I was beautiful. How will I explain my traveling alone? Nora will insist on knowing. Why didn't I listen to Daddy when he told me to wait, to get to know Trip better? What will I tell everyone? My world has changed, and I'm the idiot who changed it. Dear God, what will Waite say? I didn't listen to him when he warned me not to trust Trip.

By the time she smelled the salt water ahead, she was near collapse and looked it. The sun was climbing into the sky, illuminating a whole, fresh day in Breelan's fractured life. She found the dock by asking strangers for directions, staying just out of their reach, then tossing them a coin in payment as she rode away. She was too tired to care what was correct or incorrect, safe or unsafe. She had to get aboard the *Gentle Comfort* before she fell in the streets.

Breelan thanked the heavens once again when, at last, she saw the ship, dead ahead. It had only just arrived because the men were still tying her down at the pier. Breelan's eyes searched for Waite, but he was not on deck. Where was he? Where was he?

"Secure that line, Hendrickson."

It was his voice. Unconsciously, she released the breath she'd been holding as she caught sight of him. Reaching the dock, she dismounted weakly, threw back her hair and advanced up the ramp.

Waite was witnessing a vision. What other explanation could there be? Breelan was coming toward him, blown and mussed, yet still as lovely. He saw dried blood around her mouth as she approached with slow grace. Who had hurt her? He'd kill them. He'd expected her, yes, but not this early in the morning. He knew he'd have to be dead before he'd let her ride unaccompanied through a strange town. He went to her. She needed him. She was near, close enough to touch. Looking down on the woman with the wild hair, in the dark cape and flat boots, she seemed smaller than he remembered, more fragile.

"Waite." She whispered his name and fell into his arms.

He cradled this wisp of femininity to his chest, his heart. He was so grateful to see her. The past month had lasted longer than forever. He wanted to crush her to him, to hold her so close that she'd melt into him from the sheer sincerity of his clench. He checked himself from physically shattering her with his longing.

All the staterooms were filled with awakening passengers, some of whom would be disembarking after breakfast, yet that was still hours away. The only empty beds available right now were those of the working crew, and they were in one large berthing room. He could not put her down in the bowels of the ship for his men to ogle. She needed privacy. Although the choice seemed self-serving, his cabin was the only place possible. Still he didn't want her in his quarters, let alone in his bed because her appeal was too overwhelming.

Crew and early rising passengers hugged the wall as the captain passed, carrying a limp girl with rich brown hair hanging past his belt. He ordered Farley, his personal steward, to bring fresh water at once as he stepped over the brass threshold into his secluded realm. Waite laid Breelan gently onto his tufted mattress. She stirred and wound her arms around his corded neck. She whimpered and trembled, her arms holding him fast.

"Bree," he spoke quietly into her ear. "Darling, it's Waite. You're safe now." He reached up to her dainty wrists and reluctantly pried her arms from around him, all the while cooing to her as if she were a child. She produced a slight smile. He wasn't sure if she knew it was he who spoke in soft tones. He wanted to think so.

Breelan was dreaming. A soothing cotton hammock enveloped and cradled her. It gently swayed to and fro. She no longer was frightened or uncertain.

Waite settled her into his pillow and felt her brow with his large flat palm. She was cool with no fever. Her skirts were covered in road dust, and she appeared to be exhausted. There was no telling how far she'd ridden or why. He'd have to be patient to hear her story. She needed rest now. Farley delivered the requested pitcher of water and discreetly left the room; a stolen glance toward the beauty in the captain's bed was his only acknowledgement of her presence.

Waite removed Breelan's boots and cape and loosened her sash. With a damp cloth, he wiped her hands, her throat, her face. The dried blood came away on the wet textile. Her mouth appeared uninjured. He was glad of that. He covered her with a sheet, not wanting her to become overheated, taxing her body further.

Waite wouldn't need to resume his duties until it was time to depart. In the meanwhile, Catfish could handle things. He gave notice he was not to be disturbed until Breelan's cousin came on board. He would inform Nora of Breelan's condition. Then, he would feel more in control of himself once Breelan was back in her own assigned stateroom in the company of her family.

Time raced as Waite studied the sleeping girl. He came to know every freckle across her delicate nose, the proud angle of her brows, every dark lash, the small scar in the crease of her smile, the shape of her mouth. He made himself move his chair from beside of the bed to the far side of the cabin. Standing tall, he opened his porthole and inhaled the humid air. It offered no relief. Finally, he couldn't be strong any longer. If he failed to do it now, this very moment, he would lose all reason. Hesitantly, he turned and walked to the slumbering girl. He sat on the edge of his bed. She stirred and parted her lips. He stared. All principle left him. He knew only that he had to taste her. Bending, he touched her mouth with his. The feel of her made his blood run hot and molten. She was so soft, her breath so sweet. She wiggled beneath him and her lips fitted themselves against and between his. In his mind, he was caressing her body with his kiss.

Suddenly, she was still. Blue eyes locked onto black eyes, as he pulled back from her. Don't," she breathed, fanning his mouth with her honeyed breath.

"Don't," he heard, but did she mean don't kiss me or don't stop? He had no chance to discover the answer. A startling knock sounded at his door, and the steward announced Miss Nora Duffy's presence on board. His eyes never left Breelan's as his husky voice ordered curtly, "Send word to Miss Duffy that I'll be with her shortly." As he spoke, Breelan's eyelids fluttered closed, and she was again still.

Thus far, Waite's fortitude had faltered and he was appreciative of the interruption lest he take her here and now. No, all that pleasure would have to wait until they married. He could never allow himself to be so selfish as to make love to Breelan unless they were wed. Not this woman. Not this lady. Deprivation of any kind had never been something he sought in his life, and this particular type of torture was nearly unbearable. For Breelan alone, he would willingly endure it and more. Her love would be worth any delay. He would bet his heart on it.

Waite left his cabin, commanding Farley to stand watch outside his door. "At the very first sound of any stirring, I am to be notified. Is that understood?"

"Yes, sir."

"Good. Now, make it so."

"Aye, sir."

When Nora answered his knock on her stateroom door, she immediately knew things were amiss from the look of him. "Captain?"

"Good morning, Miss Duffy. Please don't be alarmed. Your cousin, Breelan, is unharmed. However, she's in my cabin at this moment, recovering from exhaustion."

Shocked, Nora questioned, "What? What happened? Is Trip all right? Where is he?"

"I don't know what happened. Breelan was alone when she rode here. We'll have to find out the circumstances when she awakens. And if she was with that lieutenant, as you suppose, and if he's not dead, I'll have his hide for letting her travel unprotected."

Nora could only think the worst. Poor Trip. He must be hurt or dead somewhere. What will Breelan do without her husband? She surely must have loved him greatly to have married so quickly. Nora conveniently chose to forget her encouragement in the entire matter. "Oh, my dear Bree." Nora's green eyes filled with tears.

Waite offered his handkerchief. Declining, she mumbled her thanks and drew her own from inside her waistband. She dabbed at her eyes, shaking her head.

Waite puzzled at her mournful demeanor, questioning why she was so upset. He'd told her Breelan was all right, only tired. Empty comfort was all he could offer until he knew more himself.

104

An alarming commotion on the main deck and running footsteps could be heard clear inside Nora's room.

"Cap'n Taylor! Cap'n Taylor!" shouted Wally, the new cabin boy.

Stepping into the hallway, "Has Miss Dunnigan awakened?"

"No, sir. I ran down lookin' for ya in your stateroom. Farley told me where to find ya, sir. A man's demandin' ta see ya and right now! He's real threatening about it, too, sir."

"Do you know who it is?"

"No, sir. Just that he seems pretty riled already."

"Thank you, Wally. I'll see to it. You go on about to your duties."

"Aye, sir."

"Pardon me, Miss Nora. I have a seemingly disagreeable matter to attend," and he turned, taking large quick steps away from her. Curiosity forced Nora to follow. Uncontrolled ravings could be heard as they mounted the stairs to the main deck.

"Where is she? I'll give that sonofabitch one more minute before I go and get her myself. He can't keep me from her." The man shouting looked at his watch, counting the last seconds aloud.

Reaching the cause of the disturbance, Waite challenged, "You bastard! So you are alive!"

Nora was relieved to see a well-groomed Trip in his crisp uniform standing before the captain. She didn't understand the captain's intense anger at Trip. Surely, he had grounds for leaving Bree alone. The ship's highest officer was being purposely unreasonable. Trip would explain if just given the chance.

Waite scoped the length of his rival, assessing little damage had been done him the last few hours. Clelland merely appeared to have a set of beady blood shot eyes. The captain readied himself to hear an inadequate explanation.

As passengers gathered, "I demand to see Breelan at once," Trip shouted. The confrontation added to the exhilaration of the travelers' voyage.

"She's resting."

"Your boy says in your cabin."

"Yes, in my cabin. All other staterooms were occupied."

"How convenient for you."

Waite mentally winced at the implication for Breelan's sake. Still, he would not retaliate because he knew the suggestion of improper conduct was true.

Waite charged, "How did she come to ride here unaccompanied? Journeying for who knows how long and in the darkness? She fainted when she arrived. She's been dead asleep for hours." That is, all but for a moment, he remembered with pleasing satisfaction.

Dismissing the captain's question, Trip insisted, "Show me to her, or I'll call the law and have you arrested."

"This is my ship and I am the law, or did you forget that fact? Besides, what would you have me charged with? Aiding a woman who purposely sought my help? You're a fool."

"No, Captain. You're the fool. Apparently, you haven't been informed of the entire story." Covering each word in proud poison, Trip said clearly, "Breelan is my wife."

Waite seized the collar of the soldier's uniform and twisted it tightly against his throat. With only inches separating them, "You goddamn lying white trash. You'll regret you ever spoke such slander."

Nora clutched at Waite's arm of iron, begging him to release Trip. The blonde man struggled to free himself, but the grip on him was powered by blind rage.

Suddenly, Waite heard Nora's soft, insistent voice in his ear.

"Captain, please, let him go. You're squeezing the life out of him. Please, for Breelan's sake, let him go," she pleaded, with more calm than she felt at that perilous point.

Waite released his hold. For Breelan's sake? For Breelan's sake? Turning to Nora, he grasped her shoulders, careful this time to control himself and not bruise her. Looking hard into her face, he knew it was true. This animal, clothed in the vestments of national honor, had married Breelan. The blow of truth was so physically real and powerful, Waite nearly fell to his knees. Freeing Nora from his gaze and his grasp, his expression turned to granite. Only the clenching of his jaw revealed any hint of devastation at the unwanted knowledge.

Smug arrogance radiated from Trip as he straightened his disheveled clothing. The surrounding atmosphere was so heavy-laden with hostility that most passengers remained motionless.

"There is no need for rash behavior," urged young Nora, who was growing up with every tick of passing time. "We'll all go down and see Breelan. Together. Captain, if you will lead the way."

Waite understood he had no justification in keeping this man from his wife. The word wife caught in his thoughts. It scoured his brain to leave a permanent reminder that she was out of his reach. He did as Nora recommended and walked through the parting sea of onlookers to where

Breelan lay. Facing the heavy door marked PRIVATE in bold brass letters, he entered. Breelan was still in the same position as when he'd left her. He remained by the door and allowed Nora and Trip to go to Breelan's bedside.

"She's so ashen," said Nora, "and her hands are cold."

"Step aside, please, Miss Nora." To the surprise of no one, Trip scooped Breelan into his arms. As he turned to leave, Waite stepped into his path, blocking the way. Although they were nearly the same size, the darker man's revealed anger caused him to appear larger.

Nora hurriedly positioned herself between the two men. Opposite Waite, she again grasped his forearm and lightly squeezed. Unwilling to acknowledge Nora's meaning, that he had no rights, he stood firm until stark reality forced him to step from the door and allow Clelland to take Breelan away, away into his own room.

Still sleeping, Breelan wound her arms around Trip's neck as she'd done to Waite earlier. She cuddled into him with a sigh, dreaming again that she was rocking in the hammock. She held on tight so as not to fall from the cradle of contentment in which she rode.

"You see, Captain? My wife has no objections," said Trip as he exited the cabin. Nora was about to follow when he spat at her, "No need, cousin. I'll attend to Breelan's every need, as is my duty," and his snigger could be heard as he moved away.

Retaining control no longer, Waite slammed the door closed with such power that a polished wall sconce fell to the floor, breaking the yet burning candle in two. He stepped on the flaming wick, grinding it under his heel.

"We still don't know what happened," said Nora, aghast at Trip's curt behavior toward her, and furious. "I'll find out from Bree when we're alone."

Speaking quietly, Waite said, "He's correct, you know. I have no right where Breelan is concerned. Why should I care what happens to her? She's his problem now. His responsibility. She's no longer mine. Then again, she never really was."

Nora left him alone in his room, still rambling. She had discovered a great truth. Captain Waite Taylor would always care what happened to Breelan. He would always feel responsible for her because, plainly, he was in love with her.

Chapter 15 – *The Goodbye Lie* by Jane Marie

Breelan stretched from her graceful fingertips to her tiny toes. It felt so good to be rested.

"Bree? Are you awake, honey?"

It was a man's voice. Trip! She remembered. It was dusk now and nearly dark in the cabin. Breelan saw the shadowy form. She pulled the covers to her chin and shrank beneath them. "Why are you here? How did you find me?" Her courage was growing with each syllable.

"Whoa. Slow down. Why am I here? It should be obvious. You're my wife."

"I have not been treated like a wife."

"I admit that. I can't begin to tell you how ashamed I am to have embarrassed myself and my name as I did last night. I don't know why I ordered that second bottle of liquor. I guess I'll have to blame it on a bridegroom's frayed nerves."

"I find it a tad difficult to excuse your behavior so easily. You may have shamed yourself, but you also humiliated me in the process. I felt unwanted and undesirable."

He stepped to her side. "Please, Bree, you've got to believe it was completely me. You have only to look in a mirror and know any man with sight would want you."

"Flatter me all you like, Trip. The harm to our marriage is irreparable."

"You can't mean that. We haven't even begun to be married. Not really."

"I know what you're referring to specifically, and I have no interest in that with you." She tried to even the score with mean words.

"Please give us one more try. I won your heart once. You're a just and fair person. Give me all your attention while we're underway, until we arrive in Fernandina. Let me prove myself to you."

She realized she could have her marriage annulled at this point, before things went any further between them. Yet, she did consider herself a fair person. Giving second chances didn't seem unreasonable, in most cases. This was different. A second chance meant another opportunity for things to go wrong.

Oh, how she wanted to be home. To her, home meant Dunnigan Manor. It meant living with her parents, not sharing a house with this man. Maybe she was too immature for marriage. Maybe she wasn't ready to permanently leave her parents' care yet. If she stayed married, she had no choice. Ready or not, her husband would and should come first in her life.

She didn't expect a marriage to be problem free. That was all in the course of things, but could she find enough excitement, enough exhilaration in being with Trip to make the difficulties bearable? She didn't think so. Those crazy days were over. She couldn't commit to a marriage when she had no positive feelings for the man she was supposed to cherish until she died. This was her chance to be free.

Breelan imagined the old hags with no stimulation in their own lives who cackled on and on about the littlest things, embellishing them into the must-tell tales of the season. She thought especially of Mrs. Ickles, the worst nosey-poke of them all. There was bound to be gossip no matter which path Breelan chose. She might as well steel herself for it. Everyone probably knew she'd eloped by this time. An annulment would be reason for a few unpleasant months of blistering scandal. Remaining married was a condemnation to a lifetime of certain unhappiness with a man she didn't think she could ever love. So the gossip be hanged! She would choose annulment. But she wouldn't tell Trip yet. He'd undoubtedly make a scene. And Waite, whether she wanted it or not, would undoubtedly think himself her protector and come to her rescue. Then, holy hell would break loose. As desperately as she wanted it all to be over and done with, the situation limited her degree of honesty. So, to keep peace until they arrived in Florida, she would pretend there was a slight chance of reconciliation.

"Trip, I feel there is little promise for us. A forced love is not real." His face was that of a whipped dog, cowed and hopeless. She caught herself almost feeling guilty. Almost. "Nevertheless, I can't stop you from attempting to win my affection, should you choose to try. If I still feel the same when we arrive in Fernandina, you must agree to give me an annulment. That is the only offer I will make you."

Glad expectations scratched at his being. "You married me, Bree. Why else would you have done it if not out of love?"

"That's what I'm trying to understand myself." Could her feelings for him have come and gone so quickly and still be called love?

They were silent for a long while, he pacing around the cabin and she remembering Waite's words, "You'll know without a doubt that you've chosen the right man for the rest of your life." I only know this man before me isn't the right one. He can't be.

Trip finally spoke. "I reckon we'll let one hour follow another. You won't be sorry, Bree. Things will work out."

She replied only in thought. I'm sorry, Trip, for allowing you any hope at all and permitting this muddle, but I know of no better way to handle it.

"Are you rested, now?" he asked, concern heavy in his tone.

"Yes, I am and I'm hungry, too."

"I'm so hungry, my ribs are shakin' hands with my backbone."

His attempt at levity brought a forced smile to Breelan's mouth. "Maybe after we dine, we can stroll to the bridge and find out if we're sailing on schedule."

"Why did you say the bridge? Were you thinking of the good captain?" he snapped.

"Of course not. It's about the only nautical term I know." Was that the entire truth, she asked herself? "I'm the one who should be thin-skinned, not you."

"You're right. You're right."

"I think I'm behaving rather brightly, considering everything. Let's say no more about it."

"Agreed. And ..." he hesitated. "Thank you, Bree. You're quite a lady."

While Breelan changed behind the privacy screen, she felt something hanging around her neck. She removed it for a better look and found it to be a lovely religious medal. She'd never seen it before. Who had placed it there? Could it have been Trip? He hadn't seemed to be a particularly spiritual man.

"Are you about finished, Bree? Time is getting on," Trip called, beginning to sound impatient.

She would ask him about the medallion later when he wasn't rushing her. Hurrying, she dropped it back over her head and completed dressing in preparation for the meal. They walked arm-in-arm to the dining salon, her chin angled high with dignity. Trip was aware that once again the prettiest girl on the ship was at his side. When they entered the room, heads turned and eating ceased as forks and glasses froze midway to lips. Since the earlier altercation on deck between Waite and Trip, an altercation Breelan remembered nothing about, the gossip was rampant.

She heard hushed voices as did Trip. "That poor soldier. She only married to spite the captain. What a grievous mistake it was. She regretted it immediately and returned to him the very next day! What will become of the lieutenant now? She's a hard one, for sure."

Breelan was astonished! Why are they all talking about us, she wondered incredulously. And whatever gave them the notion of something between the captain and me?

Trip discovered he liked having people on his side, thinking Breelan was heartless and at fault. He would appear the long-suffering husband for a short time. A little sympathy never hurt a thing. Of course, he would have to clear up the misconception as to whom Breelan really cared for.

He couldn't have folks thinking his wife loved another man. During their trip, he would demonstrate such affection for her that the true nature of her love for him would display itself, no matter how she tried to keep it private.

"Bree!"

Nora was running toward her. They held tight together for an extra moment, each comforted to see the other. When the young women parted, tears glistened in their eyes.

"I'm fine. Trust me." Bree could see her cousin wasn't certain if she should believe her or not.

"Tomorrow. I'll meet you tomorrow after breakfast. Ten o'clock on deck at the lounges," said the anxious redhead. "Oh, Bree," she breathed into her best friend's ear so Trip wouldn't hear. "What about tonight, alone with him?" Nora didn't know what had transpired between the two on their wedding night. She could only gather it must have been bad, bad enough for Breelan to run away.

"I'll be fine," the bride assured unconvincingly and unable to explain a word with Trip so near. "Yes, tomorrow."

"May the angels fly beside you, darling."

Breelan nodded, invoking a similar silent prayer. She watched Nora walk back and sit near Will, who bowed in greeting toward the newlyweds.

Trip was beginning to get annoyed at the continuing stares they were receiving. He didn't mind the gossip, but wanted his privacy as much as any man could expect in a public room. "May we perhaps be seated? You said you were hungry." With no further words, they followed the waiter to a corner table.

Breelan caught a glimpse of the captain and found him watching her. She nodded ever so slightly, just enough that he saw and responded in kind. He looked tired. It must be because I bothered him so early this morning. It suddenly struck her. Waite had been docking the ship. It wasn't as if she'd awakened him from a sound sleep. She didn't recall having spent any time in Waite's bed, assuming she was immediately put in the cabin she and Trip now occupied.

"Bree, would you please come out of that trance and talk to me? What are you thinking?" asked Trip, wanting desperately to get inside her mind so he could develop the right approach to winning her back.

"Nothing in particular," she fibbed. She found she was doing a lot of that lately, in spite of her principles against it. "So much has happened in my life in the last month. I'm having a difficult time believing it all, I guess."

Trip made no comment. They ordered supper, but without wine. He was obviously not going to repeat last evening's performance she decided or, more accurately, non-performance. Good God! They hadn't specifically discussed how they would handle intimate matters. What might he expect tonight in their chambers? Well, when the time came, he would just have to understand their relationship would only be platonic, and unless her feelings somehow drastically changed, that was all it would ever be.

Throughout the meal, Breelan's eyes wandered to Nora at Will's table. Despite her clear concern for her cousin's situation, Nora she was having a lovely time flirting with Will. The family always thought Nora would be the one to get into some sort of mischief. How wrong they'd been. Nora hadn't resented Waite's close scrutiny like I did, Breelan told herself honestly. I'm the idiot who fought him at every turn with sarcasm and pouting. And still he remained ever attentive to my safety. The moment I was out of his sight, I fixed things but good.

Dancing followed dinner. Trip and Breelan danced without magic. After a three melody grouping, there was a pause in the music to allow guests to rest or change partners. Trip and Breelan were on the way back to their table, when he felt a tap on the shoulder. It was Waite.

"Good evening. How are you feeling tonight, Miss Breelan?"

Her eyes brightened when she heard Waite's deep drawl.

Trip saw her expression and whipped forth a response to his direct competition. "Beautiful as ever and weary from our dance."

"No, I'm fine, Trip. I don't want to ever go to bed." Breelan had just revealed her deepest secret. She dreaded the time alone with her husband that was soon to follow. Why had she allowed herself to speak her thoughts aloud? She saw he was fuming and withholding his spousal rights certainly wouldn't improve his mood.

Waite was angry, too. He was powerless to stop the inevitable. Was he reading her face right? She didn't seem to want Trip to touch her. Then why had she danced with him? Why would she willingly share a cabin with him where Waite would have no way of protecting her? She was playing a deadly game. Say the word, Breelan, say the word, his mind called out to hers, and I'll never let him lay another finger on you. Leave the man and I'll shield you from everything and everyone. Either she couldn't hear his offer or refused to listen. Maybe, if he could get her alone long enough
…

"Would you care to dance?"

Invisible sparks crackled the air. Surely everyone can hear them as I do, she thought frantically. I must prevent a spectacle. I have to. "Maybe another time, Captain. Tonight, Trip alone fills my dance card."

Though her words sliced into Waite's heart, he believed they were insincere and she'd rather do anything than be with the soldier.

"Are you sure?" he asked, giving her one more opportunity to save herself.

"You heard my wife!"

Breelan smiled weakly at Waite. "Yes, thank you anyway," and she cast her gaze to the patterned carpet for fear she would cry if she caught Waite's eye again. She would not permit that. She chose the opposite tack and became suddenly animated. "It was fun, Captain. Your ship is a delight. However, it's time to say good night." She spun round and recovered her reticule from the table. Together, she and her temporary marriage partner retired.

Breelan was certain Trip would be angry Waite had persisted in asking her to dance and that she would catch it when they returned to their room. He surprised her with his reaction. He was quite affable and didn't say a word about it.

"Even though you slept most of the day, I'm sure you'd like some privacy tonight. I'll make up a bed on the window seat."

Breelan couldn't believe her luck and Trip's good will. "Thank you, Trip. You're so right. I am more tired than I expected."

While she changed behind the screen into her pale blue nightdress, Trip plumped his pillow and made a pallet beneath the porthole. Once she was in bed, he bent over, tucking the sheet tightly around her. Brushing her hair back, he kissed her forehead. "I do love you, Breelan."

She returned a modest smile. "Good night, Trip."

She drifted away while he lay awake, absorbed in the mystic language of her night sighs.

Chapter 16 – *The Goodbye Lie* by Jane Marie

True to their word, the two cousins met the next morning after breakfast. "Bree," Nora greeted, grasping both her friend's hands. "I could scarcely sleep from worrying what happened on your wedding night that was so awful it made you run away. I'm confused because last night at dinner, you seemed almost happy with Trip. Explain everything. First, tell me all about ... it. You know, the love making part. "

"Slow down. I'm so sorry I alarmed you." Breelan continued hesitantly, but purposefully, "You see, things are not working out exactly as I had envisioned."

For once Nora was still, aware of the strained facial features Breelan presented at this close range.

"You mustn't tell a soul. It's so personal and I'm so embarrassed."

"I promise, Bree. By our blood, I won't."

"Even your mother and father, since they're bound to learn of my unaccompanied early arrival to the ship?"

"What unaccompanied early arrival is that?" asked Nora innocently, as if she didn't know a thing about it.

"You're my dearest ally. I need desperately to confide in someone." Before she could begin her tale, Breelan heard Captain Taylor shouting orders.

Once he'd seen her, he walked a direct line her way, his face tight. Dismissing any formal greeting, he spoke softly, "Are you alright, Bree?" The intimate use of her nickname warmed her heart, but she remained prim.

"Yes, Captain. Don't I look fine?" She threw him a saucy smile.

"No," he said flatly, "You looked drained."

"Do I, really? It's due solely to an exciting honeymoon, believe me." She wasn't exactly lying. The time since her marriage had indeed been exciting. Unpleasant, but exciting. Just because she insinuated the complete opposite of the sad reality, she still had her privacy and pride to protect.

Waite took her false meaning as gospel and couldn't shed the picture of her in her husband's bed. He removed his cap and ran his fingers through his hair. "As long as you're happy and well. That's what I want for you."

"Thank you for your concern. I'm flattered. Yet, I do wonder, out of all the many passengers you ferry to and fro, that you'd take the time to think twice about me."

"Bree!" Nora couldn't understand why her cousin was being deliberately cruel.

"I wonder the same, Madame." And he was out of sight in four long strides.

"Why, for God's sake, would you hurt him like that?" Nora asked.

"Hurt him? What are you talking about? I've only ever told him the same thing over and over, that he needn't worry about me. I'm sure he has more interesting things to do and more interesting people to do them with."

"You are either simple-minded or blind or both. Are you made of marble?"

"Nora!"

"Don't you know by now that man adores you?"

Breelan laughed aloud. "You've been reading one of those yellow covers again. Seriously, you shouldn't let ..."

Nora looked her square in the eye. "Breelan, this is a man. A full-grown, masculine man we're speaking of. In fact, I dare say he's about the most masculine of men I've ever met. This is no game. You're not playing pitch and woo out behind the barn. Captain Waite Taylor is in love with you. Completely so. When you fluffed him off like some bothersome gnat, I like to have died for him. Can't you see he's in agony at the very idea of you with anyone other than himself? Now that you're married, and happily married as you so deliberately pointed out, it's hopeless for him. I've never before seen someone's heart break."

Breelan slowly lowered herself onto a lounge saying softly, "After the tornado, when he held me, I felt a connection. I don't know how to describe it. Then when we first boarded this ship in Fernandina, he was so cold in his manner toward me, I knew I had only imagined any interest on his part.

"Oh Nora, if what you say is true, I've made a much bigger mistake than I realized! I've needlessly complicated everything. Had I hung on and been patient, Waite and I might have naturally come together. What I felt for Trip was only a momentary fascination. And that feeling for him has already faded. What persists is an emotion new and glorious and romantically raw inside me that begins and ends with Waite. I was afraid to acknowledge it before. It was too powerful. I feared if I openly welcomed it and told him how I felt about him, he might not reciprocate. I wasn't willing to take that chance. My pride was more important to me."

Nora wanted to eradicate the anguish in Breelan's eyes, but was helpless to do anything.

"This has to be love, Nora. It has to be. I can't imagine any better sensation. I never want to be without it. I just have to control myself until we get home. I can't flaunt my feelings for Waite while I'm still with Trip. I can only suppose how special our mutual love will be, but we'll both find out as soon as we arrive home. Then, I'll be free."

"Free to what, Bree. What are you talking about? And if you're in love with Waite, why in God's name are you staying in Trip's cabin?"

"Hello," Trip said. "Did I hear my name?" When neither of the girls answered, "I wondered where my bride had run off to." He figured she had told Nora the truth concerning his lack of performance. He would just have to take his lumps and bear the slight to his manhood. He'd prove himself to one and all soon enough, once Breelan bore him an heir. "Come along, dear."

"Nora and I have hardly begun to talk, yet."

"You're a married woman, Breelan, and your first and only duty is to your husband." He added more sternly this time, "Come on. Now."

While the two girls hugged one another goodbye, Breelan whispered, "Pray for me," as she was led away by the man she'd wed.

As Nora watched them leave, she wanted to cry out, oh, Bree, I do pray for you. I don't know what you expect to happen when we reach Florida, but may God see it your way. And God, please help her find happiness somewhere in this awful tangle.

Breelan was determined to avoid Waite, hoping it might alleviate the ache in her heart that struck each time he came into view. Although they had yet to speak of love to one another, she felt she was betraying him when she spent time with Trip. She willed her mind to block all entrance of Waite's image as she tried to follow through with her plan, yet her spirit was not always as strong as she wished it to be.

At dinner the second night out, she found herself directing glance after glance Waite's way. He seemed completely ignorant of her attention. The early evening passed without event, without excitement, without passion. Breelan assumed the remainder of the voyage would be similar.

As she lay in bed later on that dark, dark night, she feared her scheme would be altered forever for she was not alone. Trip lay beside her. Her thin gown and the cloth of his nightshirt were the only barriers between them. Again, she had been naïve in thinking he would be patient in all things. She should have had a stern talk with him instead of allowing things to progress to this point.

When he took her hand and laid it on his hard belly, she sprang to a sitting position. "Trip, this is not what I want. I'd hoped you'd have realized when I agreed to think things over, I meant alone in bed. You have to wait for my final decision."

"This is all part of your final decision. How can you make that decision until you know the facts? You've never known the pleasure of a man and the physical is the most important part of a marriage. Once I show you how grand it will be with me, your decision will be made for you. I have no doubt."

"I'm sorry. I must ask you to leave this bed. Please."

"I'm sorry too, but you're my wife and I take what belongs to me." He pulled her back roughly, throwing his leg across her lower limbs and holding her fast. His mouth covered hers as she struggled and she gave a muffled scream. She was frightened and her panic seemed to double his strength. She kicked and scraped and managed to allow Trip to position himself directly atop her. Pinning her, he crudely forced her legs apart with his own. She felt an insistent pushing, a harsh stretching, and then a rapid pounding. It was over in a long moment. Trip collapsed and rolled off. Chuckling to himself, he soon began a slow snore.

Silent tears washed her reddened face. Waite was lost to her forever now. Had the marriage been annulled, she would have been pure for him. That was no longer the way of things. There would be no annulment because there was no virgin. This was all lovemaking would ever be in her life, a duty, a chore, a way to create children. At least, the good of a child would come from this unhappy union. That must count for something. It wouldn't be Waite's child. Still, she would care for it, nurture it. She would transfer all the love she'd reserved for Waite to a little one someday.

She had stupidly allowed her last chance at regaining control of her life to be taken from her, all in the name of some foolish fairness. What was the matter with her? She had learned what she wanted the hard way and what she wanted could never be hers. She'd married in the church and by church law, she was truly Trip's wife. She would have to cope, accept her lot or die a withering death of self-pity. And so the night was long for a young girl of new experience as she faced her eternally dismal future.

Trip was dressed and standing over Breelan, when he cast back the blankets exposing her nightie, now puddled around her waist.

Scrambling to cover herself, "I only just closed my eyes. Please Trip, let me sleep a while longer."

"You have forever to sleep. I won't abide a slug-a-bed in this family. We're young and in love, and I want everyone to know how happy you've made me. They'll all see by just looking at us. Up and at 'um, Mrs. Clelland. Lovemaking brings on my appetite."

Bare feet lethargically carried her to the dressing screen to freshen for the difficulties of the coming day. I've survived one night; I'll survive the next. I have to be strong for the child I may already be carrying, she told herself.

"You know, darling, last night was quite amazing, albeit brief." She heard him laughing under his breath.

She remained quiet, not having any comment, not even beginning to imagine what to say.

"You mustn't be so shy, Breelan. All this is perfectly normal. It won't take long before you'll relax and learn to find joy in ..." He stopped mid-sentence.

"Trip? What is it?" She tried to put the best light on her distasteful circumstances. "I need reassurance. Keep telling me everything will ..."

The privacy screen was violently thrown aside. Breelan was left to stand naked before the man she must call her husband. His face was blood red from anger. His brow was so furrowed, his eyes seemed one huge iris and pupil burning into her like a magnifying glass. Breelan grabbed for the small fingertip towel to modestly shield herself, thinking how ridiculous she must look.

"You slut!" he bellowed murderously. Foaming spittle flew from his lips, and he was on her instantly. "You let me think you were a virgin!" The back of his hand struck her delicate cheek.

She fell to the floor from the impact. Dazed, she tried to shake away the pain in her face. "Trip?" she questioned weakly.

"Shut up! I allow no one to make a cuckold of me! Who was he? Who was the first?"

"What are you talking about?"

"Don't try and deny it. The sheets tell it all. You idiot. Did you expect me not to notice? The crimson stain is conspicuous by its absence."

Breelan knelt, wild eyed, still not understanding.

"The innocent act is past. Was it the captain? Or maybe one of his crew, one of the filthy hands who works below decks and only ever comes up to relieve himself with the likes of you? I've heard stories of girls who trick their husbands on their wedding nights by spilling a small vile of blood onto the bed. How simple. I never would have known. My God. You're not only a trollop, you're a fool not to have covered your sinful tracks! I never would have mentioned the money you took from me our first night, either. After all, you're my wife. All I own is yours. But now I know the truth. You're deceitful and dishonest. You stole that money, the same as any common harlot! I might as well use you for what you were obviously born to do!" He grabbed her wrist and she fought him as he dragged her to the bed.

The medallion around her neck swung wildly, but Trip grabbed it on his first attempt. "What a hypocrite. I guess wearing this thing did make for a clever masquerade of innocence. You've no need for it now I know the facts." He ripped it from her, abrading her flesh as he broke the chain, and hurled it out the opened porthole.

Trip pushed her down and held her there with one strong arm while he stripped his clothes off with the other hand. In her struggle, in the light-of-day, she saw a purple gash that ran from mid-thigh and disappeared up into his groin. It was an ugly scar, yet not nearly so as the look on his face, the face that moments before had been so handsome. Trip raped her then. She screamed, trying to stop all sensation, all feeling, all hurt. Jerking her head from side to side to avoid his rough kisses, she wailed until her throat was raw and then wailed more. She was gasping from his weight and had little air left in her lungs. He pressed the pillow over her face to quiet her. She could only see flashes of light behind her closed eyes. She wanted all the light to go out. She hailed the advancing blackness. It would be so peaceful in its nothingness.

A powerful pounding at the door awakened Trip from his satanic state. He removed the pillow to see a pale Breelan, motionless.

"Breelan? Breelan!" Waite shouted. "Clelland, if you've harmed her, I'll skin you alive and make slippers from your goddamn hide, you sorry sonofabitch! Open this door!" the captain demanded, his fury controlled only by the warning look from an uneasy Catfish.

"A lovers' quarrel is all." As Trip spoke, his expression immediately returned to a calm, attractive mask. "I didn't realize when I married her that Mrs. Clelland had such a willful streak. Go away so my wife and I can make up."

Dismissing Trip, Waite ordered, "Breelan, answer me! I said open this door!"

Trip shook her and mumbled callously, "Tell him you're fine. Tell him, or the next time you'll get more than a little slap from me. Tell him!"

Coming around, Breelan knew Waite would break the door down if she couldn't convince him of Trip's lie. She didn't want to involve him any deeper in her misery. "Yes, yes," she said breathlessly. "I'm fine, Captain. My husband is right. Leave us. Please."

Unconvinced, he called again, "Bree?"

He has to believe me for both our sakes. Trip is capable of much cruelty, and I fear for Waite even more than for myself. "We'll be with you in a moment. We're both very hungry. They are still serving breakfast, aren't they? It isn't too late, is it?" The more she spoke, the more composed she commanded her voice to become. "See you in the dining salon soon."

"If you're not on deck in fifteen minutes, I'm coming back! Quarrel or no quarrel! Understood?"

"Yes, sir!" she said, forcing a jovial lilt to her tone.

Trip smiled at her. "Very good. Very good," he whispered through gritted teeth. "I'll remember how readily you lie. I'll remember, too, just how trustworthy you are. And you remember, Breelan, I'll be watching you!" His malice filled the beautiful room and turned it ugly.

"Dress at once. We wouldn't want your friend, the captain, bothering us again when we're so in love."

A heavy dusting of powder and a wide-brimmed hat tied with blue tulle hid the light lavender bruise rising on Breelan's right cheek. The white silk gardenias on her chapeau cascaded around the edge of the rim, so she cocked her headpiece to conceal and distract.

There was Nora breakfasting alone. There was Nora! Seeing her cousin, Breelan's mind raced back to their childhood swimming hole on Clark Creek. My innocence must have been lost when the vine I was swinging on broke and I hit the water unexpectedly! The pain was sharp, but fleeting. Any blood would've been washed away in the current. I'll tell Trip what I remember. But what's the use? He won't believe me. He's determined not to. Breelan was caught up in her past as she walked by her cousin.

"Bree!" Nora called.

Suddenly aware, she pulled at Trip's sleeve. "I have to say hello. Please."

"Very well, but only the amenities. Nothing more."

"Good morning, Bree. Why the big hat? Are you afraid Mr. Sunshine's rays will find you inside here and darken all that ivory skin?" Nora was well aware of Trip hanging on every word she uttered.

Breelan realized Nora hadn't been informed of the commotion only a few minutes earlier. "No, Cuz. Don't be silly."

Cuz? Cuz? The jig was up! Now it was Nora's mind that raced back to childhood. As children, Breelan and Nora had a code as part of their secret club. If ever they called one another "Cuz," it meant there was trouble or danger of some sort. What Nora had suspected was true. Breelan had confirmed it with a single word. There was something terribly, terribly wrong with the marriage. Something more than unfulfilled expectations.

"It's just that I tried a new coiffeur this morning," and glancing at Trip she added, "for my husband and it turned out a disaster. There was but one alternative and that was to cover my hair. Of course, I guess, I could have cut it."

120

"Not while I'm alive!" Trip interjected, playing along. "I don't know why you girls are constantly fiddling with your hair. For God's sake, just brush it and be done."

"I'm sure you wouldn't say the same if you understood that hair has to be constantly attended. Besides, we like to achieve different effects for excitement, don't we, Bree?"

Breelan would have loved to continue the aimless banter, but she could see Trip was bored. To avoid another incident, she excused them both and moved to another table, leaving Nora alone, concerned, and guessing.

Waite witnessed what appeared to be a light conversation between the three. He was relieved, yet only partially so, to see Breelan was all right. Earlier, he'd been mere seconds from bursting into her room. The only thing stopping him, besides Catfish's forbidding look, was the simple truth that she was not his. A few more days of this misery, he told himself. Once off-loaded in Fernandina - and that was how he had to categorize her, like some bothersome cargo he was contracted to deliver - then he could relax. Once she was back in her hometown, he could begin learning to live with his future, the empty future he'd masterminded because he'd listened to his conscience and logic instead of his heart. Waiting until the woman he loved was older? Hell, she was old enough. She was on her honeymoon, wasn't she? He'd missed his opportunity by thirty damn days while she was in New York City, thirty days in which she had the occasion to fall in love with someone else and even marry him! He would probably never know what happened to make Breelan run from her husband and into his arms for those few glorious hours. Miss Nora couldn't find out. Maybe it was meant to be that way. The reason would undoubtedly make him crazy with worry anyway.

He wanted to reflect on something else. Anything else. But pictures of Breelan overpowered his wishes. *Who the hell am I? Some irresistible rake she couldn't live without? Obviously not. What a fool I've been to think she would return my affection. Because I love her is no reason she should love me. She's too attractive, too beautiful, not to have her pick of men. I'm but one of the drooling dogs.*

"Only a few more days," he said aloud and the overhearing crew silently commiserated with their mournful captain, knowing his affliction would last a lifetime.

Chapter 17 – *The Goodbye Lie* by Jane Marie

Everyone was at the Dunnigan house in Fernandina this evening and everyone's humor was subdued, even the children's. Jack Patrick shushed his baby sister. He wasn't certain why they should be so quiet, but the looks the adults cast his way assured him that it would be wise behavior. His mother always told him not to make noise whenever somebody died. Now, he wondered who was dead.

Miss Ella was positioned silently on the upholstered sofa. Michael sat beside her, straight-legged, rapidly waggling his feet about, as was his fashion when he was tense and attempting to relax. While Uncle Clabe stuffed his pipe, Aunt Noreen squirmed in one of the cordovan leather wing chairs placed on either side of the fireplace. Four pairs of adult eyes grew dry as they stared at the hot flames, thinking their own troubled thoughts. The little ones looked at their picture books, turning the crisp pages, making a game of who would be the first to cause a paper rustle. Grammy and Peeper busied themselves in the kitchen, making sticky-buns for tomorrow's breakfast.

Carolena sat in the rocking chair, sketching several versions of her dream house. All she needed was the proper husband to build it for her. As of yet, she'd found any attempt at romance to be disappointing. She'd received two proposals thus far, but neither man could hold her attention for a lifetime she was certain. So she was biding her time, attending the occasional social to keep her mother and grandmothers appeased. She would not rush into marriage like her sister had. As Carolena looked at the sad expressions around the parlor, she silently declared she'd never be the cause of misery for her dear family.

Jack Patrick broke the silence. "I hear someone coming," he announced and ran to the window to push back the draperies and look out. He waited until the buggy got close enough to make out its occupants. "I see Breelan, some man, and Nora, ya, Nora's in the back seat. Yippee! Breelan's home!" he shouted with joy, forgetting about the dead person somewhere.

The fire should have been inviting. The smells should have been tempting. The house should have been welcoming, yet it didn't feel that way when Breelan stepped over the threshold. For the first time in her life, the home in which she'd been born was emotionally cold to her. The hand carved *WELCOME ALL* beneath the pineapple pediment above the parlor's double pocket doors held no meaning. Tonight, the entrance hall had all the warmth of a public building.

Breelan had asked Trip to wire ahead and say they would drive to the house, that there was no need for anyone to meet them at the pier. In truth, she was more than anxious to get to Dunnigan Manor, despite the shame in which she'd enveloped it and its residents by eloping. When they'd docked, the town gossips were in their glory, demurely hiding their vicious tongues behind sweetly scented hankies. How could she have put her precious mother through all this?

Michael was the first adult to rise as Breelan entered. The others in the room followed suit. Breelan stood like a stack of stones with Nora and Trip behind her. She was completely bewildered, not knowing how to react to her own father and mother. Michael opened his arms. She hesitated, then ran the few steps to him with all the relief of the forgiven little girl that she was. She trembled with joy and sorrow in her father's tender arms. Her mother embraced them both, and the women in the room all sobbed.

Nora hurried to her parents and they welcomed her, her mother thanking God Nora was not the one who had done such a disgraceful thing. Grammy and Peeper wept with gratitude that their girls were home at last. The youngsters, now in on the act, hugged the closest knees they could find.

Even Carolena, the smugly wiser sister, gave Breelan an especially tight squeeze. With tears dripping from her pretty chin she said, "I'm so glad you're back with us. I never thought I'd miss you this much."

Breelan chided herself for questioning her faith in her family. Waite said you could count on the ones who love you. I readily agreed until they were put to the test. I never should have doubted their loyalty to me.

"Is that your husband, Bree?" Jack Patrick questioned innocently. Silence fell as reluctant eyes turned to acknowledge Trip.

Breelan found her voice and her courage and said, "Yes, darling. This is Lieutenant Trip Clelland. Trip, this is my family," and she introduced everyone.

Civility seemed to sit atop a mountain of doubt hidden by clouds of resentment. But good stock will rise to any occasion, and this clan scaled the elevation handily. It took mettle from on high for Michael to shake the soldier's hand when it was offered. He did it for his daughter. Miss Ella presented her best artificial smile and showed Trip to a chair.

Breelan was proud of them all. It reminded her of her own forgotten inner strength. She would need so much. Slow-going conversation commenced, and Breelan was sure the unpleasant subject of her marriage would be avoided for as long as possible.

"We must hear everything, dears," Aunt Noreen babbled. "How are the Dreshers? Is their health good? The almanac says they're in for a hard winter up there."

"They're fine, Mother," answered Nora. "They, of course, send their love. Aunt Coe says she will write you a long letter, Aunt Ella."

Everyone fell quiet, again. They all knew what the letter would be about. It would be filled with apologies and regrets for their dereliction of duty to Breelan.

Michael spoke. "And where is it you're stationed, Lieutenant?"

"Here in town, sir. At Fort Clinch."

"There haven't been any real soldiers in the fort since the war," Jack Patrick challenged.

"That's correct, son," answered Trip, keeping his temper despite the interruption. "I, along with my good friend, Lieutenant Akins, am on a special projects assignment. We're with a company of men temporarily assigned to Fort Clinch to see about the feasibility of re-garrisoning her. We'll be getting her ready for inspection from high ranking officials from Washington."

"Yes, I read something in *The Mirror* about that," said Uncle Clabe.

Cheers and thanks overflowed the parlor once one of their own confirmed it was so. "You mean our little girl will stay in her own home town?" Miss Ella was beside herself with delight.

"For a while anyway, ma'am. I'm sorry you didn't know earlier. It might have alleviated some of your worry. And if I may continue?"

Another hush descended as rapid gasps of trepidation reduced the oxygen in the room. Then Michael nodded.

"Please let me apologize for our rash marriage." Expressions turned the color of clay. Still, Trip kept on. "I realize you all wanted Breelan to have a large wedding, befitting the princess she is." He looked to his wife, cuddling her sleeping baby sister and smiled. "You see, we fell in love so quickly and that love couldn't wait. Please, please try to understand that in no way is dishonor to be associated with this marriage. We were married in the church. We love one another very much. I hope you will understand and forgive impetuous devotion."

What answer could they offer? What answer did this Trip fellow expect?

"Breelan and I will find a house in town so she'll be nearby and visit often."

"That's probably for the best. Newlyweds need their privacy, after all," recommended Aunt Noreen.

Trip went on, "While I'm on duty, if she likes, she certainly can feel free to fill her time with her newspaper job. That is, until our babies start arriving."

Breelan heard nervous laughter and was unaware she was its source. She was amazed! This was the charming and generous Trip she'd first met on the ship, the same man who courted her into marriage. His manner was that of an adoring husband. She and Nora exchanged wary expressions.

Her family appeared to gradually warm to him. She speculated it was because they wanted to believe him; to believe he would be a good husband to her. Even Grammy and Peeper were hard-pressed to doubt such sincere sounding eloquence.

"Have ya et yet?" asked Peeper, firmly convinced an overly full stomach was the basis for happiness. It was her singular duty in life to see to it that anyone she took a shine to had a potbelly on them.

"In fact, ma'am," answered Trip with an engaging grin, "we have not. I, for one, smell something awfully good coming from that kitchen. Mightn't there be a dish or two out there with my name and rank on it?"

The deed was done. Peeper was beguiled. Breelan was sure of it. One by one, Trip worked his magic on them all. There was no need for her family to suffer any more than they had and any more than they would from the gossip. Breelan's only counsel was Nora. Thank God for Nora. They'd had no time to talk in detail, but Nora's heart was with her cousin, and Breelan was very glad to have it. She touched her still tender cheek where the bruise had faded and gave a tiny sigh.

During the meal of roast chicken and biscuits, Uncle Clabe mentioned Waite Taylor's name. It was such an innocent comment. No one except the three former passengers of the *Gentle Comfort* felt the tension, but the undertow from it was potent.

"Captain Taylor sends his best to you all and said he'd gladly welcome us on board his ship anytime." Nora was all jitters, rambling because she feared Trip or Bree would crack from the strain of the evening.

"He's such a nice man. I'm sure he gets lonely going from port to port with no real place to call home. We need to have him to supper sometime."

Miss Ella's remarks angered Trip. He didn't appreciate his new in-laws being so solicitous to Taylor because a mutual hatred existed between the two men. Trip couldn't envision it ever ending so long as the captain coveted his wife. Not missing an opportunity to jab his rival, Trip said, "That's kind of you, Mrs. Dunnigan. His evenings are most probably full, him being a single man and all. You know what they say about sailors. I'm sure he can keep up with the best of them at the local drinking establishments and, uh, other places." He glanced to his wife at his side. He was reminding her that the captain could be free with any woman he chose, any woman but her.

Nora couldn't let them think her compatriot in concern for Bree was a wild man, carousing every night he was anchored in some city. "Just because he's single, Trip, doesn't mean he's that type of man. He told me someday he'd like to settle down and build ships. He's just looking for the right time and location. As a matter of fact, as we were leaving the *Gentle Comfort*, he made a point of telling me he'd be out to visit us all as soon as he had the chance," she lied sweetly. Have some of that, you big phony! And she practically stuck out her tongue at Trip right then and there.

"Is that right?" he replied, his poker face holding strong. "Well, as I look at my bride, I can see she's worn out from all the excitement. We'll have to say our goodnights." He rose from the table, taking Breelan by the elbow, compelling her to give a still sleeping Marie to Carolena.

"We assumed you'd stay with us until you located a place to live," said a disappointed Michael.

"Thank you, sir. We appreciate it. However, we booked a room at the Florida House on our way here. We wouldn't want to crowd you."

Carolena surprised herself by saying and meaning, "We have plenty of room."

"Thank you, honey. Really, Trip made arrangements. I'll see everyone soon." Her baby sister was awake now and fussing so Breelan soothed, "Don't cry, Marie. I'll come back and we'll play dolls. Listen, sweetheart, since you take such good care of your dolly, Floozy Flirt, would you want to take care of Martha Bear, too? If you think you can handle both of them, I'll give Martha to you when you're just a little older. How would that be?"

"Oh, Bree, you'll give me your favorite big white bear?"

"You're darned tootin', I will. I can't think of anyone better."

The child gave Breelan the biggest and tightest hug her little arms could muster.

"Will you play with me too, Bree? But it's okay if it isn't dolls," relayed Jack Patrick, making sure he got equal time with his bigger sister.

"Of course, I will. Now, come on over and kiss me goodbye." This time she didn't have to beg. He was there in a flash.

As she and Trip stood on the family's well-used front veranda, Breelan said, "I love you all so much. See you soon!" She fled down the stairs before the words caught in her throat and her tears were visible.

Those left waving goodbye on the porch listened as dusk and distance smothered the vision of the buggy.

Thoughts varied. Michael wanted to trust the man who'd taken his daughter from beneath his roof. He had to for his own peace of mind. Miss Ella deemed herself a romantic. She'd been so wrong when she'd envisioned Captain Taylor as the man her Breelan had abruptly married. This fellow in a blue uniform was strong-minded to be sure. That was all she knew of him. Nora only hoped her sharp tongue wouldn't cause Trip to be unkind to Breelan. She'd made up the part about Captain Taylor saying he'd come to visit the family. He'd said the complete opposite, that he was well relieved of his duties with Breelan delivered to her final destination. The look on Bree's face when she thought she'd see him again, well, it was a good thing Trip hadn't noticed.

The heavens would be flooded that night and many nights to come with earthly voices beseeching blessings upon Breelan Jane Dunnigan Clelland.

It was late November and there were others walking along the Fernandina marina. Most seemed aware of time passing. Waite was not. The old planks of the dock beneath his black boots groaned under his weight, creaking a regular rhythm with each step. A shrimp trawler sailed home, its nets empty, its catch of the day sold. The many ships in the harbor between Amelia and Tiger Islands sat perfectly still on the unrippled water because there was no breeze to make waves. Only the gulls disturbed the flat dark surface, diving for their own catches. Pelicans flew in undulating formation snagging air currents with their wings. The atmosphere was wet and heavy as the low sun peeked a soft orange through the gray and white streaked sky. Despite the moderately crisp temperature, Waite's shirtsleeves were rolled to the elbow. He was oblivious to attack by the pesky no-see-'um bugs, out in full force. Nor did he hear the abrupt yowl of cats fighting somewhere in the distance. Mindlessly, he looked west to see the faint shape of wild boars roaming free on the isle across the way. He recalled only a brief time earlier when he'd felt free like that. Before all this. Before he'd ridden the beach just two-and-a-half miles due east from where he stood. Before he'd found the girl.

His mood was as the night soon to surround him. Dark. He had no family. Wanted no friends. He never felt more alone.

Chapter 18 – *The Goodbye Lie* by Jane Marie

The drive from Dunnigan Manor to the Florida House seemed especially slow despite the brisk tempo of the horse's trot. Not a word passed between the young couple. Breelan was silent in case her tears would anger Trip further, and he for fear she'd continue crying.

He didn't want to walk into the hotel and register a puffy-eyed bride - at least, not on their first night together in her hometown. Despite the darkness, he was well aware of her secret attempts to wipe away the evidence of her unhappiness. He could feel her hushed sobs vibrate the carriage. What the hell was she blubbering for? He was the one who'd been tricked in this marriage. She'd come away with a husband of fine reputation. He'd wound up with damaged goods. He'd have to make do. She would produce fine, strong children. And that, after all, was what he'd been looking for. Trip steered the buggy along side the hotel's granite stepping-stone. Helping Breelan out, he warned, "Enough of this. I won't have it. Do you hear?"

She nodded. He was right. She straightened her skirts and inhaled a deep breath of cool river air, while Trip threw coins to the attendant, directing him to return the horse and carriage to the stable for the night. They climbed the few steps of the long, white two-story establishment and entered as if they were happy newlyweds.

Breelan loved to come to the Florida House. She'd never actually stayed in any of the rooms, but her family oft-times ate in the dining room after Sunday morning church services at St. Michael's. Meals were served family style, with large bowls and platters of food passed round the big tables. This was one of the most cozy and home-like tourist hotels in all of Florida. Since the Florida Railroad built the inn before the war, the railroad folk as well as sailors, vacationers and locals all frequented it. How often had she climbed the old live oak in the back while the grownups pontificated over coffee and dessert? Now she was one of those grownups.

Breelan could smell her favorite fruitcake, but she found she had no appetite for food and even less for sweets. Could she be pregnant this soon? Could these things happen that fast? She guessed they could and with her luck, probably had.

After registering and exchanging niceties and congratulations with the desk clerk, Mr. Lindsey, they were shown to a second story room that was referred to as the bridal suite. It was quite lovely. The wallpaper spoke of romance with tiny bouquets of pastel flowers and a matching coverlet on the canopied double bed. The window trappings of lace would merely filter the moonlight. It could be an enchanted place if the circumstances were right.

"I will leave you to your unpacking, Breelan. I'll be downstairs in the tavern." Trip caught the look of concern she cast his way. "Don't worry. I'll take heed of my drink. I won't let you go unattended in such a pretty room as this and certainly not while still on your honeymoon," he said caustically.

He quietly closed the door behind him and she breathed a sigh of self-comfort. He was gone. She was free if but for a moment. He had mistaken her look for concern. It was not. In truth, she hoped he would imbibe to excess tonight and every night, so he would never be able to touch her again.

The hour grew late and Trip didn't return to the room. Worn out, Breelan was still wide-awake. Her mind darted madly from her family, to where she and Trip would live, to her job, to the gossip, to her marriage. The cacophony in her head was generously peppered with the words and features of Waite. There was his handsome face, his hair, his eyes, his lips. In part or as a whole, the likeness was exact. It teased and tempted her until wriggling among the tangled covers of the bed a minute longer would surely bring her more tears, those of hopeless frustration. She had to get out of the room, to feel the stirring of the breeze against her hot, flushed cheeks.

Concealing her nightdress beneath her cloak, she descended the rear stairs, intending to refresh herself in the rain barrel out back. She splashed the cool water on her cheeks. It trickled down to her elbows, tickling her to irrational giggles. She languished in the luxury of laughter. She hadn't laughed since, since when? She couldn't remember. Resting the heels of her hands on the edge of the barrel, she hung her head. "I wish this were the ocean. I'd put my toes in the water and let the cool waves creep up my ankles. I'd ..."

"You'd what, Breelan?"

She heard the resonant voice seek answers softly in her ear. She responded longingly, "Oh, Waite. You'll never know how I wish you were real and with me and able to tell me all the things I want to hear. It will never happen for us. Never. I deserve to suffer for my gawd-awful mistake. But to make you suffer, too. If what Nora says is true and you really love me, I can never forgive myself for causing you pain. I pray you find someone to fill your mind and bed. Don't waste your life pining for me, my love. If only that kiss I dreamed of on your ship had been real. If I could feel your lips touch mine, I could tolerate whatever comes. I ..."

She dreamed he was behind her. He was grasping her shoulder, turning her quickly, pulling her against his unyielding body. She dreamed his arms were around her, holding her fast to him. Then his mouth was on hers, hard. His breath rasped from his lungs. She breathed him into her and tasted his soul. His essence was all male. Every thought she'd ever had of how superb his kiss would be was surpassed in this illusion. Thank God for her dreams. They belonged solely to her. Neither the nightmare of her marriage nor the fear of hell would take them from her.

"Bree, Bree," he said against her lips.

And she felt strong hands on her wrists. They pried her arms from around his neck, similarly opening her eyes to reality. It was no dream. Waite's glorious face was before her in the night and his eyes danced. Here in the dim moonlight, she could only stare at him. She placed her hands on his mildly whiskered cheeks, ran her slender finger the length of his scar and kissed it. He kissed her in return, opening his mouth to take her lips between his. He held her again and this time she rubbed against him, making him moan from somewhere deep within.

Glass shattered as a disagreement broke out in the bar. She didn't care. She didn't care about anything, but kissing him. Still, the insistent tinkling of the crystal continued to interrupt her pleasure. It was taking him from her. "Don't let me go. Please, don't ever let me go," she whimpered as he pushed her away and held her off.

"Breelan. Breelan." He had again taken advantage of her. He knew it and for that too short moment, he didn't care. He was thinking only of himself. He would pay later. He tasted her on his lips, and she was finer than he'd remembered in all the nights he'd lain awake and all the times he'd walked the deck of the *Comfort*. He wanted her so badly. He wasn't sure his willpower would win a contest with his loosened desire. For her alone, he had to do what was right. He would not allow her to be branded an adulteress.

He shook her from her splendid stupor. "Bree, you've got to hear me. With all the craving a man can endure, I want you. Do you hear? Do you understand me? I want you. Finding that you feel the same brings me such joy, I can hardly ..." Waite was unable to finish his sentence. "Knowing the truth at last was worth all the hours of agony, all the uncertainty of guessing if you cared for me. I love you and realize you love me. You do love me, don't you? It isn't merely a physical attraction between us, is it? Tell me it's more."

"Waite Taylor, you've got to feel my love. It's so alive in me, I think I can reach in, grab hold of it, and show you. Believe me, believe I love you.

And only you." She answered breathlessly, leaning into him, trying to make him hold her again.

"Then, when I die, I'll be smiling."

"Shh. Don't say such an awful thing." She pushed on his arms holding her at an unbearable distance, and he let her hug him with as much strength as her delirious condition allowed. "Waite, to finally call you by your given name to your face. Secretly, you know, I've been calling you that for some time." She laid her head on his hard chest, listened to his heart beating and took in his rich masculine scent. "This is no dream. The pounding of your very being blocks out everything but my love for you."

"Breelan, please listen. We can't do this. Your husband is inside."

If he'd whipped her with a lash, he couldn't have revived her any less cruelly. Her own heart metered the triple time rhythm of the words repeating in her brain like a haunting waltz. Your husband. Your husband. One, two, three. One, two, three. Your husband. It wouldn't stop. She covered her ears with her hands trying to halt the taunting measures and only succeeded in trapping them.

Waite could do no more than bear witness to her pain. It was misery and sorrow and heartache, everything that is torture to love. It was deep. It was searing a vicious course through her innocent being, and he couldn't stop its assault on her. He was helpless to free her from the torment of it. She began to tremble, hard, racking shivers. He lowered her to the ground and held her, rocking her in his arms, trying to console the inconsolable. "Breelan. Please, sweetheart, this must be brief. You'll be missed. Willing or not, you have to return to your room. If Clelland finds you here with me ... I've known men like him before. They completely possess for no other reason than to own. He may say he loves you and he may in his way, but if he finds us together, I can't let myself think of what he'd do to you to make you pay for your indiscretion with me."

"I don't care if he does find us. I want him to know I'm in love with you. And I would have come to you tonight, as soon as we docked, but he ruined my plan. He ruined everything."

"What plan?" He had to know. "Tell me."

Still shaking, she looked into his dark eyes. Her voice quavered as she blurted out the nasty story. "I stayed with him on the ship only to keep peace until we arrived here. I wanted to be fair, to give him a second chance. You see, he got drunk on our wedding night and passed out. That was why I ran from him. I realized I didn't love him. I decided to get an annulment since we had not been ..." she paused, searching for the right word. She lowered her tearful eyes in embarrassment.

Waite doubted his hearing. Was she telling him Clelland had never touched her? Could it be true? Could she still be his? She could get an annulment, and they could be together. He was delirious from the idea of it!

"Bree. Oh, Bree! Do you know what this means for us?" He kissed her eyes, her throat. Kissed away her tears. "Don't cry, angel. You don't have to go back to him. You're safe with me."

She didn't want to stop him, but she had to. "Waite, Waite. Now it's you who must listen to me."

He held her again, trying to govern his near uncontrollable jubilation.

"I was a fool. I was sure I could convince Trip to court me as if we'd just met, with no advances except the most pure on his part. I didn't want to add to his eventual humiliation from an annulment by making him take a separate cabin. I knew how the other passengers would talk. So, since he hadn't touched me the first night we shared a compartment on the trip home, I thought I could appeal to his sense of honor and convince him not to touch me until I'd told him of my final decision. But ..."

Waite didn't need to hear the rest. It wasn't hard to guess.

Breelan had gone this far; she had to finish the tale. She had to spear the man she loved with the ghastly truth. "Waite, I can never be yours. I'm now the wife of Trip Clelland." She had to do it. "Because he spoiled me."

All the air left Waite's lungs as he dropped his head to his chest. The chill of the night entered his body. It was worse than he envisioned. If she were with Clelland because she loved him, at least, she would be happy in her marriage. But this awful way, living with a man who had the right to violate her night after night. Dear God, how could she stand it? How could he bear it?

"We'll get you a divorce! Yes, a divorce," he brightened.

"There's more."

Amazed that there could be more, Waite listened.

"He was very angry with me the next morning. Very angry." She purposely refrained from mentioning Trip's violent hand to her. What purpose would it serve? "I didn't understand why. I've been thinking long and hard. I must have done something," she hesitated, "something to injure myself because ..." She'd never talked to a woman about anything so personal, let alone a man. But this man, she could tell anything and he would stand by her. She was convinced of it.

He covered her lips with his finger, wanting to stop her. He guessed what she was trying to say. "It's all right, darling. Shh." He tried to comfort her anguish.

Breelan kissed his palm and let the rest pour out. "He accused me of having been with, with other men. Waite," she pleaded, "you've got to believe that I never have. I swear before God, I never have."

"I know, sweetheart. I know." Waite had no doubt.

She said sadly, "You're right about this man I must call my husband. If I admit to him that I love you," she looked into his aching eyes, "he'd want to hurt me as I've hurt him. He'd say and do anything to get even with me. He could have the marriage annulled, telling everyone who'd listen that I married him under false pretenses, that I wasn't pure when we wed."

Waite cringed.

"How could I prove otherwise? Annulment is what I want. You know that. But he'll make vulgar accusations about me. Already, there's talk around town. I love you to desperation. But can I be selfish enough to expose my family to more suffering?"

The elation from their newly declared love had long passed. Her shoulders caved forward from the heft of the grief she wore. She pulled away and he didn't try to stop her. She felt his emotional withdrawal.

"I have to get back." She rose with him then began to walk away. Stopping, she turned for one last word and one last look. "Waite. Our love is doomed. Don't add to my sorrow with the knowledge you're waiting for a dream. Please, let it go. God be with you, my darling." She climbed the back steps as quietly as their creaking would allow and entered a long life of learning to make due.

Waite was exhausted, but no sleep would come to him tonight. He entered the tavern on the south end of the hotel and prayed Clelland wasn't there because he'd kill the man.

As of late, it seemed the cosmos wasn't in the mood to heed the pleadings of a ship's captain. Seated at a round pine table in the corner of the small bar, Waite saw Clelland playing poker with some of his own crew. And there in the center of things was Catfish! Where was the loyalty in all this? Fish said he understood how Waite felt. To the captain's mind, he had a damn strange way of showing it.

"What'll it be, mister?" asked a bartender Waite didn't recognize.

"Scotch. Straight. And leave the bottle."

Catfish only wished Clelland had made an early night of it. Joining the card game had been his way of keeping an eye on the blonde man in case he got stupid. If and when Waite finally did show and if everybody were lucky, a confrontation might be averted. Usually, there was little commotion at the Florida House, but tonight one brawl had already broken out and he feared a second wasn't far behind. There was little hope of steering Waite to another bar if he wanted to stay.

The service was too slow for the impatient captain and he cursed the man serving the whiskey. "Get the goddamn lead out. I came here for a drink, not to watch you clean the counter."

"Yes, sir. Here you go."

Mr. Lindsey overheard and was surprised at Captain Taylor's attitude. In all the time the sailor had been coming here, the bald attendant with eyebrows like wire quills had never seen the captain in such a foul temper. He pushed his glasses back up his nose as far as his quills would permit and wondered the cause.

Trip Clelland overheard, too, and since he was losing his pocket change fast, his mood was mean. Waite Taylor was just the guy to vent his irritation on for more reasons than money. Speaking loud enough to be heard across the room, Trip said, "Well, lads, since you're doing so well and I'm doing so rotten, I'll retire to the privacy of the bridal suite where my pretty little wife hungrily awaits me," and he emitted a prideful laugh.

The barstool bounced twice as it hit the floor, propelled by the power of Waite's kick. Menacingly, he walked the few short steps to face the man who had taken Breelan from him. Everyone readied for a vicious fight. Drawing the damp, smoke-filled air deep into his chest once, Waite said in a slow, deadly voice, "I know full well you're married to her. Believe this. If I hear you've harmed her any more than the day-to-day agony of living with you, by God, I'll happily change her status from wife to widow."

The seconds slipped away as Trip read the dark eyes of the man who had just threatened him. The threat was sincere.

Waite turned and walked back to the bar. He righted the stool and standing beside it, poured himself another drink.

Trip considered throwing a punch, but remembered the men of the *Gentle Comfort* and held his fists at his side. "Next time you confront me, Taylor, I suggest you be alone and not count on backup from your crew."

Catfish tensed at the hot words tossed on the already ignited sea captain, then relaxed. Waite didn't need to prove his courage to any man.

"Good evening all." Taking into account that he was so outnumbered, Trip was surprised by his own swaggering exit. He determined himself a brave man and grinned.

Chapter 19 – *The Goodbye Lie* by Jane Marie

Looking through the classified advertisements in the newspaper, Trip found a small frame house to rent. It was in a good location, handy to downtown Fernandina on South 3rd Street. Breelan could walk to work, her father's office, Dotterer's Grocery, the Chandlery, St. Michael's, the dentist and doctor, and nearly any place that provided the mental, physical, and spiritual necessities. The double stable out back housed Breelan's horse, Noir, and Trip's mottled white mustang, Brace. The two horses were only moderately accepting of this arrangement and an occasional bite on the rump from one or the other was not uncommon.

Most mornings, after Trip had ridden to Fort Clinch to perform his duties as lieutenant, Breelan would exercise Noir at the beach. The horse had come to expect it, and she'd made it an integral part of her day in hopes of clearing her mind of negative thoughts. Noir was responsive to his mistress's moods. As if he could feel her troubles, he galloped hard and fast when she loosened the reins, trying to help her outrun her remorse.

Her outing completed this particular Thursday, Breelan entered her house to confront the hours ahead. The air was stale in the tiny dwelling. She lifted the kitchen window, allowing the lace curtains to cavort in the clean current of fresh oxygen. As she slid open the parlor door with the glass window, she noticed its construction. It seemed built for peeking on whatever activities occurred in the front room. There could be no real privacy here. But what need had she for privacy anyway? There were no romantic teases, no quick kisses, nothing in particular to hide from company, and there was little of that, as well.

Until tonight. Her family was coming for supper. Opening the bedroom windows wide, she recalled how she'd asked Trip to look for a two-bedroom rental. She'd hoped that with a second bedroom, she could occasionally have Nora or her brother and sisters over to spend the night. Trip had ignored her request, saying he wanted her all to himself. Still, she had to give him credit. He'd settled on this pretty little place that was clean with a good layout despite its furnishings that were a touch on the well-used side. When the family comes, she thought, I can be proud of our home. Her heart lamented. Our home. She pursed her lips and concentrated her energies on the evening.

Her husband had been the one to issue the initial invitation. In the four weeks they'd been married, their only visitor had been Nora. She'd conveyed valid reasons why the others were unable to drop by. Marie had come down with an indisposition. Peeper, her imagined symptoms mimicking those of the child, had likewise taken to her bed for a time. Miss Ella had emergency church meetings of some sort and her father had a deadline at his office. Still, Breelan thought the worst, that they simply didn't want the stress of breaking bread in Trip's house even though they'd superficially accepted her situation.

At the time of their marriage, Trip had no knowledge of her lack of culinary skills. They'd never discussed it. When she confessed she could only cook scrambled eggs, he'd said, "We'll need a chicken then," laughing it off. But after three days of the same meal, he ordered in a stern tone, "Open a cookbook and learn!"

Breelan had a few successes and far more failures, so the pressure was on. "What's all my worrying over anyway?" she asked her mother's family cookbook, the one Nora had been good enough to drop off. Determined to read each recipe word for word, "I only need to slow down and pay closer attention to the instructions. I've got all day to make this meal."

Hours were passing and Breelan's education was taking longer than she'd allowed. Why hadn't she heeded her mother's warning? "I can't tell you how important cooking and baking will be to you once you're married and a mother."

And why had she ever asked Grammy in the presence of Jack Patrick, "How do you make a baked potato from a real potato?" He'd told everyone and it was a running joke whenever the subject of cooking came up. Her pride had been crushed and that pride had lead to a complete disinterest in food preparation. Pride didn't matter much right now. Oh, thank goodness for the tried and true recipes. But would everything be cooked thoroughly? Would it stay hot? Would it all be ready to put on the table at the same time? There was only one way to find out. Perhaps the extra hints in the margins written in her mother's own hand would help. It might almost seem as if she were there and helping.

After much debate, Breelan settled on Peeper's deviled eggs, Grammy's cranberry orange relish, Aunt Noreen's chocolate cake, and most important of all, her mother's always delicious Brunswick Stew. She had nearly all of what she'd need on hand. Most of it. Grammy's voice sounded in her head. "A new cook should never substitute." Well, why couldn't she use a splash of honey in the deviled eggs instead sugar? All of that would be needed for the cake and more. There was no time to get to the store and back. Why not just make a little less frosting? She studied her mother's recipe in detail one last time before she began.

Miss Ella's Brunswick Stew

A twenty-five cent shank of beef or one chicken, one rabbit or two squirrels
Salt and pepper
3 cups raw potatoes - peeled and chopped into one inch pieces
2 cups cooked butter beans
2 cups raw corn
1 cup chopped onion
6 cups raw tomatoes - peeled and chopped, if canned, do not drain
2 slices middling or 2 slices bacon
1 five-cent loaf of bread or your own homemade bread passed with butter for dunking

For serving at noon, put the meat on the stove to cook at the earliest possible time in the morning, at least by eight o'clock, covering it with water (about 4 cups). Bring to a boil and then simmer with the lid on the pot. Season with salt and pepper. At eleven o'clock, remove the meat and any bones and gristle from the broth. Shred the meat. Return the stringy meat to the stew pot. Add all the vegetables and two slices of middling or bacon to enhance the flavor. Bring all this to a boil then simmer. When vegetables are tender, drop a goodly dollop of butter into your prettiest large dish. Pour the stew over it. This serves 8 to 12 folks depending upon their appetites.

I have to stop worrying, Breelan told herself. Should the worst happen and the food not turn out very well, at least, the ladies will be flattered that I've used their recipes. Her eyes fell upon her face reflected in the window over the sink. She hardly recognized herself. She looked so somber, so sad. Spitting on the back of her hand, she wiped away the trail of tears then dipped a cotton tea towel in cool water and scrubbed life back into her flesh. "I know one thing," she declared, "from this time forward, I will become the best actress this town has ever seen. Not my family nor strangers nor enemies will detect any hint of unhappiness in me. Enough, Mrs. ..." she paused, "Clelland. You've got a good meal to prepare. Tonight is your debut as hostess." Devotion to determination was Breelan's anchor. Looking deep into her soul through the eyes staring back from the glass, "I'll make this house a home. I've got to."

Breelan lay wide-awake beside her spouse, trying to tally the varied songs of the mockingbird. Usually it worked better for her than counting sheep. Usually. Tonight she remembered her first dinner party. She and Trip had greeted their guests at the front door of their home, together. Her father had presented the newlyweds with a bottle of his blackberry wine, "For after dinner toasts," he'd said.

Her mother had handed her two bouquets of yellow and white pansies. "One bouquet is for your table, dear, and these others have their roots wrapped in rags for your flowerbed. The winds off the water are turning chilly," she'd explained, "and you remember how pansies love the cooler weather."

Marie handed Breelan their mother's blue and white tulip half-apron. "Now you'll look just like Mama," the child told her big sister. Carolena gave Breelan a hand trowel and a pair of work gloves. Jack Patrick struggled in with a bucket full of rich compost for the pansies. Refusing his father's offer of assistance, he said, "I've got it, Daddy. I want Trip to know how strong I am."

The young bride ran her tongue over the small nip on her inner cheek where she'd bitten it to stop her tears as she'd recalled how her mother so often said that flowers growing outside a home represented the love growing inside. "Thank you, everyone. How many times have we planted pansy faces in the fall, Mama? Ever since I can remember. They're like a piece of home to me." Had her gratitude been too enthusiastic? Had it demonstrated that she preferred her old residence to her new?

Grammy's gift was a quart of her meat flavoring. "It's our family secret, Bree. Here's the recipe. Memorize it, then burn it. Promise?"

"Yes, ma'am. I promise."

Peeper was not to be out done, "I saved the best fer last. It's a bottle a my very own special furniture polish."

"The way Peep experiments out back in the little house," Michael explained to Trip, "it's no small miracle she hasn't blown us all up. Isn't that the stuff you make from turpentine, alcohol, and ether, Peep?"

"Yup, but you forget the balsam fir and linseed oil, Michael. That's how come I'm the chemist and you're the architect."

The laughter had been strained and everyone had been uncomfortable. The cozy glow from the candles helped hide the chipped dishes and patched linens that came furnished with the house, and no adult noticed or, at least, mentioned the shortcomings of her table. Leave it to her brother to have asked, "How come you use all these cracked plates, Bree, when you have a whole hope chest full of brand new dishes and stuff?" Everyone else had been too polite to inquire.

She'd quickly answered, "I'll bring my chest over as soon as my cooking warrants the beauty of the china." The ladies had made a sincere attempt to reassure her that the meal was delicious. She would have believed them, too, had she not tasted her own food. The salad was gritty with sand, the deviled eggs were runny from the honey and too salty, the butter beans in the stew were hard, and the chocolate frosting was so thin, the cake showed through. Breelan saw her mother throw several sharp looks at Jack Patrick each time he'd tried a new course and then opened his mouth to comment. She imagined the lecture the poor boy must have received about how to behave at his sister's house right before they'd left Dunnigan Manor.

The more the wine flowed over supper, the more impertinent Trip's remarks had become. "At this rate, lack of edible victuals will weaken me so much, I don't know I'll have the strength to ride a horse."

The veins in Michael's neck strained against his stiff collar and his skin tone reddened as he'd witnessed his daughter's humiliation. No after dinner toasts would be made this night. Her mother had looked hard at him, and Breelan knew then and there she would have much convincing to do if she were to make her family believe she was a happy bride. So she laughed at Trip's cruel comments, empathized with his suffering, and made light of her culinary disaster.

Once the meal was over, her company hadn't lingered. Carolena carried her sleeping baby sister to the buggy with Jack Patrick asking, "Where will your baby sleep when you have one, Bree? You only have one bedroom." She'd been so glad Trip hadn't overheard her brother's last question. He'd have gone into what was becoming his typical speech about all the children they were planning. As their guests piled into the over-sized rig, Trip put his arm around his wife's shoulders and waved them away, vowing, "The next time she cooks for you will be after she's had some in-depth instruction."

While Breelan had put up the last of the clean dishes and fondly folded her mother's apron that now belonged to her, she watched Trip empty the wine bottle, then stumble into the bedroom. Her final rumination as she fell asleep after a difficult day was that her husband had a very serious drinking problem.

Chapter 20 — *The Goodbye Lie* by Jane Marie

True to his promise that Breelan would learn to cook, Trip insisted she go daily to her mother's home to become schooled in the gastronomic arts. She hated the idea of him telling her what to do, but went gladly to be near her family.

This day, the Dunnigan women were making bread. "The flour should always be sunned and aired before using," instructed Miss Ella.

"When the bread rises in the oven," said Grammy, "the spirit of the housewife rises right along with it."

"Knead without intermission for one half hour, by the clock now," insisted Peeper, waggling her finger. "Oh, a'course you're a knowin' to wrap the bread with linen to keep it fresh, ain't ya?"

"That part I do remember, Peep." It was exhausting but Breelan enjoyed the process, pummeling away her frustrations on the dough.

Breelan's mother, observing her daughter's intense technique, understood the newly married wife would speak her mind only when and if she decided to. There was no sense in prying. Breelan was a grown woman now.

"Is that the sound of Jack Patrick's bottom being spanked or are the women of the manor making me some of their sweet belly-busting bread."

"Daddy," whimpered the young master, "you know I'm right behind you. Captain Taylor will think I'm still a little boy who gets in trouble. I'm too old for whippin's." His father cocked his head. "I am!"

Breelan stopped beating the flour and water mixture. She unconsciously squeezed the dough, causing it to ooze between her fingers. She stared at the thickened paste and nearly laughed at how alike her life was to the mess stuck on her hands.

"Good morning, ladies. We just docked the *Gentle Comfort* and I ran into Mr. Dunnigan on Centre Street at the tobacco shop. He invited me to dinner this noon. I told him it was too short notice." Waite stopped speaking. There she was. His beloved Breelan was even prettier in person than in his fantasies, if that were possible. The flour dust on her dress, the tendril of brown hair hanging from her temple, a tea towel flung casually over her shoulder - just to observe her nearly stopped his heart.

At Jack Patrick's mention of Waite, Breelan's own heart quivered. She closed her eyes to the welcome sound of his strong voice, casting supreme control over her exterior expression. She had two options. Run to him and hide herself in the safety of his embrace or hold her chin squarely and greet him as a dignified woman, married to another man. Sadly, her only real choice was the latter.

"Captain Taylor, we're so glad you realize the latch string is always out to you. It's been too, too long. I think you know everyone?"

"Thank you, Mrs. Dunnigan. Hello. It's good to see you all again. I've been meaning to visit the first chance I was in town." He'd completely changed his mind about staying away. If he couldn't be with Breelan, he could be with her family. "Actually, this is my first time to Fernandina since Miss Breelan's return from New York City."

"As I understand it," said Peeper, a bit confused, "don't it take your ship a week ta git from Fernandina to New York City and another week ta git back down here? By my calendar, it's a goin' on six weeks since ya been away."

"You're right, Miss Peeper. That is our regular schedule. You see, I decided I was due a holiday. It'd been years since I took some time for myself. My dear friend, Catfish O'Halleran, took over the helm for me while I stayed in New York City and enjoyed all that grand place has to offer."

"Could that mean a woman?"

"Michael, if the captain had any news of that kind, it would certainly be for him to tell us after his own fashion." Miss Ella was as curious as her husband, but that sort of question wasn't seemly.

Ignoring her daughter, Grammy continued, "Good for you, Captain. A man with no lady love in his life can't be a happy man."

Breelan gathered her courage and raised her gaze to Waite's. She'd felt him looking at her, and he was. Her grandmother had spoken the truth. Everyone needed someone in his life. Her eyes told him that for his own well being, it was right for him to see someone. For her, the vision of him holding another woman, kissing another woman, was torture. But then he had to think of her with Trip. Oh God. Oh God! Why had she ever involved herself with Trip? Would she ever stop asking the same questions? Would she ever get an answer other than all her troubles were self-inflicted?

"Miss Breelan? Bree?" Waite was calling her. "How have you been?" He didn't want to ask the obvious, "How is life as a married woman?" He didn't want to think about it. So he asked, "Are you still reporting for *The Mirror*?" A simple enough question.

Before Breelan could respond, Grammy answered him. "She's taken a short time off to master a skill essential in keeping a husband happy."

141

Damn it. Waite could think of only one requirement that would keep him content, and he was sick at the idea of her taking extra time to practice with someone other than himself. Besides, he was certain it would be perfection anyway.

Waite's jaw clenched, and Michael cleared his throat. Seeing the anguish and embarrassment on Breelan's lovely features, no one spoke but Jack Patrick. "Ah, tell him, Bree. She can't cook worth a flip, so she's gotta take lessons from Mama. I get to slop the hogs with all her mistakes," he added, laughing at his joke.

Peeper stepped in and picked up the frayed thread of normal conversation. "The robins is a singin' up the afternoon rain, agin."

"Peep?"

"Yes, Jack Patrick?"

"Now, I'm not being rude, but are you sure it's robins you hear. It's almost winter and I thought they only sing in the springtime."

Peeper chuckled. "You're right about that, boy. I guess maybe I'd best be a studyin' my birds a bit better. "

A lively ornithological discussion followed between all except Breelan and Waite. They didn't hear a word because they weren't listening. Their thoughts were their own.

"Lunch will be served shortly," said Miss Ella. "Captain? Captain?"

"Yes, ma'am. Thank you."

"Why don't you gentlemen, yes, and especially you Jack Patrick, go out and sit on the veranda," Miss Ella suggested. "There's a soft ocean breeze today. You'll have to come inside soon enough if the showers hit a little later. Now, go on and I'll bring out a tray of orange tea to you all."

"Wait!" Everyone froze in mid-stride at the command of the handsome guest. "I'm sorry to have startled anybody, but Miss Breelan, you've got an eyelash on your cheek. May I?" Without hesitation, Waite stepped forward and removed the single dark curl with a gentle touch. But to Breelan, it was a scorching stroke. "Finger or thumb?"

"Excuse me?" She couldn't follow his meaning.

"Finger or thumb, Bree?" Waite asked again.

Jack Patrick could tell an explanation was required. "Come on, Bree. You know how to play. You guess if your eyelash is stuck on Captain Taylor's finger or his thumb."

Hearing the impatient tone in her little brother's voice, Breelan became aware of the others in the room. She'd temporarily imagined she'd been alone with Waite. Patting her cheek nervously, she smiled for show and said, "Finger."

With all eyes on the outcome, Waite slowly opened his grasp on the lash and found it to, indeed, be on his first finger.

"Blow it off and you'll get your wish, Bree. Hurry up so us men can go out on the porch and talk like Mama said." Her brother was bored.

Closing her eyes, Breelan made her wish. Then, fixing her gaze on the strong finger of the man who'd been the object of that wish, she blew the lash away.

This time it was Waite whose flesh was seared by the ripple of her sweet breath. Reluctantly tearing himself from Breelan, he led the man he once hoped might become his father-in-law from the kitchen. They entered the front parlor where he'd first held her in the darkness. Outside, he tried to calm his tangled insides as he and Michael began a backgammon match with Jack Patrick offering his opinion. "Captain, you might know how to steer ships, but you stink at this game."

Breelan excused herself from the womenfolk once the loaves were rising, saying she wanted to get home and make some bread for her husband before she forgot how. She mounted Noir and rode away, not saying or waving goodbye to her father or brother or the other man on the veranda. Her male relatives wondered at her haste. The other man did not.

Miss Ella easily saw through Breelan's story and painfully accepted that she had been right about her daughter and Captain Taylor. Eyes don't lie. They were in love with one another, and it was a fate to be pitied. Her poor, poor little girl would never love Trip the way she loved Waite. Her daughter would have many difficult moments and nights before her. And the mother hung her head at the very idea of it all.

Chapter 21 – *The Goodbye Lie* by Jane Marie

"Breelan. Breelan, wake up! Good God, your family must have some kind of sleeping sickness, is all I can say."

Her heart pounded hard against her ribs, as it always did whenever she was startled awake. She'd been proofreading an article she was writing, and the heat of the late afternoon sun coming in the window had made her sleepy. She felt no remorse for dozing off on the sofa so refused to acknowledge Trip's criticism. "What is it? What's all the commotion?"

"I thought you might be interested to see what I have here." He dangled an envelope above her, just beyond her reach.

"I'm not going to leap for it like a dog. If you'd like me to read it, please turn loose, and place it in my hand." He did so and Breelan accepted the already opened envelope, noticing it was addressed to Mrs. Trip Clelland. As she read the contents, her face took on a sort of pinched appearance.

"What's the matter with you? You should be thrilled that the other soldiers' wives are having a tea and you're to be the guest of honor since you're the most recently wed. From your expression, you'd think they'd appointed you washer woman for the entire camp."

"Oh, I'm sorry. I'm just surprised they'd bother, me being a stranger and all."

"That's exactly the point. They want to get to know my wife. Every one of them thinks I'm quite a prize, and they're anxious to see what sort of woman I took a liking to."

Breelan was becoming accustomed to her husband's conceit. It was unattractive to her, even repulsive. That a man could stand before a mirror and preen the way some women did was beyond her. How many times had he asked if his hair was in place? When there was any dust on his boots, he'd re-polish them, sometimes taking so long he'd make them late to an engagement. His uniform was the most crisp and clean of any at the post. He'd made it clear to Breelan he would tolerate only perfection when it came to her care of that uniform. She might feel differently, less resentful, if the reason he wanted to look good was for the honor of his company. It was not. It was solely for his own vanity.

"Write to Mrs. Maveney, the major's wife, and tell her you accept. I'll deliver your reply tomorrow when I go to the fort."

She recognized this tea as a gracious gesture. What she didn't relish was sitting through the afternoon with a lot of strangers. If what Trip said was true about them adoring him, she'd have to answer questions concerning her marriage with them pointing out how lucky she was. The whole prospect was most unappealing until she was reminded it was far less so than having to share a bed with him. "You're right. I look forward to the tea and will write my reply right now."

"Good. Oh, and while you're writing, be sure and mention that your husband will personally escort you to and from the event. Mrs. Maveney will like that."

It was a pretty winter afternoon in Florida, and as Trip drove the buggy east to where Breelan's party awaited, she felt fresh despite the warmth of the day. She noticed how the ocean air smelled particularly fishy. Rust-hued wild grapevines tangled themselves among live oaks to form a canopy festooned with silver tassels of Spanish moss, which shadowed the path leading into the fort. Two soldiers were filling potholes along the entrance with sand and shell, and saluted Trip when the buggy passed.

Breelan knew quite a bit about Fort Clinch because she'd heard Major Fairbanks tell stories of the place. And too, being a thorough investigator, she'd done extensive research and found construction on its five-sided contours was begun some thirty-five years before in '47 by the Federals. It was named after General Duncan Lamont Clinch, who'd fought in the Second Seminole War, and left unfinished when the War Between the States broke out. With no heavy armament or guns in place at that time and only two of the five bastions completed, the Confederacy had easily taken the citadel for their own. By 1862, the capture of Georgia and South Carolina's coastal islands by the Union isolated Fernandina, so the Confederate troops withdrew and the North regained control. Most fascinating of all to Breelan was that neither side ever fired any great guns in battle there.

One wall of the pentagon-shaped brick structure sitting strong at the ocean's edge came into view. Since joining the handbell choir three years earlier, Breelan had played here each Easter Sunrise Service. That was when all of Fernandina's Christian denominations came to worship as one. Perched high on the wall, the panorama of the rising sun cresting ray-by-ray above the water's horizon, the dolphin bounding on the waves as the chaplain preached, men seining for shrimp from small dinghies, the United States' flag twisting on the temporarily placed loblolly pine pole in the middle of the parade ground, and her own mother singing Amazing Grace to the accompaniment of the delicate tinkle of handbells were memories of a lifetime for her.

Trip interrupted her reverie. "Well, here we are. I certainly hope you're more friendly with these ladies than you are with me. You'd better not shame me, do you hear? If I learn that you, in any way ..." He was interrupted by a gaggle of chattering women as their carriage crossed the wooden drawbridge.

Breelan was forever shocked at the degree of anger displayed by this man. She guessed she'd never get used to his tempers. Trip calculated most times just when and where to show his true demeanor. He was careful and practiced and had achieved expert status at the concealment of his ugly nature.

Breelan put on a congenial expression for her hostesses while they warmly received her as one of their own, a fellow army wife, dignified and patriotic. She wished Trip warranted the devotion to their husbands that these wives freely expressed. Had he, she could more readily have expended the same efforts for him that they did for their men.

Trip removed his hat and wished them a fine time at the party, but not before manufacturing a mournful expression. "Too bad this gathering is for women only. How about I borrow a dress from one of the laundresses and come incognito?"

The younger wives were aghast and tittered saying how he, of all people, could never, ever pass for a woman. That fed his ego a healthy dose of praise as he intended. The older, more worldly-wise females hardly acknowledged his remark and swarmed over Breelan.

Mrs. Hale, an attractive lady somewhere in her forties, smiled brightly and tightly gripped the hands of her guest. "It's so lovely to meet you, Mrs. Clelland. We're a unique group, and we want you to fit right in."

Charmed by her sincerity, "Thank you, ma'am. I'm very honored you've gone to so much trouble for me." She tried hard to retain the name of each of the ladies as she met them. Everyone was so busy chatting, Breelan soon realized they didn't expect her to remember who they were. Relaxing, she joined in the talk. All wives lived in town, not at the fort, which would be a much more difficult life for a woman. It would be particularly hard to make a home, especially in a temporary duty station, with all the horses, cannon and drilling soldiers. The new bride suddenly appreciated her little house. She also realized that thus far, not one remark had been made concerning her good luck at having landed Trip. In fact, no one had mentioned him since her arrival.

The fort was clean and well-maintained. There was no tall grass or sand spurs to catch your skirts here. Delicately embroidered cotton cloths covered two pine tables. These freshly sanded tables and benches had been set up in the shade of one of the tunnel-like brick galleries leading from the interior wall of the fort all the way out to the beach. "What lovely tea cakes," Breelan noticed. "And so uncommon." She bent over to examine their floral garnish more closely. "Each one is different. They're almost too pretty to eat, but not quite." Everyone laughed as the daffodil cake disappeared into her mouth. "My own cooking needs a lot of work. I don't think I'll ever get to the point where I create fancies like these."

Joan Richards, the woman who'd made the dessert remarked, "Now ladies, let's all make it a point to write down one or two of our easiest and best recipes for our newlywed." Heads nodded. "She'll have them within the week?" she asked. Again the women agreed, and a discussion broke out about who made the best corn pudding.

"Time to present the gifts," announced Mrs. Wagoner.

Breelan was overwhelmed! Never had she guessed she'd be getting gifts. "I'm Patricia Smathers and this is Sue Watkins. We've gone together and bought you an appointment book so you can keep track of your exciting new life."

"How kind of you both." The recipient flipped through the date book then passed it around.

"Anna Crossley, here," squeaked the small, rotund woman with huge teeth and blonde curly hair. As Breelan removed the muslin covering tied with a blue ribbon, Anna explained proudly, "It's a glass paperweight with a drawing I made of downtown Fernandina glued to the bottom."

"Look, the glass magnifies the scene," Breelan pointed out. "You're a wonderful artist." Necks craned until she shared her present with everyone.

Lois Barnibus said, "Mine and Josephine's Turner's next. We hope it comes in handy."

The thin wrapping paper crinkled excitement as they all impatiently waited to see. "It's a pewter thimble. And isn't that a tiny shrimp carved into the side?" Breelan asked.

"It is, Mrs. Clelland," confirmed Josephine, her long legs poking off the end of the bench for comfort.

A pink-cheeked beauty across from her informed, "Josephine is the best seamstress in town."

"I'm sure," Breelan agreed politely, not wanting to argue with that assessment since she knew her own mother and Grammy were the best.

"I've something I hope you like." Mrs. Maveney held up a white cotton hanky with hand rolled borders, edged with some of the most intricate lace Breelan had ever seen.

"It's lovely. Did you make it?"

"Yes. I have to tell you about the lace. I was given a spool of this lace when I married and was told it was very special. No matter how torn or tattered it becomes, it will always retain its beauty. And once mended, it will never look worn."

"What a sweet story," Breelan told her.

"Truly, it's no story. That lace is a lot like love." She was momentarily interrupted by troops marching to the orders of a small red headed sergeant with a very big voice. Once they'd passed, Mrs. Maveney finished. "Remember dear, true love can always be mended."

Breelan appreciated the sentiment, but realized her love of Waite, her true love, would never get the chance to be mended. The party was winding down and so was the guest of honor. Looking over all the gentle faces she had come to care for in such a short time, she spoke from her heart. "Thank you seems so inadequate. I can say how you've created a feeling which honors me so that whenever I experience loneliness, I'll hearken back to this day and remember the warmth that a woman can only know amongst her own kind. You've all touched me deeply."

"You can tell this one is a writer, can't you?" Lois teased, trying to make light of Breelan's words before she dissolved into tears like most of the rest of the ladies.

"Whoever said I was a writer?"

"Your husband, for one, and Lieutenant Akins, too. They were telling us all about how you work for the newspaper."

The fact that Trip would brag about her was a shock. Maybe Will. He held nothing against her, but Trip?

As the sun dropped over the marsh, the new friends said goodbye with the promise to meet again at the upcoming Community Christmas Dance at the fort on December twentieth. Climbing into the buggy for the ride home, Breelan was happy for the first time since her marriage. She hoped that if, indeed, she had any skill as a writer, her thank you note to each of the ladies would demonstrate her appreciation to its fullest magnitude.

"Miss Breelan!" She recognized the voice calling her name and turned in her seat to find Will running toward them.

"Hey, Will. I'd hoped I'd see you here. It's been a while."

"That it has. You off duty, Trip?"

"Ya. Just taking my gal home."

"You going to the Christmas dance, Will?" she asked.

"Yes, ma'am."

"I'll bet I don't have to ask whom you'll be taking," Breelan sweetly taunted the cheery young man. He was so unlike her husband. Will always made her smile. Why were the two such close friends? Their personalities were so different.

"I'm pleased to report that Miss Nora has kindly accepted. Oh, speaking of reporting, since I'm the company secretary, I've made a log in the official book of your shindig, oh excuse me, reception here today. You'll be famous!"

"How thrilling to be written about for all posterity." She could hardly wait to tell Nora.

"I don't know about you, but it's dinner time for this old man," said Trip. "You probably aren't hungry from all the sweeties you ate at your party, Bree. How's about we stop by the Florida House and I'll grab some of their fresh fish. That way you don't have to worry about cooking supper. Care to come along, Will?"

"Thanks. Sounds tempting, but I'm on the job until ten tonight."

"We'll see you at the dance then."

"You bet. Bye, Bree."

When they pulled away, Breelan had to speak. "Thank you, Trip. It's very thoughtful of you to eat out tonight."

"I try. Well? Was I right?" he asked as they rode.

Breelan shielded her eyes as the last glow of the sun shaded the sky a near match to the rust of the brick fort. She hoped the weather would stay as lovely as this for the dance.

"Right about what?" she wondered, only half hearing, feeling special kinship toward the women of the soldiers of Fort Clinch.

"Breelan," Trip said impatiently. "Right about all those females telling you how lucky you are that I married you."

"Yes, Trip. You were right," and she offered no more. It was just easier that way.

Chapter 22 – *The Goodbye Lie* by Jane Marie

Melinda counted the days until the Christmas dance. Yet, her excitement was curbed because of the character of her escort. Thank the good Lord, the man's loutish behavior was always in check in open society.

Breelan was disheartened by her writings. She felt the cold surf grazing her toes and dropped her pencil. She looked about and seeing no one, pulled her skirts a little higher because what was left of the evening was sweet and warming. Straightening her legs, she extended them further into the water. The chill of it stimulated her sense of touch and she ground her heels into the rough sand, mindlessly observing the multi-colored grains burying her feet. Throwing her head back, her arms wide, she stretched every muscle from her fingertips, up her arms, and clear through her back. The hem of her skirt was wet now from the rising tide, so she walked a few feet from the ocean to weigh down her papers, shoes and stockings with a heavy shell. Time progressed to near darkness and the beach was just the way she liked it, isolated except for Noir. She knew she should ride home soon, but the night here never frighten her. Instead, it wrapped her in a shawl of comfort. She tried to block out the vision of her husband's eyes devouring her. Fortunately, Trip was on overnight maneuvers. Tonight, she wouldn't be pawed.

Scarcely able to discern the stones and shells on beach now, Breelan nevertheless took position. Hands behind her back, head bowed down, gaze focused but widespread, she scoped the shore for triangle-shaped sharks' teeth. Over the years, she and the family had found enough to fill three quart jars to the brim. They were on exhibit in the Dunnigan kitchen window, meant to astonish out-of-towners. They ranged in size from the tiniest, a sixteenth of an inch, to the biggest, four-and-a-half inches long, unchipped with a serrated edge. That rare tooth was brought out last to dazzle and never failed to deliver. Breelan had a theory about the art of shark tooth hunting. If one got lazy and didn't go to the effort and discomfort of lower back pain by picking up the tiny ones, then the Almighty wouldn't let one find any large teeth. It was silly. Still she followed the practice as if it were the written law. Any for all. This intensity of pursuit kept her from feeling, temporarily.

He accepted his decision. It would be best. What options were left him? What more harm could he do to himself? This might save his sanity. Something had to.

Atop the dune, Waite's dark eyes watched. There was something fluttering in the pale of the early dark, a small white bird, maybe an injured baby gull. From this distance he couldn't make it out. He dismounted and walked his horse, keeping as quiet as possible, so as not to startle the little creature. Suddenly, the bird leapt into the air, managing only to snare itself among the slender sea grass. "Probably not much I can do for the poor thing," he whispered to his golden palomino horse. "Come on, Rory boy. We'll do whatever's necessary." Ending a life was never easy.

Close now, he laughed out loud with relief. It was no bird, just a stupid piece of white paper. He snatched up the thing he'd steeled himself to kill if need be, then crumpled it into a tight wad. He raised his arm, ready to toss the document into the sea. He stopped. Sitting down on the sand, he carefully smoothed out the many wrinkles against his hard thigh. In the dusky light, he read, not recognizing the handwriting, but appreciating the words because they could be sentiments she might have written.

Would it never stop? Would she forever afflict him? Then, out of the advancing night she appeared to him, the moonlight directing her course. Breelan was exquisite. A powerful wind lifted her hair from her shoulders, leaving it floating on the air like a stole. She was close, within his reach. He rose to capture her, and lifted her high above him. Slowly, very slowly, he allowed her to slide down his length to stand against him. She would permit him anything he wanted. He knew it because he knew her. Lowering his mouth over hers, he touched her lips, and they were blended, enraptured by the complete fascination of one for the other. Their lips never parting, never wanted to part, he laid her on the sand. Pulling back for but a moment to see the outline of her beautiful face, he heard her whimper. Then she captured his strong jaw, dragging him down. She couldn't abide being without his touch any longer.

Eager to oblige, he lay atop her, feeling the woman, lingering, thrilling, loving her. "Breelan, dear God, you can't know. You just can't know how I've wanted this with you. Only you. No one can fill my heart, but you. I'm alive again for the first time since you left me."

"Waite. Oh, Waite. I didn't realize it would be this sweet. It's almost too much to endure. I think if you don't make love to me right here and now, I'll die from want of you. Don't let me wait any longer. Don't make me wait any longer." And again she pulled at him, caring only to give herself. All of herself.

He tensed and grabbed hold of her shoulders. Running his hands down the length of her arms to her hands, he held them tight inside of his. "How I crave this. It's so strong, it panics me."

She wanted the weight of him upon her again. "Don't let it. We'll carry the burden of ecstasy together. We'll ..."

He stood and left her lying there - alone. "Stay where you are and listen to me! Listen to me!" he ordered.

With much difficulty, she did not move.

"I want you so badly, I'm numb with the ache of it."

She smiled radiantly and sat up, holding out her hand for him to take hold of again.

He jammed his hands in his pockets to keep them away from her. "You're the one woman in the entire world for me to love. If you were any other I wanted this much, married or not, I'd have you. But you aren't just any woman. And I won't do that to you. More importantly, I won't allow you to do it to us. I can only imagine the joy of lying with you. Imagining is all we'll ever have, Bree, so long as you're his, whether you want to be or not. The hard, ugly fact is that you are. What kind of a life would it be for us? Your family would disown you if you left him for me."

A speck of worry penetrated her brain. Was he turning from her? No. She got to her feet but kept her distance. "You're just reluctant because you're a good man with a good heart. That's one of the reasons I adore you." He didn't respond. "I don't think my parents are so sure about Trip themselves. The more they're around him, the more suspicion I see in their eyes."

He'd picked up on that fact from Michael as well. It didn't matter. "That's not the issue, Bree. Even if you stayed with him and went sneaking around, the moment we were out of one another's arms and the reality of the hideous situation showed itself, you'd despise our weakness. And what if, heaven forbid, you got pregnant?"

"At least, we'd know it was your baby, Waite. That would make up for everything."

"Could you ever be sure it was mine, honey?"

"Yes. I'd know your child, our child. He'd be dark, like his father."

"Okay. Say it was my child for certain. In good conscience, could you allow Trip to raise my baby? I couldn't. How would fighting over the innocent little thing affect him or her? Something of that nature would never remain private. Trip would see to it. And I couldn't blame him. For your own peace of mind and the happiness of the child, you'd have to leave this town and the family you love.

"You have two choices," he told her. "You must go back to your husband, or leave him and live a celibate life because you'd still be legally married. There is, of course, a third choice. Divorce him."

"Trip would probably charge me with adultery, whether or not you or I had ever lain together." Breelan's mind raced as did Waite's for much of what she was saying could have been said by him. "I've never told him or even hinted I'm in love with you. He may be a lot of things, but the one thing he isn't is stupid. I think he can sense it. He's jealous and hates you. I wouldn't want to have a divorce shame the Dunnigan name. Now, after being apart from you for so long, I could be that selfish. I won't live without you. I'll allow my family to pay the price so we can be together. I'll be excommunicated by the church. And while I don't want that either, I'll accept it all and more to be with you."

"Well then, after a divorce, you'd legally be free to love whomever you choose. But it couldn't be me because morally, excommunicated or not, in your honest heart, you'd know you still belonged to him. My darling, you married before your God. He's my God, too, and I will not condemn you to the fires of damnation so I can enjoy the thrill of loving your body. I find myself not believing that it's me who's saying these things," Waite confessed. "Me, the bachelor, the lover wherever and with whomever I choose. You've changed me, Breelan. I'm a different man now because of you. I'm sorry, sorry for us both. Know that I suffer with you, my beauty, out of devotion. We've mangled our lives and the only solution is to pay the price, the honorable price. And that's with silent love."

Breelan threw her arms around her head, trying to block out the cruel reality of his pronouncement.

"I can't handle being alone with you anymore, Bree, not and keep my reason. You ask too much of me." His eyes burned with deadly pain and he was glad she couldn't see it in the darkness. His rough hands took hold of hers. He pulled her down to her knees along with him. He needed her to understand he meant what he'd been saying. Keeping her at arm's length, Waite begged for her comprehension. "I can't take this any longer. I just can't. I'm not as strong as you think. Not with you here. Not with the breeze swirling the very scent of you around me and through me. In a saner moment, you'd remember we've been over this once before and it was you who did the proper thing when you stopped me from making love to you. Now I stop you. You must let what I say register inside you - for all our sakes."

He was right. It was that simple. She loved him too much to continue to torture him by her nearness. Yet, she couldn't help what involuntarily escaped from her lips and she wailed, "All right! All right! I'll do my best to stay away from you." Forcing herself to calm, "Just know, it's all for you. I'd give my soul away to be with you," she paused, "but you won't let me."

There in the cool, with the sloshing sea beside them, the peeking stars observing, and an isolated patch of fog engulfing them, they kissed a final time. It was a soft, slow, lingering kiss. When he withdrew from her, he helped her to her feet because she needed help. Once again, as he'd done at their first meeting so many aching heartbeats ago, he handled her tiny foot and raised her onto her horse, though the shock of her bare skin on his hot palm startled him.

"Your boots?"

The absurdity of his question startled her as well. "Oh, the surf probably has taken them. No matter. If only it would take away our pain as easily."

"If only." He slapped Noir's backside hard and the animal reared up at the unaccustomed cuffing to bolt down the shoreline.

The beacon from the Amelia lighthouse threw its pale brilliance high overhead in unceasing intervals as Breelan rode north. Its pulsing intruded upon the solace she searched for. Many minutes later, she gentled her animal and dismounted. She stood in the pounding breakers, her heavy, wet skirts slapping her legs. With agony beyond endurance, she howled into the black night. The insatiable ocean gulped away at her despondency, swallowing all sounds, leaving only its own. At that moment, she hated God.

Chapter 23 – *The Goodbye Lie* by Jane Marie

Stuffing her small reporter's notepad and pencil into her reticule, Breelan was ready for the dance at Fort Clinch. If she had an extra moment, she'd jot down a thought or incident and submit it to the society editor, Heleen Cydling.

Nora tried very hard to keep the mood light inside Breelan's bedroom, the room she shared with Trip. The redhead remembered how giggles would be heard whenever and wherever the two cousins could be found. These sobering days, laughter seemed almost a chore.

"Breelan, come along. Don't make us late to the ball."

"We're coming, Trip." One girl hurried out to meet her escort, the other followed more slowly.

Breelan was struck upon first sight of Trip and Will, standing undeniably handsome in their formal dress uniforms. They were mirror images of one another. The difference between the two was that Will was about two inches shorter than his friend and just a handful of pounds heavier. She noticed their pristine white gloves laid side-by-side across the arm of the sofa and realized how much larger Trip's hands were than Will's. She'd heard her husband complain he had to special order his gloves because of the size, but until this time she'd never really appreciated his problem. She sighed as she considered what a simple problem glove size was in comparison to the complications in her own life.

"You're so pretty, Nora. You make me glad I'm alive," Will gushed, taking her hand in his.

The words were sweeter than Nora could have ever imagined. Beaming, she answered, "Thank you, sir. You make me feel like a fairy princess." Looking into the eyes of her confidante, she asked, "Don't you, Bree?"

"Yes. A beautiful gown will do that to a girl every time." Breelan could have been more coquettish by substituting the words "attractive escort," for "beautiful gown," but Trip didn't seem to notice the difference.

After helping the ladies with their cloaks, the men donned heavy military capes. They all piled into the carriage to begin the cold journey to the ball, for winter had finally chosen to pay a visit to Fernandina. As the sun set, the lighted buggy lanterns shown brighter as each minute passed. The elaborately embroidered crazy-quilted lap robes helped some, but even encased in all her bundling, Breelan shivered.

Trip slid closer to her on the front seat, holding the reins with his right hand, encircling his wife with his left. "There now, honey. Let your husband warm you. No need for you to catch a chill while I'm around."

Breelan did her best to participate in the inane conversation that transpired. She condemned herself for being judgmental. Time was, she'd have thrived over his insipid words. Time was ...

Pulling onto the long path to the fort, they followed the lamps from proceeding conveyances through the dark. Nearing their destination, they found the traffic had slowed to creeping as ladies and gentlemen alighted from their transports.

Single candles in each brick framed window glittered star-like against the thick, wavy glass. A huge bonfire sent sparks up into the night, swirling wild from the bitter wind off the ocean, until they burned themselves out. Even the shelter of the fortifications did little to alleviate the piercing cold.

Music was heard, softly, then loudly again at each opening of the door to the second floor common room where the dance was being held. Once inside, Breelan took it all in. The entire length of the banister of the straight wooden staircase was swaged with a pine needle garland and the garland was draped with a red and green paper chain that had been her particular contribution. The smells of gingerbread and apple cider wafted down as they climbed up into the excitement. Add the fires burning in the fireplaces at both ends of the room, their logs strewn with cinnamon sticks and dried orange peel, and Breelan was carried back to earlier, happier Christmases.

Eager eyes were fixed on the entrance to see who arrived with whom and in what fashionable garb. As Trip removed her black velvet cape with burgundy satin lining, Breelan's friends found her. Tonight, she wore the prettiest dress she'd ever possessed. Her mother and grandmother had created an entire gown of horizontally sewn rows of ivory lace. The drop shoulders were edged with four-inch white fringe, which allowed her upper arms to peek out. Pink and gold silk rosebuds intertwined in a vine of ivy leaves to diagonally cross the bodice. More rosebuds sat atop pale bows scattered over the drape covering an underskirt of ecru satin. An oval coral brooch outlined with tiny seed pearls and pinned to her mother's string of pearls, was positioned at the base of her throat, her earbobs matching. White gloves only long enough to cover her forearms, an amethyst ring on her right hand overtop the glove, and a tussie mussie of small pink poinsettias in a lace cone completed the picture of loveliness that she was. The women touched her gown, admiring its grandeur and the beauty of the woman who wore it.

Trip enjoyed the envy in every man's eyes as he proclaimed Breelan his possession by staying nearby and playing with her sleeve trim or touching the back of her neck. She wanted to swat him away like some bothersome fly.

Breelan looked about the room for Nora and Will. She saw them sipping red punch from delicate crystal cups. They were talking and laughing with Carolena and Graham Winger, an assistant draftsman in her father's firm. Breelan hurried over to her sister and cousin while Trip followed reluctantly. He wanted to dance, not visit. He wanted to hold his wife in his arms.

"Carolena! What a surprise to see you here! I knew Mama was under the weather and wouldn't attend, which of course didn't break Daddy's heart any. You know how he feels about this sort of affair. I heard her trying to talk you into coming. You said these parties were always the same. What made you change your mind?"

"Frankly, I got to thinking about it. Yes, these balls do tend to blend one into another. But I decided since I'd never really seen the inside of many of the buildings here at the fort, it would be a wonderful opportunity to observe the construction and mix a little socializing with education." She glanced over, saw her escort's hurt look and amended, "And it will be ever-so much more fun with Mr. Winger here to explain the architecture. He's extremely well versed about these things, and you know I'm only just learning." Carolena dipped her chin and shyly looked at the floor.

Lord Almighty! Breelan couldn't believe her eyes or her ears. Her serious sister, her sister who'd rebuffed invitation after invitation from boys and men, was actually playing feminine games!

"I think Miss Carolena looks lovely tonight," Graham stated. "In that jade dress her eyes glow like honey-dipped emeralds."

Carolena took his arm. "I'm sorry my gown isn't new, Graham. There wasn't time to have another one made since I decided to come at the last minute."

"I, for one, am very pleased that you did."

"Are you sure my dress is pretty enough?" They disappeared into the dancing crowd with him reassuring her that it was and her smiling, as were Nora and Breelan, happy to see the bookish Carolena enjoying herself.

While Trip and Will found amusement between them, Nora commented, "You'd never think this was a military establishment from the looks of the holiday decorations. I heard that huge pine tree in the center was donated by Mr. Beltzer of all people. You know, that bent-over old man whose wagon is so ancient, his supplies fall out the bottom. Why he doesn't get himself a new one is beyond me. Daddy says he's tighter than

157

the bark on a tree though he's got lots of money. Heck, I heard he's got more money than - well, than your family!" She had to laugh at the silly she'd made. "I'm getting quite good at this party chat. Don't you think?"

"Yes, you are." Breelan shook her head, never knowing what outrageous thing might come from her cousin's mouth next. "Maybe the Christmas spirit moved him to donate it. All I can think of right now, though, is biting the head off one of those frosted snowman cookies hanging from the red ribbons,"

"Didn't you have any supper?"

"I mostly pushed my food around the plate because I was so excited about the dance. I didn't actually eat much."

"That's not a problem. There's a long table filled with finger food at the front of the hall."

As they headed straight for the delicacies, they passed near the tree. This caused the flames of the small white candles on the pine boughs to flicker. A young lad was stationed by the water bucket, patrolling for any wild sparks and called out, "Ladies, tend your skirts. Ladies, tend your skirts."

Breelan recognized him as the son of the commander of the fort. "Thank you, Master Maveney." A nod was his acknowledgement, and he was quick to catch a penny someone tossed him for his trouble.

The raised platform in the south corner of the room held the musicians from town. They were playing seasonal songs amongst some of the more popular tunes of the day. A beautifully printed sign decorated in red and green read *Courtesy: Mrs. Luella Smitty* and sat atop the handsome harpsichord. Violin, fife, double bell euphonium, clarinet, trumpet and snare drum made for quite the orchestra.

The girls nibbled on triangular egg salad sandwiches, rolled ham, and sugared nuts while watching Mrs. Bleether. The stout widow was still dressed in black for General Bleether who had passed away in the line of duty before Breelan was born. Tonight, the widow nodded periodically to the conductor with instructions. A self-described expert tunesmith, she could always be found near the hapless leader of the band at any social function she attended.

"Wasn't that last song *The Jack-in-the-Pulpit Waltz?*" Breelan asked.

"I believe so." Nora checked her dance card hanging from her wrist. "It says the next is to be the *Sweet Brier Polka* followed by the *Fort Clinch Cannon Brigade*. Oh, look here, in parentheses it says *Haymakers Reel*."

Breelan recognized the name. "I think we've played that one on the handbells. I'll know that when I hear it." And she did.

She danced with Trip each time he asked despite his occasional cutting remarks. She didn't understand why he was becoming increasingly nasty as the evening advanced. Usually that happened as he drank more alcohol, but the dance committee was only serving spiced punch and mulled cider heated with a fire poker. When Trip crushed her to him in an indelicate moment of lust, she felt the hard flask under his tunic and understood.

The glowing fireplaces kept most of the cold at bay. They blazed high, casting a golden haze on everyone and everything. Passing the door in dance, Breelan felt a rush of raw wind enter the room, along with a late arriving couple. The cape the man wore was not military. She saw the woman next. The blonde hair, piled a little too high on the head, left no doubt that it was Leona Visper, a figure not seen since New York City and more importantly, not missed. Looking again at the silhouette of shoulders, Breelan realized the identity of the singer's escort. It was then that eyes met, expressions hardened and polite nods were exchanged.

"What the hell's he doing here?" Trip railed.

Having no answer, Breelan offered none.

"Look everyone," said a voice from somewhere in the room, "Captain Taylor and his lady brought the snow with them to Fernandina!" The floor cleared as couples rushed to the windows to see the rare white flakes drop softly to the earth, melting on contact with the warmer sand and sparse grass.

Trip grabbed Breelan's hand and yanked her to the window farthest from the entrance. He threw his arm tightly about her waist, pulling her roughly into him. "Don't fret, my darling. You won't spend a cold moment once we get home." And he murmured a vulgarity against her ear. She tried pulling away, but was fused to his side by his overpowering strength.

"Trip. Say, Trip." Witnessing her distress, Will tapped his friend on the shoulder. "How's about we switch partners for a while. What do you say, Miss Breelan?"

"Yes, please. Let's do. I'd love to dance with you, Will."

Nora never felt less like dancing with anyone, yet she too saw her cousin needed help. "Yes, Trip. Bree tells me you're quite the dance partner. I have it straight from Mrs. Bleether that the next is to be a waltz. How fortunate for us all," she lied, sounding only vaguely sincere.

"I can't turn away a woman who begs, now can I?" And Trip hauled Nora to the center of the floor, ready to show off his talent.

Breelan saw that her husband was hobbling a bit. Turning, she confided, "Will, I've never found the right moment to ask Trip why he sometimes limps. Do you know? Could you tell me?"

"Well," he stammered, seemingly hesitant to reveal the reason. "It happened in the ... it happened when ... come over here into the cloakroom. I'll tell you."

"Is it so private as all that?"

"Yes, ma'am. Very private."

"All right, then." I should know, she thought. It might help me understand the man. She followed Will into the tiny chamber where the myriad of cloaks hung. With the door closed, it was dark except for the light coming in at its bottom. He whispered for her to lean closer. She did, ready to hear the horrible truth. He grabbed her upper arms, pitching her against the capes. She reached out to him, but only for stability. He misread her meaning and tried to plant a kiss on her protesting lips. Wrenching and writhing, she freed herself, then slapped him backhanded across the face, the ring on her right hand making mean contact with his cheek. "Will Akins! Of all the men in this wide world, I just knew you were a friend to be trusted. You're all the same, the whole lot of you! Rough, nasty jaspers!"

"I'm so sorry, Bree. Trip and I've had a tiny bit to drink, and I lost my manners and my heart. Forgive me."

"All I have to say is, 'Poor Nora!'" and she turned to leave, tears in her eyes for her cousin. As she twisted the knob, the door was thrown open and, for a split second, she was blinded by a fully lighted candelabra in the hands of a passing solider.

"Breelan? What is it? What are you doing in here? And with that little weasel?" It was none other than Waite, the one person she'd wanted to avoid out of the crowd of hundreds.

"We had something private to discuss," she offered quickly.

"I can see by the bruise on the silly fool's cheek that you had the last word," and he burst out laughing.

Breelan was shocked by his reaction. Watching him, seeing his handsome, happy face, she temporarily forgot her concerns and easily did the same.

The guests around them, not knowing the reason but ready for a good joke, joined in. Mirth was the call to order and everyone willingly obliged. Everyone except Leona Visper. She didn't appreciate missing out on the gag. Worse yet, she wasn't the center of attention. Hurrying over, she caught the last few words Waite spoke. They were directed at some soldier in a closet. He looked familiar, but she didn't care to trouble herself with trying to remember from where.

Waite cautioned Will, "May I recommend that you never attempt ..."

"You need say no more, sir. I've learned my lesson - too well," and Will winced when he touched his tender bruise.

Fearing once again that brunette was involved, Leona curled her arm through that of her escort and purred, "Why Waite Taylor, whatever is all the fuss about hanging up my wrap? Oh, Mrs. Clelland, is it? I see you admire my fur, as well as my companion." The last she said under her breath, knowing Waite didn't like her to be too possessive. She wouldn't want to make him angry. Not yet anyway. Not this soon. Her next words sounded casual although they were purposely calculated to be cruel. "My fiancé gave it to me as an early Christmas present. Isn't it the most beautiful fox fur you've ever seen?"

"Fiancé?" Breelan's skin paled to the color of her gown.

"Yes. Waite? Darling? Haven't you told everyone you've met? I certainly have. We're planning a spring wedding. Waite wanted to marry me before the holidays. He's crazy about me, you know. Anyway, I recommended against doing it so soon. My fans would be sorely disappointed if we ran off and had a piddly little wedding with no one there. What kind of a stupid thing is that to do? Oops. Now, isn't that just what you did?"

"Leona," Waite said firmly. "I'm sure Mrs. Clelland did what she wanted at the time."

Breelan thought how gallant this man was. Then the word echoed in her thoughts. Fiancé. Fiancé. This union would be as empty as was her own.

As his dance with Nora ended, Trip overheard the news. "Congratulations, Taylor," he said, purposely leaving off the title of the person he addressed. He didn't want to be reminded that this man was a success - in business and in love. "It appears you, too, will soon be unavailable to the female population. You'll have to make do with what you have." Gazing obscenely at the singer, "And I don't mind saying that you'll bear no hardship by the looks of that pretty gem beside you."

Leona gloried in the compliment, Waite hated the public offense, and Breelan was shamed by the crude remark. Here, for any and all to hear, her husband had revealed just how much his wife and their marriage meant to him. Nothing.

"Come on," called Nora. "Let's all go outside and try and make snow balls before the snow melts." Seeing Will for the first time since he'd disappeared with Breelan, she ran to him. "Sweetheart! What on earth happened to you? Did you run into a door jam?" She patted his cheek with her hankie.

Batting away her hand, "That's not exactly it. More like a brick wall," he said sarcastically. "It's fine, Nora. Leave it be."

"Let's do go out of doors, Waite darling, and you can watch me catch snowflakes with my tongue. You should like that." Leona nuzzled her slim nose against his starched collar, enjoying the smell of him.

Turning away, Breelan walked to the cloakroom to retrieve her wrap. Trip followed, laughing. "Will has some knot on his cheek. What female clobbered him?"

Breelan wanted everyone to be as miserable as she was, so she informed her husband as to the source of the bruise.

"Aw, come on. You're overreacting. I'm sure it didn't mean anything. Forget it."

Her husband wouldn't even defend her honor. She shouldn't be surprised.

The hall was almost empty but the musicians played on. The melody of Jingle Bells was faint, yet still audible enough for the throng outside to hear and sing along, all except one tall dark-haired man and one small, dark-haired woman. Tonight neither would be in good voice.

Trip rolled onto his back, drunk and mad as the devil that his libido had deserted him and was swimming in the whiskey in his belly. "I want an answer. Now," he demanded. "Or do I admit the truth. God knows you won't." Without pause, he said, "You're barren."

His low, guttural tone cut Breelan deeply. Still, no heartless utterance could outweigh the pain of the validity of the remark. She refused to believe him. She would know. Surly she would be able to feel an emptiness? A hollowness. Whatever you called it, he was wrong. He had to be.

She wondered what kind of father Trip would make every miserable time he took her to bed. He wanted a child so badly. So did she, but for completely different reasons. He wanted a smaller image of himself to groom and train. Someone to brag on. She only wanted someone to love and care for. But she, too, was beginning to worry that there was no baby. Hard as it was for her to admit, if he were right, it might be better for the child's sake. Trip was cruel to her. What would he do if disobeyed by an independent son or daughter? Oh, surely she could protect her child. Or could she? She hadn't done much of a job protecting herself so far.

"Give it time. Maybe it will be all right. We've been married only a short while."

"Short while? It only takes once with a fertile woman. It would appear, dearest, that you just ain't. Hell, I'm fast becoming a laughing stock at the fort. "What's the problem, Clelland? You shootin' blanks? Why aren't you passin' out the cigars yet, Clelland?" You're a looker all right, Breelan, but the real and only reason I married you was because you'd breed me a lot of strong sons. Guess the joke's on me."

She rose, careful not to bounce the squeaking springs, hoping he would drift off. At the window, she leaned into the breeze that blew ice cold against her face. He'd insisted the window be raised. She suspected he hoped the chilled air might revive his physical prowess. Tomorrow when he was sober, he'd be nicer. He'd probably not even remember his cruelty. But she would remember his words. She hoped he wouldn't speak of it too often. It was such a hurtful thing.

Wait a minute! She turned on her bare feet and ran to him in the dark. "Maybe it isn't me. Maybe it's you! Maybe you can't because of that scar on your thigh. Maybe you were left sterile when ..."

He leapt from the bed and had her throat in his hands before she could finish her supposition. "Don't say another word," he screamed. "Not another damned word! I know it isn't me. That scar has nothing to do with it. Nothing!" He pushed her away from him into the open window frame. She grabbed the wooden casing to keep from falling out. Ignoring her struggle, Trip calmly crossed back to the bed. He fell on his stomach and was asleep.

I'm right! Dear God, please let me be right, she prayed. It's him! He's the sterile one! I must be crazy because I feel sorry for him somehow. His want of a child and his inability could explain his erratic moods, she thought, surprising herself at her charity. What was wrong with her? How could she feel kindly toward him? She was becoming as crazy as he was!

Exhausted from the dance, her encounter with Will, hearing of Waite's betrothal and realizing her husband's infertility, Breelan needed to sleep and wanted to so badly. In slumber, she might loose herself in dreams of what could have been.

Chapter 24 – *The Goodbye Lie* by Jane Marie

Four days and nights ago, there had been snow in the air. Now at midnight mass on Christmas Eve, it was almost too balmy to be comfortable. That was the way of the unpredictable weather in north Florida. Guests on the island often said it didn't feel like Christmas when the weather was like this. The natives knew better.

St. Michael's Church was exceptionally hot. Breelan was as anxious for the service to begin as was the tightly-packed congregation of warm and worshipping bodies. The throng waved a vast array of fans, some store bought, some homemade, some from the funeral parlor, and a few discourteously fashioned from church bulletins. All the Dunnigans were in attendance with Miss Ella singing soprano in the holiday cantata. The Duffys, the Clellands and nearly every family in town were there as well.

When the offering was taken, little Marie shook all the coins from her ceramic Saint Nicholas bank into the wicker basket. The gentle clatter of change touched the hearts of nearby worshipers who were smiling at the charming lesson for all.

Now the lamps and candles were extinguished, save for the ones lighting the empty manger. It Came upon a Midnight Clear was played on the pump organ as Jack Patrick Dunnigan walked up the aisle, dressed in a black cassock covered by a crisp white surplice. He cautiously carried the wooden statue of Baby Jesus to the miniature manger, placing it upon the bed of straw. The entire congregation let out a hushed sigh of relief when the task was successfully completed. All knew the boy well and were justifiably worried that his propensity toward antics might overtake his good sense. It had not. This time.

To Breelan's distress, a golden-robed Leona Visper stepped onto the altar to lead the choir and worshippers in song. This was no place to be unkind reminded Breelan's conscience. She said a tiny prayer, very tiny, of remorse. Sleeping children and old men continued their cacophony of soft snores to the consoling melody of everyone's favorite Christmas carol, *Silent Night*. No one referred to the hymnal for this song. From many years of practice, folks had absorbed the lyrics to each verse and knew just when to sing out and when to quiet their voices for dramatic effect.

Breelan glanced across the aisle to scarcely make out the profiles of Nora and Will who had appeared blissful when they arrived. She was torn, wanting to save her sweet cousin's pride and heart from such a miscreant. Breelan decided then and there to give Will more time to break off the relationship. She wouldn't ruin Christmas for Nora if she could help it. There would be a better opportunity to fill her in about Will later on.

Everyone felt the jar of an explosion as it tore at their eardrums, leaving a temporary humming behind. Windows cracked and glass shattered. A blinding flash illuminated shocked and frightened faces. Then the sanctuary was plunged back into darkness as screams and cries rang out.

"It's an earthquake!"

"A train wreck! My God, it's a train wreck!"

"It's Armageddon! I knew we should have come to church before this. I knew it!"

Men and mothers threw themselves upon their children. Babies squalled as they were thrust under the pews for protection. Some people ran from the church, certain the roof would cave in and bury them alive. Some in the balcony pushed and shoved their way down the steps, forgetting their Christianity while others climbed over the railing and leapt down. But the structure stood strong, and no one in it appeared to be seriously hurt. The great sound had come from the west, the docks. Candles were lit to reveal puffs of dry mortar here and there coming from between the interior bricks. That, in combination with the dust loosed from the rafters, wafted throughout the church to cloud the air, polluting lungs enough to bring the congregation to coughing.

"Where's my pew baby? Where is it?" Little Marie wept, her voice the high squeal of brakes on a train.

Jack Patrick discovered the handkerchief doll beneath the boot of his father. "Here it is, Marie. You can quit crying now. "

"Good boy, son," his mother praised, absently patting the top of his head.

"Trip, see to it that the older woman and children make it home safely," commanded Michael Dunnigan of his son-in-law. "Clabe, come with me. Let's try and find out what happened."

"Sir," Trip responded, "I think I could be of better service with you. I'll have Lieutenant Akins take everyone home. He's a good man."

"Very well. Ella and Noreen, let Peeper and Grammy tend the little ones. We may need your nursing skills."

"I pray God you don't, Michael," Ella answered her husband as she quickly stepped out of her choir robe. "We'll ride with you to Centre Street and see what's happened."

Unashamedly admitting her weakness at the sight of blood, Carolena volunteered, "I'm not much use in a crisis, Mama. I'm sorry, but I can't help it. I'll go home with Peeper and Gram. I can at least keep Jack Patrick and Warren Lowell busy."

"Good idea, honey," Miss Ella said.

"Daddy," Breelan pleaded, "Let me go with you. I can help and I'll need to report on the explosion for the paper."

"It's not up to me, honey. It's up to your husband now."

Breelan detested asking permission of that man, but in the interest of time, she didn't argue. To her huge surprise, Trip was readily agreeable.

"I'm coming, too," cried Nora, disappointed at being separated from Will, but seeing her duty and doing what needed to be done.

Watching the glow in the western sky, the good intentioned walked or drove south two blocks to the main street in Fernandina.

The instant they passed the brick building blocking their line of vision to the wharf, Breelan saw the waning moon emptying its crackling lava down upon the water, bursting the liquid surface into a reservoir of fire. Drawing closer, intellect overcame imagination.

Black smoke crawled toward town, threatening to engulf everything. A deafening inferno roaring out on the river was nearly two blocks in length. Smaller blazes randomly raged all along the island's shore as bucket brigades had already begun work to quell them. Flaming debris from an ill-fated freighter or barge was thrown a quarter mile in the blast. Even the rooftop of *The Florida Mirror*, clear across the north and south running railroad tracks, shown with unnatural light.

Miss Ella did what she could to assist as limp bodies were carried on shore from incoming rescue boats. Figures lay about, some faces covered with blankets, others reassuringly alive, but contorting in pain.

"I can't do this," Aunt Noreen confessed. "I just can't. It's too gruesome. I'll have bad dreams."

"Go sit on the bench then and get out of the way." Miss Ella wasted no words on her useless sister-in-law. She hadn't the time or, particularly, the patience.

"Now really, Ella. If you're going to take that tone, I don't want to work with you any longer."

"Go away, Noreen"

Breelan, Nora, Michael, Clabe, and Trip were otherwise occupied, throwing water onto the remaining scattered fires. They took no notice of the emotionally wounded woman who was doubly offended at their lack of concern for her suffering.

Once everything except the conflagration on the river was under control, Breelan stepped out of the line of water bearers and ventured as close to the dock as was safe. She had heard the speculation of what was out there burning, but until this moment, she hadn't realized the truth. Dear God. She knew that silhouette. It was the *Gentle Comfort*! She bit into her tight fist as she pressed it against her lips, squelching her scream.

Where was Waite? Where was he? She hadn't seen him at church. Oh, God. Oh, God! Was he on board when it happened? Her eyes bounced here, bounced there as she ran about, searching for the brawny form she cherished. "Daddy! Daddy!" she shrieked. "It wasn't a freighter that exploded. It was the *Comfort* and I don't know where Waite is! I only know Major Fairbanks said the ship was having some work done to her decks over the holidays. Have you seen him? Tell me. Tell me!"

Michael saw the panic in his daughter's wide eyes highlighted by the glow of fire reflecting in their depths. "Here now, darlin'. Calm yourself. Come with me. We'll go to your mother. You remain with her until I find some answers."

"Daddy, you don't understand. I can't wait. I have to stay with you. I have to!"

Michael did understand. He understood clearly from the fear in his daughter's voice. "Yes. All right, angel. All right. You must be brave, braver than you've ever been or thought you could be. Do you take my meaning?"

Breelan nodded slowly, looking deep into her father's mind. "I understand."

Michael and Breelan walked hand-in-hand to where women worked among the bodies lying on hard packed Front Street that paralleled the river. They watched the amateur nurses from around town apply soft linen rags soaked in limewater, linseed oil, and laudanum to relieve the pain of the few still breathing. Michael peered into each prone face, covered and uncovered. Lifting the last blanket of the two dozen or so there, his own breath ceased.

His daughter observing, took the corner of the wool cover from her father. She dropped her gaze. The victim was very badly burned and unrecognizable but for the opened eyes. Her stomach took a tumble and she ignored it. She knew this person by the sky-blue orbs staring at her. It was Catfish, Waite's oldest friend. But it was not Waite. It was not Waite. Her knees gave way and she fell across the body of a man she didn't really know. Breelan wept for Waite's loss and for her own relief.

And while she wept, her husband watched.

"Breelan, dear. Breelan. We've found him. Come away from here, darling," she heard her mother's soft voice and felt a tender touch on her arms.

Wiping her tears with the cotton of her lace hankie, she clutched Miss Ella's hand asking, "Where is he, Mama?"

The older woman turned northeast and indicated Waite's direction with a nod. Breelan saw the only man she would ever love, heading her way, taking long deliberate steps. A crowd of sympathizers was beginning to gather round him. Neither stopping to accept condolences nor slowing his pace, he continued on. Breelan thought he was coming to her, but he ignored her as well. Walking past, he headed toward his burning ship. He halted when he saw all the blanketed forms on the ground. One by one, as Michael had done, he peered onto the tortured faces. Unlike Michael, he knew all these men. Every one. Here before him was his crew, or at least many of them. More were sleeping in the deep warm water of the Amelia River. Farley, Billy Boy. These were the lads who had sailed and served with him. Coming to the last blanket, he stared down. He wasn't sure if he had the courage to discover who lay beneath. Silent tears fell from the eyes of the bystanders as they stayed back, letting the captain deal with his grief alone, for there was no comfort they could offer.

Waite raised the cover. What he feared most was blindly looking at him. It was the scorched face of his confidant, his ally, his mate; the face of the man who had cared for him and about him for so many, many years. Waite closed his eyes tightly. Everything was gone now. His friend, his men, his ship, his livelihood, the woman he loved. Replacing the shroud over his beloved departed comrade, Waite looked out, staring into the flames of the sinking *Gentle Comfort*.

In the telling grasp to her mother's hand, Breelan revealed the depth of her sorrow for the man she watched. She knew she couldn't go to him. It wasn't her place. Michael and Trip were at her side now, and along with the other spectators, remained silent out of respect for the dead.

"Waite! Waite! Someone told me what happened. Poor dear. You all right?" Out of breath, Leona caught up with him and was hanging onto his arm like a limp dishrag. "Thank goodness you wanted to be alone. You could have been on board that awful thing." Demonstratively crying and flailing her arms, she went on and on about what might have befallen him. "Why, it could have been you, burned beyond recognition instead of one of your boys. You're beautiful face. My God! What if something hurt your face?"

He grabbed her and shook her. His words were muted as he growled, "Shut up. Shut up. Not now. Leave me be. Please, I'm begging you. Just leave me be."

He left his fiancée standing in the center of town, quite puzzled. Actually, she didn't mind as much as she pretended. She could hear a buzz of whispering now and just naturally knew empathy was directed her way. Waite had been so mean to her.

He disappeared into the night. No one followed him. No one dared.

Chapter 25 – *The Goodbye Lie* by Jane Marie

"They're here! They're here!" Jack Patrick hollered, running into the parlor, the screen door slamming behind him.

"Thank goodness. Now pay attention, everyone." Miss Ella looked about the gaily decorated holiday parlor and saw the sad expressions of her family. "We shan't say a word about it. Is that understood? Jack Patrick? "

"Yes, Mama. I wouldn't hurt Captain Taylor's feelings for anything. I'll be careful. I promise."

"Good boy. We must act as if everything is fine. I'm very sure the captain would not want our pity. So no matter how hard it is, appear as if it were a normal Christmas. Remember, it's a thousand times more difficult for him." Her lips smiled, "Merry Christmas," but her eyes were cheerless.

Michael was helping Waite up the front porch stairs. He was dusty, red eyed, and very tired. "Miss Ella. Look who I found out and about and in need of a Christmas dinner. Our good friend, Captain Taylor."

"Welcome once again to our home. It's lovely to see you," she said sincerely.

"Thank you, ma'am. Please excuse my appearance. I've been out most of the night and I'm not fit company on such a grand occasion as this."

"You needn't worry. Michael, show our guest to Jack Patrick's room."

"My room?" the boy's grin was all teeth.

"Thanks for the use of your quarters, Pat," Waite said, not realizing he'd just nicknamed the boy.

"Certainly, sir," responded a very grown-up sounding eight-year-old saluting his weary hero. Jack Patrick was not only thrilled to have the captain honor him by using his room, he liked the word quarters. It sounded very military to him. And the topper was his new name. Maybe his mother wouldn't approve, but his buddies in school would surely take to calling him Pat. He'd make certain of it. What a great Christmas present, he decided.

"Take as long as you need. Dinner won't be served for several hours yet. Would you like a light breakfast in the meanwhile? I can have it ready in a jiffy."

"That sounds pretty tempting, Miss Ella. I'll be down in a few minutes. Thank you, again." Waite was dead on his feet and Michael stepped in and assisted the larger man up the stairs.

Once out of earshot, Waite was the topic of Aunt Noreen's conversation. "Where do you think he's been? It's not right that he should be unavailable for questions. After all, it's his responsibility to contact the families of the crew. What a horrible time of year for such a tragedy. Thank goodness the boat was being repaired and no innocent passengers were on board."

Miss Ella said a quick prayer. Dear God, I don't want to embarrass Clabe or Nora. Help me find the right words to stop Noreen.

Peeper interjected her thoughts. "Noreen. If'n you don't shut your trap and start a listenin' to what Miss Ella said about not talking about none of this, I'll fill your head with mashed taters and tie a rag around your neck sos ya can't speak no more. Now, come help with supper. You can stir the boiling water or sit over there and pout. Makes no nevermind to me or anybody."

"That would sure look funny to see Ma stuffed with potatoes." Warren Lowell caught a warning look from Clabe, which was sufficient for him to cease and desist from further comment about his mother.

Changing the subject, he whined, "I wanta see what Santa brought me." When can we open presents, Ma? How much longer do we have to hold off?"

Determined to be the better person and ignore all the abuse of late, Aunt Noreen stated, "This year, we're at your Aunt Ella's house and we'll follow her schedule. You'd best do as she says."

"Yes'm," he unhappily replied.

Miss Ella appeared with a tray of fried eggs, sausage and biscuits, a cup of tea and half of a homegrown broiled grapefruit covered with a heavy sprinkling of melted brown sugar. Purposely choosing Carolena over Breelan, who was sitting near Trip, she called, "Cary, would you please take this up to Captain Taylor?"

As the older sister mounted the stairs, her descending father met her halfway. Seeing the food, he took the tray from her and said, "He's out for the count. Don't expect him to appear again before nightfall." He whispered to his wife, "Found him wandering the beach." Determining it time for happier matters, he decided everyone had been patient long enough, including himself. "Is there anyone here who'd like to unwrap their presents?"

The children and adults all raised their hands, all except Breelan.

"And don't worry about the noise, Grammy," Michael told his mother-in-law who was not certain this was the proper time. "That man won't hear a thing until he's ready to re-enter the world of the living. Trust me."

"If you say so, Michael." Grammy nodded and watched her solemn-faced granddaughter trying to put the tragedy of it all from her mind.

Once gifts were exchanged, the house was tidied of wrapping paper and ribbon. Following the traditional dinner of roast turkey, the ladies did the dishes while Michael picked the bird. Apart from eating, it was his single contribution to the annual feast. As he separated the white meat from the dark, he made certain he didn't break the pulley bone which, when dried, would be much needed for good wishes. Anticipating the mouth-watering sandwiches he would consume when he went down to the kitchen for his midnight snack later, he occasionally tossed a scrap to Monstrose. The larger than normal cat was uncharacteristically waiting patiently under the table, but only because his furry tummy was as near to bursting as his master's. Both Jack Patrick and Warren Lowell had been feeding him and Blackie-White-Spots all during dinner.

"Mama! Jack Patrick's done it again! Look at the angels," Carolena whimpered.

Miss Ella crossed the parlor to the mantle and rearranged the porcelain kissing-angels, placing them in their proper posture. Her son's running game was to turn the cherubs back to back. He didn't mind the angels. It was the kissing and puckering part he couldn't abide. How many more years would it be before he'd be doing the same to some little gal of his own, his mother wondered.

"Bree, you're mighty quiet," Peeper noticed, addressing the new bride in deep green taffeta. "Did ya eat too much of my punkin' pie?"

"No, ma'am. I'm fine."

"My wife is concerned for the captain, upstairs. Seems they got to know one another pretty well on her trip to New York. Isn't she the nicest girl to be so worried about his well being?" asked Trip sweetly. He took her hand and kissed it.

Breelan was really surprised by his remark. He sounded sincere, but what wrath would befall her when they got home? Right now, she didn't much care. All she could think of was Waite. What would become of him now?

"If you will all excuse me, I must run to town. I have one more present to collect for Breelan."

"What?" asked Peeper. "All the stores is closed."

"Yes, ma'am. But this isn't a store bought present. I'll be back before long." Trip dashed out the door and rode off in the buggy before Breelan had a chance to respond.

"I can't for the life of me imagine what he's after." She surveyed her booty from him: perfume, a pair of white knit gloves with tatted cuffs, an ink pen, and a leather pouch for her writer's notes. He'd been very thoughtful. She in turn had purchased for him a wall-mounted mirror on a crisscross extension, which she felt was quite appropriate. His was the only gift she'd paid for. She had knitted sweater vests or scarves for everyone else, working since last Christmas to complete them all in time. Trip once asked her if she were knitting baby clothes - but only once.

Michael came to his middle girl and offered her a chestnut from the long-handled pan in which he'd been roasting them over the fire that had been blazing since sundown. Careful not to burn her fingers, she accepted one. Together, father and daughter silently cracked shells and nibbled the nutmeats after dipping them in melted butter.

"Breelan, don't drip that greasy mess on your dress now," cautioned Aunt Noreen.

"No, ma'am."

"Don't you think my child has enough sense not to let that happen?" Michael scowled at his sister.

"Really, Michael. I was just looking out for her."

"You were just meddling as usual. If I've asked you to butt out once, I've ..."

Miss Ella hurried to the pump organ, "Come on. Let's all sing *Deck the Halls.*" Welcoming the distraction, they all sang for a spell, but gradually the others fell away, preferring to let her sing alone.

Peeper passed cups of eggnog while Grammy assisted Warren Lowell and Marie in creating thank you notes from potato stamps carved into moons and comets. These were dipped into blackberry juice, then pressed onto colored paper. At least that was what Warren was doing. No one was quite sure what Marie's intentions were.

Jack Patrick was still for a time, fascinated with the new picture book sent to him by Aunt Coe and Uncle Fries. It contained real photographs of real people. "Hey!" he declared in awe. "Boys from Ohio look just like me, Mama!"

"Yes, dear. Isn't that something?"

"What's funny about that?" he asked, irritated when everyone else in the room got to chuckling. Adults!

Uncle Clabe reread last week's *Florida Mirror* and Aunt Noreen peeled an orange from her stocking, commenting that this year's crop had too many seeds. Nora and Will took turns shaking and looking through the viewing glass that magnified the tiny sea shells, sharks' teeth and flower petals it contained. Carolena gazed out the window, watching for her sister's handsome husband, and trying to guess what other gift he was bringing.

"Good evening everyone. Let me apologize for the late hour. I must have been worn out to sleep through dinner."

All the ladies but Breelan rushed to the captain, assuring him they understood, to take no mind of it, and could they fix him a plate? They scurried off, each fussing, wanting to spoil the man.

He stepped into the parlor to sit near the fire and held his open palms toward the heat until the flames stimulated a horrible recollection of the previous night. Waite turned his back and walked to the sofa.

Michael and Clabe exchanged small talk, mentioning everything they could think of except the one thing that was on all their minds. Clabe continued his tale. "Yes, my Pa got so mad when the alarm clock woke him up two hours early, he threw it out the window. When he got home that night, he worried how he'd get up on time the next day without the clock. So carrying a torch, he scoured the yard and bushes until he found it. Trouble was he could only get the dang thing to work by laying it face down in a pan of coal oil!"

"How did he discover that?" asked Michael, temporarily engrossed in the mystery.

"I never did hear that part of the story!" The brothers-in-law laughed, holding their too-full bellies.

Breelan watched Waite pick at the tray of food balanced on his lap. He didn't seem to notice she was even in the room. She wanted him to glance her way, to reassure him without words, to let him know she was there for him. But if he did look at her, they both knew it would be a lie. She couldn't comfort him. She was not allowed to.

"Everyone! Close your eyes! Especially you, Bree," Trip called out, eager to present his gift. He was so enthused he didn't acknowledge Waite had joined the family.

The front door to slammed shut and feet shuffled. Breelan could hear her husband whispering, yet she couldn't make out what was being said. As instructed, she didn't peek.

"You can all open your eyes now. Merry Christmas, Breelan!"

There before her was a small boy! He was about Jack Patrick's age, maybe a little older and well dressed in a brand new jacket, trousers, and shirt with a cherry red bow tie. He politely held his cap in his hand and smiled sheepishly at her.

"Breelan, may I introduce your new step-son, Roy Clelland IV?"

"What? Roy Clelland IV?" She didn't believe her ears.

"You're darn tootin', ma'am," and the boy offered his hand.

Not hesitating, she shook it and studied the child, trying to gather her wits. He had the same slim bone structure and blue eyes as her husband, although his hair was a shade or two darker. "How do you do, Roy? Merry Christmas," she said tenderly.

Stunned, the adults in the room looked on. Peeper felt her heart move over in her chest from the astounding news.

Even Will looked somewhat surprised to see his friend's son, Waite noticed.

"God bless you, child," was what Grammy found to say.

"Hey, sis? Can me and Warren Lowell and him shoot my new marbles? It's always better with three playin'." Leave it to Jack Patrick to break the tension.

"Well, yes, I suppose so." She paused and added, "So long as it's alright with his father."

"Sure, you go on. This is your new family now, son," and Trip hugged the boy to his side.

Michael picked up the conversation. He could see this was a severe jolt to his Breelan. "Lieutenant," Michael said, angry with Trip that the family knew nothing of this man's previous history. "Tell us about the lad's mother, if you'd be so kind."

"Maybe it's better Trip privately explains the details to his wife." Miss Ella feared her husband would loose his temper all together for having this responsibility so abruptly thrust upon his daughter.

"It's fine, ma'am. I have some explaining to do, I know that. Shall we all sit down?"

Everyone found a place, some morbidly curious, all personally affected.

"While I was stationed out west at Fort Smith in Arkansas, I met and married a fine woman." Seeing the boys in the corner, he lowered his voice. "Or, at least, I thought she was fine. After our son there was born, while I was on maneuvers, she ... let's simply say she was not a faithful wife. Never did understand how a person could change so. Be nice one minute and evil the next. Anyway, I couldn't have my boy growing up around all that bad talk about his mother. That's when I asked for a transfer. They sent me to Washington, D.C. We moved, but it didn't change her. She was still a runabout. With no alternative left, I was fixin' to get a divorce ..."

Nora's mouth fell open in fascinated shock.

Trip continued. "I was sure I had grounds to get custody of my son. I can tell by your faces you're all stunned."

"That's an understatement for damn sure," cursed Michael.

This time, Miss Ella didn't even think to correct him.

"You see, I was going to call on our family lawyer in Connecticut concerning the legalities. It was on that very trip, I met Breelan. Also on that trip, I was wired the boy's mother had been murdered." Gasps, one after another, stole the air from the room. "They suspected it was some old beau she was readying to throw over. He'd hit her on the head with a burning log, then turned a gun on himself."

Losing her senses, Aunt Noreen put her head in her lap as best she could, considering her middle took up a generous portion of that lap. Grammy and Peeper listened carefully, judging each syllable.

"I felt I didn't need a mourning period before I remarried because my entire horrible marriage was little more than that anyway. I was legally free to marry once I was a widower. I didn't want to bring melancholy to Breelan at our wedding, so I didn't say anything. My boy's been off at boarding school in South Carolina. He's ridden the train for two days to be with us this Christmas. I hope all of you will forgive me not telling you sooner."

Breelan spoke, "We can discuss this later. Right now, we'll feed Roy and have no more talk of it. Let's remember the reason for this holiday, shall we? The world was saved by a newborn son. I think the least we can do is welcome a child in need of some family love."

The women were on their feet before the last of Breelan's words were uttered. They hugged Roy, jostling him away from his game and into the kitchen in search of some of Michael's freshly picked turkey.

Waite's boundless admiration for Breelan was interrupted.

"You-who. Merry Christmas! May I come in?" came a sing-songy voice, seeking a self-initiated welcome.

What next? Breelan couldn't imagine the nerve of the woman. Then again, she could.

"Merry Christmas all!" called Leona. "Waite is here, isn't he? Where is my poor baby? He needs me so. Waite Taylor, you naughty fellow," she reprimanded when she saw him. "You went off last night without a goodbye. Why, if I hadn't seen Lieutenant Clelland there from my hotel window a while ago," she smiled, nodding in his direction, "and he hadn't told me you were clear out here, I would have worried myself sick, not to mention, I would have had to spend Christmas night all alone."

Peeper had heard stories of this woman and with her typical warmth, commented, "We'd best be getting' out the straight razor. We gotta slice the turkey thinner."

Unaware - or uncaring - of the antagonism toward her, the intruder imparted a simpering baby whine. "Now that Miss Leona is here, she'll take care of her special boy. Don't any of you worry about that." And she hurled a deadly glare at her rival across the parlor.

Breelan's expression matched the rest of the women in the room. Their unspoken response was simple. Poor Waite.

Another year was passing and as they did annually, the clan gathered on New Year's Eve, this time at Duffy Place. Aunt Noreen had invited Waite. Uncle Clabe, bewitched by Leona, personally invited her. "They're a unit these days," he'd said. "Almost considered one since they're engaged. We can't very well have him over without her. Besides, she'll be a comfort to the captain." As such, aunt felt charitable and uncle felt daring.

Breelan accepted Waite's continuing presence. Her family had developed a strong affection for him and she was glad because he needed friends. More importantly, he needed a family and her family was the best there was. Her trials couldn't hold a candle to his, so she bucked up as best she could whenever he was around.

The evening meal of ham, sweet potato casserole, and black-eyed peas for good luck in the coming year was a group effort. Jack Patrick had learned a new blessing and pleaded with his aunt for permission to say grace. Always happy that her relatives took their religion seriously, Aunt Noreen readily agreed.

With everyone seated, all hands clasped to form a circle around the table. Jack Patrick began:

We thank You for our daily feed.
Now open wide.
Eat all you need!

Eyes glared, lips thinned to tight lines, teeth gritted. Michael excused himself, shoved the heavy chair away from the table, and escorted his son outside into the dark night and away from the open windows. There was little sense in upsetting the ladies further with the sounds of a boy being severely scolded on the last day of the year.

The countdown to midnight was ticked off in unison with the swinging pendulum of the Duffys' grandfather clock. When the hour struck, Trip took Breelan tightly in his arms. His kiss was grinding.

Waite saw the performance, pointedly demonstrated for him and looked away, the sight leaving him angry and half sick. Leona's reaction was the opposite of her fiancé's. It left her wanting to out-do the marrieds. She threw her arms around Waite's neck, pulling him down to her, and passionately smothered him with tiny, loud, smacking kisses.

Bewildered by the noise, Breelan broke loose from Trip and watched the spectacle. She tasted bile and swallowed it back, governing her hands at their sides. With no effort, she could reach over, grab a handful of fluffy blond hair, yank, and have a grand souvenir of her hatred for Leona Visper.

"Breelan, there's someone over there who could use a hug from his mama," Trip suggested, causing a wave of guilt to wash over his wife.

"Oh, of course. I'm new at this mothering business. I'm sorry, Trip." She hurried to Roy who was sitting quietly on the floor near the hearth and hugged him tightly. It did her heart good to hold a child. Looking at him, she saw the dark circles under his eyes and could see he'd had all the late night he could stand. Jack Patrick and Warren were already curled up on the sofa, the well wishing from everyone not disturbing their slumber.

When Michael finally got the chance to embrace Breelan, he whispered in her ear, "Your little brother told me it was Roy who put him up to saying that irreverent blessing - for an aggie marble, no less. Then, I caught Roy smelling the seats of the dining chairs after we'd eaten, telling Jack Patrick that Uncle Clabe had sat here and Grammy, there. It's comical really, but we can't have it. Looks like you'll have your hands full. Thank goodness you've had a lot of practice with your brother's shenanigans."

"Roy surely would be a challenge to raise, but I won't get the opportunity to find out. Trip told me today his son will be returning to school in a few days. I tried to talk him out of it. Told him the boy needs family around him, but he wouldn't hear of it. Said he needed discipline. I thought he sounded awfully harsh, yet after all this, maybe Trip's right. I don't know. I don't know much of anything anymore," she said half to herself.

Michael patted her cheek and turned to his mother-in-law to exchange best wishes.

Breelan looked for Nora and saw through the front window that she was sitting on the joggling board close to Will. The two rocked from side to side on the long bowed courting board. Maybe he did care for her cousin. He was certainly attentive enough. Perhaps he deserved a second chance. Here was another thing she didn't know much about. Her list was lengthening.

Leona was at the piano playing *Auld Lang Syne*. Aunt Noreen and Peeper passed steaming mugs of Smoking Bishop and the scent of the spiced wine filled the room. A toast was raised and cups clinked.1883 had begun.

Chapter 26 – *The Goodbye Lie* by Jane Marie

"Oh Nora, when was the last time we were alone like this? I've missed you somethin' fierce!"

"Me too! Me too! Remember how we dreamed together under the magnolia last summer, dallying with the minutes of our lives, wondering what escapades we'd enjoy away from home? Well, now you're Mrs. Trip Clelland and I'm soon to be Mrs. Will Akins." Nora continued her stroll up the beach as if her proclamation was a mere comment upon the heat of the day.

Breelan expected her cousin's announcement, just not quite this soon. With a smile on her lips, "Have you two decided when the ceremony will be?" she began. "What did your folks say? How many bridesmaids will you have? Will you wear your mother's gown? We have so much planning to do. I'm thrilled for you! For you both!"

Nora loved Breelan's enthusiasm. She didn't want to admit she had a doubt or two. But then every bride worried a little. "First off, it goes without saying you'll be my matron of honor. We'll marry here in St. Michael's Church, of course. And with a few tucks in the side seams and darts, I think my mama's dress will fit fine. I haven't told her or Daddy yet, Bree. You're the first."

The girls stopped on the sand and embraced. They realized growing up was separating them more every day physically, yet they were becoming closer in their hearts.

"Tell me about your life, Bree. I miss hearing the details." Nora anticipated a few exaggerations in her cousin's response. Seeing her with Trip was always quite a show. They both thought everyone believed they were happy together. Although Trip spoke of his adoration for his wife, he was troubled. And his torment had become Breelan's. No, Nora didn't expect much of a truthful answer and after hearing a short, unconvincing dissertation on the joys of wedded bliss, she asked the only real question that mattered. "Bree, have you heard from Captain Taylor since New Year's Eve?"

Unconsciously, her companion's pace slowed. "No. Only talk around home that he and Daddy are making plans to design and build another ship. Since the *Gentle Comfort* was insured, financing won't be a problem. They're going to do it right and spare no expense. The new ship should be grand, but Daddy says the life has gone out of Waite. He's near inconsolable at the loss of his crew, especially Catfish. That man was his second father. Ya know," she went on with her unbroken monolog of concern for the man Nora knew she really loved, "Daddy told us he's talked with the sheriff since the investigation and his office concluded it was sabotage. Something about a deliberately jammed pop-off valve. Pressure built up, had nowhere to escape and just blew the whole blessed thing apart." She emitted an odd little laugh thinking how the same was done to Waite's life.

"At least he's engaged."

"Ha, he's engaged to Leona Visper. She's pretty, I guess, but her heart is cold, Nora. Marriage to her would be like jumping off a cliff into a shallow lagoon. The water is inviting enough from a distance. You'd better watch out though. Once you've leapt, there's only suffering ahead." Breelan's cheek tickled and she was surprised to wipe away a small tear.

Breelan hoped Nora hadn't noticed, but she had. And there was no comfort Nora could think to offer. Maybe talk of babies. Babies always warmed a body.

"A cold heart is one thing you don't suffer from. Why, when the tiny ones start coming, you'll be the very best of mothers. You'll have more help from the women in the family than you can shake a stick at. Do you want a boy or a girl? I imagine after that short, intense spell with young Roy, you'd probably like a little girl. I think little girls with long locks are the most adorable creatures. I can't wait until Will and I have a family. Gee Bree, I thought for sure that you'd be expecting by now. Our children will grow up together and be the best of friends just like we are. We're all so lucky."

Breelan couldn't stand to hear any more. She'd revealed too much of herself to Nora already. Though she also understood it would stay with Nora, she didn't want to continue this particular conversation. "Look up yonder," she said nodding toward the white object at the edge of the water. "It's a jellyfish. And a mighty big one at that. I'd hate to have stepped on it in the water. How dreadful!" They both shuddered at the very idea.

Meandering along the beach, eyes directed downward to spot sharks' teeth, each was lost in her expectations and anxieties. Nora was the first to lift her gaze. She threw her arm out in front of her cousin, stopping her from advancing another step.

"Did you find one?" Breelan asked. "You stinker, you have the keenest vision for picking out the tiniest teeth. What's your secret?" Breelan squinted over at Nora, the sun shining in her eyes. Nora was pale, deathly pale. "Darling, what's the matter? What is it? Tell me," Breelan pleaded. Nora could only stare.

Breelan followed the direction in which her cousin was gawking. There was no large jellyfish on the shoreline. Dear God! It was the bald head of a dead man, the rest of his body buried to his neck in the sand! The incoming waves pounded against his face, tilting his head backward, forcing his mouth open in a grin of horror. The wide eyes stared blankly out to sea, frozen in terror at the realization of the inevitable. Patches of flesh were gone from the skull where tiny sea creatures had nibbled when the tide was higher. Never had the girls seen a sight so gruesome. Who could do this to another human being? Who was this poor man? The outgoing waves washed the sand away from the pathetic creature's shoulders, slowly freeing his hairy, lifeless arms.

Nora finally spoke. "We've got to get help, Bree! Come on, before I'm sick. Come on!" She turned to run back to their waiting horses.

This time it was Breelan who stopped her cousin. "Nora. Nora!" Her panic increased with each word she spoke. "I know this man! I know him!" She had difficulty breathing now. "He's the monster from the Birch Bark Inn! The one who attacked me! The one I bit on the arm!" And she pointed to the purple cavity, now shriveled, but clearly visible on the right forearm of the corpse before them.

While Breelan and Nora slept in Breelan's old room at Dunnigan Manor, drugged to slumber by the potent shots of brandy their fathers had insisted they drink, the men and friends of the family spoke of the murder. Piecing together the grizzly details, some wondered if it were coincidental or connected in any way to the sinking of the *Gentle Comfort*. Since Breelan knew the identity or at least recognized the man from New York, many figured it likely he was somehow more than an innocent victim.

"I cannot pass judgment on any of this," commented Major Fairbanks. "Naturally, I have my own theories. In my position as editor of the paper, however, it wouldn't be prudent for me to speak such in public. I must remain unbiased."

"Shit," Uncle Clabe looked about for his wife, making sure she was still in the kitchen. He was in no mood for one of her vulgarity lectures. "I can understand you can't say what you feel, George, but I freely state I believe the two incidents could be linked. Why else would that ruffian be clear down in Florida? "

"I've already heard that some may not be coming to church Sunday next because of what's happened," Father O'Boyle worried. "I don't want this evil deed interfering with the souls of my parishioners. It's bad enough that one brother has found his Maker in such a horrible fashion."

"Back up, Father," Michael challenged. "That so-called brother you speak of assaulted our Breelan and I, for one, won't call him anything other than the devil's disciple! I'm glad he's dead and I hope he's in hell. I would have killed him myself if I'd had the chance."

"Michael, you don't mean that."

"Then you don't know me as well as you think you do, Padre." He turned from the priest. "I'm inclined to agree with Clabe. Breelan said the dead bastard was a dirty drunkard of a man. Her first impression was he would only be motivated by money. Since Captain Taylor has never seen him, I conclude he's merely a hireling. If that's the case, who would have put him up to it? And why?"

"May I state the obvious?" asked Will. "The saboteur of the *Comfort* has a grudge against Captain Taylor. Enough of a grudge that he was willing to destroy the man's ship. Willing to not only kill him if he were on board that ship, but also willing to let the entire crew perish."

In the corner of the front room, the priest made the sign of the cross.

"And if what we surmise is correct," Trip took over, "he's still out there somewhere. Still able to give his orders, although it now appears he murders his own henchmen to keep them from talking. I'd say it was a recently formed alliance, probably based on cash. Captain Taylor sits there in the eye of this hurricane, pondering our opinions, but offers nothing." Then looking directly at Waite, "I'm not saying any of the disruption is of your making."

Michael put his hand on Waite's shoulder, feeling the muscles in his back tense at the unspoken inference.

Trip finished his thought. "But there's someone out there who has a hankering to cause you great grief, let alone, wants you dead."

Waite drained his glass of whiskey, his eyes not leaving the face of the blonde lieutenant. He couldn't let this last pass. "You're standing mighty close to the horse's head, son," he counseled, alerting Trip he was walking a dangerous path. The tension was obvious to everyone. Not waiting for a response from the seething soldier he'd warned to back off, Waite spoke his piece. "To the rest of you gentlemen, I can only tell you, I've been no saint over the years. I've never pretended to be. For the life of me, though, I can't think of one person I've knowingly wronged or of any difference I've left unresolved. I may not always agree with a man nor him with me, but he'll know my feelings on a subject, like it or not. He'll know." Adding, "I clean up my own scrapes." Reflexively, his finger followed the path of the saber scar across his cheek. "My concern now is that nothing more happens to endanger your homes or your people."

"We all rather hoped you'd begun to think of Fernandina as your home, too, Captain," said Father O'Boyle. A rumble of agreement crescendoed through the parlor.

"Thank you, Father. This is a fine place, and I'm proud you're all so warm and welcoming to me." Saying this, he watched Trip clench his jaw with envy.

"A fine place or not," Michael interjected, "I recommend to a man that until this is behind us, we should be on our highest guard. If we're smart and it's possible, we shouldn't ride out alone at night. And, of course, the ladies are to be warned, not panicked, but honestly warned. Even in the daylight, I recommend they only go out in pairs or, better yet, be accompanied by a man carrying a pistol. And everyone should stay to the main roads. Trip, I know my Breelan has her early morning routine of riding the beach. She's not to go by herself until we all feel it's safe."

Trip didn't want any instruction from his wife's father, especially not in front of these men. Still, he withheld a sharp remark. "Certainly, Mr. Dunnigan. She will hear the word."

"That goes for Nora and her mother, Clabe. Have your man, Joey, go with them."

"I've already spoken with him, Michael."

"Good. Now gentleman, I think it best you retire to your own homes to secure your property and your persons most dear."

 Grumbles of good evening and the whirl or two of spinning revolvers followed the men out onto the veranda and down to their mounts.

"Clabe, let Nora stay over tonight. I'll be here and Clover's out back. She's just now got settled. We shouldn't disturb her. Her quiet dreams may soon enough be replaced with nightmares."

"You're quite right, Michael. Noreen is still in the kitchen with Miss Ella. Maybe she won't pitch quite the fit if you reassure her with me." Clabe sounded like a man who couldn't handle his wife. That was because he couldn't. He was worn out from trying. "I'll wait for you in the kitchen."

"Trip, you and Will might as well say good night. You heard what I told Clabe. The girls will be fine here."

"That will work out for everyone, Mr. Dunnigan," Will explained. "We have to be up at sunrise, ready for duty. Goodnight, sir. Oh, and please give my warmest regards to Nora for me, would you?" The young soldier's face reddened with his remark. He'd soon be saying such endearments as a matter of course once he was married, so he'd better get used to it.

"Certainly, Will. Good night, Trip," said Michael.

"Aren't you coming too, Taylor?" Trip questioned, not hearing his father-in-law.

Remaining civil in another man's home was more important than discharging any number of retorts that flooded his brain. Waite said simply, "Michael and I need to discuss some details concerning my new ship. Good evening."

Waite's dismissal and personal address of Trip's father-in-law did not go unnoticed by Michael's son-in-law. Mr. Dunnigan had not yet given Trip leave to use his first name. The captain had the final word this night only because Trip also realized this was not a place for challenge.

Chapter 27 – *The Goodbye Lie* by Jane Marie

When the last of the visitors had gone and the houses, big and small, were buttoned up tight, Michael and Waite had a talk. The later the hour, the more liquor consumed, the more candid their words became.

"I want to apologize, Michael, for not keeping Trip away from Breelan when I had the chance on the *Gentle Comfort,*" Waite disclosed.

Her father wasn't really listening. Instead, he was making comment upon his middle child as he saw it. "I don't understand Breelan. She's the one with spirit, and it's that same spirit that gives her problems. I guarantee, if she hadn't gone off on that damn trip to New York City, you'd be my son-in-law by now. Not that insincere, primping ass she married in some fit of temporary insanity."

Waite was imbibing a little too much. Had Michael said he wished he, not Trip, were Breelan's husband?

"Crimus, that can't be quite right. If Bree hadn't gone off on that trip, hell, then she never would've met you to begin with. But then again, you met her the night of the tornado. Whew! You'll have to pardon me, boy. I think I need a little shut-eye. Lack of sleep is making me stupid." It would never occur to Michael that the problem might be drink. "See you in the morning."

Waite got to his feet with hardly a struggle and escorted the older gentleman to his bedroom. He rapped quietly on the door. Miss Ella, wrapper clutched at her throat, answered. They assisted Michael to the double bed, the beautiful bed Breelan had been so relieved to find unharmed that first night he'd discovered her. The captain removed Michael's boots, while Miss Ella loosened his clothes. She touched Waite's arm. Turning, he looked down on the small, strong face. Craning her neck, she kissed the sailor on the scar on his cheek. Their eyes held for only an instant, but in the candlelight, they exchanged the truth of his heart and the acknowledgement from hers. She was glad. He was relieved.

Closing the Dunnigans' door behind him, Waite stood in the carpeted key hall. Ahead was the door to Breelan's room. Cracked open, it beckoned. Reason departed and instinct took over. He entered to see her lying beside her cousin, their hands clasped. They were there for each other. Breelan was nearest him. On the bedside table, an oil lamp was dimly glowing. Its purpose, he was sure, was to provide a sense of security in case the girls awakened suddenly. He crossed closer and with a weak assist from the flame, was able to study the sleeping silhouette of his princess, returning him to that time in his cabin aboard his ship. The first time he'd watched her like this. The first time he'd kissed her.

Breelan stirred. Waite startled. He left the room and descended the staircase, gripping the banister until he was back in the parlor where Michael's statement chose to reenter his brain. You'd be Breelan's husband now. Breelan's husband. Breelan's husband. Waite sat on the sofa, holding his spinning head. Damn it. Why had he drunk so much? He leaned back for a moment, just until the room and his head stopped their reeling. Waite thought about Michael's comments. Since they had become close friends, he understood Michael rarely said anything he didn't mean, drunk or sober.

Waite was awakened from a fitful sleep by a sound he didn't recognize. At first glance he was disoriented. Then, looking about at the moonlit furnishings, he recollected the earlier hours, the speculation, the concern, and the drink. He was still at Dunnigan Manor. He stretched. His shoulder had a cramp from the too small sofa that supported his too large frame. Ignoring the discomfort, he got to his feet and listened. There it was again. The noise was coming from the direction of the kitchen. The heavy oriental rugs muffled his careful footsteps, but he worried the creaking of the wooden floor might be audible down the hall. He dared not go for his gun that hung in the vestibule. It would take too much time to retrieve - not to mention the extra noise.

Four large steps and he was at the open door to the kitchen. Flattening himself against the wall, he peeked around the corner to see the bushy rump of a cat, his head rummaging beneath the white tea towel that effectively protected the next morning's muffins from night dust and bugs, but not felines. Peeper would skin Monstrose if she could catch him, Waite guessed. He had to chuckle to himself at the picture of this furry master of the house. At least to the cat, he was the master. And Waite suspected that probably to everyone else in the family, he was, too.

Advancing to the table, Waite hoisted the flabby feline in the air, brushing the crumbs from his fat belly. The cat had finished dining, so he allowed the intrusion. Waite could hear his rumbling purr and feel the tickling vibrations from the fuzzy throat against his palm. Heading for the front door, he whispered, "Mr. Monster, I'd say it's about time I leave this wonderful home of yours for a while. You're a lucky boy, I hope you know that."

In the dark, Waite collided with someone. A ball of fur yowled and with claws unsheathed, pushed away from Waite's body with its powerful hind legs. "What the ...? Why you mean old ... !" was the big man's cry at

186

the nasty scratch. Instantly, he felt foolish for cooing sweet sentiments to a male cat in the shadows of a house not his own and, worse yet, crashing into God knows who. He struck a match and almost fell into the shimmering blue eyes that focused on him. It was Breelan. "Are you all right? I'm so sorry, Bree. Being startled by some strange man in your family's house is not what you need right now. Go back to bed. I was just leaving."

She breathed his name. "Waite."

He had to listen closely to hear, her words were so soft.

"Did Monstie leave a bad scratch? I know he hurt you."

The flame burned his finger and he shook it out. Having forgotten altogether about his injury, it took him a second before he understood. "No. It's nothing, I'm sure. He's quite a boy, that one."

"Let's at least go into the kitchen and light a lamp so I can take a look."

Her concern tore at his heart. He needed to leave, but he wanted to prolong any time alone with Breelan. He'd missed her so. Doing as she ordered, he sat on the edge of the table. She took a candle from the sill, and he offered her a lighted match for it. As the flame caught the wick, they looked at one another, saying nothing while deep emotions swirled within them both.

"Let me see."

Waite unfastened each mother of pearl shirt button, growing more hesitant as the opening widened.

Breelan forgot to breathe as she watched him remove the ripped cotton shirt to expose his finely sculptured torso. At her angle of vision, his wide shoulders blocked the moonlight from entering the room behind him. His arms and belly were ripe with muscle and a soft shadow of dark hair covered his upper chest. He was magnificent to see. Breelan's lips thinned at the sight of blood that oozed from the straight, single gash running diagonally about four inches across his midriff. "Good God Almighty! Look at what that Monstrose has done! You'll have a nice scar as a reminder of his hospitality."

"I have many scars. One more will go unnoticed."

Not by me, she wanted to say. If it were possible, I'd know every mark on your body.

"It's my fault anyway. I've been warned about him, but he was purring in my arms."

"Once again, it proves that sweetness can't always successfully hide a vicious nature," she philosophized. Her thoughts were of Leona, his of Trip.

Breelan cleansed the laceration with cool water and cooking sherry. She retrieved a roll of bandages from her mother's pantry and began encircling Waite's strong frame with the soft gauze, leaning in close to reach clear around him. With each pass of the gauze, her senses took him in, savoring his every cell.

Waite's muscles were tense, but not from the pain. He couldn't relax. She was much too near. Her nightdress-covered breasts brushed his skin each time the binding wound around him. He had to look away, out into the night.

"Your shirt is ruined. I can wash and mend it for you."

He wouldn't have Breelan doing his laundry. He wasn't entitled to expect it. "It's not worth your trouble."

Washing a shirt for a friend would only be a kindly gesture. With Waite, it was somehow intimate. She longed to touch the fabric that touched him. "Please. Mama will have my head if you don't let me. You can wear Daddy's." She was up the stairs to fetch one of her father's before he could stop her.

God, what had he started? She returned quickly, a fresh garment in hand. Waite was losing control. He could take her here, here on her own family's kitchen table, burn in hell for it, and not regret a moment.

Breelan held the clean shirt tightly to her. Surprised at her own brazen stares at him, her embarrassment finally made her look away.

But she didn't want any of this to end. "This kitchen is so horribly hot." Throwing him the clean shirt, "Let's ride to the beach! I'm not supposed to go alone. When you're with me, I'm never alone. Or in danger. Please, Waite. Please, come with me." She ran to the front door not waiting for his reply.

For safety's sake, he needed to go. For his own selfish sake, he wanted to. Pushing his arms into the long sleeves of the clean shirt, Waite closed the door, hearing the satisfying click of its lock.

Breelan was already walking Noir out the long drive. Waite followed with Rory. Once she figured she was far enough away so the beat of the horses' hooves would go unheard, Breelan pulled herself onto Noir's bare back and was gone in a gallop. Waite did likewise, his horse eager to catch up. Together man and woman rode, side by side, loving the moist air, loving the salty sea, loving each other. Her intention was to ride as far south as the island allowed to stretch the distance from Fort Clinch on the north because that place reminded her of her husband.

Waite was blissful, watching her hair whip behind her, seeing the skirt of her nightdress fly wide as she rode astride, her bare ankles and calves revealed to him. He was with her and that was all he cared about.

When the land ran out, they slowed their heaving horses. "Poor baby," Breelan patted Noir's sweating neck, feeling guilty for riding him so hard. He probably didn't mind, she thought. He loved the freedom of the gallop the same as she. She dismounted and Waite did the same. They strolled the beach like any other couple in love. But both realized they weren't any other couple, and they both chose to disregard the fact.

Then he spoke. "Bree?"

How she loved the sweet sound of her name on his lips.

"I'm glad we're here. It's a privilege to be in the company of the most beautiful woman I know. You do know you're beautiful, don't you?"

"Oh, I'm attractive, I think. Maybe kind of pretty, but I'd hardly qualify as beautiful."

"Then your definition and mine are different."

"Maybe I look beautiful to you because you're in love with me, Waite."

He was startled to the core at her bold, but undeniably true remark. Suddenly, he was fiercely pleased she could speak of his love. "Yes, I adore you, but even if we were strangers, I'd still find you stunning."

She was giddy with the joy of being with him. "Am I beautiful even like this?" She stuck out her tongue and crossed her eyes.

In the pale light from the waxing moon, he laughed at the delightful girl with him.

She laughed, too. Laughed until tears trickled down her cheeks. Laughed until her laughter turned to sobs.

He reached for her and held her, supporting her light weight. "Your father told me of the murder and that you and Nora were the ones to find the body. He said you were shaken but unharmed. I wanted to come to you, to see for myself that you were really all right. Had it been any man but Michael, I'd never have taken his word. I didn't know you were staying at your parents' home until I was already there. I thought if I'd excused myself and left as soon as I found out, it might cause more talk and there's too much of that now."

"You mean talk about who killed that awful man?"

"No. I mean about your marriage."

Breelan was shocked. "What about my marriage?"

"Let's just say that some folks have mentioned off-handedly that you and Trip don't look like the two love birds he's telling people you are."

"I had no idea anyone could see we weren't happy. I thought for sure he was fooling everyone. He's so smooth and caring in public." She hesitated for a moment. "It isn't Trip who is unconvincing, is it? It's me. It has to be me. Waite, I felt sure they all believed me. I didn't want to worry my family. I've caused them enough heartache already."

"I know you're trying, sweetheart. It must be so awful for you. To be with a man you don't love. We all do what we feel we must." He looked out to sea and counted the rolling waves as they crashed on the shore.

"Yes, we all do what we ... Waite! Is that why you're marrying Leona? To stop any rumors about you and me? Of course, it is! You're doing it for me! If people can read me so easily, then they can undoubtedly see I'm mad about you. You're marrying her to try and quiet the talk about us!" He didn't answer. He didn't have to. They both knew Breelan's supposition was correct. It made her love him all the more for what he was willing to endure for her. "I don't want you to marry her. She's, she's self-centered and nasty, and wants you only for your magnificent body." She blushed at her remark and the remembrance of him in the kitchen, but meant every word.

"Who does that remind you of, my love?"

He was right. Leona was just a female version of Trip.

"Don't do it, Waite. Don't do it for me. Please."

He remained silent.

"Say something to me. Say you won't."

Still no answer.

"Well then, maybe you're going through with it because you really do want to marry her. She certainly does stand out in a crowd. I'll give her that. And you know why? I'll tell you why. It's because she looks so different from the rest of us. Her face is thick with cosmetics. Her dresses are cut so low you can see everything she's got to offer. And her perfume, that'll take your breath clean away. Oh, I imagine she's capable of satisfying a man. Lord knows she's had plenty of practice."

He interrupted her tirade. "You little imbecile. I never would have believed it. With all your natural beauty, you're jealous of Leona Visper."

He was laughing at her! How could he laugh at her? "Stop it! Don't make fun of me!" She was angry and ran from him.

He watched her run several steps, enjoying her silhouette until it struck him she was trying to get away from him. He dashed after her, catching her round the waist and dragging her down upon the sand. He wasn't laughing anymore. He took her wrists and held them fast.

Breelan was shamed by her exhibition because he was right. She was jealous to the point of violence. "Maybe I am, but I can't help myself, and it's not over her looks. It's because she'll have you the rest of her life. I never will."

As he stroked her face, he felt her warm tears. God, he loved her so much. "My darling, yes. I will marry Leona. I'll do it because if I can't have my way and be with you, the very least I can do is not complicate your life further by public chatter about our love. When I marry Leona and move away once my new ship is ready, maybe you'll find some kind of mutual understanding with Trip."

Releasing her, he removed his open shirt and spread it out on the beach. She lay on it and her hair fanned around her. She reached up to him. He was poised above her, ready. She was ready, too, waiting for him. She'd waited too long. She'd wanted too long. Nothing was worth the torture of never knowing his love, never feeling his love. He lowered his body onto hers and she felt the tremor of his muscled arms as he restrained himself from grinding her into the sand. He doubted he could curb his desire much longer. He craved to taste her again. This time his kiss seared her lips with an intense physical heat. It didn't hurt her. It engulfed her with satisfaction and left her thirsting. He was so unlike her husband, the essence of him, the smell, the shape of his face in the hollow of her hands. She groped for him, lusting for more of the same.

He wouldn't stop the inevitable. Not now. He couldn't. Happily, the ribbons on her nightgown were in the front. Still, he cursed his fingers, impatiently struggling with them. Not breaking his kiss, she willingly took over the task. Once she finished, he parted the delicate fabric and placed his hand upon the curve of her breast. She listened to the tenor of the groan rising from deep within him, and her heart palpitated to the melody of it. Even through her gown, she could feel his need for her.

"You can't know how badly I've wanted you to hold me like this. You're the only man I require. I'll ever require. The only one."

Her compliment exploded in his brain. Sonofabitch! How could he loose complete control like this? Again. Why did he allow himself this sweet fancy, then pay with the inevitable denial of pleasure of it all? He knew the answer. Because it was Breelan. The woman he loved. He kissed her again. He had to burn this image of her into his memory. Forever. He pulled back then.

"You're married and I'm engaged," he said over her, his breath fanning her lips.

"To hell with them both. It doesn't matter to me." She sat up and rubbed against him, driving him to madness with every teasing movement. "And if you're still worried I'll get pregnant, I won't."

"Of course, you might. You know that."

"No. I won't because I can't." Grabbing hold of his neck, she kissed him hard, refusing to starve her appetite for him.

Clasping her shoulders in his hands, he held her off. "What do you mean?"

"I mean I don't care about anything, but you making love to me."

"No. You said you can't get pregnant."

"We can see one another and need never worry about complications again. Maybe it's a blessing."

"Breelan, you know you want children more than anything. And I know it, too. Why are you sure you can't have any?"

"Why are you spoiling this for us?" she screamed at him. "Why should we talk of serious matters now?"

"Because what almost happened here is deadly serious."

"I don't care, I tell you! I don't care." Her words faded away as she curled herself into a small, tight ball.

He wrapped his arms around her and lifted her onto his lap. For a long while, he listened to her wracking sobs.

Finally, "I didn't think it would matter to you. Not you."

"What, darling?"

"My not having babies. I hoped you would love me in spite of it."

His heart twisted at her pain. "It doesn't matter. I swear before God, it doesn't matter to me. I love you for you. And because you love me so fiercely. No one has ever loved me like you do." He tried to remember some of the women in his life over the years. There was no hint of comparison. "Please, tell me. Why are you convinced you can have no children?"

She wanted to tell him the truth, but the thought revolted her.

He insisted. "Tell me."

She swallowed twice. "Because Trip is constantly at me."

His brain took a peek into hell.

"And I'm not yet pregnant."

"Maybe it's him."

"It can't be. You met his son. No, it's me. There's something wrong with me. I'm sorry, Waite."

He shook her hard. "As long as you live," he was livid, "don't let me ever hear you say there's something wrong with you! Do you understand me? Do you?"

She was whimpering. "Yes,"

Realizing his harshness, he cried, "Did I hurt you? I'm sorry. I'm so sorry."

"Shh. You didn't hurt me. You could never hurt me."

They sat under the stars and watched the clouds change shapes to darken the night and then expose glimpses of the Man in the Moon tittering down at them. He, at least, was not taking their dilemma any too seriously. He obviously has matters of greater import to contend with, thought Breelan. But to her, this was everything. She hid her face in the contours of Waite's hard chest to enjoy the tickle of his hair against her cheek. Her life was a knot and she couldn't find the free end to begin its untangling.

"I remember when we were little. Daddy would take us out to the beach at night. We'd watch for sea turtles laying their eggs. They must have wanted babies very much because they really struggled up the sand. Their efforts to lay eggs seemed so great and selfless. I remember the tears in their eyes, Waite."

"It's all right."

"No, I mean real tears of agony. Or were they tears of knowing they'd never see their own babies? The little ones would hatch while their mothers were out to sea. The mothers would never lay eyes on their own children. At least, they'd have the joy of delivering them. I never will."

She was doing it again! Feeling sorry for herself. She dried her eyes with her hem. They should be talking about him. She wanted to try and share his pain somehow. He'd lost so much more than she had. Taking a deep breath and expelling her selfishness, "Waite, what can I do to help you?"

"Your being here with me like this is more support than you can imagine."

"It's precious little. I'll never understand the depth of your anguish at the loss of so many of your friends. Please, please know I pray for you. I hope time fades the memory of your disaster. A lesser man would have been destroyed by all this. The man I love is strong. He'll survive. Look how you and my father are already working on your new ship."

"Yes, Michael Dunnigan is a good man." Waite smiled and Breelan kissed his beautiful mouth, sharing his feelings. In the short time the two men had known one another, she'd watched a deep respect develop between them, something her own husband and father would never have.

Thoughts of Trip reminded her of Leona. "Waite? Would you tell me something if I asked? It isn't really any of my business."

"There isn't a thing I would hold back from you, Breelan. What do you want to know?"

"Do you get as" she searched for the word, "as aroused with Leona as you do with me?" There. She'd needed to know for so long.

"Breelan Dunnigan!" Waite innocently forgot that she had a married name.

"I'm embarrassed to ask you, but I want to know. And the truth, please."

"No, I don't." He would say no more. Not because he was too much of a gentleman to discuss this subject with a lady. It was because there was no real comparison between the two women. He desperately wanted to physically prove it, yet he really didn't need any proof. The difference was love.

"If I can't stop you, and you're determined to do this foolish thing, marry her. I mean, I hope your life as her husband will be more fulfilling than mine is as Trip's wife. Everybody knows Leona isn't good enough for you. On the other hand, she'll be entertaining. And she can give you all the babies you want. Be happy, my darling. Just be as happy as you can."

There was goodbye in Breelan's words. He felt it and for the first time, too, he felt the cool spray blowing off the ocean as the breeze shifted direction. The touch of the seawater roused his common sense, enough so that he was able to admit there was nothing more to say, and so he took her home.

Nora watched from the second story window of Dunnigan Manor as a man and woman walked up the drive leading their horses. She recognized Breelan's outline and suspected her husband was not the man accompanying her cousin. Turning, Nora crawled back into bed and curled around her pillow. In the dark, she smiled for the happy moments her sweet cousin had stolen this night and imagined the parting kiss of the lovers concealed under a coverlet of soft clouds studded with stars.

Chapter 28 – *The Goodbye Lie* by Jane Marie

'Twas an early spring evening and a spirit of renewal could be felt in the briny breeze as it tantalized some of the more fervid in the merry crowd. The Atlantic, Gulf and West India Transit Company had only six years previously erected the grand seventy-five-room Egmont Hotel at South Seventh and Beech Streets. Tonight, Michael Dunnigan and family were the proud hosts of a reception there to honor the famous architect, Mr. Robert Schuyler from New York City. Mr. Schuyler, now a resident of Fernandina, was celebrating the second year of construction of a Gothic Revival style cathedral in the downtown to be named St. Peter's Episcopal Church. The immense undertaking was set for completion in two more years and this evening's gala celebrated the halfway point. It was meant to recognize all the tradesmen who had thus far worked on the project.

The lively orchestra entertaining in the grand salon braved fierce competition from torch-lit outdoor croquet and lawn tennis. Inside, included in the game rooms, were billiards and a bowling alley. This being only her fourth time in the alley and her third time actually playing, Breelan was attempting to knock down all the smartly shaped white-and-red striped pins. Her total concentration on the game was a tall task considering what she'd witnessed earlier in the evening. Leona Visper's behavior, or rather misbehavior, had been noteworthy. Breelan had frequently noticed a speculative look on Leona's face when the woman was near Trip. Bree usually ignored the hussy since she didn't really give a hoot anyhow. But this last time was different. Leona was on Waite's arm. The chanteuse in the silvery gown cast a feline glance over her shoulder at Trip. With her hand almost but not quite hidden in the folds of her skirt, she covertly waggled four gloved fingers his way. Breelan was incensed when Trip responded with a lascivious grin. Waite apparently missed the entire performance. And he was going to marry the woman?

Breelan's left arm was becoming weary from many failed attempts to score in this bowling game. She found the weight of the black ball excessive. Unaccustomed to the crashing noise of the sport, she felt the stirring of a headache. Attempting to ignore all discomfort, physical and mental, she focused her attention on one objective - to knock down at least one of the blasted pins.

"Careful, darlin', or you'll drop that big old ball on your toe."

Startled by Leona's unexpected and disingenuous voice, Breelan did just that. The pain was awful and only Will's quick response kept her from crumbling to the floor.

"Oh, Bree! Honey! What can I do to help you?" Nora scurried over. Not waiting for any response, she ordered, "Will, carry her to that sofa over there. Then go find a doctor at once!"

"Yes, Nora." After gently setting Breelan upon the soft, wine-colored cushions, Will went out through the thick, soundproofed double doors in search of a physician.

Despite the horrible throbbing of her foot, Breelan was humiliated at having done herself such a careless injury, particularly in front of Leona.

After retrieving another glass of Chablis to help his nerves in the harried circumstance, Trip was at her side. He felt wobbly on his feet, so sat on the edge of the couch with her and skillfully balanced the glass upon his knee despite his not quite sober state.

As Nora fussed and tenderly removed her cousin's slipper, Leona tried her hardest to contain her laughter. She knew if once she smiled, she'd be a goner and would giggle uncontrollably. So instead, she sauntered over to the injured girl, feigning sympathy.

Dr. Tackett led the entire Dunnigan family into the bowling hall. The crowd surrounding Breelan grew and grew. The folks in the back, hearing the need for a physician, imagined ailments ranging from heart attack to childbirth.

Once the stocking was taken off, all parties could see purple toes adorning a slender foot. "No more dancin' for you tonight, missy, and especially no more of that danged bowling game. Seems the more the worldly-wiles come to Fernandina, the more our people get hurt." The doctor was off on one of his notorious harangues. The older gentleman liked things the way they were when he was growing up and had little use for change.

Miss Ella smelled the condition of her son-in-law. She strongly suggested her daughter be driven to the family home where the women could tend to her for a several days.

Trip didn't want to be without Breelan's warmth beside him in bed, not for one night, let alone a few days. But even with a few drinks in his belly, he decided it wasn't worth the storm he'd raise should he refuse her mother in front of her father. Pasting on a dutiful smile, he agreed.

Assured he could do no more for Breelan and that she was in the competent care of his wife, Michael returned to his guests, taking Carolena with him.

As the always helpful Will carried Breelan away to the buggy, she overheard a dreadfully sweet voice say, "Yes. We've moved into this palatial hotel, but my Waite has run off to do business. He left me all by my lonesome." Having tired of pretending to be a lady, "I'll venture we could make one another some excellent company with very little effort. Don't you agree, Trip?"

Breelan heard no debate on the subject from her husband as Leona brazenly reached up and straightened his tie. His response was to motion to the waiter for a round of drinks.

It took Breelan three days to convince Grammy, Peeper, and Miss Ella she was able to do for herself and allow her to go home. Her father asked Clover fashion a crutch from a straight oak limb, and the ladies of the house thickly padded the upper support, not wanting their girl to suffer any underarm strain or irritation.

As Trip escorted his hobbling wife to the carriage, Jack Patrick left her with one last observation. "Look there, Mama," he said pointing to her bruised extremity. "Bree looks like Peeper, the way she carries on about her feet always being swole up."

"Jack Patrick! All I can tell you, my boy, is it's a very good thing Peeper didn't hear you make such a disrespectful remark or she'd clobber you like a long-tailed rat!"

"I didn't mean no disrespect, Mama."

"Any disrespect is correct, son."

"Yes, ma'am. Any disrespect. But Peeper is always saying her feet hurt her, isn't she?"

"You're running out of wiggle-room, young man. Now carry your sister's bag to the buggy."

"Yes, ma'am." Jack Patrick was forever getting a scolding and could never quite figure why. What he'd said about Peep was the truth. Once he'd transported the valise to the carriage as his mother requested, his thoughts strayed to spending the night at Warren Lowell's house. It would be fun, provided they kept clear of Aunt Noreen. He'd need permission, of course, so decided to ask his father, since so far today, the two of them hadn't had a fuss. But it was still early and there was plenty of time for him to get into trouble. Caution was Jack Patrick's watchword. After his sister and her husband had driven out of sight, he dashed around back of the house to chase the chickens. Then he spied Clover. "Hey, ole pard. What cha doin'?"

"Just dumpin' a little salt and vinegar on the weeds along your ma's walkway."

"Seen any slugs around?"

"Matter of fact, Pat, I did see one crawl under Grammy's backdoor hydrangea bush there. Now that was 'bout five minutes ago, so you might have to go lookin'."

Jack Patrick knew he could count on Clover to use his new nickname, at least when his mother wasn't around. "Got any extra salt?"

"All ya need."

"Thanks!" On his belly in the sand, Jack Patrick determined that a slug melting from salt was a thing of mystery. Besides, he was safe with Clover. He rarely caught any grief when they were together. As he searched for the slimy creature, he called out, "It was sure good to have Bree home for a spell, wasn't it, Clove?"

"It sure was. Real good."

Breelan had ridden away and couldn't hear what they'd said about her, but she'd noticed how her family had gone out of their way to be particularly solicitous to her while she'd stayed at the manor. Even her little brother had tried not to holler so much and so often, and she'd thanked him for his efforts. The bouncing buggy jarred her foot like the devil and if she could have, she'd have stayed with them forever. But it was time to return to her wifely duties.

With some difficulty she managed to put supper on the table. Poached eggs and toast with Peeper's kumquat jelly wasn't much, but it was easy to prepare and seemed to satisfy Trip. After they'd eaten and the dishes were done, Breelan maneuvered herself with crutch out the back door, down the three wooden steps and across the small sandy yard to the barn. Noir was snorting pathetically. He'd missed the attention of his mistress far too long. Clover had been kind enough to take Noir out for a ride once while Breelan was laid up, but looking at her horse through her mother's front parlor window wasn't nearly the same as petting his velvet neck and inhaling his rich equine smell.

"Tomorrow, Noir. I've got it all arranged. Nora will ride over and help me get up on your back. We'll ride together to our usual spot on the beach. How does that sound?" He answered her with a positive whinny, or so it seemed to her, as she pulled a carrot from her apron pocket.

Breelan turned to go back inside because it was getting late. A sparkle caught her eye. Something was peeking from between the seat cushions of the buggy. Naturally curious, she reached for it and found herself holding a woman's brooch. Leona's brooch.

Breelan was in a sour mood anyway because her foot smarted, so she decided to pick a fight and spread her misery around a bit once she limped back indoors. "What have you been up to, Trip, while I've been at my folks? They wondered why you came to visit me only one of the three nights I was there."

"I told them what I've told you. I was busy at the fort. There're some top brass visiting tomorrow and the entire place is on alert for inspection. Don't you ever listen to me, Breelan?"

"Oh, I do more than you think I do."

"What does that mean?" he asked, sounding defensive.

"Only that I saw Leona wave in your direction, unbeknownst to Waite, at the Egmont the other night, and I saw her sit down at your table as they carried me out. You didn't seem to mind much."

"Why should I mind? You know I'm not overly fond of Taylor. It gives me a bit of satisfaction knowing Leona flirts with me behind his back. Besides, she's a beautiful woman and when I'm alone, she offers her company."

"Just how often does she flirt with you?" Breelan was disgusted.

"Every chance she gets."

"And I suppose you'll tell me you were fighting her off in our carriage when the clasp on her brooch broke." She presented the pin, expecting his denial.

"That's right," he responded unconcerned. "So you found it. She's been pestering me about that thing."

"I can dismiss her behavior because we all know what she is, don't we? You, on the other hand, are supposed to be an officer and a gentleman. One thing is apparent. You're sorely lacking in honor."

Trip burst out laughing! Breelan was taken aback. That was the last reaction she'd expected from him.

"Are you jealous?"

She probably did sound like a wounded, heartsick wife. "Oh bother. Think whatever you like. You will anyway."

The rest of the evening, she sat silent while he glowed with triumph. At last, he thought, she's finally come around.

Chapter 29 – *The Goodbye Lie* by Jane Marie

Reluctantly mesmerized, Leona watched Breelan through the etched glass of the girl's front door, loath to be captivated by the delicate features of the younger beauty. The celebrated entertainer felt a trickle of perspiration run between her breasts and cursed the moist dark spot it left on her lavender and white flowered bodice.

Breelan was ragged from her internal argument about whether or not to alert Waite to his fiancée's faithlessness. While her heart detailed why she should involve herself, her head commanded her to stay out of the entire affair. She huffed aloud that such an appropriate word had come to mind. The thud of the doorknocker startled her from her worries over Waite. Reaching the front entrance, suspicion was her immediate and intuitive response at seeing Leona Visper on her porch. "Yes? What is it?" she coldly greeted her uninvited visitor.

"My goodness, Breelan. May I call you Breelan? We seem to meet around every corner, don't we? You may call me Leona."

Dismissing all civility, Breelan said, "I asked you what it is you want, *Miss* Visper."

Leona could have slapped the stunning brat. Instead, she held her tongue, calling upon her plentiful acting abilities to appear at ease. "You see? I've brought you some lovely daffodils. The first of the year according to the shopkeeper. I'm hoping your foot is about healed by now."

The flowers were pretty enough, but Breelan wanted no part of them in her house. Their soft yellow reminded her of their bearer's hair color. "I can't see why you would take any notice of my health or lack of it," and she slammed her door closed, turned, and as gracefully as one could with a bum foot, crutched her way down the hall toward the kitchen.

If that's how it's to be, dearie, it's just fine with me, seethed Leona. Vehemently chucking the bouquet to the floor of the wooden porch, she thrust open the barrier blocking her entry. Closing it as quickly and none too quietly, she advanced on a shocked Breelan.

"I underestimated your crust! Get out of my house!"

"I will leave, but not before I educate you on a subject or two."

"There isn't a thing you can say that holds any interest for me."

"No? Shall we start with Waite?"

Leona had presented the perfect opportunity. Breelan could not retreat from the chance to do battle with the shrew challenging her.

The brazen blonde helped herself to a glass of sherry from the parlor tray table then settled neatly onto the stripped upholstered chair beside the opened window.

Breelan followed, expending great effort to govern the poisoned passion she was experiencing. Seating herself directly across from the enemy, she laid her crutch on the oriental carpet beneath her own chair, envisioning it a first-rate weapon, should the need occur.

"I surmised my mention of Waite would get your attention. You see, being the sensitive woman I am, I'm aware of your fascination with him. And in a small way, I emphasize small, his with you."

Breelan said nothing.

"I admit, at first, I thought his attentions might have developed into something deeper. However, you deftly ended all possibility of any liaison with him by marrying Lieutenant Clelland. I credit you completely for giving me free rein to love Waite."

Breelan couldn't remain still another minute. "You love Waite? That's an impossibility for a person like you. You're selfish, leeching and shallow. All in all, I'd have to say you're the most unappealing woman I know."

Judging the insults as empty words with no basis for truth, Leona replied, "Unappealing, you say?" Lowering her lashes coyly, "Waite finds me appealing enough to share my bed every night. In fact, he often shares it with me in the light of day. He can't have enough of me. He mentions with regularity how he so enjoys a woman of experience compared to girls who merely try and imitate the women they hope to become."

Breelan was shaken. She never imagined Leona and Waite were together every night. She admitted to herself that occasionally they must be, but every night? And in the daytime, too? Bravely overlooking the torment that was so obviously being piled upon her, Breelan responded, "Granted, he uses your body. You're his diversion. And if you're implying my life's goal is to follow in your dark, demented shadow, well, we couldn't be more different. Waite likes me the way I am. He's in love with me. He's told me so."

Leona blanched.

With a victorious grin, Breelan felt sure she'd hit a bull's eye! She was certain Leona didn't doubt for a second that Waite had professed his love to her. Suddenly realizing the gravity of what she'd said, she bit her cheek at having been foolish enough to be goaded into saying she and Waite had been together and spoken of such matters. Still, she hadn't said when they'd met, had she? She'd not disclose it was after she'd married Trip.

"When? When did he tell you?" Leona was standing over Breelan, yelling down upon her. Her breath smelled of the sherry she'd finished in one gulp.

"Tsk, tsk." Breelan shook her head. "I can see you're insecure. You'd better sit down." She spoke as if she were addressing a child. "Besides, what does it matter when he told me? If you're so confident of Waite's devotion to you, then it had to have been before Trip and I married, hadn't it?"

Breelan had her. Leona would have to admit Waite was vacillating about their marriage if she continued with her questions. Pride would not permit that. Reaching into the hand painted vase behind her, Breelan said, "Since you're here ..." She pulled forth the diamond and emerald brooch she'd found in her carriage. Tossing it at her intruding guest who deftly caught it, Breelan concluded with, "I'm telling you to stay away from Trip."

It was Leona's turn to smile as she made no attempt to deny they'd been socializing, to say the least. "Why, I'm engaged! Why would I go near Lieutenant Clelland?" Her freshly applied and unnaturally chaste simper couldn't mask her true nature, that of perpetual liar.

"God only knows why you'd seek another man if you could be with Waite." Damnation! Breelan had admitted her feelings for Waite again. She was making the situation worse, not better.

"What makes you think your husband would be interested in me? Unless, it's because he's not satisfied at home. Yes, that must be it. You see, little one, Waite is right in marrying an experienced woman."

"I believe by your definition that experience and promiscuity equate to the same thing."

Leona mumbled something unpleasant under her breath that Breelan couldn't make out. Nevertheless, the meaning was easily decipherable.

"Bottom line. Waite and I simply have no use for you now we're betrothed."

Breelan noted Leona neglected to say she had no use for Trip. "Just when will your marriage take place, Miss Visper?"

"Soon" was the last word uttered. It was followed by the slam of the front door.

In Waite's suite at the Egmont, Leona sat and fumed while he read the newspaper across the room. She was exasperated with the beautiful Breelan Clelland. If that bitch told him of her flirtations with Trip, Waite might believe her. Like most men, he'd undoubtedly throw the usual possessive tantrum, huff and puff, and go off mad. For a while. She could certainly woo him back, but such scenes were so tiresome. Leona was well schooled in that aspect of romance. Men were continually upset because of her wandering attentions. Waite, on the other hand, was different from the others. That was why she'd chosen him to marry. She must make the effort to be true, at least, until they wed. After that, it would be safe for her to do whatever she pleased. Waite would never divorce her because he'd told her once that when he married, it would be for life.

She began humming *Our Dream by the River*, humming and thinking, thinking and humming. Yes, Captain Taylor was respected, more handsome than anyone she'd ever been with, so very strong, and a wild man in bed. The last she liked best since it was the most important of all his characteristics. His other virtues were good, certainly, but his performance when they lay together was simply outstanding. Her experience as a lover of men told her she had a prize in her future husband. She was not about to turn loose of him.

"Waite, darling. Shall we sup here in your suite tonight? I'm weary of the attention I'm getting downstairs in the main dining room." She leaned over his shoulder and snatched the newspaper from his hand. "What you're concentrating on can't be nearly as entertaining as what I have planned for us this evening. Don't you think it's warm in here? How about I take a few of these suffocating under things off? You go on and order us a light dinner. I wouldn't want a heavy meal to slow you down for dessert, if you understand my meaning. Then again, nothing has ever slowed you down before."

As she slithered around his high-backed chair, Waite smelled her expensive and overpoweringly sugary perfume. She kissed him full on the mouth, inserting the tip of her tongue between his lips. He said nothing, suddenly feeling a craving for a thick juicy steak with onions. When she had gone to her own room, he walked to the gold braided cord that hung in the corner of his sitting room, tugged and patiently waited for the bellman's arrival to give his dinner order.

Checking her appearance in the mirror and splashing a few extra drops of Waite's favorite fragrance on her inner thighs, Leona was ready. Her timing was excellent. She could smell through the walls that their dinner had arrived, so she cracked open her door and peeked out, inspecting the corridor for witnesses who might see her sneak into Waite's room. She personally felt the entire game was folly. Waite, however, did not. He had stipulated discretion, so she'd obliged. What an inconvenient and utter burden it was to uphold an angelic persona in public.

Tiptoeing in her dyed rabbit fur slides, she entered Waite's unlocked suite. He was at the window, looking down upon the scurrying parade of people on their way in and out of this trendy establishment. He heard her come in and turned to see a vision in pink, so brilliant a hue that at first it startled him. Would he ever become accustomed to Leona's flamboyant fashions? Holding her chair for her, he looked down to see her smile up at him while batting her long black lashes. He'd found her to be no true blonde and imagined fleetingly how she'd look as a brunette.

"Why, Waite Taylor. I told you to have a light meal and just look here. Those imbeciles in the kitchen have given us pieces of meat so big and rare, I'll bet each would moo should we prod them with a roll."

"Leona? How did I ever get along before you?" he mocked.

Undaunted, taking him at his word, she rambled, "I don't know myself, darling. The first thing in the morning, I'll march right down to the uppity manager and let him know this is no way to be running the place. When I think of the fine service we could be receiving in New York City, and here we are, stuck in this tiny unsophisticated wilderness, with no real theater for me to perform in and ..."

"Leona," he began, "I ordered the steak. It sounded good to me. And as for us being in Fernandina, this is where my new ship is being built. You know I can't leave her until she's done. Hell, if you don't like it here, go on another trip and perform. It's fine with me. I've told you that before."

"Honey, you sound like you wouldn't even miss me. That can't be true. You'd surely miss my lovin'."

"Let's eat our dinner, shall we?"

Leona dismissed his grumpiness and resigned herself to delight in her own repartee, thinking it quite amusing. The last joke she'd told about the preacher and the dead nun had sent her into fits of laughter so loud the occupants in the next room had pounded on the walls.

Waite laid his fork aside, having uttered not one syllable during the meal. He drank the final drop of his wine, pressed the linen napkin to his mouth, slid back his chair and walked around the square table to Leona's side to grasp her firmly by the arm. She rose to stand beside him, certain his need for her couldn't wait another moment and that this just might be the best and most wickedly wild encounter thus far for them.

Speaking softly, he said, "My dear, I'm used to better than this." Accompanying her to his front door, he opened it, took in her puzzled expression, gently pushed her through then slammed it behind her!

In stunned silence, she heard him turn the key. Leona Visper was dumbfounded! There she stood, in her best frilly lingerie, locked out of her fiancé's room with people passing and staring. If they wanted a spectacle, she sure as hell would oblige. She pounded and screeched at Waite's door. He would not respond. With fists red and throat raw, she glared at the crowd gathering, gave one last piercing scream, a perfect *A* note, and entered her own room.

Chapter 30 – *The Goodbye Lie* by Jane Marie

Five days later, Breelan's bandages and crutches were gone and so were Trip and Leona, he on overnight maneuvers, she in Savannah at a singing engagement. Breelan had confirmed the songbird's travels by paying a visit to Heleen Cydling, the society editor of the newspaper. Since Miss Heleen kept abreast of all that went on in town, she concluded immediately that Breelan's deeper purpose was to gain information concerning Waite Taylor and his broken engagement, a subject on which Breelan seemed, as yet, to have zero knowledge. However, Miss Heleen had a strict policy against spreading gossip. Her source was the head housekeeper at the Egmont Hotel. Although the news was probably reliable, it would be unforgivable to embarrass Captain Taylor, if it weren't true. He was a fine gentleman who had helped her Monday last when the train's whistle spooked her horse. She would say nothing until she'd spoken with him directly.

"I'm sorry, Breelan. I can offer you no more information. You know how I feel about scattering unsubstantiated stories until I verify them personally."

"Whatever information do you think I'm trying to find, Miss Heleen?" Breelan's initial inquiry had been innocent enough. At the suggestion of other details, her mind flooded with questions.

"You mustn't play these games, dear. You're just no good at them. Leave them to the likes of Miss Vesper." Heleen's hand went to her mouth when she realized she'd spoken ill of the great lady herself. Well, maybe Leona Visper could sing, but she wasn't very nice to reporters and the elderly editor mentally refused to take back her comment.

Miss Heleen had been right, Breelan decided. She wasn't very good at stratagems. She was used to the direct approach and chose Nora as her helper. "I know Daddy will get after us if we go out alone," she told her cousin, who was spending the night with Breelan for security purposes and the peace of mind of the family. "But I must see Waite to caution him about Leona and her disgusting behavior with Trip, Nora. And, too, I have to return Waite's shirt to him."

The how, when, and where of Breelan's possession of Waite's garment was a curiosity that required discussion at a later time. First things first. "We can't, Bree," Nora told her. "It's dark already and your foot is just now on the mend. The killer or killers may well still be out there and ..."

"We have to. At least, I have to. Leona said the wedding would be soon and if he marries her without hearing my warning, I'll be unhappy the rest of my life because I know he'll be miserable with an adulterous wife."

"Bree, be realistic. You'll not rest easy ever again whether you warn him or not. You love the man, and the fact that he's to marry another will haunt you forever."

"I admit it! I do love him, but believe me when I say I'm learning to live without him. At least, I'm trying like the devil. It's okay. I'll go alone. I don't mind. Really I don't. I mean it."

Nora threw up her hands. "You win. I'll go. I'll go! Come on. Let's not dawdle. We need to get back quickly because Will said he might stop by. He'll have our heads right behind Uncle Michael and my father if he finds us gone."

"Will's not on maneuvers with Trip tonight?"

"No." Nora thought nothing more of it.

Breelan did. Was Trip really on military business as he'd said or with Leona or worse? Was he somehow involved with the death of that awful man from the Birch Bark Inn? They could have met one another when Trip awakened from his drunken stupor after their first night married. And what about the destruction of the *Gentle Comfort*? Could the sheriff be wrong? Could more than the jamming of a valve have caused the massive explosion of the ship? Could gunpowder have been used? Trip did work with weaponry of some sort, she knew. The opportunity was there. Was the motivation? His hatred for Waite ... could it be strong enough for Trip to have murdered an entire crew in order to see one man dead? Was he insane? Dear God, it wasn't possible.

Breelan and Nora checked with the front desk clerk of the Egmont Hotel, but were informed that Captain Taylor's key was not in his box. He had yet to retire to his room for the evening.

"Since we're already here, let's look around. This is such a large place. Maybe, he's in one of the game rooms."

"Breelan, do you think we should? Go into the card rooms, I mean. Someone may recognize us and tell our families."

"Quit being such a silly-billy. If we see anyone we know, we'll simply make up something, like we're looking for Major Fairbanks. Have they seen him? He was here a minute ago."

"How did I miss him, Bree? I've been with you the entire time." Nora was confused.

"Nora," Breelan replied a little exasperated with her cousin. "I said we'd make something up. The major isn't here. At least, I don't think so."

"Oh," Nora said, embarrassed it had taken her so long to comprehend the plan. She blamed it on her anxiety at being caught out after dark.

Breelan shifted the bundle containing Waite's shirt to squeeze her friend's hand. "Besides, I'm a grown up married woman, and I deem it necessary to find Waite. If you'd like to remain in the lobby while I look for him ..."

"Alone?" Nora was scandalized. "Heavens no. Someone might think I'm a street walker and approach me!"

"Sweet girl, I don't think you need worry about that happening with you in that dull gray gown."

"What's the matter with my dress?" Nora queried, insulted.

"Not a thing. It's just that women of ill-repute usually dress in clothes more daring and attention-getting."

"You mean like Leona Visper?"

"Exactly like Leona Visper."

A pleasant search through the lobby allowed the girls to enjoy the elegance of the decor, the beauty of the fresh flowers and delicious scents from the dining room. They continued looking for Waite in the bowling hall, the gaming rooms, the shooting gallery and at the outdoor lawn tennis arena. There was but one place left to look - the main drinking saloon. The dark, rich room possessed a prominent sophistication. It was filled mostly with men, which caused Breelan's to flash back to the Birch Bark Inn in New York. She shuddered at her memory of the experience.

Waite had a habit of facing the door in a public place, particularly a bar room. You never knew who or what might enter or just when. Seeing Breelan and Nora startled him. What was wrong? Something serious had to draw them out alone.

He downed his second double bourbon, folded his poker hand of three jacks and a pair of eights, excused himself from the game, retrieved his chips, and walked steadily over to the girls whom he'd naturally assumed had come for him. Keeping his voice low, "Tell me what the matter is, Bree, but let's all get out of here first. You ladies won't need any more talk than what's already started, I'll wager."

Nora smiled nervously at his unintended pun.

He escorted the girls through the front door and out onto the main veranda. They were in shadows as he turned to face his callers. His eyes settled longingly on Breelan.

Observing, Nora offered, "Captain Taylor, would it be safe for me to sit over there on that glider amongst those blooming azaleas? They're so inviting, and I'm a bit weary from our fast ride over."

"Yes, please. You rest while I speak with your cousin. I'll keep watch over you." He added, "I promise." Waite and Breelan both appreciated Nora's thoughtful consideration in such delicate circumstances.

Then looking up into the face of the man she adored, Breelan stated firmly, "You can't do it." Not and have any peace in your life."

He bent down closer and she smelled the liquor on his breath, "I can't do what, Bree? What are you telling me?"

"You can't marry Leona."

He straightened. "You foolishly dragged Nora out into the scary night to tell me that?"

She nodded, knowing he'd be grateful she cared enough to alert him, even at her own peril. I admit it was dangerous, but you have to be informed."

"Informed of what?"

"That she'll be unfaithful. She's just an old rip, Waite. I've seen her flirt shamelessly with Trip. I'm sorry to tell you, but I found her brooch in my own buggy. If she's untrue to you now, she'll certainly be disloyal once you're married."

Gazing down into the sincere eyes, he couldn't help himself. He laughed at her.

Breelan couldn't imagine why. "Didn't you understand me? You can't do it."

His expression became serious. "God Almighty. I can't believe your naïveté. You are inexperienced, aren't you?"

It was exactly as Leona had said. Had Waite spoken of her to that woman?

His tone was flat as he bent closer over her. "Do you think I'm an idiot? Give me some credit for having lived a more enlightened life than you, my dear. I know Leona is all but a woman of easy virtue."

Breelan didn't understand. What was he telling her? Her questioning expression seemed to spur his annoyance. "If you know that, why would you ever consider marrying her? Why?"

She grabbed for his arm, but he was quicker and caught her slight wrist first. "Because I'm past caring, past loving. My only desire now is to seek diversion and, like it or not, Leona is capable of giving and receiving much of that. She's never at a loss for surprises. No tangles, no complications. Pleasure on demand for us both. Need I say more?"

Breelan felt sickened. Her skin chilled against his hot palms, and he released his hold on her, stepping away. She couldn't believe he was simply a man who lived for physical gratification. She wouldn't believe it.

"Waite, I know you don't mean that. I worried you were burying your grief too soon, that no one, no matter how strong, could endure what you have and bounce back unscathed. You're broken hearted at losing so much, so quickly. It will take a while, but you'll recover and then you'll find a decent woman. One who ..."

"Damn it all!"

She raised her hand as if to protect herself from the blow of his words.

"How much clearer can I make it for you? I don't want a decent woman. I'm tired of prim and proper. I want what I want when I want it. I want wild times in my life and wild love. Hell, Leona would come to me whether I married her or not. She's a real female, unlike most. Believe me, I know first hand."

His words were meant to lance her. They hit dead center. "I've severely misjudged you, Captain Taylor. You deserve all that woman can and will give you. I won't bother you again. I apologize for my unwanted words of warning."

As Breelan and Nora rode into the clutching fog and deep night, hot eyes watched and thoughts were savage.

Chapter 31 – *The Goodbye Lie* by Jane Marie

The steaming air forced Michael to wipe his brow and it was only eight a.m. He'd been unaware of a sudden shower the night before, but as he made a morning inspection of his garden he saw the birdbath was filled to capacity. It hadn't been so when he and Clabe had taken their evening walk after supper. That was one less chore for Clover to do since Mother Nature had contributed her part toward the good grooming of her feathered friends.

Continuing on, he picked up the morning post to discover a note underneath addressed to the family in Breelan's script. Michael wondered why she was writing when he'd seen her just two days earlier. He concluded Trip must have delivered it on his way to the fort. The father of four gingerly climbed the stairs to the bedroom he shared with his beloved wife.

Miss Ella was running her ivory-handled brush through the long hair blanketing her left shoulder, the occasional sparkle of silver glinting handsomely in the sunlight washing in through the window. "Good morning, honey. Have you gone into the kitchen yet? I can smell Peeper and Grammy's breakfast. They told me they were making something special this morning, but wouldn't say what. I hope it's waffles. I love it when they make that orange butter and sprinkle everything with dark sugar."

As his wife happily chatted about the cooks in her kitchen, Michael opened the note.

"I find myself laughing about those two so often. They indulge all of us." Miss Ella glanced up to catch her husband's expression reflected in her vanity mirror. Spinning around on her padded bench, she asked calmly, "Michael, what does that letter say?"

He gave no answer.

"Michael?" She rose and walked to him. She encountered no resistance when she removed the paper from his hand. Miss Ella read a note that turned her heart to stone. Her second born had faced her own heartache and chosen to flee. Breelan had run away.

Miss Ella always thought herself hardy and handy in a crisis. Until now. She wanted to scream in the streets that her daughter was gone. Considering her husband's temperament, she knew she must keep control. He didn't need his wife dissolving into hysterics. It would only make matters worse.

"Damn it! Where did that girl go? And why? What's got into her head? Hell, no one has a completely carefree existence. Why should she be any different from the rest of mankind?"

Miss Ella wondered how many times she'd said this very thing to Michael. I've worried so over the years that our children would not be able to cope as adults because they've been spoiled when they were small. This proves me right and, dear Lord, I don't want to be right. "Michael, you've got to find Trip." he hesitated then added, "And Waite."

"I'll find Trip. You can bet on it!"

He was hiding his fear and worry with anger. It was always his way. She watched him walk to the wardrobe and grab his spare pistol from the top shelf. As he checked the ammunition, making sure each chamber held a bullet, Miss Ella crossed the room to where he stood, snatched the gun from his grasp, and fled the house. Michael followed in cursing pursuit. Miss Ella cast the weapon into the well and heard it hit the water with a heavy plunk!

Dumbfounded, Michael leaned over and watched the ripples until they disappeared. Turning to her and seeing a stunned Grammy and Peeper and Jack Patrick standing by the back door watching, he let out a long sigh. "Maybe you're right."

Clover had heard the commotion, too, and came running.

"Breelan's run off, Clove. I've got to find her. Saddle my horse, would you."

"Now why's she gone and done that?" Clover asked, expecting no answer. "Yes, sir. Want me to go along or stay here and mind the family?" Already guessing Michael's reply, Clover waited for a response, just the same.

"It's best you stay with the women and children. I'll be back as soon as I can. Hopefully with Breelan in hand."

Knowing that Nora had spent the previous night with Breelan, Michael caught sight of Joey, stacking rocks in the decorative stone fence he was making around Noreen's recently planted sunflower seeds. "Hey, Joey. Seen anything of Miss Nora this morning?"

Joey waved a greeting. "Just caught a glimpse of her riding in early this morning. Said she'd had a fine time with Miss Breelan and was going to grab a few hours extra sleep."

Since Joey didn't say anything to give Michael reason to believe Nora had any knowledge of Breelan's shenanigans, he called out a quick, "Thanks," and rode to find Trip, feeling the weight of his everyday derringer in his coat pocket. Then, it came to him. What if Waite and

212

Breelan had taken off together? He'd seen the looks that passed between them, and he understood too well those were no innocent glances. He only hoped it was emotional and not physical. You've got to be a realist about this, he told himself. What if your daughter is pregnant by a man other than her husband? She'll never be able to live a peaceful life in Fernandina. If that's the case, it would be best that she go away. I, sure as the devil, won't be the one to suggest it to her mother though.

He needed facts fast. Reaching his son-in-law's house, Michael rattled the glass in the front door with the force of his pounding. He heard Trip calling out, "I'm coming, I'm coming. If you bust a window, I'll ... Mr. Dunnigan! Good morning, sir. You look excited. Is there something the matter?"

"You damn well ought to know the answer to that question. Where is she?"

Trip's face reddened despite the lather that was hiding half of it. His outraged father-in-law must have heard something about Leona and him. Sonofabitch. "I'm sorry, sir. Please tell me what you mean."

Michael pushed his way into the parlor and stormed, "I might be twice your age, but right now I think I can whip your ass. I know I'd enjoy it."

The younger soldier rather admired the older man's ferocity, but the outburst was ridiculous. As he wiped the soap from his cheeks with the towel hanging around his neck, Trip asked, "What are you talking about? Why are you so angry?"

"She didn't tell you she was leaving us a note, did she?" Michael held out the evidence and Trip took it, reading silently.

"Sir, I swear to you, as an officer in the United States Army, I have no knowledge of Breelan's leaving. None. This shocks me as it does you."

"Well, when did she leave? Surely you know that. You two live in the same house, for God's sake."

"I was on duty all night. I just got home. When I saw she and Nora weren't here, I naturally assumed they had ridden out to the beach.

"Well, wherever Breelan is, she's alone. Nora's home in bed! I thought I told you to make sure she doesn't go anywhere by herself." Michael hollered. Any smattering of tolerance for his relative by marriage was long gone.

"Sir, you know well your daughter and her, excuse me, her stubborn ways. I have cautioned her repeatedly not to go out unescorted, but she does anyway. Why, when I was riding home just an hour ago, I passed a buddy of mine who told me my wife and her cousin were seen wandering the Egmont Hotel after dark last night! I was going to ask Bree about it the first I saw her, but she wasn't here. She'd probably come up with some vague story to cover her tracks, but I've learned at this early date in our marriage to drop some matters for fear pressing them will make her secrecy worse."

"Are you calling my daughter a sneak and liar?"

"I'm just trying to be as honest as I can."

Michael didn't want to admit that Trip could be right, so stated, "In the note, Bree says the blame is all hers. I find that quite hard to believe. Hell, she's been miserable since the day you two ran off together."

Trip flinched at the hurtful yet true words. Breelan was unhappy, very unhappy, but was it his fault? It was that damn contemptible sea captain she was pining over.

"Have you any notion where she could have gone?"

"No, sir. All I can do is look for her. I'll have to let the fort know I've had a family emergency. Major Maveney is very understanding about women since he's married himself. Where shall I join you in looking for my wife?"

"By God, you'd better be telling me the truth, is all I can say."

And you'd better shut-up, old man, and get off this porch or I'll knock you down, Trip raged inwardly.

"I'll be at the Egmont seeing Waite Taylor. I hope he can help me find my girl." As a parting shot to a man he disliked, Michael informed, "They're real close, you know."

The usually well-tended grounds of the Egmont Hotel were littered with debris from last night's wind and rain. Gardeners, raking the fallen Spanish moss and pine needles from the lawn and drive, jumped from the path of the galloping horse that bore down on them. The cruel bit cut into the delicate mouth of the steed that carried Michael to his next best hope for clues of Breelan's whereabouts. Waite Taylor.

From his parlor window, Waite saw Michael race up the stone avenue to the hotel, his horse's hooves hurling the gravel like grapeshot from a cannon. Alert patrons dodged the flying pebbles, but a few unfortunates were pelted. Matters must be gravely amiss because in all the time Waite had known him, Michael had never hurried. He guessed about the only thing that could upset his friend was trouble in his family. He hoped he was wrong.

Waite met up with Michael as the architect was fumbling to tie his horse's reins through the iron hitching ring out front. Taking the ribbons, Waite swiftly secured the heaving beast and then escorted the winded gentleman to the wicker chaises on the veranda. With no preamble, "What is it, Michael?"

"Breelan, my Breelan."

The man who loved her listened with alarms going off in his head.

"We awoke to this note." Pulling it from his pocket he tenderly smoothed it against his waistcoat, the same as he would have done with his little girl's tangled curls.

Impatient, Waite wanted to grab the paper from her father's aging hand. Realizing he was wasting time, Michael thrust the letter at his ally. Reading, Waite stood, uttered a vile curse under his breath, and began pacing.

"You know where she is? You must have an idea from your reaction," said an optimistic Michael.

"I'm sorry, sir, for my outburst. No, I do not."

"Then why such a response?" At no time did it enter his head that Waite would lie to him. He trusted this man.

"Michael, it's my fault. Dear God, she's gone because I hurt her."

Michael bristled when he heard the word hurt then, just as quickly, realized the only hurt this man could inflict upon his girl would be emotional. "Sit down, son, and tell me."

Waite hated the nosy passersby looking at them. Nodding for Michael to follow, they walked to the formal gardens while Waite told his guilty tale. Reaching the cast iron bench among the Japanese yews, "I threw her warning about Leona in her face. I laughed at her. I told her I was sick of her kind. That I wanted to live my life for pure physical delight. I exaggerated every word I told her. I couldn't stand any more of her loving attention. Not because I don't care. I can't say how much I do. But she must somehow conquer her feelings for me. It isn't right or fair to any of us involved."

"Can you tell me that you'll ever get over your love for her? Honestly?"

"Honestly? No. Never. I don't matter. She's married and not to me. We must live with that, the both of us. Michael, please know that anything I said to hurt her, I said only to help. To drive her away from me, not you, but it's all backfired now."

"It took little figuring to know Breelan came to see you at your hotel last night, Taylor."

Waite turned to lay eyes on Trip whose brutal expression was a representation of his consuming jealously.

Trip hadn't arrived in time to hear all Waite said, but he was sure it was about him. "The fact that you'd been drinking in the bar all evening had nothing to do with the vile things you told her, I suppose?"

"Could one of those vile things be that Breelan is aware you've been with Leona?"

"What other lies did you put in her head?" Trip lunged at Waite, but Waite side-stepped and the assailant fell to his hands and knees. Rising, Trip looked at the dirty britches of his usually pristine clothing and again advanced.

Michael sat firm, knowing that until the two men came to blows, there would be no cooperation in the search for his daughter.

Catching Trip by the shoulder, Waite strategically landed a punch just above the shining belt buckle of his attacker, knocking the wind from his lungs. Inhaling short quick gasps, Trip backhanded Waite to leave searing red finger marks across his right cheek. Shaking his head to clear it, Waite seized Trip around the neck and the two fell to the ground, each brutally pummeling the other.

Blow upon blow landed, blood dripped and gashes oozed. It was time. Michael had seen enough. Putting his first two fingers in his mouth, he blew a shrill whistle that startled the combatants enough for Michael to hook Waite's arm and pulled him off the struggling man beneath him. "That's it, boys. This has been long in coming. Now we find my daughter. Together."

Trip saw his opportunity and could not let it pass. As Waite straightened, dusting off his clothes, he felt a kick to his upper chest when the spur from Trip's boot sliced his shirt and his flesh. This time it was Waite's turn to drop on all fours.

"You call yourself a gentleman?" Michael demanded of Trip, as he helped Waite to his feet.

"You can't tell me you approve of his behavior with my wife."

"I will only tell you I've had enough of this endless hostility. Find my girl. That's all I give a great goddamn for. Now, let's get to it!" And the party of three left in search of the missing woman, each having his own motivation for finding her.

Chapter 32 – *The Goodbye Lie* by Jane Marie

It was well past four in the morning and the lamps still blazed at Dunnigan Manor. Only the children slept. Miss Ella was replacing the front window candle with a taller, newer taper. It helped her somehow.

Played out from their search, the men gathered, each telling his tale of unproductive results. Since her horse was gone, it was assumed Breelan had ridden off somewhere. Just in case, the train and boat schedules had been checked, but no one thought she would have taken either if she genuinely wanted to remain missing. Her face was too well known in the area.

Michael had ridden around town asking friends in hasty, but casual conversations when last they'd seen Breelan. Clover had done the same with his friends. Will, who'd joined the hunt as soon as he could be released from his duties, had ridden the roads up to Old Fernandina, the original location of Fernandina, just north of the city proper. He'd even scoured Bosque Bello Cemetery on his return. Trip reported he found only disheartening answers. He'd combed the west shore of the island along the riverbank to the marsh. No luck. Waite haunted the beach, riding the entire length of the island and back, looking for a sign that would tell him Breelan had passed that way. He discovered nothing.

Uncle Clabe and Joey had stayed behind with the women and children for their protection and as Clabe refilled the whiskey glasses of the returned men, heads hung low from equal parts of exhaustion and despair. Where had she gone?

"Mr. Michael?"

"Yes, Clove?"

"I don't want to be sayin' this and you don't want to be hearin' it, but if we believe her note, sounds like Miss Bree will come home when she's ready."

"Maybe Clover's right, Michael. There isn't much we can do if she really wants to disappear," Clabe agreed.

The protestations from the younger women were expected, but the older ladies and men did not argue. Nora patted Carolena's hand with feigned reassurance, watching her uncle stare blankly at the handwritten letter from his daughter. "Uncle Michael, can I see what Bree wrote?"

"It isn't much."

Nora took the paper, almost afraid to read its short message. Sitting down again by Carolena, she hesitantly looked over each word, as if it would be the last she might ever hear from her sweet Breelan. To everyone's shock, Nora sprang to her feet, her face pinched.

"Baby, what's the matter?" squeaked her mother with dread.

"Dear God! Dear God!"

"Damn it, Nora! What in hell's the matter with ya?" hollered Peeper, her nerves wound tight as violin strings about to break. Hearing the old gal utter a cuss word was enough to startle anyone out of a stupor.

"The note!" squeaked Nora. "See, it's right here!"

"What's right here?" Carolena asked, eyes wide as nickels.

Waite, on his feet now, too, narrowly refrained from shaking the answers out of the girl.

"She wrote this note for me!" Nora cried, beating the paper with the back of her fingers. "No one but me would understand her message! If only I'd seen this earlier. Breelan didn't run off. Something or someone has forced her to leave and I'm guessing that this time, it's much, much more than an unhappy marriage!"

Trip's spine starched at the spoken truth. Those who weren't aware that Breelan had run from him on their honeymoon didn't notice or care what Nora intimated because their concentration was back on the letter. As it was passed around for all eyes to see, each hastily read the overlooked, seemingly insignificant postscript:

P.S.   *Remember me to My Cuz.*

Nerves were frayed, tempers were short, and physical strength was sapped. Miss Ella, with advice from her mother, agreed Michael must be made to lie down a few hours before he renewed the search for their missing child. Filled with weariness and whiskey, he reluctantly capitulated and headed upstairs to their room, protesting the entire way there. It would soon be time for the children to awaken, so Grammy and Peeper trod to their little house out back to gather energy for the long day or days they feared might follow. Miss Ella would have plenty enough to do what with contending with her own worry and that of her husband.

The Duffy family went next door to their beds, praying for their lost relative. Nora, of course, argued that she should go with the younger men when they went out again after they'd eaten because she was strong and could keep up and especially because she knew Breelan better than anyone did. Unhappily for her, she was made to follow her parents home to think about who would have done such a horrible thing. Trip and Waite would not be deterred. In an extraordinary consensus, they arranged to meet in Waite's room at the Egmont after each had freshened up. There would be plenty of time for sleep once Breelan was found.

Neglecting to respond to the early morning greetings from the hotel cleaning crew, Waite ascended the staircase on his way to his suite, pondering the situation. He considered not only who had wronged Breelan by taking her against her will, but also what punishment he would inflict upon the perpetrator. The captain compelled himself to dwell first on finding her because his thoughts of slow and premeditated recompense were playing with his concentration.

Waite hadn't wanted to make accusations in front of the womenfolk, although he strongly suspected Trip of involvement. Trip was a skillful, self-centered liar. Waite had found many narcissistic people to be so. Trip could readily have played the innocent, pretending concern for Breelan's disappearance, all the while smack in the center of it. His accomplice might easily be Leona. Waite understood too well that she was dishonest. Too many odd events had occurred in this little town in the short time since her arrival. He would not, could not point fingers until he was certain, however.

The hall to his room was long and empty. He slowed his pace as he neared his room. Ear to his door, he could hear the rustling of petticoats. That did it. Leona was in his room! He'd have the job of the maid who'd let her in! He caught himself thinking like the witch awaiting him, wanting to fire every man jack who was slipped a penny under the table. The staff worked hard and should they collect an extra a coin or two once in a while, it was fine by him. Few people were paid their actual worth these days. His lost men immediately came to mind. He regretted that he hadn't allotted them more salary. He wouldn't make that mistake with his new hands. That settled in his mind, it did nothing to alleviate his temper. He didn't need Leona's kind of trouble. Not now. Thrusting his key in the lock, he threw back the heavy mahogany door so hard it slammed against the wall behind, sending vibrations throughout the room and causing a figurine to shatter when it fell from the mantel to the polished oak floor.

The crash of it produced stirring from the woman in his bed. He marched over, threw back the coverlet, and had the shock of his life. There lay Breelan, her dress damp and muddied! She was on her side, facing away from him. Her wet hair covered his pillow and the sight of her there aroused feelings of love and desire he didn't want to control. He removed his holster and slid it under the bed.

At the first touch of his hand on her arm, she moaned and rolled into a tight ball, jerking away from him. "Don't hurt me anymore. Please, don't hurt me."

"Bree, darling. You're safe with me now. I'm here, baby. I'm here."

"No!" she screamed at him. "Not you. Leave me alone!"

He couldn't understand why she was acting like this toward him. Granted, he'd said mean things to her that he regretted. Surely he could explain them away if she'd let him. She must be confusing him with Trip. "Breelan, this is Waite. You're in my room at the Egmont Hotel. Don't be angry with me. I'll find the man who took you. I'll deal with him, I swear. Let me hold you. I love you."

She laughed a peculiar laugh. It was nothing like Leona's shrill, irritating guffaw. It contained resignation, defeat. Waite had to stop this. Somehow he had to reassure her. Again, grasping her arm, he moved to roll her over to see her better.

"Don't look at me!" she shrieked. "Don't you dare look at me!" She buried her in the pillow and wept.

He could tolerate no more. He had to help her. "What's the matter with you? How did they hurt you?" Fearing the worst but facing it, he forcibly turned her onto her back. Her struggle was a mere tussle against his brawn. Throwing her head from side to side, her hair blanketed the features he needed to see. He pinned her to the bed, holding her wrists with one hand across her breasts. She kicked at him, but her legs only tangled the covers. He lightly lay against her body. Despite her wild wiggling and verbal objection, with his free hand, he brushed away her tresses to expose her filthy face and upper torso. It was then she fell silent, offering no more resistance.

The early daylight's glimmer lit the room to gray, but it took little light at this close distance to see she was not unharmed. He winced at what he saw, and she observed his reaction with frightened eyes. What had they done to his Breelan? Who could have committed such a deed?

She made a soft groaning from somewhere deep inside. He had to see more, and she knew it. She endured the humiliation because he, of all people, had to understand she would never be as she once had.

Releasing her, he struck a match and touched it to the bedside lamp. Before him was the woman he adored, a woman who was lovelier than any he'd ever known. Now she was different. The dirt that covered her could be washed away, as could the smeared dried blood on her neck and shoulders. But this injury had not been caused by a fall from her horse or a tumble from a buggy. Where once he gazed upon her skin like ivory snow, now there was crusted blood, yet it was not blood alone he saw. It was mixed with something that appeared to be dark indigo. He felt as if he would vomit. It was worse to him than any battlefield wound because it had been done to Breelan with deliberate malice. He swallowed hard once before he found the courage to say the word silently to himself. Tattoo. She had been tattooed! Had she at least been given liquor to deaden the pain from it all? He wanted to kill someone.

He was staring at her without blinking. "Please. Let me turn away," she whispered. "You've no need to see me any longer. You'll remember me as I am now. Of that, I have no doubt."

He cursed his own soul for not having been stronger for her. "Forgive me, darling. Forgive me. I'm thinking only of the man who hurt you like this. I will have his life. Before God, I will."

"Don't call me darling, now or ever. I am as I will be, a curiosity to be pitied. People will hear of this and lump me with the likes of women of the night who proudly bear such marks, who lure men to their beds with their bizarre brandings. I will forever carry this thing, whatever it is. I can't tell now. Once the scabs fall off we'll know. But does it really matter? I'm marred for life. I can never wear a revealing gown of any sort for you. If I do, I will only be inviting gossip and shining an unwanted spot light at myself. I didn't realize how vain I was until all this. I guess they knew me better than I knew myself. Well, they've accomplished their task. I'm no longer a threat to anyone."

She knew who they were! His brain screamed for names. His heart demanded blood. He told her, "I'll call you whatever endearment I damn well choose. We tried apart. It was torture for us both. I'll be without you no more. You've been through enough in your young life. So have I."

"You could never make me understand why you'd want me, Waite. I'm no longer pure; I've been with another man. I'm barren. I'm grotesque. What attraction is there?" Bitterly, she answered her own question. "None."

Raising her reluctant chin with his strong hand, he forced her to look into his dark eyes, then ordered, "Be still. Do you hear? I'll have none of that talk. Later. We'll argue later." His mind was made up, as was hers. It would come down to a battle of wills. In that, he would be victorious. He had to be. Taming his voice, "Tell me who did this to you and I'll watch them take their last gasp."

"I can't."

"You know and yet you won't tell me?" He was livid!

Her eyes turned cold. "Do you think if I knew, I'd not wish them the same fate as you do? I saw no one. I heard a man's voice I didn't recognize. Maybe it was disguised. I'm not sure."

She said no more and he needed more. "Try and think. Was there any other sound, a touch, a smell?"

His suggestions stimulated her memory of senses. "I smelled perfume!"

"Was it familiar to you?"

"It was the same scent Leona wears!"

"Damn her to hell and the lackey who helped her! Tell me everything you can."

"Okay. Okay." She didn't want to relive any part of the ghastly experience, but he would hound her until she told him what she remembered. "It was sometime around three in the morning, I think. Nora was deep asleep, yet I just couldn't tame my thoughts. I paced and paced the house. It was so miserably hot, I went for a ride on the beach in hope of tiring myself out. I knew I shouldn't go alone, but I didn't have the heart to wake my cousin. Besides, it was only a little earlier than usual."

"A little earlier? It was hours earlier than your usual ride. I couldn't sleep that night either and I remember thinking how pitch black it was because there was no moon." He wanted to throttle her as an angry father would his disobedient child for being so foolish.

"Things are damp and fresh at that time of night. When I ride, I become oblivious to everything but the serenity around me and my own thoughts. The man who took me had to have been spying on my house. He must have followed me to the shore. Out on the sand where the roar of the sea would cover my screams, a horse I didn't recognize carrying a man dressed in black wearing a hood over his head, overtook me. He grabbed my reins, and his voice thundered. He told me to come along peacefully or he'd shoot my horse. You know how dear I hold Noir. I had no choice except to go with him. I was blindfolded, but I listened. As we rode, it began raining, which was good for him, since it almost guaranteed our tracks would be hard - if not impossible - to follow. We rode away from the ocean, turned north, and I think sure we ended up in some hovel in Old Fernandina. I listened closely for sounds of people passing us, but his luck held and I heard nothing like that."

"What about the note you wrote? Did the man recite the words for you to pen?"

"Yes, partly. He kept me blindfolded until I was to write the letter. Then, he sat me at a table and held my hair fast so I couldn't look around. A copy of what I was to write was thrust in front of me and his gloved hand gave me a pencil. I wrote slowly, trying to come up with some kind of a plan. When I finished his phony message, I thought to add the postscript. I convinced him his words were too detached sounding, that mention of Nora would make it more believable. I hoped Nora would see it and know I was in trouble. Apparently, she never did."

Breelan cried and the salt from her tears fell to her shoulder and burned her wound. She unconsciously reached for her treasured hanky to dab her eyes before any more fell and was amazed to find it still tucked in the cuff of her sleeve. That simple discovery was gravely overshadowed by her complete misery. "Please, blow out the lamp." He did and the muted darkness slightly soothed her, so she continued. "I was blindfolded again and he forced me to lie on a musty mattress and tied me to the bedposts. He went to the door, and I think handed the note to someone because I heard the rustle of paper and harsh whispers. It was then I smelled the perfume, but the woman left without entering the room. After that, I felt the pain. He stuck me with needles or the point of a knife over and over again then poured a liquid over the cuts. I screamed. He stuffed a foul rag in my mouth and threatened Noir again. I could only lie there, a blind witness to my own disfiguring." Waite gathered her to him as she let out ragged, choking sobs. "If only Nora had seen the note."

"She did see the note." He refrained from calling her a sweet endearment. She didn't want to hear that now. "But she didn't see it until shortly before I arrived here. We've been out all day and night searching for you, wondering where you'd run off to. I was sure it was because of the cruel things I'd said. You've got to know I only wanted you to stop loving me for your own sake. I never wanted to marry Leona. I did once in a moment of insanity and that quickly passed. After loving you, no one, particularly her, exists for me. I threw her out. I broke the engagement even before you came to warn me. The only thing I want of Leona is to see her dead for her part in this." He'd never wished death on a woman before. He felt no guilt now.

"I came back to this room to splash cold water on my face. We're all to meet here, then ride out again."

"Who is we?" she asked trembling. "Who is to ride with you?"

"Why your husband, dear. Who else?"

Waite marveled at Trip's timing as the man in question walked in the door. Setting Breelan back against the pillows, Waite stood up, cursing himself for having left the door ajar when he'd entered his room so hastily.

"I'm here, too, Bree," said Will, following close behind Trip.

Although the sun had grown stronger, the room was still dim, shaded by heavy velvet drapes. Breelan's face was in the shadows.

"She's been here all along!" Trip shouted. "You led us right to her! Very slipshod of you, man. Did you think we'd wait in the goddamn lobby like a couple of your deck hands? You, Taylor, will never again have the same pleasures with her that I do. I will kill you first." Trip pulled his gun and aimed it dead center at Waite's heart.

"No!" screamed Breelan. She jumped from the bed and in front of Waite. He pushed her away and she landed, bouncing on the jumbled and soggy bed linens.

"Stay where you are, Bree," ordered Waite. "We all knew things would come to a head between us. I'll find immense enjoyment in destroying the animal that did this to you. That is if he has the guts to let me get my gun and make it a fair fight. And if his hey-boy behind him will step aside and stay out of it."

"I'm a military man, sir. I know of no way to fight, but with honor." Trip's eyes fixed on Waite and he pointed at the corner of the room to his left. "Will, stand over there. Taylor, get your gun."

As Waite reached under the bed, Trip said, "You think she's had such a hard life with me? I admit, I could've been more considerate of her feelings, but let me tell you it's damn hard when you know your wife is in love with another man."

"Let's skip all the self-pity, shall we, and get down to the real nut cuttin'. Never could you justify what you've done to this girl. You'll pay with your life," uttered Waite, anxious to extinguish the existence of the man in front of him.

"At least, you've been made to suffer too, knowing I was sleeping with her any time I wanted. That had to rile the hell out of you."

"The image drove me out of my head," Waite confessed.

Trip was grinning. He could hardly believe he was standing here listening to the proud Waite Taylor admit to suffering at another man's hand. This was better than he could have ever hoped for.

"You call yourself honorable? It takes little courage to scar a woman."

"What the hell are you talking about? You're a fine one for shifting blame. Here I find my long lost wife in your bed and you accuse me of scarring her? It's you who's scarred her good name. If it weren't for you, there would be no scandal. Once you're dead, the whole town will know the truth about her. Hell, few people will blame me for shooting her lover."

Breelan spoke, "Please, Trip. Hear me. I've only ever been with one man and that's you. I've been faithful to my vows. Now, looking like this, no respectable man will want me, just as you wished."

"Looking like what? You're all wet and your hair is in knots. That can't detract from your beauty any. What are you talking about?" Trip demanded, seemingly confused.

"Don't play innocent, Clelland. Come clean." Waite's hand held his gun, but put it in his holster and lunged at his nemesis.

Suddenly light flooded the room. All eyes blinked back the brightness. "I heard the yelling from my chambers. What's going on in here?" Leona held her lamp aloft. "Are you two still fighting over that bitch? Well, let me be the one to provide illumination for the final battle," and she set the light on the bureau, then laughed viciously.

Trip nearly dropped his gun when he laid eyes on his wife. "Dear God, Bree! What happened? Who did this to you?" Trip pried Waite's strong grip from his wrist and rushed toward her.

Waite moved in to bar his way. "You lying sonofabitch!" cried her defender, grabbing Trip by his shirtfront. "We know it was you. You tried to ruin her for me."

Leona was smiling wide as she looked Breelan over.

"But she'll always be beautiful to me despite what you've done to her."

Breelan felt more love for Waite at that moment than she ever had before.

Trip was deathly pale and he shook his head from side to side. As tears rolled down his cheeks, he choked out, "Breelan. Breelan. I didn't do this. Please, believe that. I love you."

Waite let go of the weeping man.

Trip was unaware of anyone except Breelan in the room with him. "No more lies. I'll tell you everything. I promise I will. Everything. I've never been jealous over a woman until you. I wink and they all come running. They want to do for me, take care of me in every way. And all my life I've allowed it. It gave them happiness and me enjoyment. But somewhere inside, I knew I was on a quest for the one woman I could truly love. I went through so many before I met you. And once I did, there was no other." He was on his knees now, holding Breelan's hands as if he were praying to her.

Waite hated Trip's touch on her. Still, he listened and remained silent, along with Will and Leona. The situation was too precarious for anyone to make a move.

"You were reluctant at first to marry me. I know that. Once you'd agreed, I was ecstatic. I wanted to elope before you were talked into a long engagement. When I told my folks, Ma said I'd be marrying up. She's a wise lady, my ma." The soft remembrance lifted the corners of his pretty mouth for a fleeting moment to be quickly replaced by tight lips as he told his harsh tale. "Once we set foot inside the Birch Bark Inn, I knew it wasn't a fit place for our wedding night. I picked it only because it was close to where we were married and I had to consummate our marriage. Since our courtship was so brief, I worried you'd change your mind about the whole thing and I didn't want you to get away. I admit I was anxious, too anxious. I drank too much and passed out. When you told me you'd give me another chance, I was so hopeful. The more time we were on the *Gentle Comfort*, though, the more danger I felt of losing you to Captain Taylor. That's why I forced myself on you in the room we shared. I couldn't risk him having you. When I found you'd been with someone before me, I was crazed. I didn't want you to ever be with anybody else besides me."

Her hands ached as he squeezed the circulation from them. She had to tell him again. She would not have him doubt her word. "Trip, I have never been with anyone but you. It was a childhood accident. I swear before God it was."

Such familiarity between them sickened Waite; nevertheless, he credited Breelan for knowing how to handle the man she had married.

"I should've believed you, I guess. I was blind with jealousy."

Breelan was beginning to think Trip might be sincere. Maybe he was capable of cruelty, but not to the degree imposed upon her last night. Then, she remembered something and stiffened. "If you didn't hurt me, how can you explain this away?" Opening a button on her bodice, she pulled out a white military glove, now stained.

"Where did you get that, Bree? As if I need to ask." Waite glared at Trip, confirming his suspicion. Again, he grabbed at Trip, roughly pulling him to his feet by the arm. "You don't know how I relish the idea of splattering your guts around this room with my bullets, Clelland, but I don't want your life to end that quickly and easily. I'll take you to the sheriff and let him deal with you. Better yet, you're a soldier. A military trial might be more punishing and certainly more disgraceful. Or would it? We all know integrity means little to the likes of you. I want you to linger in prison, turn old and ugly and dirty and flea-infested. After that, I'd like to see you paraded in front of all your women and watch them laugh. See them kick you away, just like you hoped men would do to Breelan." Waite looked at the tears streaming from her brilliant blue eyes.

Almost unaware of Waite's menacing words, Trip wiped away his own tears with the back of his sleeve and repeated Waite's question. "Bree, where did you get that glove? Let me see it."

"You're done giving her orders." Waite punched Trip square in the belly. He doubled over, losing his breath.

"Waite!" Breelan leaped from the bed and clasped his arm. She was afraid he'd already forgotten his words concerning a trial and would beat Trip to death here and now.

Trip spoke. "Please, Bree." He gasped. "Please tell me where you got the glove."

"I'm mighty tired of this act of yours, Clelland," Waite said, but he was respectful of Breelan's wishes and refrained from attacking Trip.

"Tell me, Bree. Please, tell me."

After a frustrated sigh, she complied. "When I was blindfolded ... when I was so frightened and crying in the shack ... the man with the disguised voice told to me to quit bawlin'." He slapped me across the face with something, then threw it at me and said to dry my tears. He said they were wasted on him."

Trip offered his only defense. "That glove could belong to any number of men from the fort."

"That may be so, but I know one way to prove it isn't yours. Try it on, Trip." It was Breelan who ordered him. "Go on. What are you waiting for?"

The others stood silent. How would trying on a glove prove his guilt when all gloves were standard military issue?

Trip took the soiled glove from his wife. Inserting his fingers, he could only get it on as far as his knuckles. It was too small! Before anyone could comment, Trip sputtered, "I remember something! Trying on the glove brought it back to me. I was so concerned about Breelan's disappearance, I'd forgotten. Yesterday morning, when I went to the fort to ask for leave to look for my missing wife, I changed into these civilian clothes. Since being in the service, I've become extremely careful and orderly with my possessions. It helps when there are surprise inspections."

"We're all happy to hear you're such a tidy criminal." Waite lowered his voice to threatening. "Get the hell on with it!" His patience was used up.

"When I opened my trunk there, I immediately noticed my spare pair of gloves was missing. They had been there the day before. Obviously, someone needed extra gloves because his were lost or dirty. He got them from my locked chest. There is only one other person with a key to that lock."

Chapter 33 – *The Goodbye Lie* by Jane Marie

"If I may interrupt," said Will, still dressed in his uniform. Heads turned in the direction of his voice and before all eyes, he somehow seemed to grow in stature. Was it the way he held his shoulders more squarely or his chin at a higher angle? "Are these what you're looking for?"

Trip caught the gloves so casually tossed his way. Trying one on, his hand easily fit into its entire length. They were his pilfered gloves.

"You aren't as slow as I thought, Trip. Yes, I'm the one who borrowed your gloves. I seemed to have," he smirked, "misplaced one of mine. I was in such a hurry I forgot about the enormous size of your stupid hands. That it would take weeks to special order a replacement pair in the mail. So you'd undoubtedly have found me out sooner or later. It makes little difference because I'm ready to tell my story anyway. It's been rough all this time keeping quiet, not getting the proper credit."

Dismissing the subject of the gloves, Will went on, his attitude almost breezy. "Oh, first I must tell you, I find all this personal crap between you and Breelan boring beyond belief. Would you mind if I interjected a little more interest into the conversation? This groveling of yours before mankind has to stop, Trip. You call yourself an officer in the United States Army? I'd tell the men at camp of your sweet, whining performance, but I'd be too humiliated to mention it, them all knowing that we, at one time, were the best of friends. It would reflect poorly upon me. I took up for you for years. No more."

Waite's hand found his holstered gun again.

Trip looked upon a stranger. "Will? This is a whole new posture for you."

"Wouldn't you say it was about time? I'd rather cut a tin bill and pick shit with the chickens than be your bootlick any longer."

"I never realized you felt like that about me. I thought we were close ever since we were young, when my family took you in."

"That's just what I figured you'd say. All your life you've made me feel beholden to you. Living together doesn't make somebody a member of a family. I was made to sleep on the back porch, remember that?"

"We had a small house. That way you had your own room."

"Own room, hell! If it hadn't been for the body warmth from that mangy mutt, Gyp, I'd surely have been frozen as hard as the water in his drinking bowl every morning."

"We worried about that. We asked you to come inside on the cold nights, and you refused."

"I knew my place and kept it. Your parents never adopted me. I wasn't given their name. And you, especially you, didn't treat me like a friend. Always like a servant."

"I'm sorry. Never once did I think of you like that. If I bossed you around, it was the way I'd always heard the older brother should act. And that's exactly how I regarded you, as my brother. I never meant you any disrespect."

"It's too late for apologies. I don't believe you anyhow. What's done is done."

Trip's heart was pounding. "What's done? What are you talking about?"

Not hearing him, Will went on, "While you're baring your soul, dear brother," he spat the last word, "be sure and tell your wife about your problem. I think a spouse has a right to know that her husband is sterile if not before she marries him, then certainly after. Don't you, Breelan?"

Her head snapped from Will to look at Trip.

Trip was nodding. "What I put you through, thinking you could have no children. The truth is that I wouldn't admit my wound from a knife in a skirmish out west left me with anything more than a limp. I've wanted children all my life since I was an only child myself. I'm the last male in my family, the last chance left to carry on the Clelland name. The possibility that I'd be unable to father a child was so abhorrent to me I refused to accept what the doctors said. I would have fessed-up one day to you. At least, I would like to think so, Bree. I'm sorry you had to find out like this."

"Oh, Trip. You can't fathom how glad I am that one day I'll have babies of my own! This has changed my entire future!" She turned and saw the expression in Waite's eyes. And everyone else in the room saw it, too. Then, she stopped. "What about your son, Trip Jr.? We all met him at Christmas."

"Hell, he has no son!" Will was alive with the thrill of exposing Trip's sworn secrets. "It was only some orphaned wharf rat he hired to play the part."

"That's it!" Waite figured out, astonished. "The child looked familiar to me and I couldn't place him, all cleaned up like he was. Bree, think back. You remember the boy who helped your father and uncle with the trunks when you and Nora left for New York City?" Waite asked, supplying reminder to her memory.

"You mean that poor thing was paid money to play the role of your son?" Thunderstruck, she asked, "What about the woman you said was his mother?"

"I've never been married before you, Bree. It was a crazy concoction of lies."

Leona broke in. "I have to agree with Will. This whole scenario is tiresome. What galls me is that regardless of your good looks, Trip, you're dumb as a stump. You could have had me anytime you wanted with no permanent attachments. That's generally how I prefer things anyway. Still, you saved yourself for that prude over there." She sneered at Breelan, trying to rub in her immoral practices as everyday-wholesome and acceptable. "I was willing to marry Waite when he begged me. We would have done so until I discovered he was not the worldly-wise sophisticate I originally thought him to be. I concede I had him all wrong. I guess it only proves that just because you're the captain of a prestigious passenger liner, it doesn't mean you're not small town at heart. So, I broke off the engagement. There's no sense wasting my life in this miserable, bug-infested hole of a toy city when I can be out there with royalty. Those are the kinds of circles I prefer to run in. Believe me, I have my choice of suitors. As a matter of fact, this just arrived for me yesterday and because of it, I leave for the London at noon." She pushed up the sleeve of her black lace dressing gown to reveal a ruby bracelet.

Waite and Breelan knew she was lying about the details of the broken engagement, but it was of little significance to them at this point. They knew, also, that she would not be leaving on schedule.

When no one seemed impressed by the gemstones, Leona railed, "What is the fascination for her, you fools? My only guess is her looks. Oh, pardon me, was her looks. Need I lecture all of you on the facts of life? Comeliness alone isn't enough. You would soon be disappointed by her lack of, shall we call it, spontaneous excitement and inventiveness?'" Leona's lashes dipped to touch her cheeks in pathetic flirtation.

Trip didn't hold back. He had no reason to. "Breelan will eternally satisfy me as only an honorable woman can. That is something you can't conceive of, Leona."

Never having actually exchanged complete passion with Breelan, Waite, nevertheless, found himself in agreement with Trip's statement.

Waving off Trip's critique, the chignoned actress detailed, "Will, here, is another story. He was after me from the first time he saw me. Quite bothersome, really. Once, just for sport, I let him have me. It was shameful. He couldn't keep up."

Will's face darkened at her insults. Every word of dire humiliation she spoke caused the veins in his neck to swell more and more as his kerchief visibly choked him. This was his chance to shine. Leona was trying to smother the light of his brilliance.

"Will's told me of his ridiculous delusions of himself with Breelan," the singer jabbed.

Trip took a step in Will's direction. Waite took hold of his arm, halting Trip when the barrel of Will's gun pointed in his former friend's direction.

"Don't you people see? Will fails with all beautiful women, boring or bold. He's an idiot and the rest of you aren't far behind!" Leona screamed, savagely eyeballing everyone in the room.

"Ah, yes. Leave it to Miss Visper to understand affairs of the heart," Will said. "I thought Breelan and I made a logical couple because we shared a common interest in writing." He huffed. "She isn't as devoted to her work as I am. Instead, she wasted her time playing one lover against the other." Will was disappointed when his last statement didn't goad Trip or Waite to a response. If they needed more needling, he had plenty for them.

"What about Nora? You two are engaged." Breelan demanded the truth. "Was it all a ruse?"

"Oh, no. I would have married her. She's sort of pretty and respectable enough. We'd have wed, and I'd have taken my interests elsewhere when the need arose just like every other poor bum does who lives a mundane marital existence. But then the culmination of the shabby treatment I've received all my life led my destiny on a course of its own making. And here I am. People will remember my name. I'll be famous!"

"You mean infamous, you bastard," charged Waite. This time Trip stopped Waite from advancing on the loaded gun.

Will couldn't have halted his narrative had he wanted. "There will be quite an account compiled in the old company book concerning these events. For years, I logged other men's deeds. Now, they will write about me!" His eyes glazed as he read aloud the imagined copy he knew would be recorded. "The legendary soldier of Fort Clinch, Lieutenant Willis G. Akins, commanded the ingenious destruction of the *Gentle Comfort*. Akins lured Perly Nast, king of rabble, from New York to Florida with the tempting proposition of revenge upon Breelan Dunnigan, the woman who marked Nast with her bite. Per Akins order, Nast did willingly obstruct the release valve of the *Gentle Comfort's* engine, causing the ship to explode."

Will's eyes cleared, but those clear eyes were part of the countenance of a madman, witnessed by an audience of four. He became a braggart as he continued his saga of atrocity. "Best of all was Perly's demise. Watching a man dig his own burial pit, forcing him to stand in the hollow of it, then letting the sea fill the sand in around him - it was nothing short of brilliant.

You can't know the exhilaration I felt. The look on the poor wretch's already repulsive face changed to horror as he watched the waves run in and out, each wash of the water binding him firmer and bringing his death closer. You all ought to experience it for the sheer thrill."

Will had just confessed to sabotage and murder.

"It worked so smoothly. Breelan recognized the dead man on the beach and I knew suspicion would be cast on Trip, since they'd all been at the Birch Bark Inn together. It was easy to find an accomplice in an establishment like that, especially since Breelan had such an interesting exit from the place. She was still the main topic of conversation when I arrived there, weeks later. Remember Trip, that time I was a messenger to Washington? A fast horse and rail got me to New York and back to seal my plan. No one was the wiser."

"You and Leona did this to me?" Breelan, in trying to find reason where none existed asked, "Why would you seek her help when she'd treated you so badly?"

Leona defended herself. "I'm just here to pick up my things. Can't you all understand that I don't need to perform acts of violence, when it's acts of passion that get the results I want?"

Will now considered Leona to be useless white trash so let her words go. "Allow me to make this easy for everyone so you can get it all straight. It wasn't that slut who helped me." Will hadn't answered the question of who his female cohort was. He held the gun and it was his timetable they all followed. "It was a shame to mess you up like that, Bree. But you see, this way, I was getting even with Trip for a lifetime of subjugation because he really does love you, getting even with Taylor, the man you love instead of me, and getting even with you for rebuffing my advances.

"Hey, no one's commented on my handiwork yet. I guess it is kind of hard to make out, what with all that blood and dirt covering it. Take the corner of the sheet there, Captain, and dip it in that pitcher of water on the bedside table. Wash off some of that goo on the right side of her neck and have a look-see at my artistry."

Waite obeyed. To do otherwise would mean a bullet in the gut. With each swipe of the cold, wet cloth to her skin, Breelan flinched, but she didn't tell him to stop. The sheet turned filthy and Waite had to repeat the process a second time and a third in order to wipe away all that was nasty. When he'd revealed the fresh wound, his hand stalled above it as an icicle of hatred for the man who had done this despicable act stabbed his very essence.

"What's the matter, Captain? Can't read my writing? Let me help you out. It's a four-inch letter *W* and it sure as hell doesn't stand for Waite! I was going to make it bigger, but I wanted it to be in good taste and not too showy."

While Will laughed, Waite and Trip, both, ground their teeth and with all that was in them, restrained their natural instincts to crush the vermin speaking.

"I've branded Breelan for life as Will's woman. I may have never actually enjoyed her," he winked, "but damn, it's her word against mine, and everybody knows she's married and in love with another man. Anyone who is worth their salt will spurn her and that's my whole purpose, you see, because that all that high society garbage means so much to her."

No one could find words to respond to this lunacy.

Having more to tell and appreciating the rapt attention of his hostages, Will went on. "Now where was I? Oh, yes. So far, the only one left scot-free is Leona, but she'll insult me no more." In an instant, Will turned the point of his gun at the performer's slender throat and fired. The songbird fell in a heap.

In a panic, Breelan couldn't think what to do. Trip dived toward the maniac and grabbed the hot barrel of Will's gun to direct the next shot into the floor. Waite attacked Will's back, snagging him around the neck with the crook of his arm and dragging him down and off Trip. Will still had possession of the gun and pulled the trigger again. This time, the bullet entered Trip's left thigh and he fell beside Leona, her hands dripping blood from the bullet hole through her throat. Her open mouth was silent but for bubbling gasps as her lungs tried for air. Breelan threw her body across her husband's to protect him as best she could. Her back was to Will but over her shoulder, she kept her eyes fixed on the vicious clash.

Waite and Will grappled savagely. They tumbled around the room, knocking over Leona's oil lamp, snuffed out by a small miracle and darkening again the suite that had been a showplace. Trip held his thigh, feeling his own blood seep between his fingers. Deeply touched and grateful that Breelan should forgive him enough to lay her body over his in defense, Trip pushed her aside, his right hand holding his gun as he tried to get a clear shot at Will, who held onto his gun despite the pounding he was taking at Waite's hands. Periodic and random discharges of gunfire rang out.

Breelan was possessed by fear for Waite and dread at her own death. "Shoot, Trip. Why don't you shoot?" She looked again at her husband. Crimson covered his face, spilling onto his starched blue shirt. A wild bullet had pierced his right eye, delivering a death wound. "God no. Trip! Trip!"

Her scream at his demise didn't penetrate the barbaric contest raging between sanity and madness. Neither Will nor Waite held a gun now. Will slammed Waite's head into the iron bed frame and saw his chance to break and run. Heading for the door, he couldn't help but gloat at his escape, further tales of renown bombarding his brain. One last blow for glory. Reaching deftly inside his boot, Will produced his blade. Many's the time, he'd expertly stilled the beating heart of an enemy with this toad stabber. One more heart to stop. He turned and observed Breelan, weeping and disfigured, Leona, suffering heavily for her insults, Trip, permanently unkempt and incapable of ever issuing orders to him again and Waite, duly trounced for once in his life. "Who's in command now?" Will wasn't really expecting an answer. He didn't need one for he felt triumphant, and his victims could not and would not claim otherwise. He raised his arm to throw the blade at Waite, the persistent survivor. "It won't be you for much longer, *Captain* Taylor," Will said aloud, his thoughts so slick with evil he was unable to contain them within his psychotic psyche. They oozed off his tongue. "Let me do the pleasurable honors."

Everything seemed to slow. Will watched his knife fly through the dawning at its target. Strangely, its course went askew. The same instant the small silver sword left Will's fingertips, he heard a deafening, yet recognizable snap of bone. Excruciating pain immediately followed. He looked down to see Breelan tumbling clear. She'd driven her left shoulder into his left knee, snapping it backwards. His calf bone was jutting out his ruptured skin and split trousers just above the top of his boot.

It was then Will felt the slam of a bullet. Blood poured from his stomach. Its wet heat ran freely down his wobbling legs. Despite his physical suffering, Will wore the demented grin of a lunatic. Another bullet. This time high in the shoulder blade. Only moderately displeased at the agony, he cocked his head, mildly curiosity as to where that slug had come from. He fell on his belly, unable to inhale. Gasping, he rolled to his back, looked into moss green eyes swimming with tears and breathed one heavy, final sigh.

"It's all over," spoke a quivering voice amidst the acrid smell of gunpowder.

Chapter 34 – *The Goodbye Lie* by Jane Marie

The commotion was full blown. Following the gunplay, servants and occupants of the hotel crowded the suite, a few stunned to quiet, most spouting questions. One maid in a frilly cap swooned into the eager arms of the nearby custodian. The desk clerk arrived and parted the drapes, letting in the light. He shook his head, shrieking, "Good Lord! Look at this place! This is a respectable hotel, mind you." Shaking his finger wildly, "Someone will pay dearly for all this damage and destruction!"

Breelan studied her sister. Carolena looked like a stranger. The older girl visibly trembled as she stood alone in the corpse-littered room, puffing pistol in hand, but Breelan could offer her no comfort without comprehension.

Waite called to several snooping men to rush Leona to Doctor Tackett's office. A path cleared for the group to pass. While one fellow held a clean towel to her wounded throat, the others supported her small frame. Mercifully, Leona had passed out from the pain. Her future was grim.

And then Carolena began. Her voice was threadlike and frail sounding. One by one, those present caught the gist of her mumblings and became still. She was talking to Breelan alone. "I'm your big sister, Bree. I, like you, could have my pick of beaus. I had the offers. I could have married first as everyone said I should. When I heard you were wed, I admired you for your independence. As the family waited to meet Trip, though, I saw how upset they were and I vowed to never be the cause of more misery. That promise was immediately forgotten when I laid eyes on your husband. I was envious for the first time in my life. I didn't care a lick that he was a Yankee. I only cared that he wanted you. Not me. Eventually, I got over it. As I think back, I don't know exactly what my fascination for him was beside his obvious charms that everyone else could see.

"Captain Taylor became a frequent visitor. He was betrothed to Miss Visper, but I could tell he didn't love her. I hoped he might find me appealing, since I was more mature than most of the girls my age. He looked at you the way I wanted him to look at me. To him, I was only a nice girl, not one he found attractive, not once he'd seen you. So I eventually got over him, too.

"Finally, I noticed Will Akins. I wanted him. I think it became a competition, a challenge because you'd been taking the men I desired away from me. Maybe I couldn't take someone from you, but I was determined to beat out somebody, anybody. So much for my mature outlook on life and romance. I didn't want to hurt our cousin, yet I was sure I was falling in love with Will, and he with me. He told me he would end his engagement to Nora. But he delayed and delayed the breakup, still seeing us both. He and I would meet late at night while everyone was asleep. It was easy to sneak out of my room and away from the house. Will and I would go on long walks, and he'd declare his love for me. I was bewitched by him and all I thought he stood for.

"He told me how one day they would write books about his deeds. He talked of tales in his past, of glories in his future, and how I would become famous along with him as his wife. This was my first serious involvement with a man. I was mesmerized because I allowed myself to be.

"I see now that Will continually led the conversation back to you. He got me to talking about you. He'd ask me intimate questions about your likes and dislikes. I put it off to him wanting to know my family better. The more we spoke of you though, the more I found myself telling him of resentments I had about you. Resentments I never recognized before. Breelan, the fun-loving one. Breelan, the one with the beautiful hair. Breelan, the independent one, already employed in a man's world. Will told me how you'd bragged to him that you were so much more popular than I am. How all I had to offer men was brains and that wouldn't be enough to hold any man's attention for long. I guess I was more insecure than I realized because he succeeded in turning me against you. He played on my bitterness and convinced me to help him in a devilish plan to teach you a lesson, telling me all along it was just a game.

"He said he'd take you to a shack in Old Fernandina. I was to meet him there and then deliver your note to our house in the early morning. Everyone would believe you had left Trip. We all knew you weren't happy with him. Will said you'd be blindfolded and you'd never know it was our scheme. He gave me *Blushing Jasmine*, but told me only to wear the scent with him. Now, I know it was the same perfume Leona wore. I can faintly smell it right now. His plan worked. He hated her so much; he wanted you to suspect her. Don't think for a second he did it to protect me. He just needed an accomplice and guessed I would do his bidding because I was so taken with him. He guessed right.

"He told me to bring a fresh vial of ink to him when I picked up the letter. He said he'd pour the ink over your hair and stain it so you'd have no choice but to cut it. I liked that idea. Anything to make you just a little less attractive. I started to have serious doubts when Nora alerted the whole family to the fact you were in trouble and hadn't just run away. Everyone was so upset. Family and friends were out all night searching for you. And I worried, too, how Daddy would feel if he ever found out it was

236

I who caused you to have to cut your hair. He might never forgive my meanness.

"When I arrived at the dingy shanty where Will had taken you, he wouldn't let me in. We argued in the doorway and I could tell he'd been drinking. I guess he needed the whiskey to bolster his courage. I whispered to him to let you go, that I'd thought better of things and I didn't like his plan any more. He turned on me like some rabid dog. He threatened to tell everyone that it was all my doing, that I was the mastermind. No one would doubt it with my known intellect. He'd say he'd only taken you because I threatened to tell Nora he'd made advances toward me and he wanted to protect her. I was scared at the way he'd changed so quickly. Now, I realize he hadn't changed; he'd been bad all along.

"He admitted to me he'd once wanted you. He didn't say you'd rejected him, but it was clear you had feelings for no one other than Captain Taylor. That was why he wanted to destroy you. He said you'd be found in the bed of a man not your husband and your reputation, along with your beauty, would be a thing of the past. He laughed that he would ruin you for any other man. That sounded like much more than you having to cut your hair. If I'd argued, I feared he might be capable of killing us both. I was right because that's when he told me to go home and keep quiet or I'd pay with my life. I went home all right, but to get this gun."

Carolena still held the grip by thumb and forefinger, looked at the thing and dropped it to the floor, her eyes closing as if she were trying to erase the memory of it forever. "I guessed he would take you to the Egmont, since he spoke with such loathing of Captain Taylor, the man you wanted, and he knew the captain would be out looking for you. When I arrived here, I was too late to get the first shot off, but I was in time to fire the last. He's dead now and so is all my resentment of you. I'm sorry, Breelan. I'm so sorry. Please forgive me."

There was no hysteria in Breelan. She sat on the bed, leaning on Waite's strong shoulder, surveying it all. She'd forgotten her own torment and was unaware of staring eyes. She'd been wrong about so many things. There, dead before her, lay her husband, Lieutenant Trip Clelland, who had stopped the man he knew his wife loved from advancing on Will's loaded gun. A dark stain of blood on the floor was all that remained of her nemesis, Leona Visper, the woman she despised from the moment they'd met, who had been involved in immoral liaisons, yet not her kidnapping. If she survived, Leona's throat would never emit sweet song again. And Lieutenant Will Akins, a soldier her husband had trusted, turned madman and murderer, lay still beside his once best friend.

Waite spoke. The venom on his words was palatable. "How, Carolena, can you have the nerve to ask for your sister's forgiveness after what you helped that maniacal monster do to her? Never mind the terror of the whole experience or her pure agony as something brutal was happening and her not knowing what. Hell, for all she knew, the next pain she might have felt was having her throat cut! She'll have to live a lifetime with what he's done to her. You might not have used the needle on her yourself, but you ... how can you call Breelan your sister ever again? How?"

"But Bree, you don't understand. He didn't scar you permanently. It'll be all right."

Breelan touched the raw of her injury realizing fully that she would never be all right again.

Carolena saw the look of disbelief on her grimy face. "Hear what I'm saying. It wasn't ink in that vial I gave Will. It was Daddy's blackberry juice. Will was so deranged, he never noticed the difference. Breelan, your neck will heal! It will heal!"

Chapter 35 – *The Goodbye Lie* by Jane Marie

It had been two years since they'd begun construction on the ship. This mid-afternoon, all was at the ready. The powerful sun shone brilliantly and the river air carried perfectly synchronized streams of gliding pelicans overhead. They, too, had heard this was launching day for the new liner commanded by Captain Waite Taylor. It was a celebration not to be missed, and even songbirds were doing their part in accompanying the festivities.

Breelan spotted friends and family in the throng of spectators who'd come from everywhere. There was Heleen Cydling, Father O'Boyle, Clover and Joey and Aunt Coe and Uncle Fries. Her Aunt Noreen was centered between Uncle Clabe and Doctor Tackett. So many faces were recognized. So many were not. She took a moment to listen and appreciate all the wonderful things around her in the present and the wonderful things that had happened to her in her recent past as Mrs. Waite Taylor.

"Don't stand so close to the edge of the dock, Marie," Miss Ella was warning, her arm looped through Aunt Coe's.

After a year's official mourning, Breelan had wed her captain. Miss Ella wrote in the family bible that the marriage took place at St. Michael's Church with Nora Duffy as maid of honor and Michael Dunnigan as best man, something quite extraordinary. This had been of particular concern to Aunt Noreen. Breelan imperceptibly shook her head as she recalled all the squawking about such a break with tradition, the father of the bride also being the best man. Aunt Noreen had reminded everyone repeatedly that Father O'Boyle was just too progressive for her taste, concluding her chronicle of Breelan's shame with, "At least it's not my Nora who's going against all that's socially holy." Somewhat still resentful to this day of her aunt's sour intrusion on such a special occasion as her marriage, Breelan turned away to look at her father.

Michael was walking about, shaking the hands of the crew. "You've done a fine job of readying this vessel," he said to a sweating seaman. "She's a grand specimen, she is, that will ferry passengers in style and grace. Thank you." A slap on the back punctuated his sincerity.

"And while I'm a thinkin' on it, Michael Waite Taylor," Breelan heard Peeper scold the boy with the rolled sleeves and already dusty trousers, "don't be pullin' any more tricks on our old cat, Monstie, once we get back home to Dunnigan Manor."

In short order, Peeper, along with everyone else, had come to think of Trip's imposter son as part of the family once they'd heard the sad orphan's tale. It took little persuasion from Breelan to convince Waite they should adopt the child, seeing as how he needed them so. Although not entirely innocent in Trip's plan, he was too young to be aware of Trip's motivation. It all ended for the best, and no one regretted the decision for a minute.

"That animal is near ta reachin' his pucker-point," Peep cautioned, "He members everythin'. The next time ya go a puttin' peanut butter on the roof a his mouth, you'll be lucky if'n ya don't pull away a bloody stump of an arm. If I have to slap the fire out of ya with these here poor upside-down-turned rumatiz fingers a mine, I will!"

Of course, it took Mickey, as he was soon nicknamed, little time to realize Peeper could holler up a storm, but her artificial threats were soon and always followed by a cookie or a piece of pie.

"And your cousin, Jack Patrick, I mean Pat, has learned enough mischief from ya already," the old woman persisted. "Behave and make your mother and Captain Taylor proud, won't cha? You two skeedaddle over there and sit on them pilings with Warren Lowell where's I kin see ya. Now git!"

Breelan spied a blonde man in a blue uniform and for a second's ticking, her skin crawled as a flash of her distasteful past brushed her memory. Trip, Leona, and Will were all gone now. What a horrible waste of life. Trip was a sad soul, only to be prayed for these days. The soldier in blue disappeared into the crowd, a stranger just passing through since Fort Clinch was once again overgrown, garrisoned only by the ghosts who kept her secrets.

No ghost was Nora. Alive and happy, she was darting glances at a husky crewman wearing the insignia of an officer on his shoulder boards. Breelan watched as he flexed his muscles in a performance calculated to send willies down the spine of her red-haired cousin and successfully so.

Grammy was carrying her tiniest treasure, a squalling baby girl with dark hair and deep dark eyes. "Another country heard from," she said of this child, as she'd said of so many others over the years. The little girl was a feminine replica of her handsome father, Captain Taylor. Just two months old, Grammy conjectured to Miss Ida, a woman in her sewing circle, "I predict this tiny one will be a dickens." Then again, she said that of most newborns.

Breelan smiled as her baby squinted into the sun, the same as she always did, and her mother watched Grammy pull the infant's bonnet forward to shadow her eyes the same as she'd done for Breelan when she was born. Nora and I were so silly back then, Breelan thought, worrying as if there were something wrong with us.

"Attention. May I have everyone's attention," called Major Fairbanks. And the ceremony commenced with speeches.

Breelan's eyes landed on Aunt Noreen again. She was surprised that her plump aunt was still present, an unusual occurrence since the woman detested any perspiration whatsoever on her person. Was always-short-on-praise Aunt Noreen proud of her brother, Michael, and his success for once in her life? Breelan quickly pushed her question to the back of her mind as she watched Waite, standing tall on the temporary platform with the other dignitaries. Her husband was beyond handsome. The crisp new captain's uniform he wore had been her present to him. He'd mentioned something about giving her a gift in exchange, but would offer no hint. With great self-control she hadn't pressed him, wildly wondering what his surprise might be.

Concluding the formalities, Waite looked to his beautiful wife. Her flawless face reminded him how blessed he that she was alive and well, left only with a crude tattoo across her throat to remind her of her horrible ordeal. Although Carolena had, at the last minute, tried to save her sister from the beast that was Will, she had been wrong. The blackberry juice left a mark, but that mark was fading. Breelan covered it with theatrical makeup and powder. Anyone not knowing it was there would never guess its presence. The hope was that time would eventually lighten the scar further and take with it the ugly memory of its application.

Speaking for all the assembly to hear, Waite said, "Carolena Dunnigan, my men and I would be glad, happy and proud if you would do the honors on, this, the first anniversary of my marriage to your sister, Breelan." He presented Carolena with a bottle of champagne and covering her hand with one of his, kissed her forehead.

In doing so, Waite had complied with Breelan's wishes. It had been a mighty struggle for him to forgive his sister-in-law, but his love for his bride was that great. All of her family was at peace. Seeing tears of joy roll down her cheeks, he recognized that Breelan understood his gift to her had been his victory in this battle of resentment toward Carolena.

Turning to the crowd, Carolena said loudly, "I christen thee, the *Miss Breelan*! May God grant her a steady course, and may all who voyage upon her arrive safely on new shores." With an impressive swing, she smashed the green glass against the pointed hull. Foaming champagne flew. The ship slipped her bonds of rope and slid stern first down the wooden way into the Amelia River. The excited spectators roared with approval at the perfectly timed seafarer's ritual.

Waite jumped down from the stage and walked straight to his wife through the parting crowd. He raised her high above him. Slowly, he lowered her into his tight embrace then set her gently on her toes. He kissed her hard before all assembled, and she was weak in his arms.

A blur of joy, more champagne, and celebration followed. Michael made a toast that touched the hearts of all attending. "Waite, may you love and cherish Breelan as much and as long as I have loved and cherished her mother."

"Hear, hear!"

"I believe I have something that belongs to you, boy."

"Sir?"

Michael held out the silver flask Waite had given him the night they met, the night of the tornado. "I kept this as a reminder of a good and honorable friend. I hope you didn't miss it too much."

"It's I who am honored you'd say such a thing. Please, it's yours. You've given me the most precious prize in my life, one I'll revere the rest of my days, and that's your daughter." The two men united their four hands as one. They said nothing further as Breelan watched the love of father and son pass between them.

The hours grew long. Was there anything more that could possibly add to her happiness? She hid her face in the softness of her mended and still lovely lace hankie.

Waite went to her. Lifting her chin, he guessed what was on her mind and excused them both from the late night activities on board the *Miss Breelan*. As they headed in the direction of the captain's cabin, he told her, "I believe Nora has an eye on my new second officer, and we need to steer your big sister in the direction of ..."

Breelan had to comment. "Waite Taylor, I never realized you were such a matchmaker."

"Until you pointed it out, I guess I never did either. Must be because I'm so happy with you. I love you more than my next breath of air, darlin'. I want everyone to know my happiness, but with their own special someone, of course." She laughed and he squeezed his arm around her slender waist. "It's amazing how you've gotten your figure back since our baby was born, Bree. I'm a lucky bastard. Don't think I don't know it."

"We're both lucky, Waite."

The birth of her daughter flashed through Breelan's thoughts as they strolled. The baby hadn't been expected for three weeks. Waite was with Michael at the nearby Chandlery, ordering the last of the brass fittings for their ship. She and Nora had been alone at the Taylors' cottage near the

242

docks. Her labor had started with only a backache. Being a novice at child birthing, Breelan figured she'd simply strained her muscles lifting the laundry and forbade Nora to seek the assistance of Doctor Tackett. When the contractions reached around her front and came frequent and hard, her water broke. Both afraid, Breelan from the pain and Nora from witnessing it, they futilely tried to comfort each other. As the wet dark head entered the world, Nora squealed with delight until she realized the cord was caught around the fragile neck. At that moment Waite crossed the threshold to see his wife lying amid tousled sheets and blankets on the horsehair sofa, delivering his child. Exhibiting a calm demeanor, he unwound the life-endangering noose from around his baby's throat, and Breelan completed the birth with no other difficulties.

Waite saw a sweet light come into his wife's eyes there in the corridor. His quizzical expression sought an answer.

"Oh, I was remembering when we were trying to come up with a name for the baby. I recall looking down into her tiny, tiny face wearing the white bonnet with the lavender ribbons I'd knitted and how, although the pattern said it was newborn size, it was huge on her."

"I remember." He was smiling, too, now.

"Then when I suggested we name her Halley after your special friend Catfish O'Halleran, well, if I told you I think I saw a tear in your eye back then, would you admit to it?"

"I'll never lie to you, Bree. I was deeply touched."

"And when I was trying to decide what a complementary middle name would be, without hesitation, you said ..."

He finished her sentence. "I said I think it proper my first daughter carry the name of her mother, since it was because of her that she came healthy and strong into this world. I thank you and I love you, Breelan, and I love our daughter, Halley Breelan Taylor."

"You're most welcome," she'd responded, "I thank you, too, for so much - my joy, my contentment and now our little Halley." Breelan reached up and fiddled her fingers in his thick hair. "I'm glad there're only our friends and family on board tonight, that the public won't get on until tomorrow. The ship is so big; it's almost as if it's just the two of us. Tell me what you're thinking this very moment."

"I'm sure you can probably guess my exact thought," and he caressed the back of her neck.

She could hear delight and devilment in his answer without looking up at him. He was a man with strong physical needs and his lucky wife temporarily halted her teasing, thinking it best to turn his focus from her to more business-like matters before they got carried away right then and there. "When do you think Mr. Rockwell will be ready to take over some of your runs up the coast and back, Waite? I'm awfully anxious to have you home for more than a few days a month."

Knowing full well that Breelan had purposely changed the subject, he went along for the time being. "I'm anxious to be home with you, too." He loosened the top buttons of his tunic. "The word home sounds and feels the way I've always imagined it should. I haven't had a real home since my mother died when I was still a boy. I loved going to sea with my father, but since I found you, I'm so glad to settle here in Fernandina. To answer your question, Bree, Rockwell is an experienced man. A couple of months at the longest, until he knows precisely how I want the ship handled."

"In the meanwhile, we'll just have to have a honeymoon every time you dock. How would that be?" she coyly asked, giving up her efforts to hold him at bay since they were almost to his cabin.

"I'd have it no other way." Waite backed her into the corner where the wall made a right angle and let his hands slip down from her waist and around behind to pull her to him. He saw the beating pulse in her throat and kissed her there. She shivered in his arms. He experienced her tremors and approved. "Hey, did your father tell you we're already talking about building a second ship together? Carolena will be a major contributor, we think, particularly with the interior design. She may have finally found her calling."

"I've heard. It's her turn to find happiness, honey. She's been through as much as we have with her own private guilt."

"Mrs. Taylor. You're a marvel. Your capacity for forgiveness is enormous."

Never comfortable with effusive compliments, Breelan dismissed the praise saying, "We'll have a grand time once the baby gets a little older. I look forward to all of us occasionally traveling on board the *Miss Breelan*." Enjoying the sound and appreciating the honor of the name of the ship, she gave an extra squeeze to his muscled arm. "Mickey, Pat and Warren Lowell are so anxious to go with you tomorrow on the maiden voyage, I'll be surprised if they close their eyes tonight."

"Aha." He wasn't listening, only watching her. Her fiery glance back at him ignited his coal black eyes and he dropped his gaze to her lips, full and pink and impatient for his kiss. Remember, we only get one chance to celebrate our first anniversary," he teased as they arrived at his quarters.

She needed no enticement because her husband and temptation were the same to her. They entered, and Waite quickly took his wife into his arms and walked her backwards into his cabin after securing the door. Again, he nuzzled her neck, inhaling the rich ripe scent of the perfume he'd given her, the same perfume he'd originally suggested she wear. It had become her favorite now, too. There in the dark mahogany-paneled room, lit by a single oil lamp, he clasped her to him, kissing her again and again. Looking into his shadowed face, he seemed almost anxious. She tore her gaze from him and turned her head. Her eyes found the massive focal point of the room. The bed! Her parents' bed! To see it in her husband's cabin like this set off sparks that prickled every cell of her femininity. She'd often wanted to ask her father and mother about it, but it was not her place. It was for them to give to whomever they wished in their own time. She threw her arms around Waite's neck. He lifted her against him in a robust embrace as they toppled as one onto the mattress.

"I've known since our wedding day, Bree. Your father came to me and said this bed would be his and your mother's gift to us once the ship was finished. Of course, we can move the thing to anywhere we live. For right now, I like it on board the *Miss Breelan*. What do you think?"

"I'll tell you exactly what I think, Waite Taylor. You're the best secret keeper ever! You and my father, both!"

"We'd better get the baby before we, uh, retire. You can't know how you tantalize me." He turned from her. Breelan's beauty was almost more than he could endure. "Well now," he breathed, removing his mind from the pleasure he and his wife would soon share. "Peeper must be exhausted."

"I'll bet," Breelan answered. "We'll have our time soon."

They were quiet as they entered the cabin next to Waite's. Peeper, in the rocker, had nodded off, her hand still on the infant to be sure she was breathing.

"Peep. Peeper," Breelan called, gently shaking the old shoulder.

"I'm awake. Never did close my eyes. And you two thought this child would be a might too much fer ole Peep? You's both too young ta know much a anythin' anyhow."

Waite helped her from the chair. "You're right, Miss Peeper. We couldn't do it without you."

"That's just what I been a tellin' ya all along." Turning to Breelan, "One more feedin' and the child should sleep a good long time. That is unless the two of you is loud." And she gave them her evil eye in warning.

"We'll be good, Peep. Thank you," promised Breelan as she kissed the satiny wrinkles on her cheek.

"As soon as I carry the cradle into our room, I'll walk you upstairs, Miss Peeper," said Waite. "I'm sure the others are ready to go home. It's pretty late."

"Speakin' a late, don't ya think it's past time ya call me Peeper, like the rest a the family? If'n you ain't careful, I might be assumin' ya don't like me none."

"What?" He was shocked. "Not like you? Why, I'm plum wall-eyed crazy about you! And yes, ma'am, you've been after me all along to address you as Peeper. The only reason I don't most of the time is out of respect, being that you're such a grand lady."

Peeper had to agree with him. "Well, if'n ya feel that strongly 'bout the matter then I guess I'll let ya go on and call me Miss Peeper once in a while. But you's the onlyest one allowed. Hear?" She touched his arm.

"Yes'm. It will be just you and me."

Breelan couldn't believe it! Peeper was flirting! It was another precious memory to add to the tapestry of sentiments filling her heart.

"There you go, Halley," Waite whispered setting the cradle beside their bed while Peeper watched, making sure he was doing it gently enough. "I'll be back here with you and your mama in a minute."

"Just holler now whenever ya need me ta sit with her, Bree. She's a baby angel, just like you was." Peeper exited beside her attractive attendant, stuffing his ear with yet another biased story of his wife as a child.

Returning three-quarters of an hour later, Waite found his bride in the glorious bed holding their sleeping infant. "I'm so sorry. I just couldn't get away up there. Your father insisted I have one last drink. He sure can celebrate."

"That's an understatement if ever there was one."

Waite took the child, full and contented, and placed her in the cradle. He blew out the flame in the lamp. "Let's let the moon be our light tonight, darling." He crossed to the porthole and pushed back the cotton covering, letting the room wash with sparkling moonbeams.

She rolled to the far side of the bed, anticipating the moment he would begin touching her in his particular way. No one but he could pierce her barrier of passive contentment to send her into romantic escapades that they alone could share. Their private heaven had scarcely been surveyed, though they'd been together like this so many times. Yet to be scaled pinnacles of pleasure awaited, enticing them.

Waite sat on the edge of his desk, impatient to hold his wife. He prided himself on his forbearance, yet with Breelan, he had no physical control.

Had he his way, they'd become one at any and every opportunity presented. However impractical, that was the way he felt. No other woman held sway over him. With Breelan he could be any damned way he wanted. She would understand. He was as sure of that as he was of her love for him.

Breelan, dressed only in her chemise, was not embarrassed. She was proud to let him see her. All of her. She knew it was more than carnal with him. With his every touch to her skin, he demonstrated his wide range of emotions for her. How could she ever get used to this? To her dying day, his flesh to hers would spur ribbons of delight inside her. His moods were often different, and she read and understood him by the way he caressed her. Sometimes he was gentle and sweet; she was the mother of his child. Other times, his touch was strong and powerful as he escaped from worry or disappointment by way of her. Here, at this very hour, at peace with love's deliverance, this particular union would be a highlight of their lives.

Her outstretched arms invited him into her warmth. He kissed her palm. Turned it over and kissed the back of her hand. Trailing a path of more of the same up her arm, he stopped at her throat, laying his lips where the tattoo was.

"Waite," Breelan took his head in her hands. "I want you to understand that whenever I'm reminded of the ordeal," as she'd come to call it, "or see the *W* in the mirror, I think of you, the man I love, the man who saved my life in more ways than the physical. Someone told me once that true love can always be mended. She was so right."

He drew her to him. He would always inwardly shudder at the idea of harm coming to his Breelan. But right now he wanted to distract her from any past pains and bring her back with him into their perfect present. He hesitated but a moment, goading her with want for him. When she began to whimper, he could stand no more. He dragged her from the bed, maneuvering her against the hard wall, pressing his body against her length. She pulled at his back, demanding, unreasonably craving him to be closer than was physically possible.

Waite kissed her with deliberate force. His mouth was insistent. His slight growth of beard sanded her lips and chin and cheeks. She didn't mind. Her single desire was to taste of him. She felt wanton and wild, and she loved the feeling. Breaking free from him only because he let her, she rushed back to the bed, dived beneath the covers, and hid in pretense. His clothes shed, the moonbeams showed his white teeth. She smiled too, anticipating his next move. She'd been right. With one grasp of the blankets, he threw them back, tugging them completely from the bed. "There will be no hide and seek tonight, darlin'. It's been a long and glorious day, and I can think of only one thing that I need from you now that will make it complete." Waite added, "For us both."

She giggled and rolled on her stomach. With one hand on her shoulder, he turned her over and her mass of hair covered the pillows. With his other hand, Waite untied the bows at her breast. Tossing aside her bothersome frills, she lay unclad beneath him.

There was little doubt he was ready for her, but she wanted him to wait, if only for a twinkling. She teased him with her mouth, her breasts, her hips. She wound her legs around his muscled thighs, holding him off until the right instant. And it would be her decision as to just when.

She chose now. His drive was unending, his strength and stamina inconceivable. Over and over again, he sent her into convulsions of pleasure, some slight, most intense. She was near delirium when his endurance was no more. Then one final jolt of euphoria for two. They saluted the zenith of their passion with a deep kiss, silently pledging to love throughout their lives and beyond.

Waite straightened the rumpled sheet over them both as they recovered their senses and returned to their comfortable, secure world of mommy and daddy, husband and wife, best friends. "I've got one last surprise for you, Bree." He reached beneath his pillow and pulled out a necklace. Holding it in the path of the moonlight, he asked, "Recognize it?"

She could see its silver sparkle there in the dark. "It's the medal of Jesus' mother that Trip threw out of the porthole. My God, Waite! Where did you get it? I thought it was lost forever. How did you know about it? Unless ..."

"Yes, I was the one who hung it around your neck the day you rode to the *Gentle Comfort*, the day you ran away from Trip."

She studied the small oval, marveling that she again had it in her possession.

"The next time I saw you, after Trip claimed you for his wife," Waite swallowed hard, the idea still bothering him as it probably always would, "you weren't wearing it. I'd hoped you'd put it away for safekeeping. When I never saw it again and you didn't mention it, I guessed it was gone, for whatever reason. I was astonished when one of my men found it snagged on a rough piece of wood on the side of the ship. I knew you'd never have thrown it away, no matter who you guessed gave it to you because it's such a pretty piece. I kept it for you, hoping someday I could place it back where it belongs." He made sure the silhouette of Mary was facing outward and draped it around her neck. "My father gave it to his wife to acknowledge her extraordinary capacity as a mother. I feel the same way about you. And you can give it to Halley someday."

Flattered beyond belief, Breelan asked, "You're not comparing me to the Blessed Mother, are you?"

"Well no, of course not, but I'm not being blasphemous when I say that to me, you're the closest thing on earth to a saint."

She shook her head, amazed at the overwhelming adoration this man had for her. She kissed his cheek and looked over at their daughter, rocked to sleep by the soft sloshing river. In the strong curl of her lover's arm, Breelan was content to dream her own private thoughts that weren't much different from those of Waite. While each stared at the cabin's ceiling awash with lunar light, they knew only that their devotion would grow, as would their family. Their love could never be destroyed. They wouldn't let it. Nor could it be denied. To live without one another ever again would be known to them and all who learned their story as *The Goodbye Lie*.

COMING SOON from
Jane Marie and greenlightWRITE

VELVET UNDERTOW

Volume Two in *The Goodbye Lie* Series

The devastating Johnstown Flood washes away secrets of the past for Carolena Dunnigan. But who will survive to claim her love?

ABOUT THE AUTHOR

A native of Erie, Pennsylvania, Jane Marie Harkins Malcolm makes her home at the edge of the world in beautiful Fernandina Beach on Amelia Island, Florida.

Visit **http://www.GraciousJaneMarie.com** to discover more about the fascinating Dunnigan family. Sign up for Jane Marie's free monthly newsletter and Celebrate HEART & HOME with roses, recipes and romance.

Printed in the United States
21115LVS00007B/187-240